12/17

SpongeBob™ COMICS #1

Silly Sea Stories

ALSO AVAILABLE
SpongeBob Comics: Aquatic Adventurers, Unite!
SpongeBob Comics: Tales from the Haunted Pineapple

PUBLISHER'S NOTE:
This is a work of fiction. Names, characters, places, and incidents
are either the product of the author's imagination or used fictitiously,
and any resemblance to actual persons, living or dead, business
establishments, events, or locales is entirely coincidental.

Cataloging-in-Publication Data has been applied for and may be
obtained from the Library of Congress.

ISBN 978-1-4197-2319-3

Copyright © 2017 United Plankton Pictures, Inc.

Cover illustration by Sherm Cohen with additional SpongeBob
character art by Jacob Chabot and Gregg Schigiel

Book design by Pamela Notarantonio

The stories included in this collection were originally published in
SpongeBob Comics no. 2 (April 2011), 3 (June 2011),
4 (August 2011), 5 (October 2011), 6 (December 2011),
7 (February 2012), 8 (April 2012), 9 (June 2012), 12 (September
2012), 14 (November 2012), 21 (June 2013), 23 (August 2013),
and 29 (February 2014).

Published in 2017 by Amulet Books, an imprint of ABRAMS.
All rights reserved. No portion of this book may be reproduced,
stored in a retrieval system, or transmitted in any form or by any
means, mechanical, electronic, photocopying, recording,
or otherwise, without written permission from the publisher.

Amulet Books and Amulet Paperbacks are registered trademarks of
Harry N. Abrams, Inc.

Printed and bound in U.S.A.
10 9 8 7 6 5 4

Amulet Books are available at special discounts when
purchased in quantity for premiums and promotions as well as
fundraising or educational use. Special editions can also be created
to specification. For details, contact specialsales@abramsbooks.com
or the address below.

ABRAMS The Art of Books
195 Broadway, New York, NY 10007
abramsbooks.com

SpongeBob™ COMICS #1

Silly Sea Stories

STEPHEN HILLENBURG

EDITED BY CHRIS DUFFY

AMULET BOOKS
NEW YORK

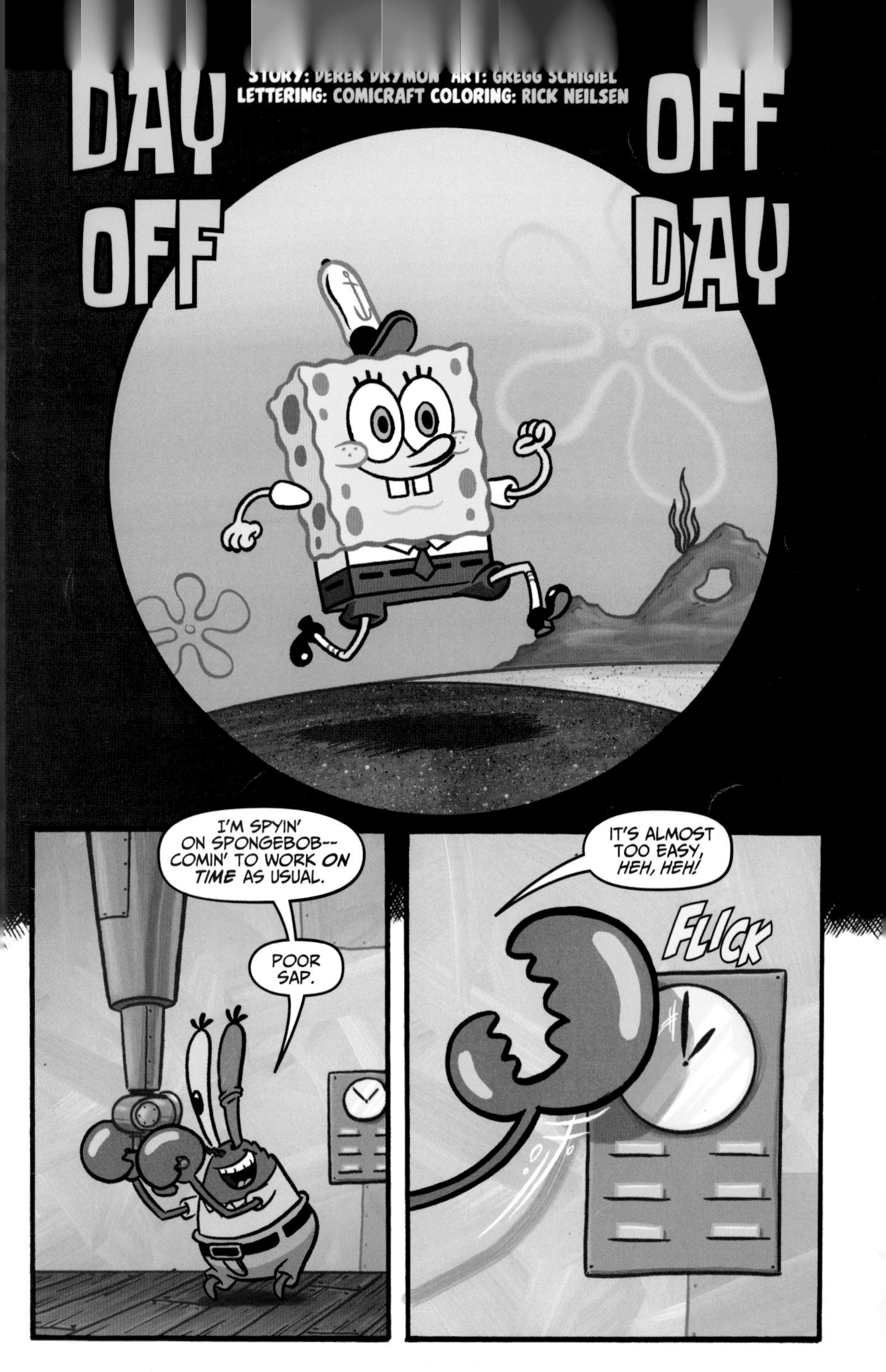
DAY OFF
OFF DAY
STORY: DEREK DRYMON ART: GREGG SCHIGIEL
LETTERING: COMICRAFT COLORING: RICK NEILSEN
I'M SPYIN' ON SPONGEBOB-- COMIN' TO WORK ON TIME AS USUAL.
POOR SAP.
IT'S ALMOST TOO EASY, HEH, HEH!
FLICK

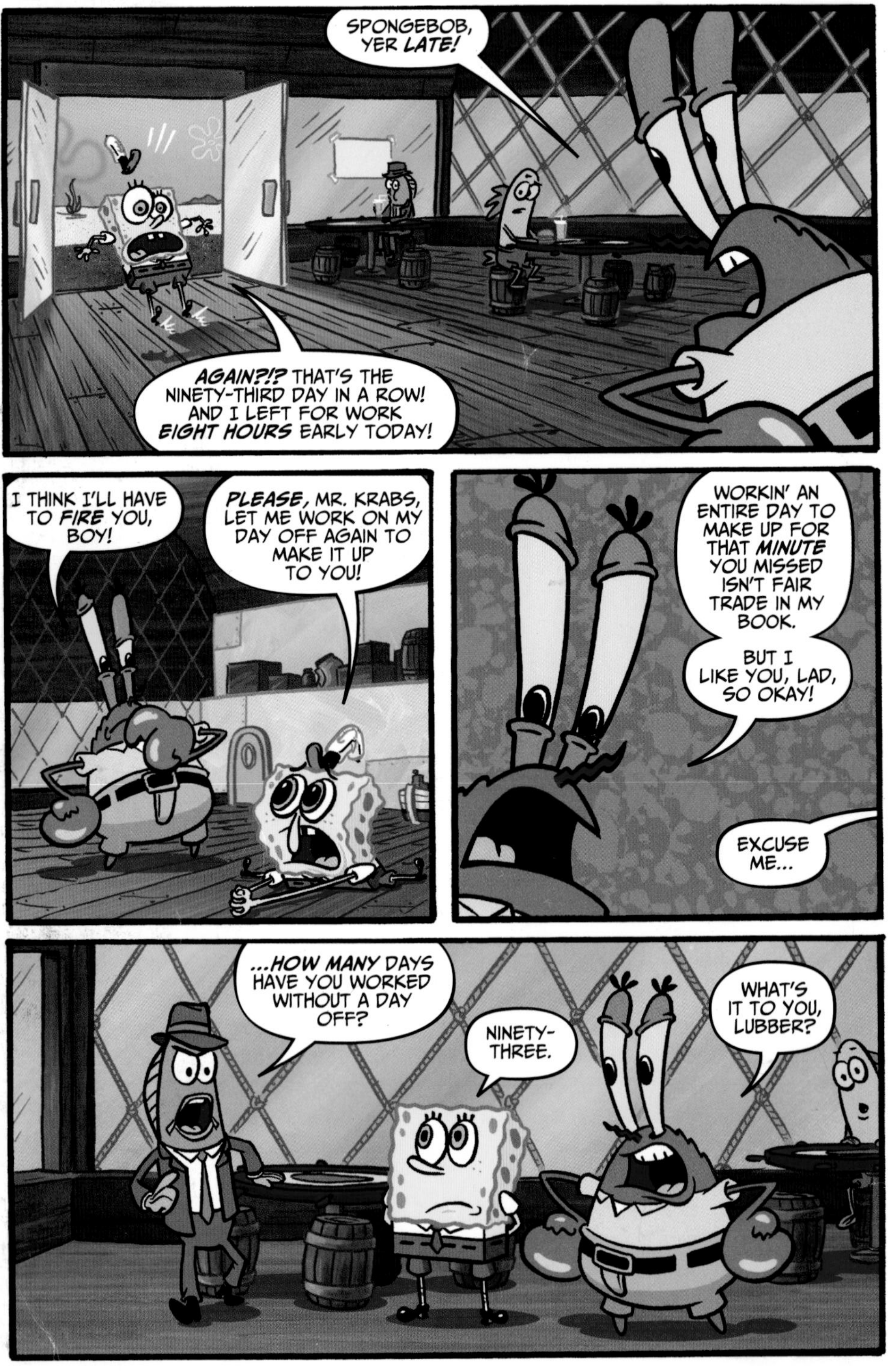
SPONGEBOB, YER LATE!
AGAIN?!? THAT'S THE NINETY-THIRD DAY IN A ROW! AND I LEFT FOR WORK EIGHT HOURS EARLY TODAY!
I THINK I'LL HAVE TO FIRE YOU, BOY!
PLEASE, MR. KRABS, LET ME WORK ON MY DAY OFF AGAIN TO MAKE IT UP TO YOU!
WORKIN' AN ENTIRE DAY TO MAKE UP FOR THAT MINUTE YOU MISSED ISN'T FAIR TRADE IN MY BOOK.
BUT I LIKE YOU, LAD, SO OKAY!
EXCUSE ME...
...HOW MANY DAYS HAVE YOU WORKED WITHOUT A DAY OFF?
NINETY-THREE.
WHAT'S IT TO YOU, LUBBER?

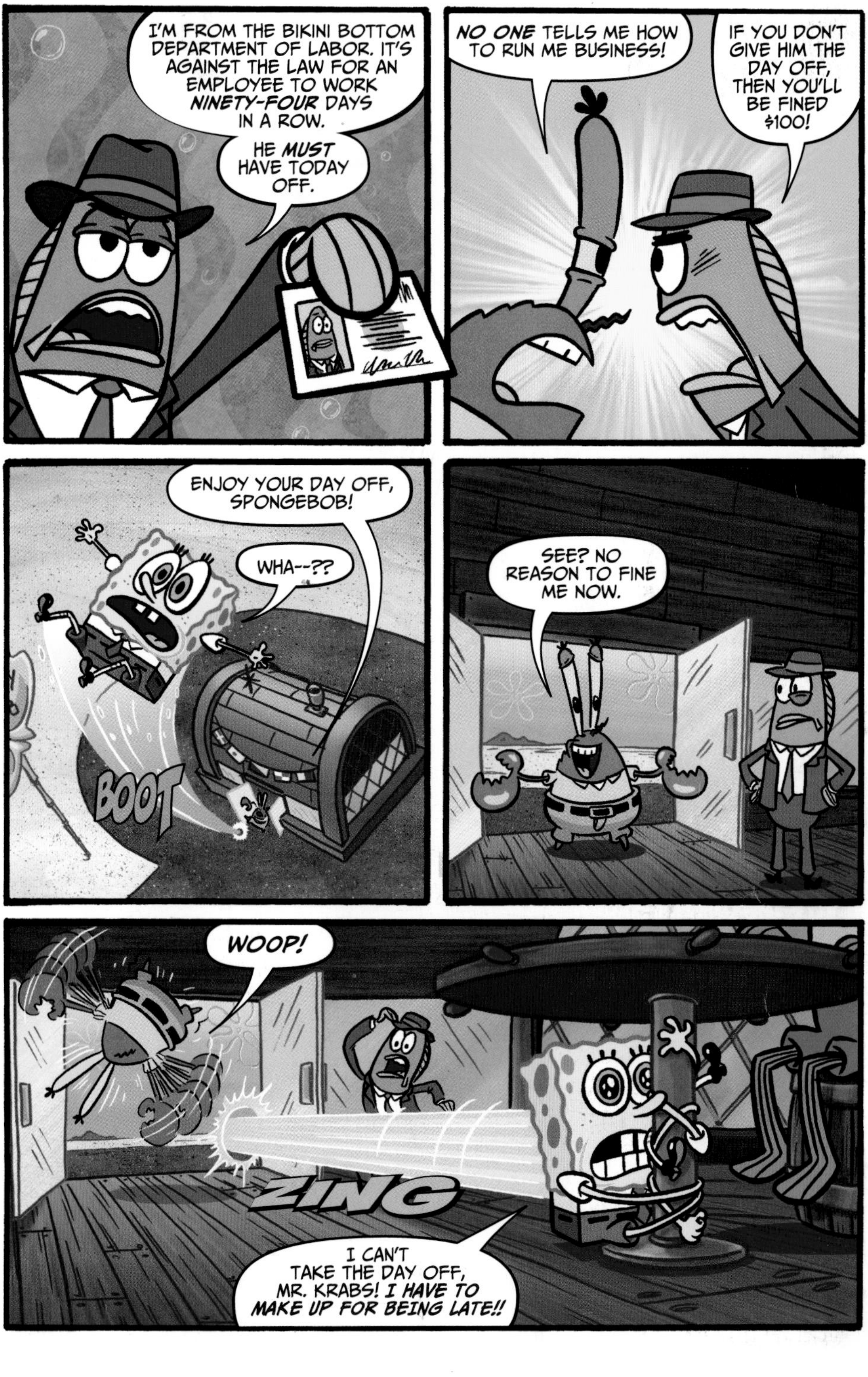
I'M FROM THE BIKINI BOTTOM DEPARTMENT OF LABOR. IT'S AGAINST THE LAW FOR AN EMPLOYEE TO WORK NINETY-FOUR DAYS IN A ROW.
HE MUST HAVE TODAY OFF.
NO ONE TELLS ME HOW TO RUN ME BUSINESS!
IF YOU DON'T GIVE HIM THE DAY OFF, THEN YOU'LL BE FINED $100!
ENJOY YOUR DAY OFF, SPONGEBOB!
WHA--??
BOOT
SEE? NO REASON TO FINE ME NOW.
WOOP!
ZING
I CAN'T TAKE THE DAY OFF, MR. KRABS! I HAVE TO MAKE UP FOR BEING LATE!!

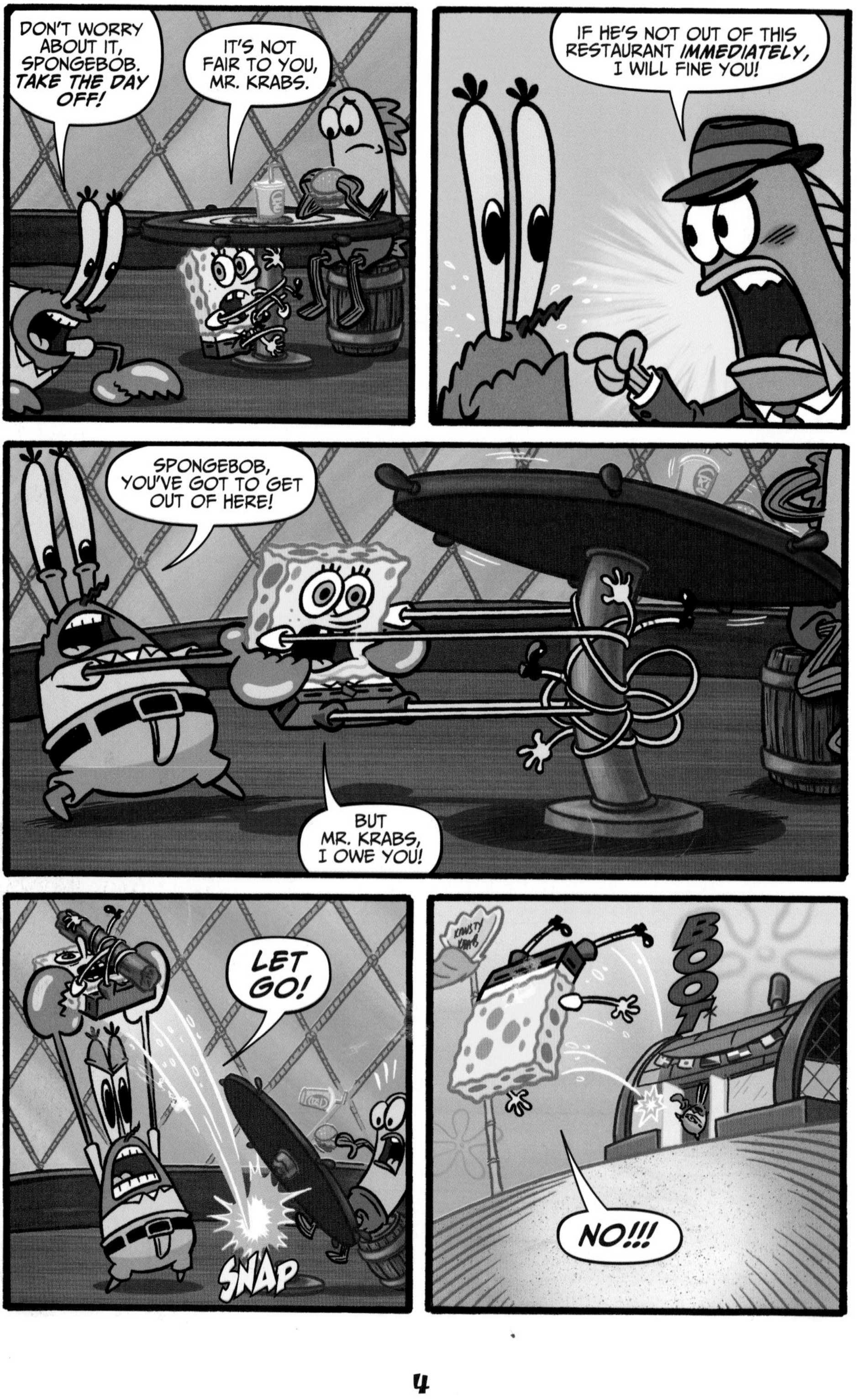
DON'T WORRY ABOUT IT, SPONGEBOB. TAKE THE DAY OFF!
IT'S NOT FAIR TO YOU, MR. KRABS.
IF HE'S NOT OUT OF THIS RESTAURANT IMMEDIATELY, I WILL FINE YOU!
SPONGEBOB, YOU'VE GOT TO GET OUT OF HERE!
BUT MR. KRABS, I OWE YOU!
LET GO!
SNAP
BOOT
NO!!!

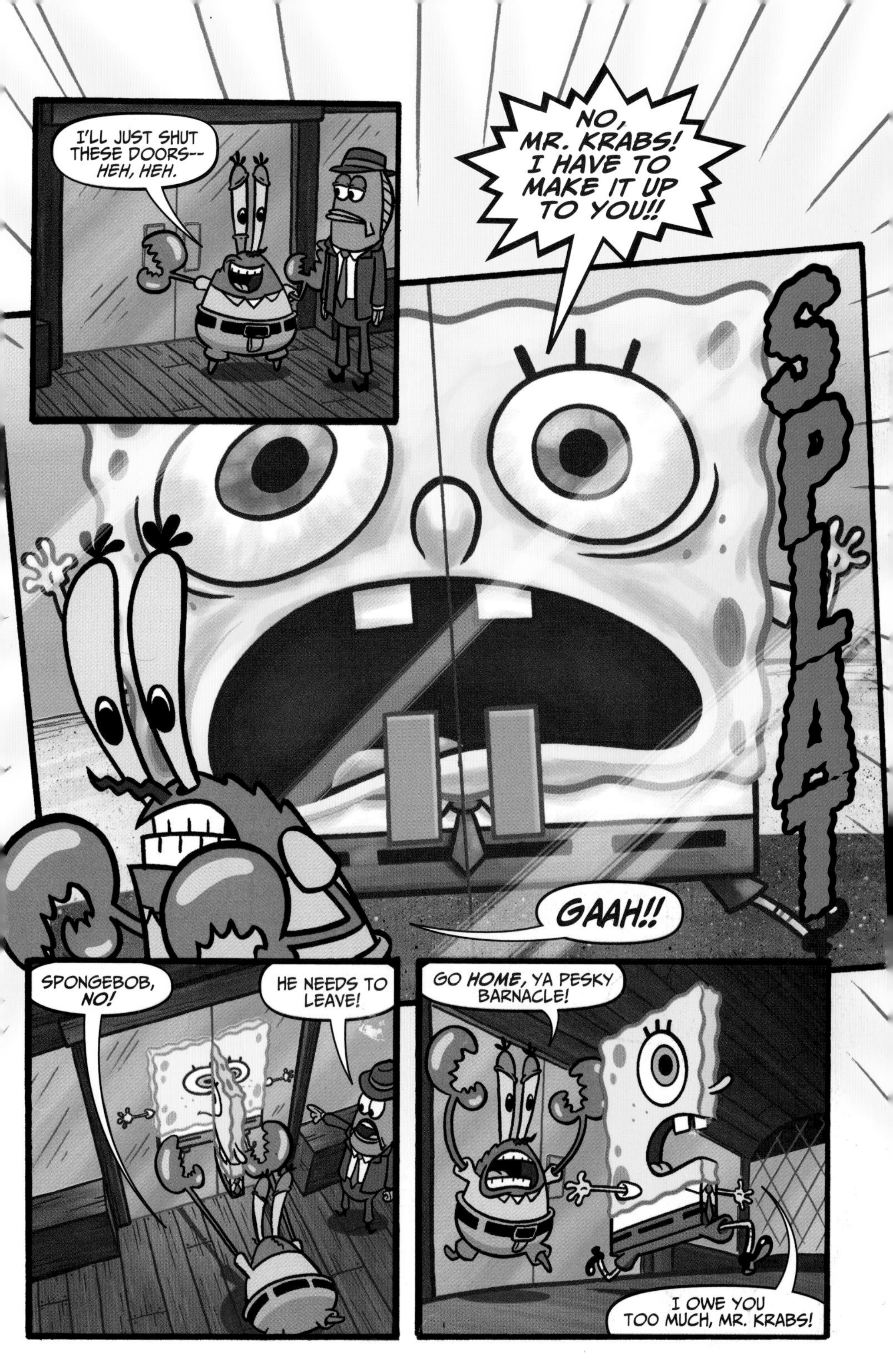
I'LL JUST SHUT THESE DOORS-- HEH, HEH.
NO, MR. KRABS! I HAVE TO MAKE IT UP TO YOU!!
SPLAT
GAAH!!
SPONGEBOB, NO!
HE NEEDS TO LEAVE!
GO HOME, YA PESKY BARNACLE!
I OWE YOU TOO MUCH, MR. KRABS!

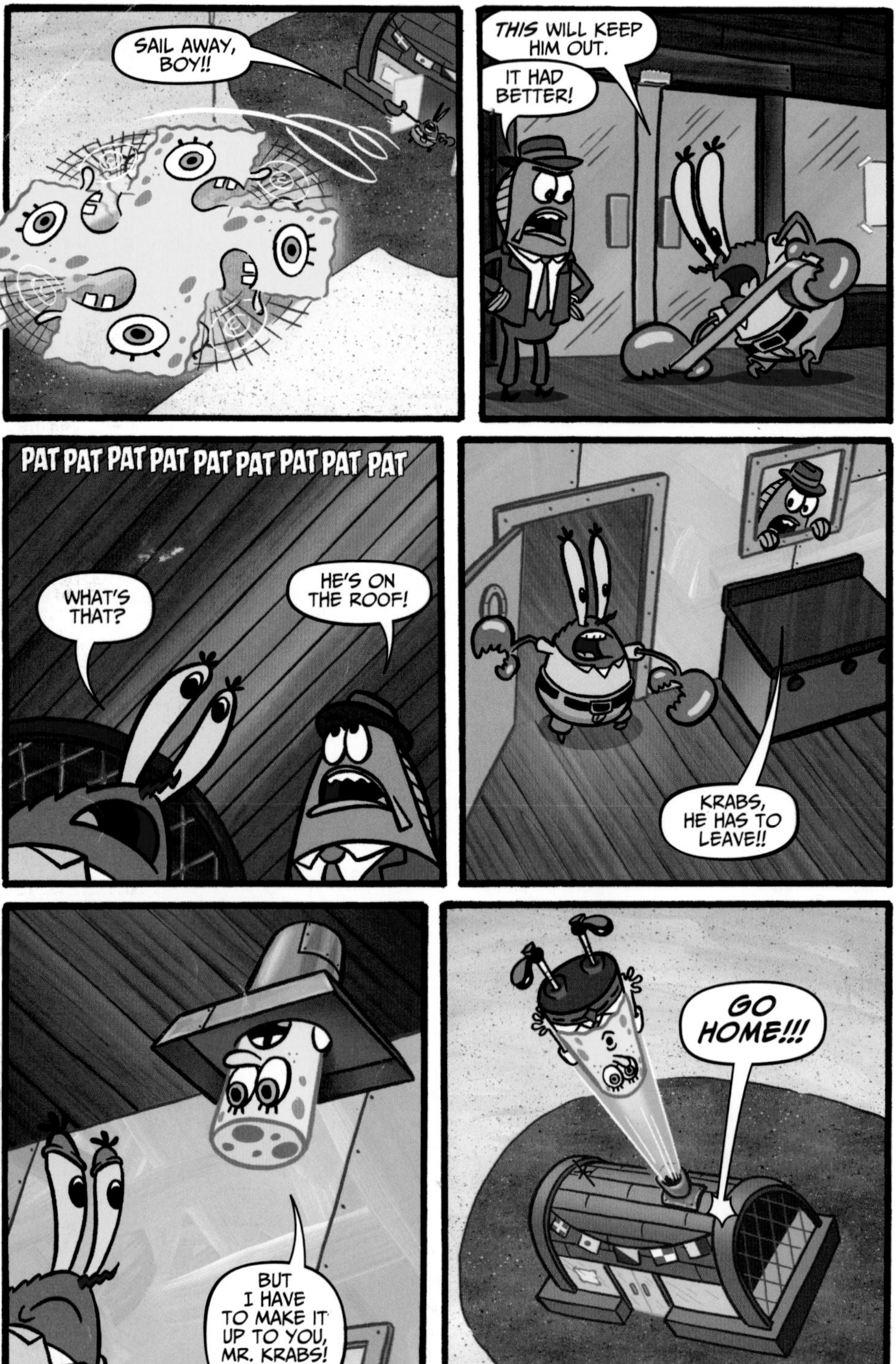

SAIL AWAY, BOY!!
THIS WILL KEEP HIM OUT.
IT HAD BETTER!
PAT PAT PAT PAT PAT PAT PAT PAT PAT
WHAT'S THAT?
HE'S ON THE ROOF!
KRABS, HE HAS TO LEAVE!!
BUT I HAVE TO MAKE IT UP TO YOU, MR. KRABS!
GO HOME!!!

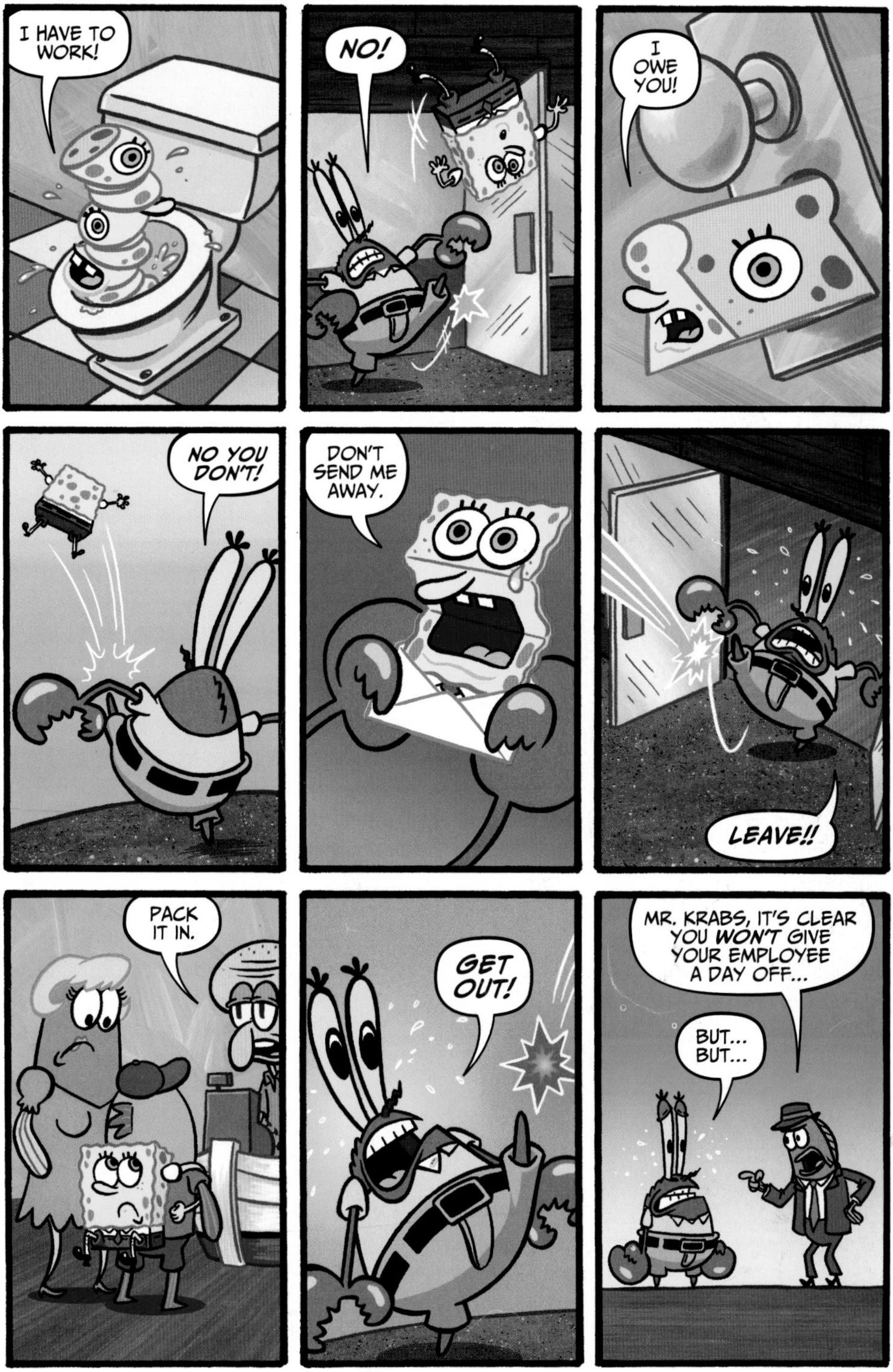
I HAVE TO WORK!
NO!
I OWE YOU!
NO YOU DON'T!
DON'T SEND ME AWAY.
LEAVE!!
PACK IT IN.
GET OUT!
MR. KRABS, IT'S CLEAR YOU WON'T GIVE YOUR EMPLOYEE A DAY OFF...
BUT... BUT...

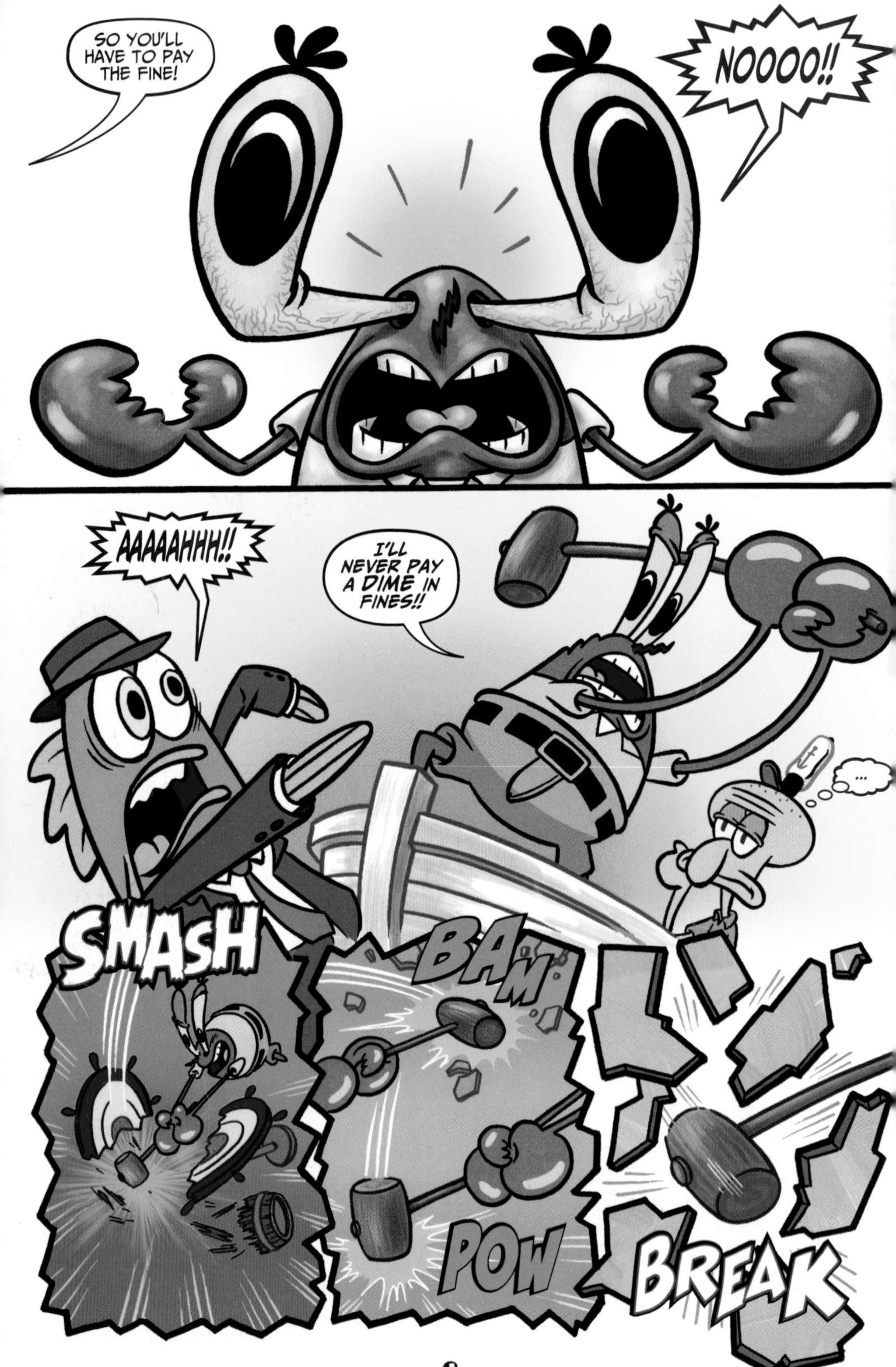
SO YOU'LL HAVE TO PAY THE FINE!
NOOOO!!
AAAAAHHH!!
I'LL NEVER PAY A DIME IN FINES!!
...
SMASH
BAM
POW
BREAK

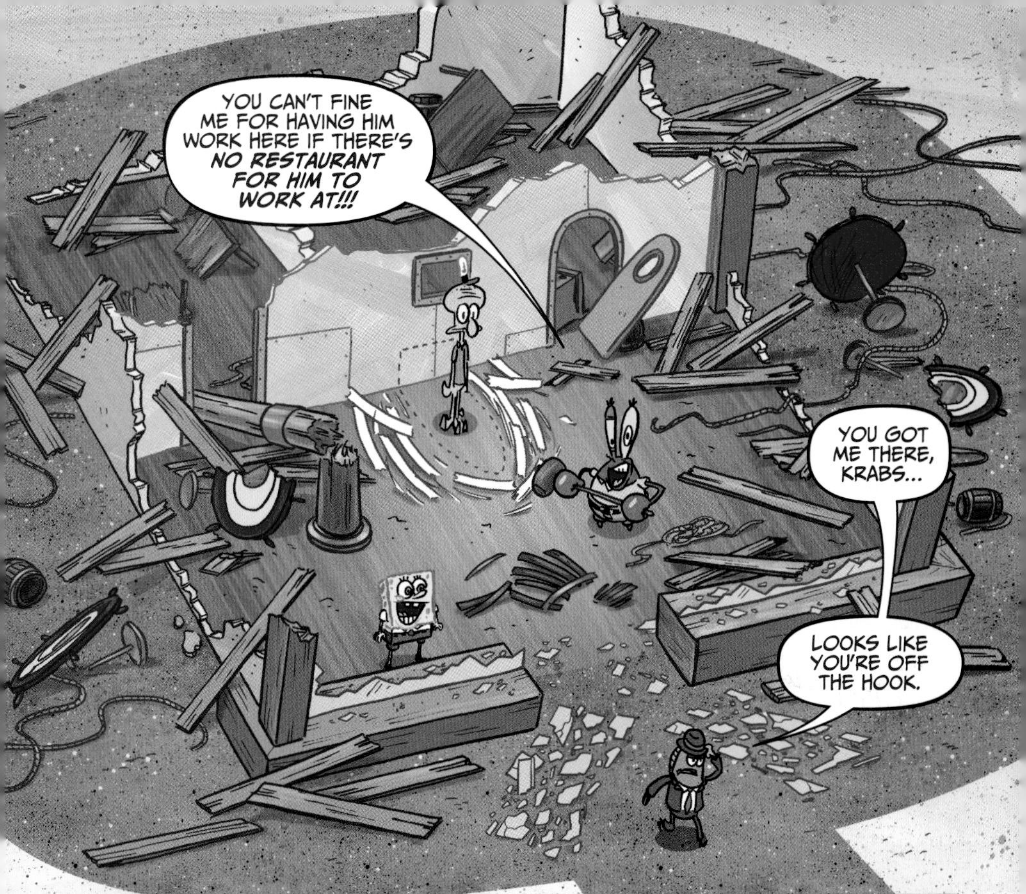
YOU CAN'T FINE ME FOR HAVING HIM WORK HERE IF THERE'S *NO RESTAURANT FOR HIM TO WORK AT!!!*
YOU GOT ME THERE, KRABS...
LOOKS LIKE YOU'RE OFF THE HOOK.

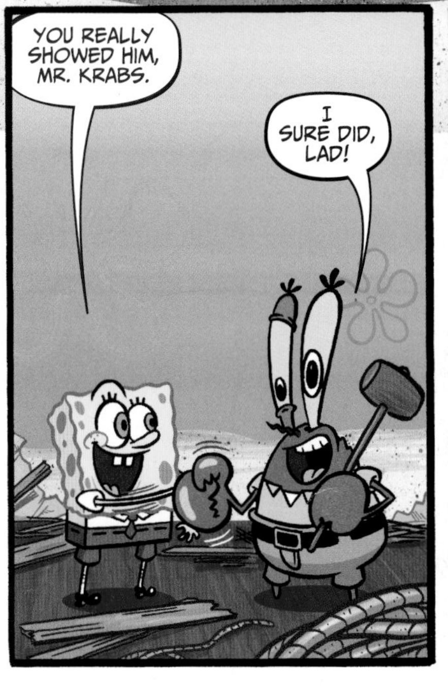
YOU REALLY SHOWED HIM, MR. KRABS.
I SURE DID, LAD!

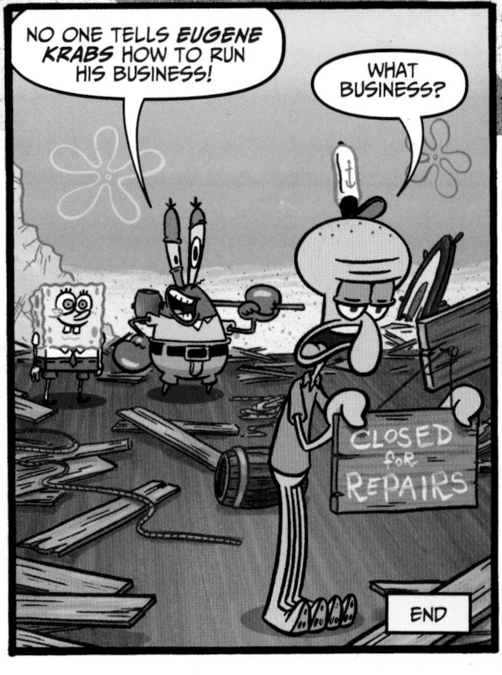
NO ONE TELLS *EUGENE KRABS* HOW TO RUN HIS BUSINESS!
WHAT BUSINESS?
CLOSED for REPAIRS
END

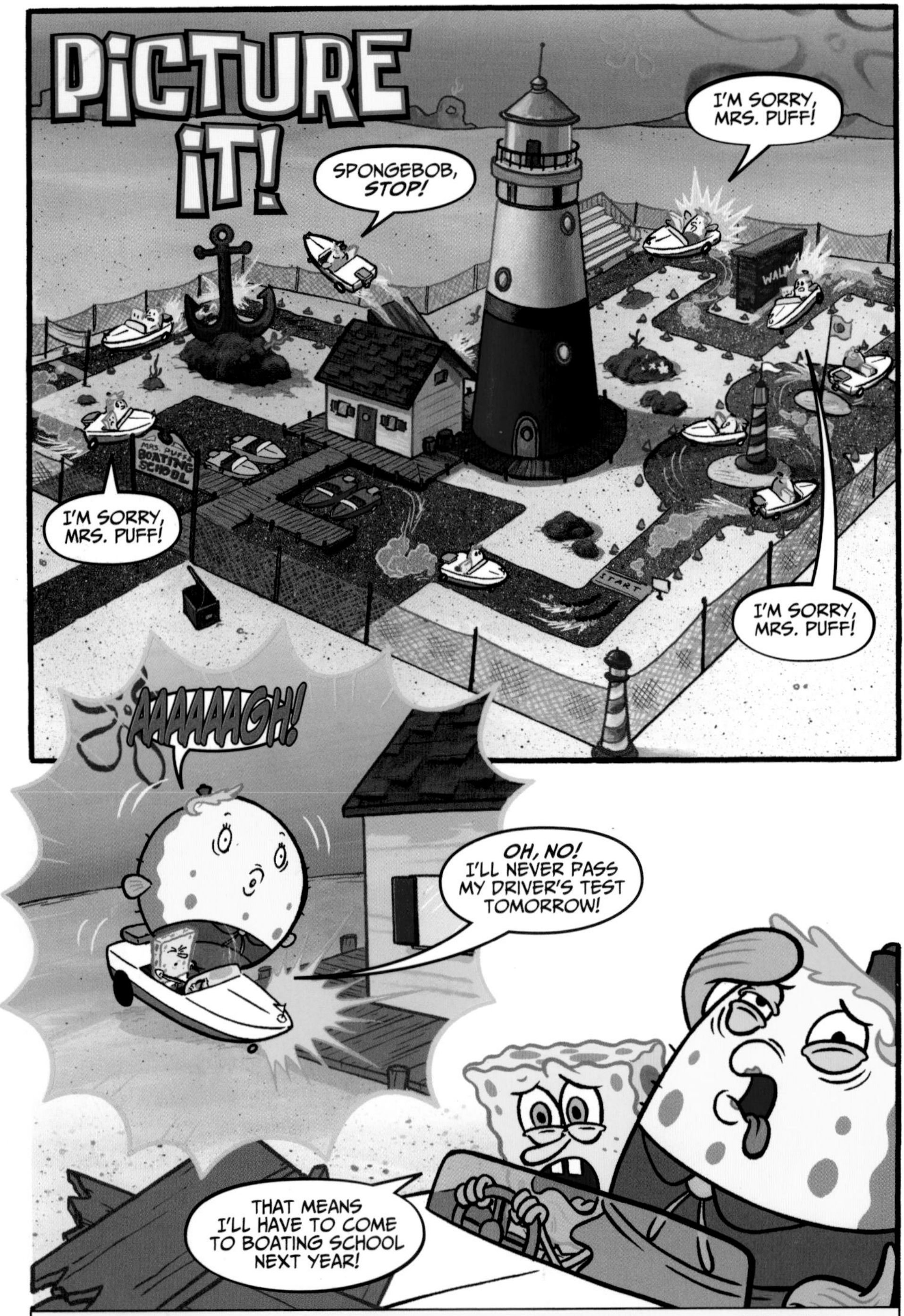
PICTURE IT!
SPONGEBOB, STOP!
I'M SORRY, MRS. PUFF!
I'M SORRY, MRS. PUFF!
I'M SORRY, MRS. PUFF!
AAAAAAGH!
OH, NO! I'LL NEVER PASS MY DRIVER'S TEST TOMORROW!
THAT MEANS I'LL HAVE TO COME TO BOATING SCHOOL NEXT YEAR!

STORY	ART	LETTERING	COLORING
DEREK DRYMON	**GREGG SCHIGIEL**	**COMICRAFT**	**MOLLY DOLBEN**

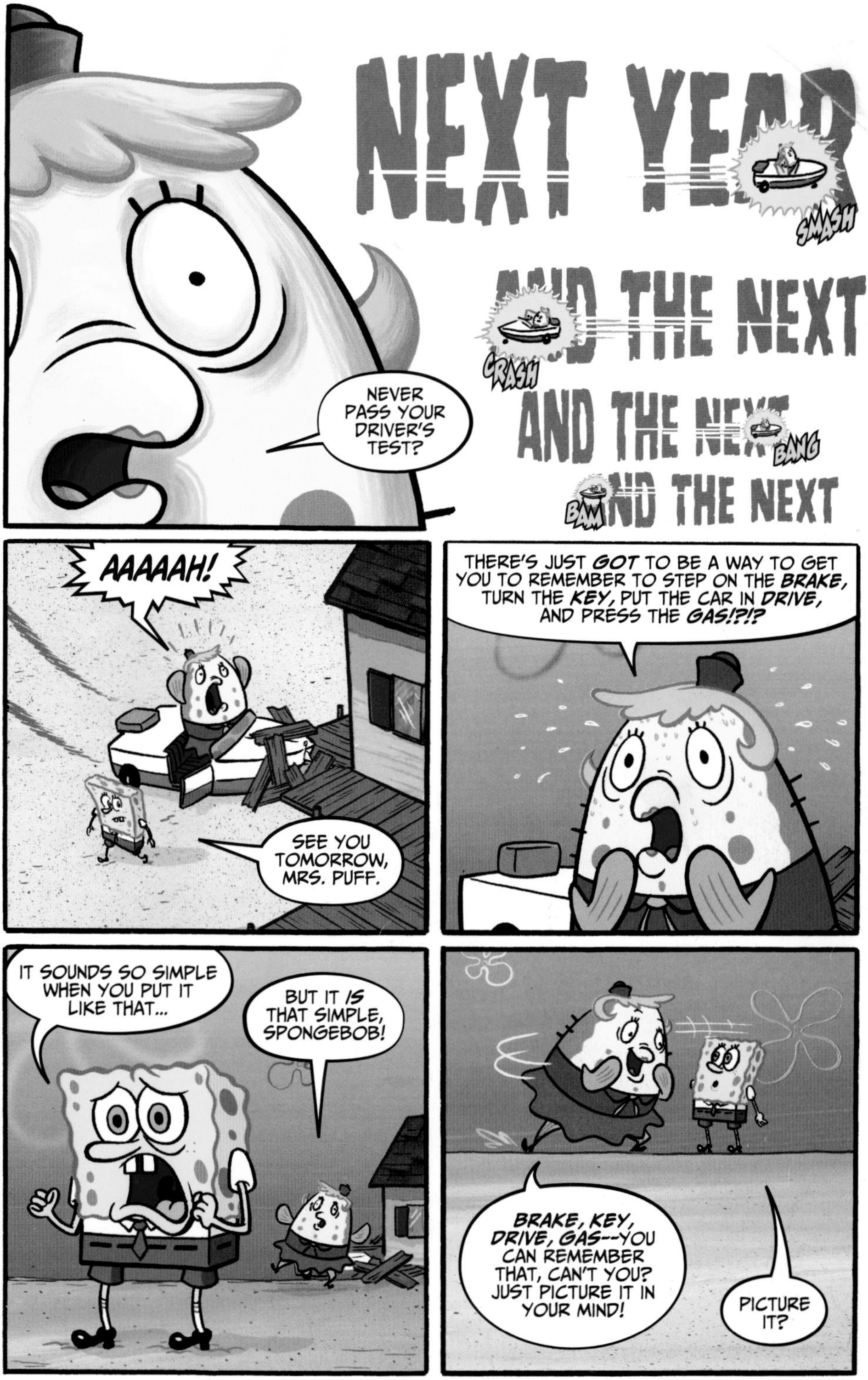

NEVER PASS YOUR DRIVER'S TEST?
NEXT YEAR
SMASH
AND THE NEXT
CRASH
AND THE NEXT
BANG
AND THE NEXT
BAM
AAAAAH!
SEE YOU TOMORROW, MRS. PUFF.
THERE'S JUST *GOT* TO BE A WAY TO GET YOU TO REMEMBER TO STEP ON THE *BRAKE*, TURN THE *KEY*, PUT THE CAR IN *DRIVE*, AND PRESS THE *GAS!?!?*
IT SOUNDS SO SIMPLE WHEN YOU PUT IT LIKE THAT...
BUT IT *IS* THAT SIMPLE, SPONGEBOB!
BRAKE, KEY, DRIVE, GAS--YOU CAN REMEMBER THAT, CAN'T YOU? JUST PICTURE IT IN YOUR MIND!
PICTURE IT?

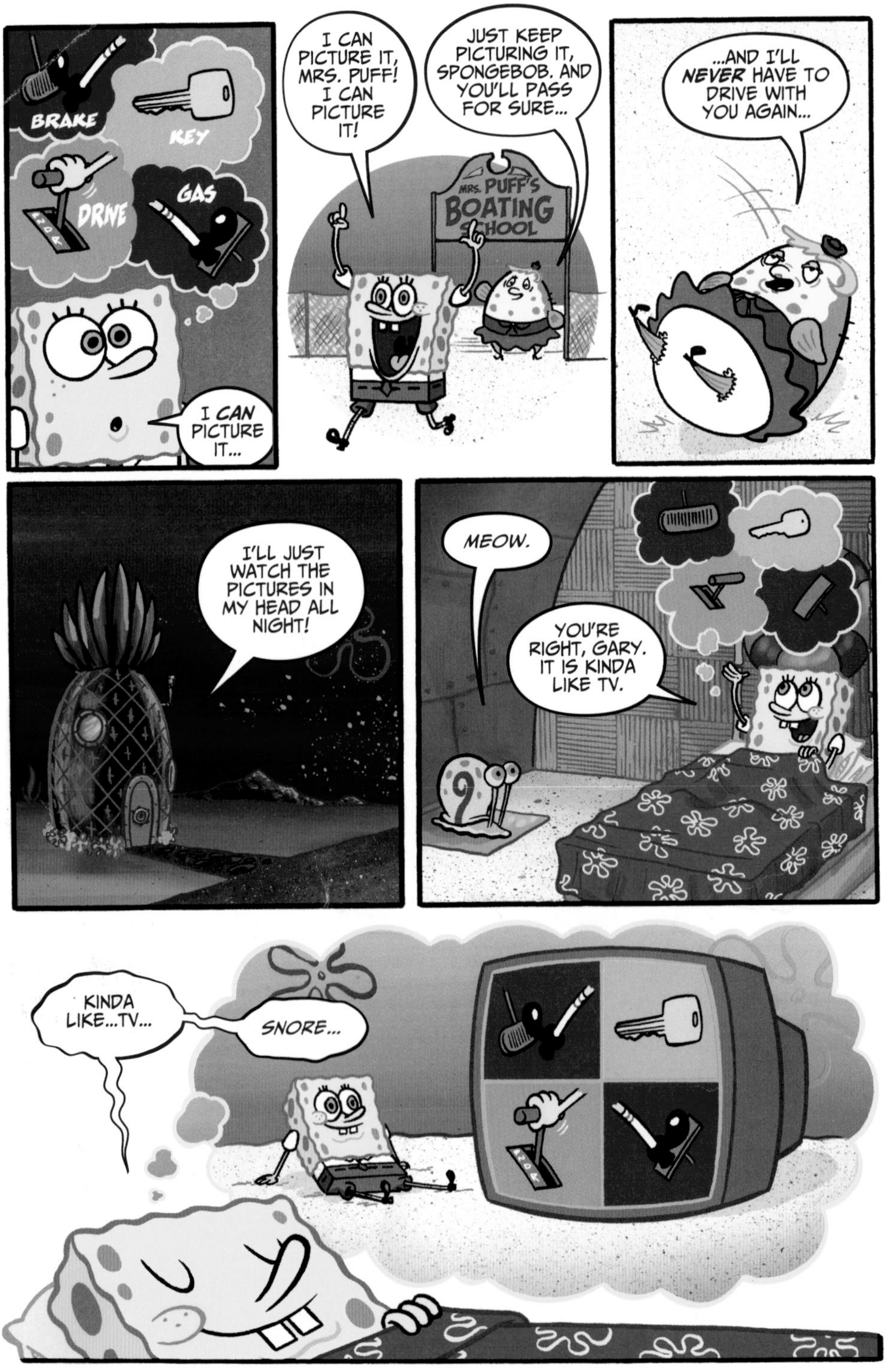
BRAKE
KEY
DRIVE
GAS
I CAN PICTURE IT...
I CAN PICTURE IT, MRS. PUFF! I CAN PICTURE IT!
JUST KEEP PICTURING IT, SPONGEBOB. AND YOU'LL PASS FOR SURE...
MRS. PUFF'S BOATING SCHOOL
...AND I'LL NEVER HAVE TO DRIVE WITH YOU AGAIN...
I'LL JUST WATCH THE PICTURES IN MY HEAD ALL NIGHT!
MEOW.
YOU'RE RIGHT, GARY. IT IS KINDA LIKE TV.
KINDA LIKE...TV...
SNORE...

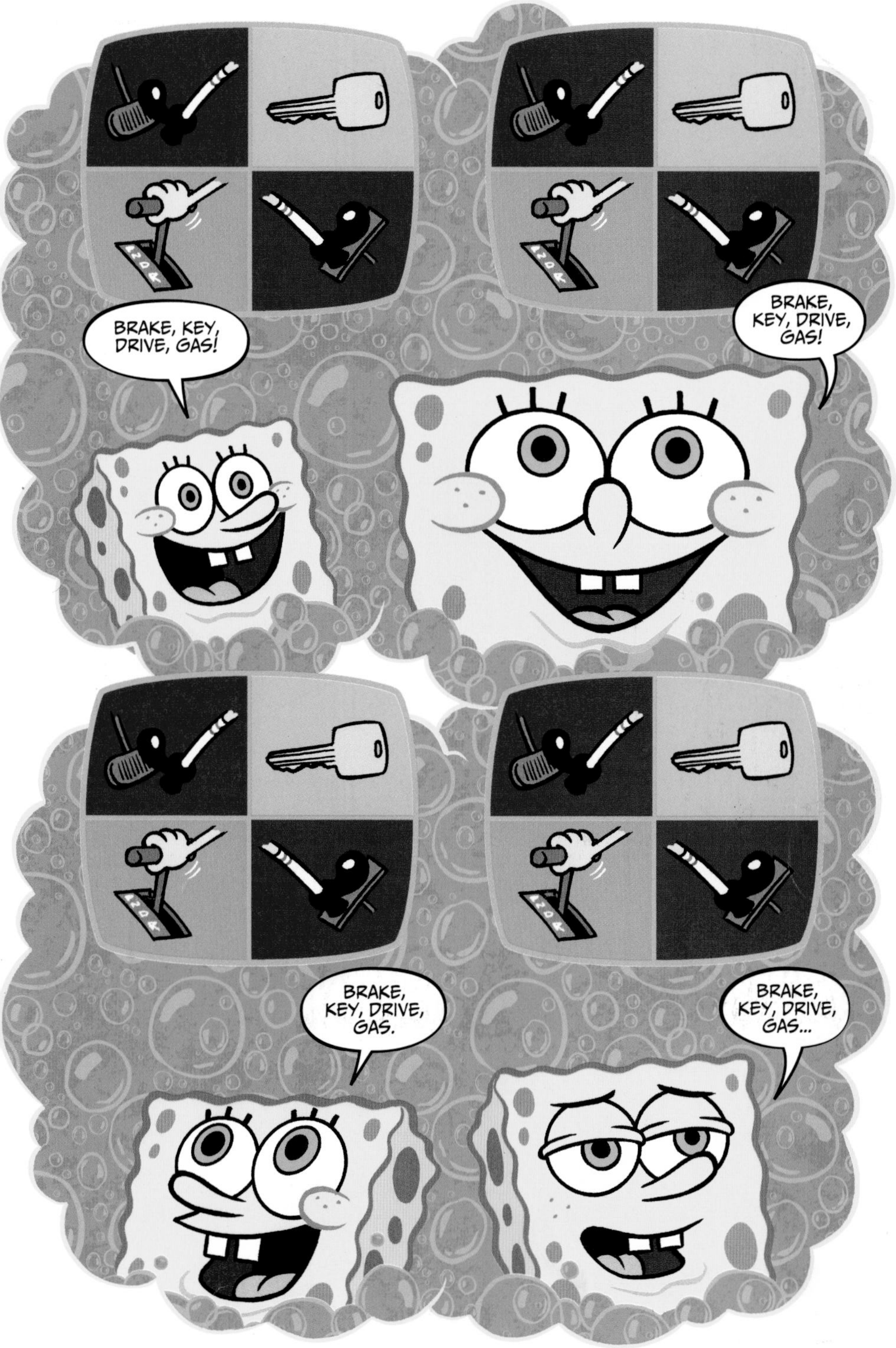
BRAKE, KEY, DRIVE, GAS!
BRAKE, KEY, DRIVE, GAS!
BRAKE, KEY, DRIVE, GAS.
BRAKE, KEY, DRIVE, GAS...

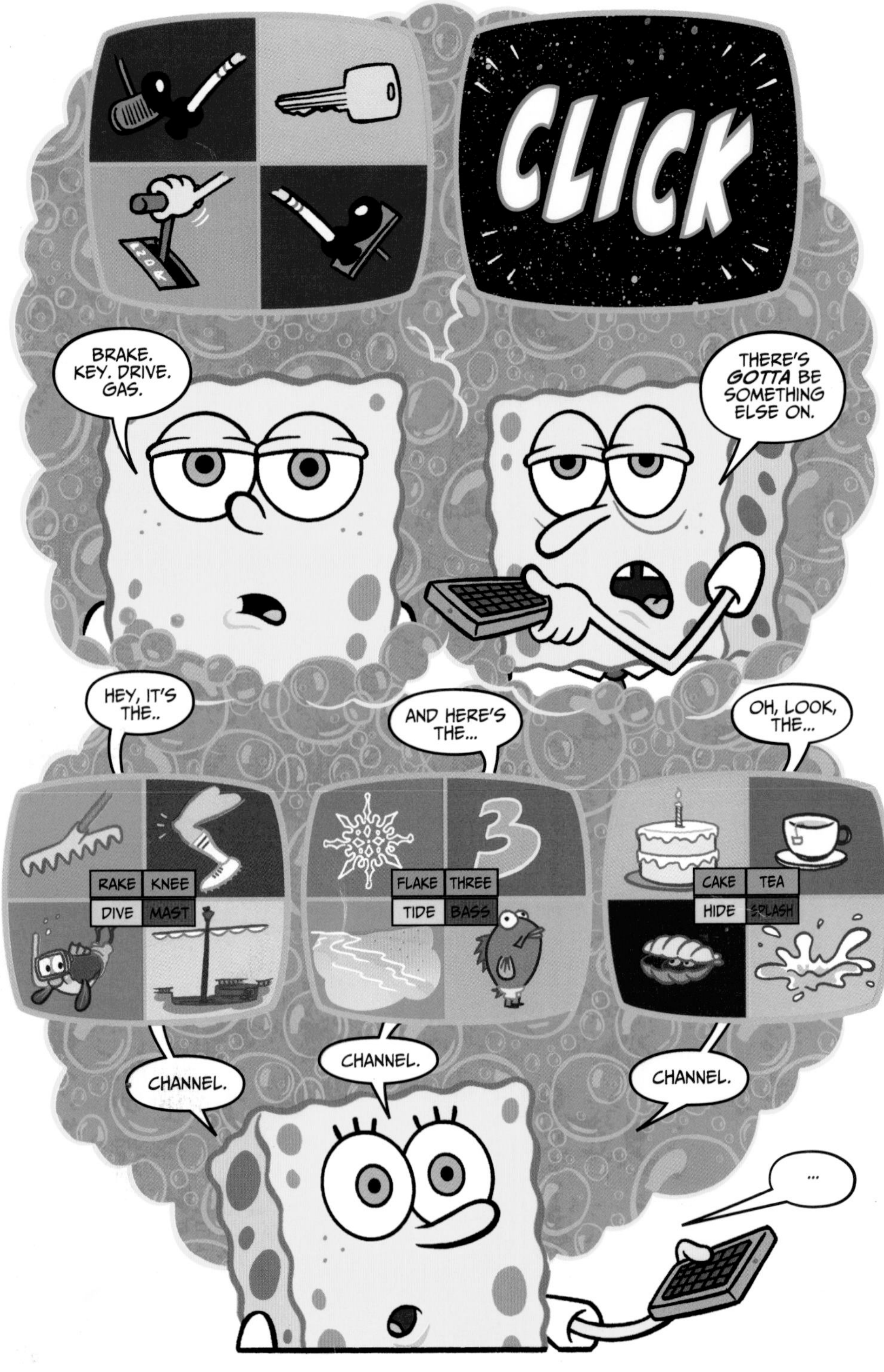
CLICK
BRAKE. KEY. DRIVE. GAS.
THERE'S GOTTA BE SOMETHING ELSE ON.
HEY, IT'S THE..
AND HERE'S THE...
OH, LOOK, THE...
RAKE
KNEE
DIVE
MAST
FLAKE
THREE
TIDE
BASS
CAKE
TEA
HIDE
SPLASH
CHANNEL.
CHANNEL.
CHANNEL.
...

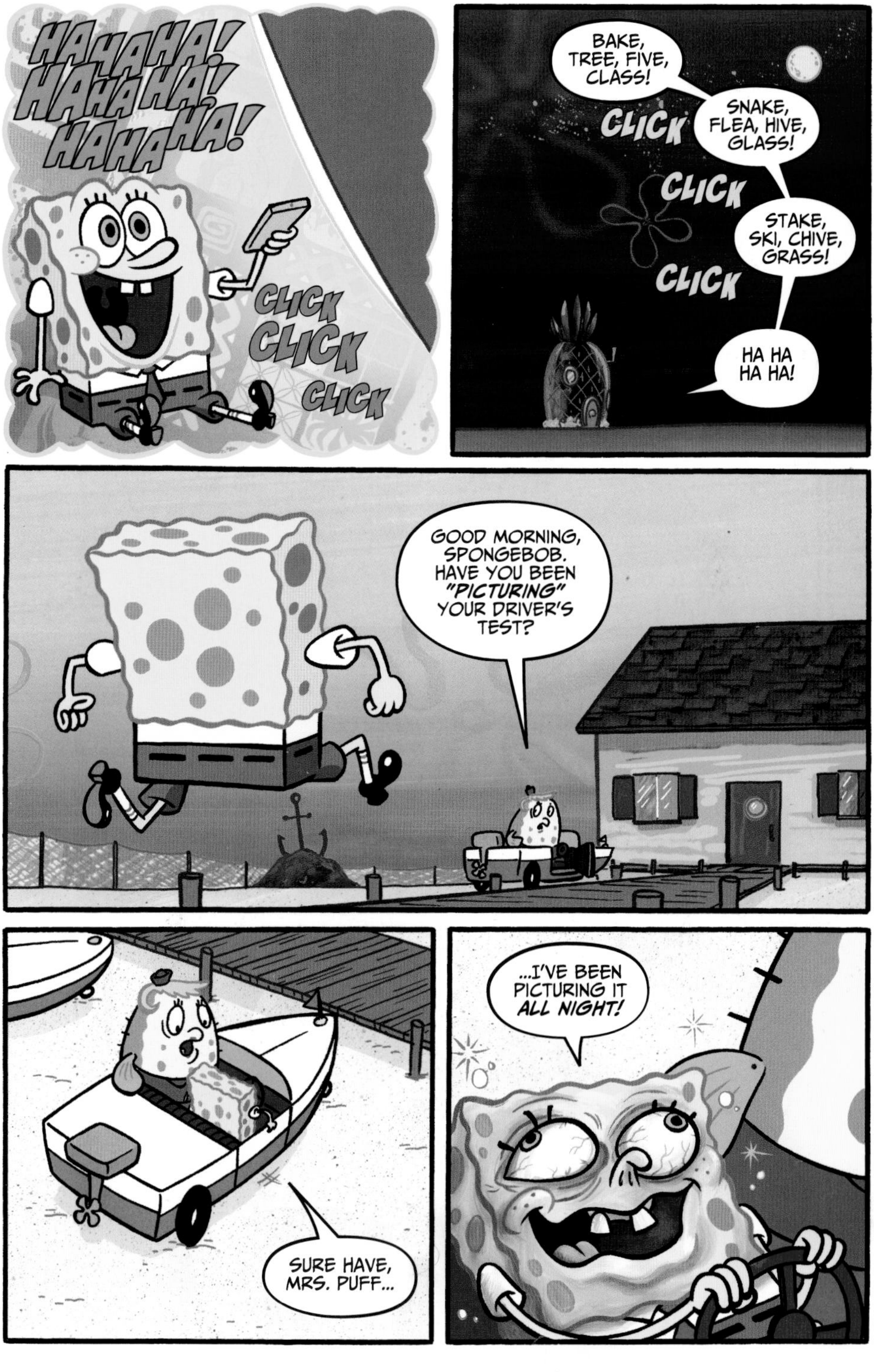
HAHAHA! HAHAHA! HAHAHA!
CLICK
CLICK
CLICK
BAKE, TREE, FIVE, CLASS!
CLICK
SNAKE, FLEA, HIVE, GLASS!
CLICK
STAKE, SKI, CHIVE, GRASS!
CLICK
HA HA HA HA!
GOOD MORNING, SPONGEBOB. HAVE YOU BEEN "PICTURING" YOUR DRIVER'S TEST?
SURE HAVE, MRS. PUFF...
...I'VE BEEN PICTURING IT ALL NIGHT!

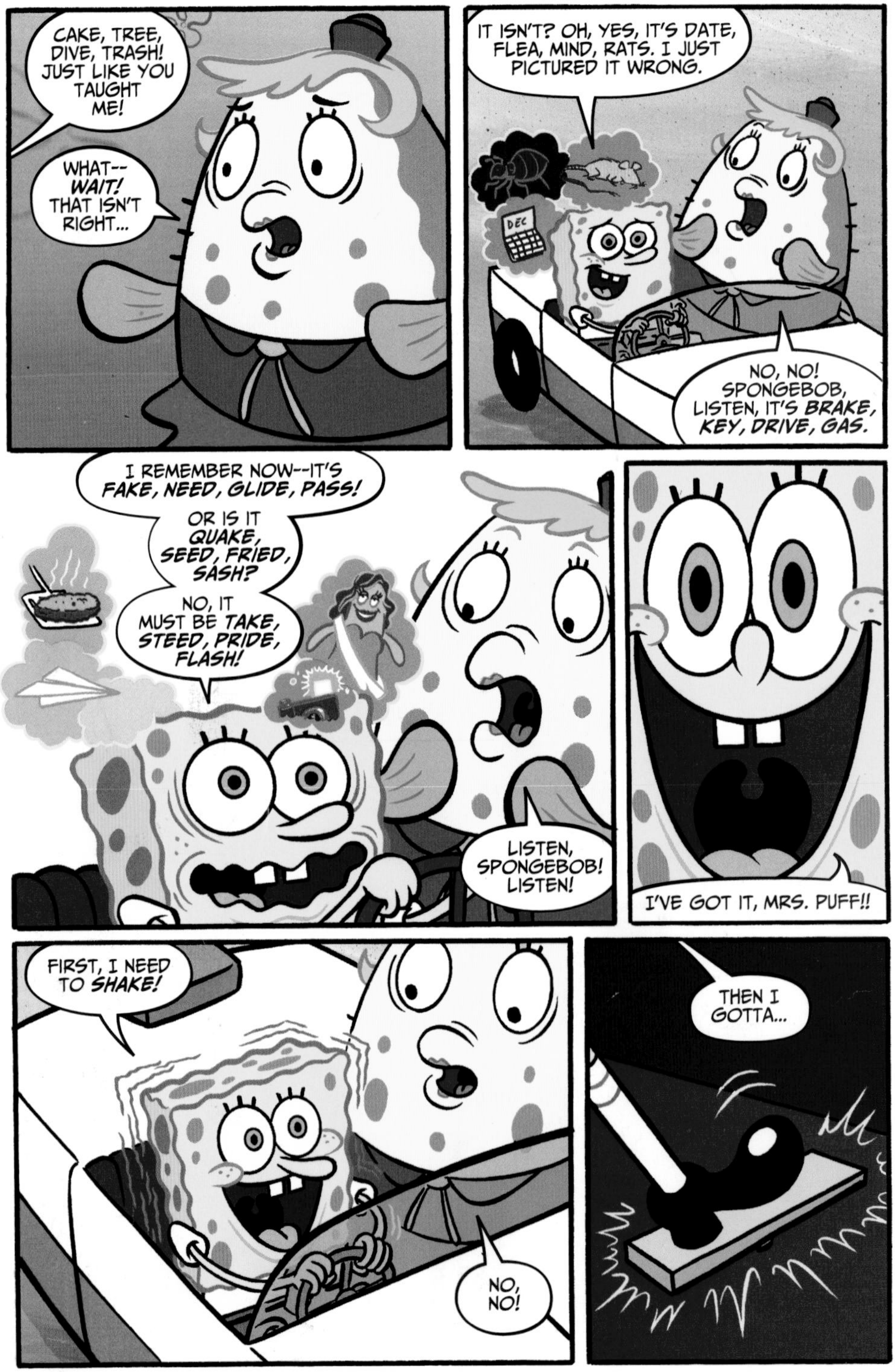
CAKE, TREE, DIVE, TRASH! JUST LIKE YOU TAUGHT ME!
WHAT-- *WAIT!* THAT ISN'T RIGHT...
IT ISN'T? OH, YES, IT'S DATE, FLEA, MIND, RATS. I JUST PICTURED IT WRONG.
DEC
NO, NO! SPONGEBOB, LISTEN, IT'S *BRAKE, KEY, DRIVE, GAS.*
I REMEMBER NOW--IT'S *FAKE, NEED, GLIDE, PASS!*
OR IS IT *QUAKE, SEED, FRIED, SASH?*
NO, IT MUST BE *TAKE, STEED, PRIDE, FLASH!*
LISTEN, SPONGEBOB! LISTEN!
I'VE GOT IT, MRS. PUFF!!
FIRST, I NEED TO *SHAKE!*
NO, NO!
THEN I GOTTA...

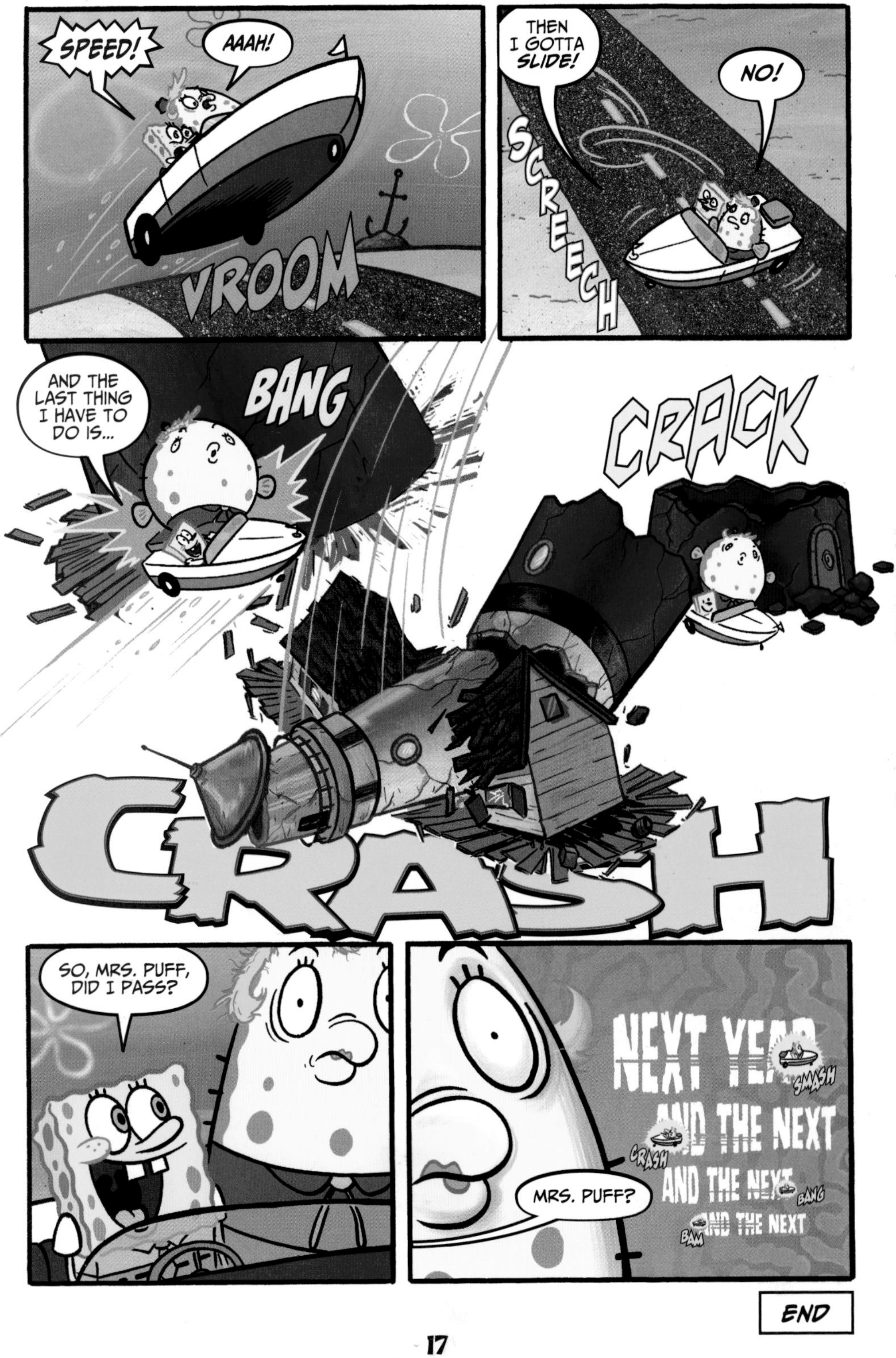
SPEED!
AAAH!
VROOM
THEN I GOTTA SLIDE!
NO!
SCREECH
AND THE LAST THING I HAVE TO DO IS...
BANG
CRACK
CRASH
SO, MRS. PUFF, DID I PASS?
NEXT YEAR
SMASH
AND THE NEXT
CRASH
AND THE NEXT
BANG
AND THE NEXT
BAM
MRS. PUFF?
END

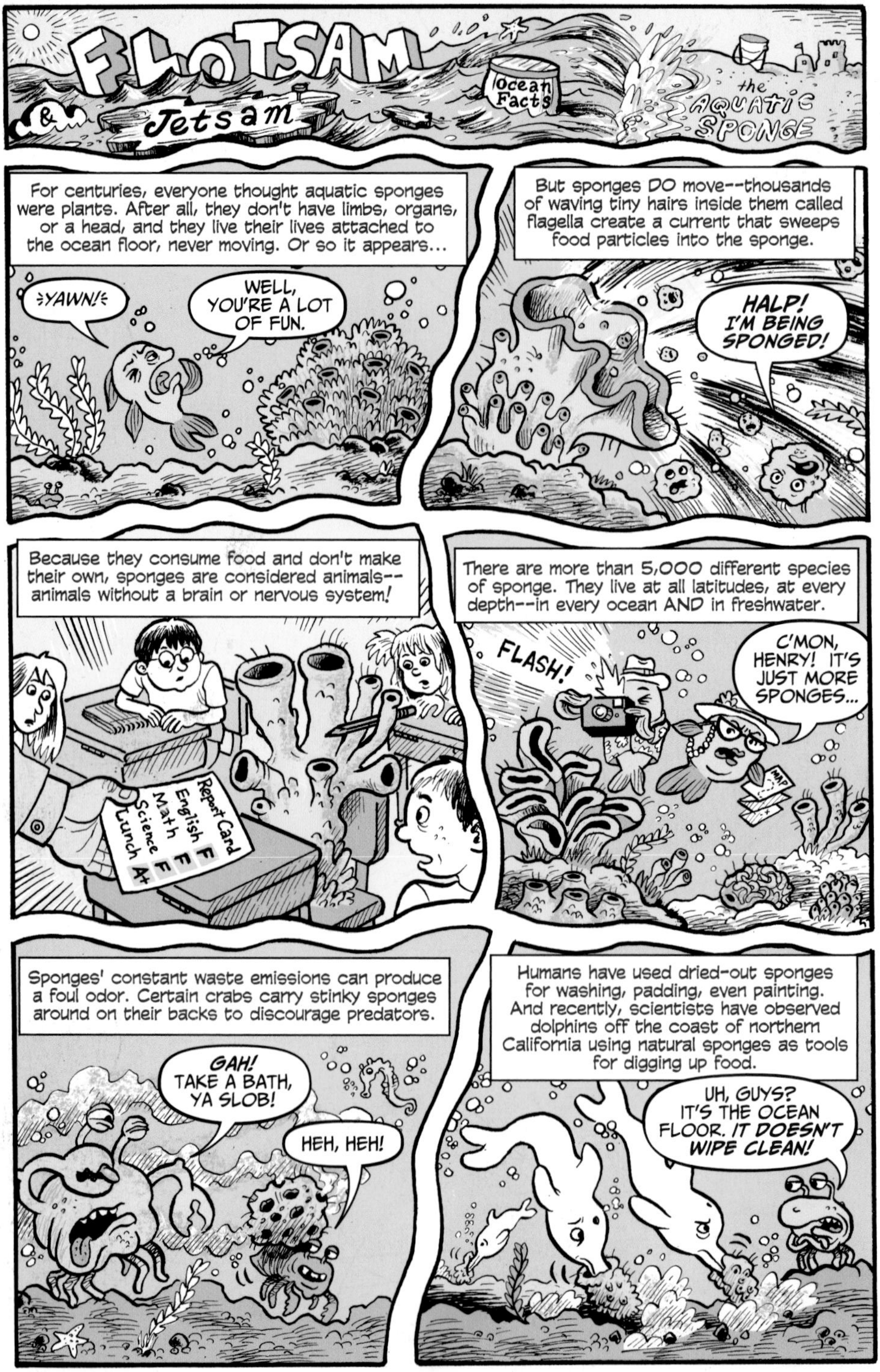
FLOTSAM
&
Jetsam
Ocean Facts
the AQUATIC SPONGE
For centuries, everyone thought aquatic sponges were plants. After all, they don't have limbs, organs, or a head, and they live their lives attached to the ocean floor, never moving. Or so it appears...
YAWN!
WELL, YOU'RE A LOT OF FUN.
But sponges DO move--thousands of waving tiny hairs inside them called flagella create a current that sweeps food particles into the sponge.
HALP! I'M BEING SPONGED!
Because they consume food and don't make their own, sponges are considered animals--animals without a brain or nervous system!
Report Card
English F
Math F
Science F
Lunch A+
There are more than 5,000 different species of sponge. They live at all latitudes, at every depth--in every ocean AND in freshwater.
FLASH!
C'MON, HENRY! IT'S JUST MORE SPONGES...
MAP
Sponges' constant waste emissions can produce a foul odor. Certain crabs carry stinky sponges around on their backs to discourage predators.
GAH! TAKE A BATH, YA SLOB!
HEH, HEH!
Humans have used dried-out sponges for washing, padding, even painting. And recently, scientists have observed dolphins off the coast of northern California using natural sponges as tools for digging up food.
UH, GUYS? IT'S THE OCEAN FLOOR. IT DOESN'T WIPE CLEAN!

WRITTEN BY CHRIS DUFFY DRAWN AND COLORED BY NATE NEAL LETTERED BY COMICRAFT

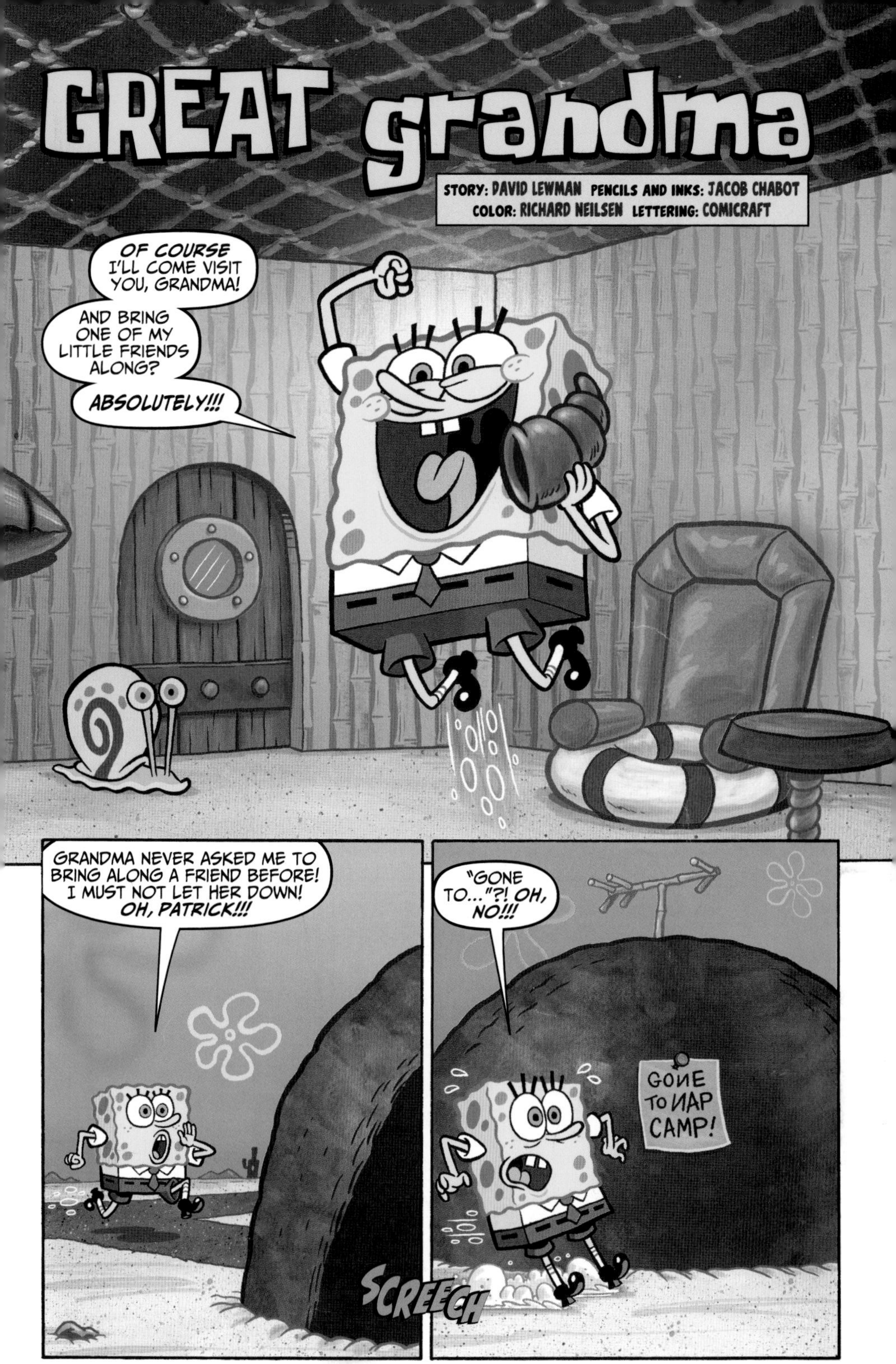
GREAT grandma
STORY: DAVID LEWMAN PENCILS AND INKS: JACOB CHABOT
COLOR: RICHARD NEILSEN LETTERING: COMICRAFT
OF COURSE I'LL COME VISIT YOU, GRANDMA!
AND BRING ONE OF MY LITTLE FRIENDS ALONG?
ABSOLUTELY!!!
GRANDMA NEVER ASKED ME TO BRING ALONG A FRIEND BEFORE! I MUST NOT LET HER DOWN! OH, PATRICK!!!
SCREECH
"GONE TO..."?! OH, NO!!!
GONE TO NAP CAMP!

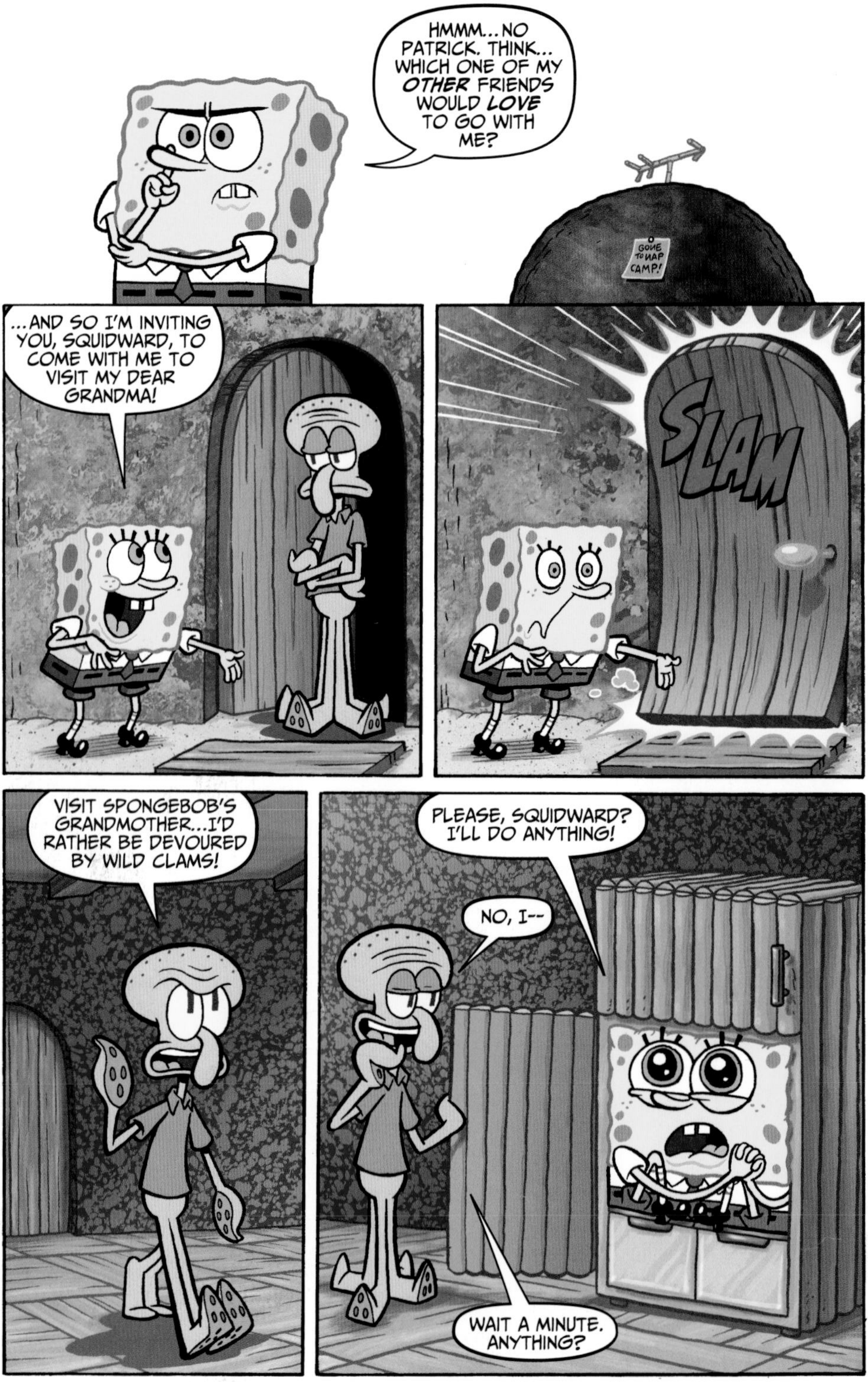
HMMM...NO PATRICK. THINK... WHICH ONE OF MY *OTHER* FRIENDS WOULD *LOVE* TO GO WITH ME?
GONE TO NAP CAMP!
...AND SO I'M INVITING YOU, SQUIDWARD, TO COME WITH ME TO VISIT MY DEAR GRANDMA!
SLAM
VISIT SPONGEBOB'S GRANDMOTHER...I'D RATHER BE DEVOURED BY WILD CLAMS!
PLEASE, SQUIDWARD? I'LL DO ANYTHING!
NO, I--
WAIT A MINUTE. ANYTHING?

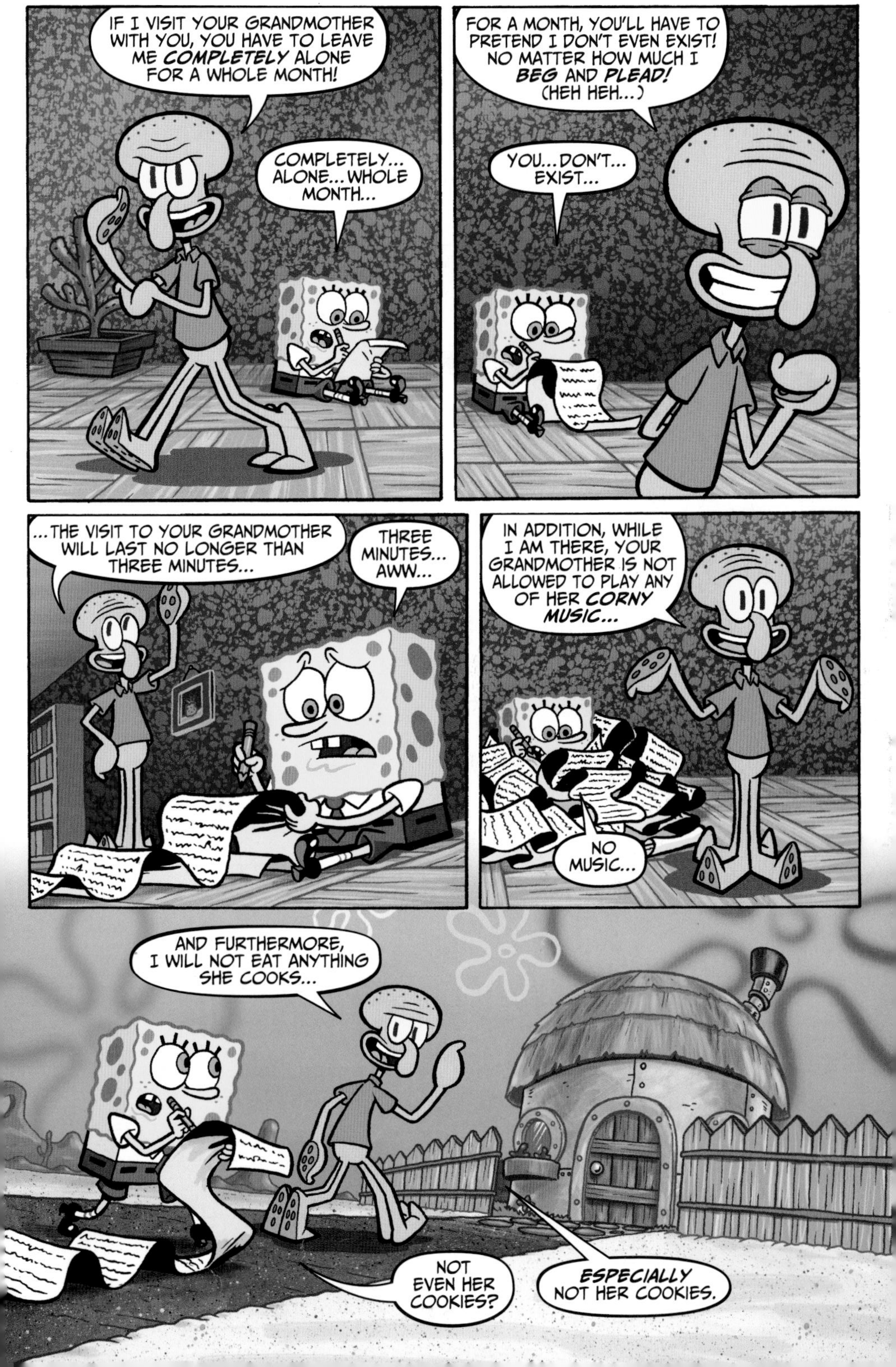
IF I VISIT YOUR GRANDMOTHER WITH YOU, YOU HAVE TO LEAVE ME COMPLETELY ALONE FOR A WHOLE MONTH!
COMPLETELY... ALONE...WHOLE MONTH...
FOR A MONTH, YOU'LL HAVE TO PRETEND I DON'T EVEN EXIST! NO MATTER HOW MUCH I BEG AND PLEAD! (HEH HEH...)
YOU...DON'T... EXIST...
...THE VISIT TO YOUR GRANDMOTHER WILL LAST NO LONGER THAN THREE MINUTES...
THREE MINUTES... AWW...
IN ADDITION, WHILE I AM THERE, YOUR GRANDMOTHER IS NOT ALLOWED TO PLAY ANY OF HER CORNY MUSIC...
NO MUSIC...
AND FURTHERMORE, I WILL NOT EAT ANYTHING SHE COOKS...
NOT EVEN HER COOKIES?
ESPECIALLY NOT HER COOKIES.

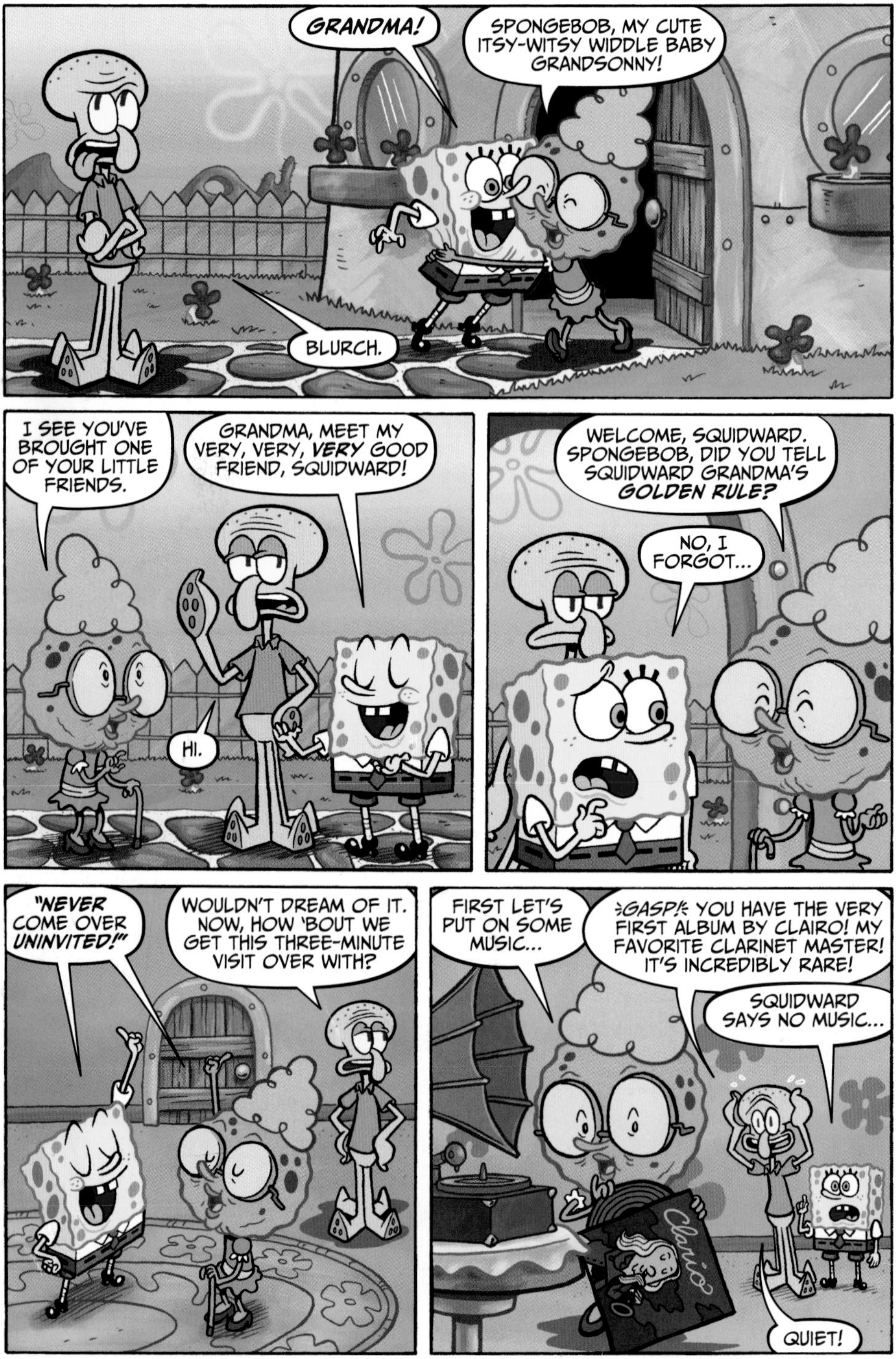

GRANDMA!
SPONGEBOB, MY CUTE ITSY-WITSY WIDDLE BABY GRANDSONNY!
BLURCH.
I SEE YOU'VE BROUGHT ONE OF YOUR LITTLE FRIENDS.
GRANDMA, MEET MY VERY, VERY, VERY GOOD FRIEND, SQUIDWARD!
HI.
WELCOME, SQUIDWARD. SPONGEBOB, DID YOU TELL SQUIDWARD GRANDMA'S GOLDEN RULE?
NO, I FORGOT...
"NEVER COME OVER UNINVITED!"
WOULDN'T DREAM OF IT. NOW, HOW 'BOUT WE GET THIS THREE-MINUTE VISIT OVER WITH?
FIRST LET'S PUT ON SOME MUSIC...
GASP! YOU HAVE THE VERY FIRST ALBUM BY CLAIRO! MY FAVORITE CLARINET MASTER! IT'S INCREDIBLY RARE!
SQUIDWARD SAYS NO MUSIC...
QUIET!
Clairo

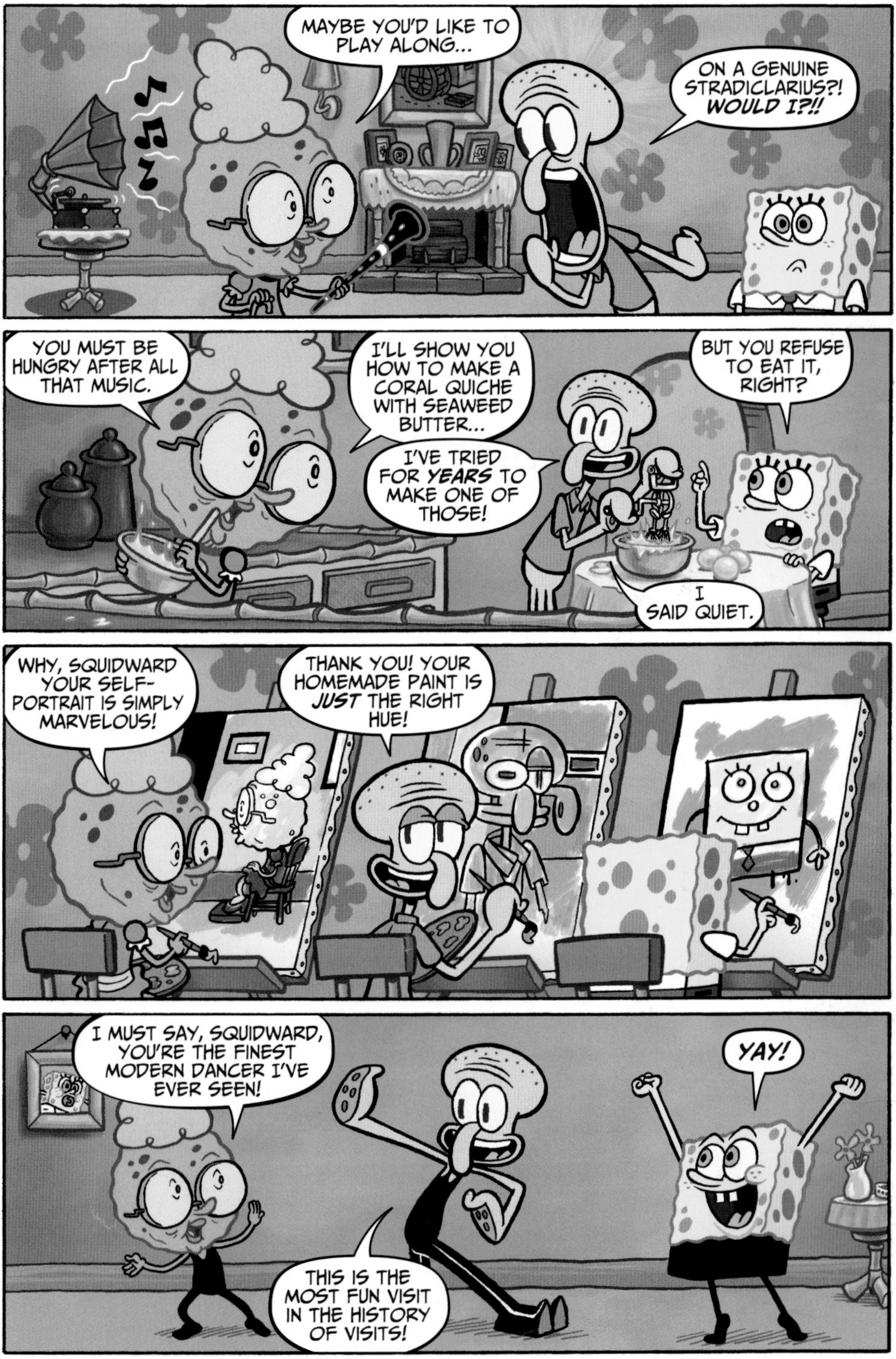
MAYBE YOU'D LIKE TO PLAY ALONG...
ON A GENUINE STRADICLARIUS?! WOULD I?!!
YOU MUST BE HUNGRY AFTER ALL THAT MUSIC.
I'LL SHOW YOU HOW TO MAKE A CORAL QUICHE WITH SEAWEED BUTTER...
I'VE TRIED FOR YEARS TO MAKE ONE OF THOSE!
BUT YOU REFUSE TO EAT IT, RIGHT?
I SAID QUIET.
WHY, SQUIDWARD YOUR SELF-PORTRAIT IS SIMPLY MARVELOUS!
THANK YOU! YOUR HOMEMADE PAINT IS JUST THE RIGHT HUE!
I MUST SAY, SQUIDWARD, YOU'RE THE FINEST MODERN DANCER I'VE EVER SEEN!
YAY!
THIS IS THE MOST FUN VISIT IN THE HISTORY OF VISITS!

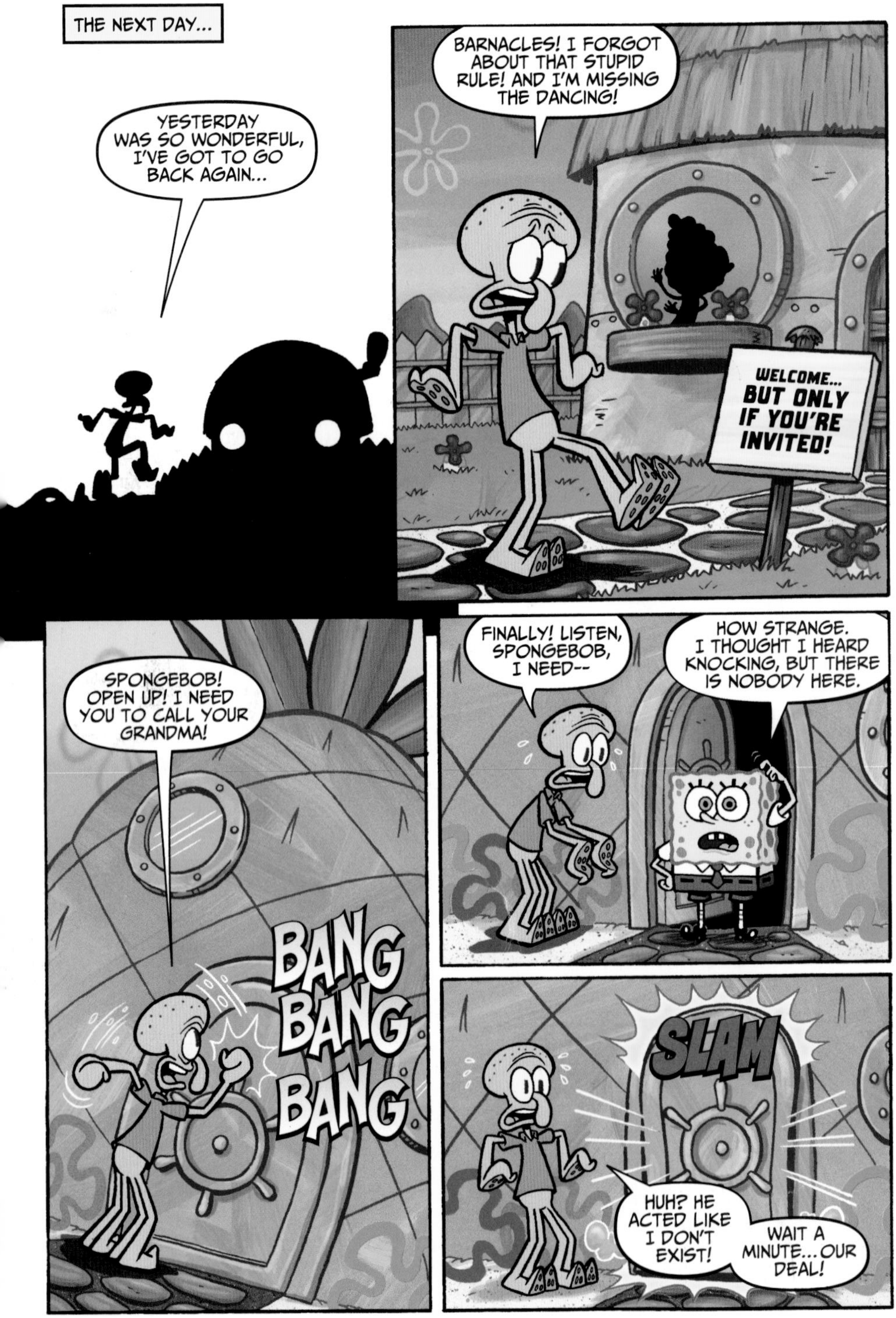
THE NEXT DAY...
YESTERDAY WAS SO WONDERFUL, I'VE GOT TO GO BACK AGAIN...
BARNACLES! I FORGOT ABOUT THAT STUPID RULE! AND I'M MISSING THE DANCING!
WELCOME... BUT ONLY IF YOU'RE INVITED!
SPONGEBOB! OPEN UP! I NEED YOU TO CALL YOUR GRANDMA!
BANG BANG BANG
FINALLY! LISTEN, SPONGEBOB, I NEED--
HOW STRANGE. I THOUGHT I HEARD KNOCKING, BUT THERE IS NOBODY HERE.
SLAM
HUH? HE ACTED LIKE I DON'T EXIST!
WAIT A MINUTE...OUR DEAL!

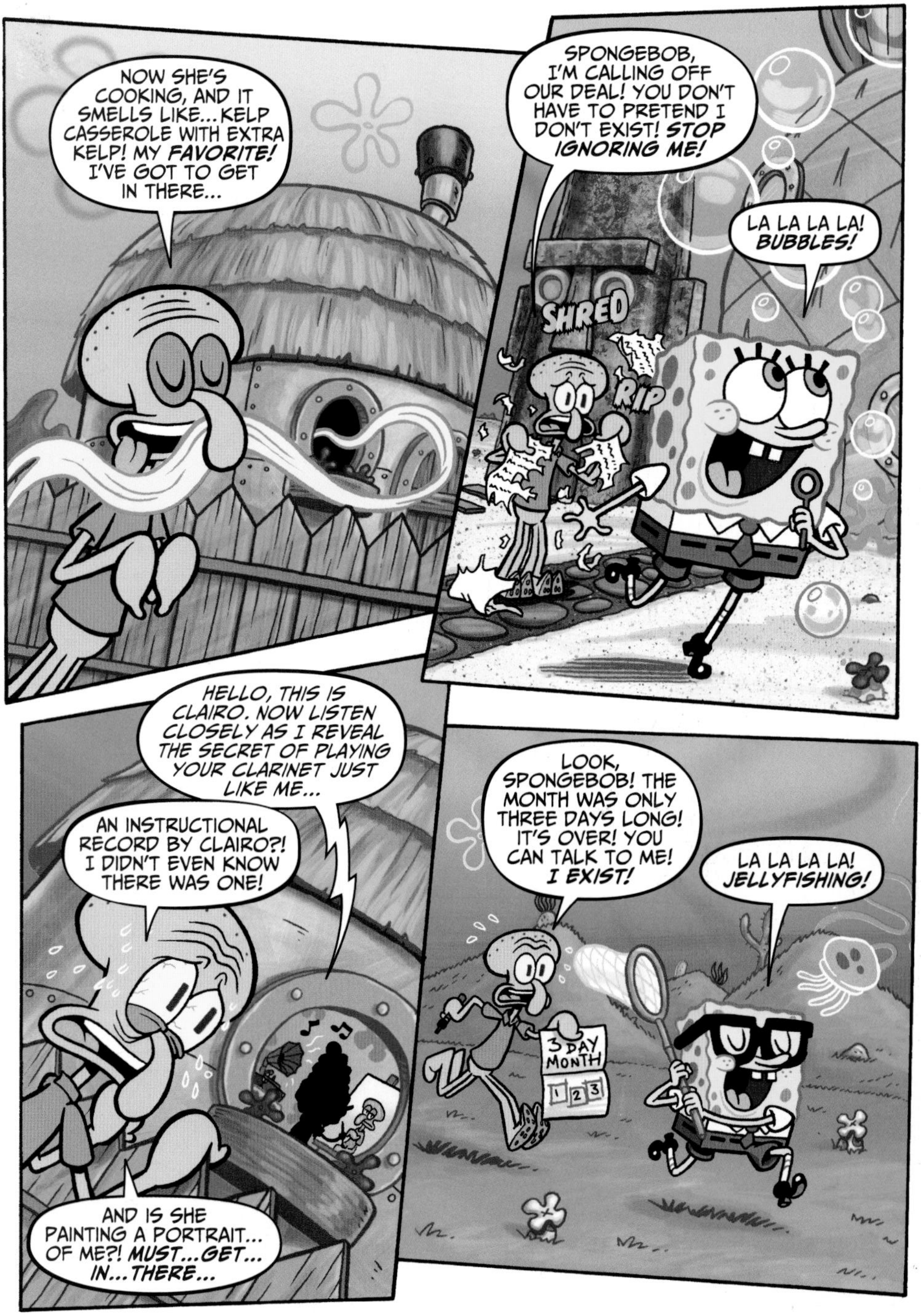
NOW SHE'S COOKING, AND IT SMELLS LIKE... KELP CASSEROLE WITH EXTRA KELP! MY *FAVORITE!* I'VE GOT TO GET IN THERE...
SPONGEBOB, I'M CALLING OFF OUR DEAL! YOU DON'T HAVE TO PRETEND I DON'T EXIST! *STOP IGNORING ME!*
LA LA LA LA! *BUBBLES!*
SHRED
RIP
HELLO, THIS IS CLAIRO. NOW LISTEN CLOSELY AS I REVEAL THE SECRET OF PLAYING YOUR CLARINET JUST LIKE ME...
AN INSTRUCTIONAL RECORD BY CLAIRO?! I DIDN'T EVEN KNOW THERE WAS ONE!
AND IS SHE PAINTING A PORTRAIT... OF ME?! *MUST... GET... IN... THERE...*
LOOK, SPONGEBOB! THE MONTH WAS ONLY THREE DAYS LONG! IT'S OVER! YOU CAN TALK TO ME! *I EXIST!*
3 DAY MONTH
1 2 3
LA LA LA LA! *JELLYFISHING!*

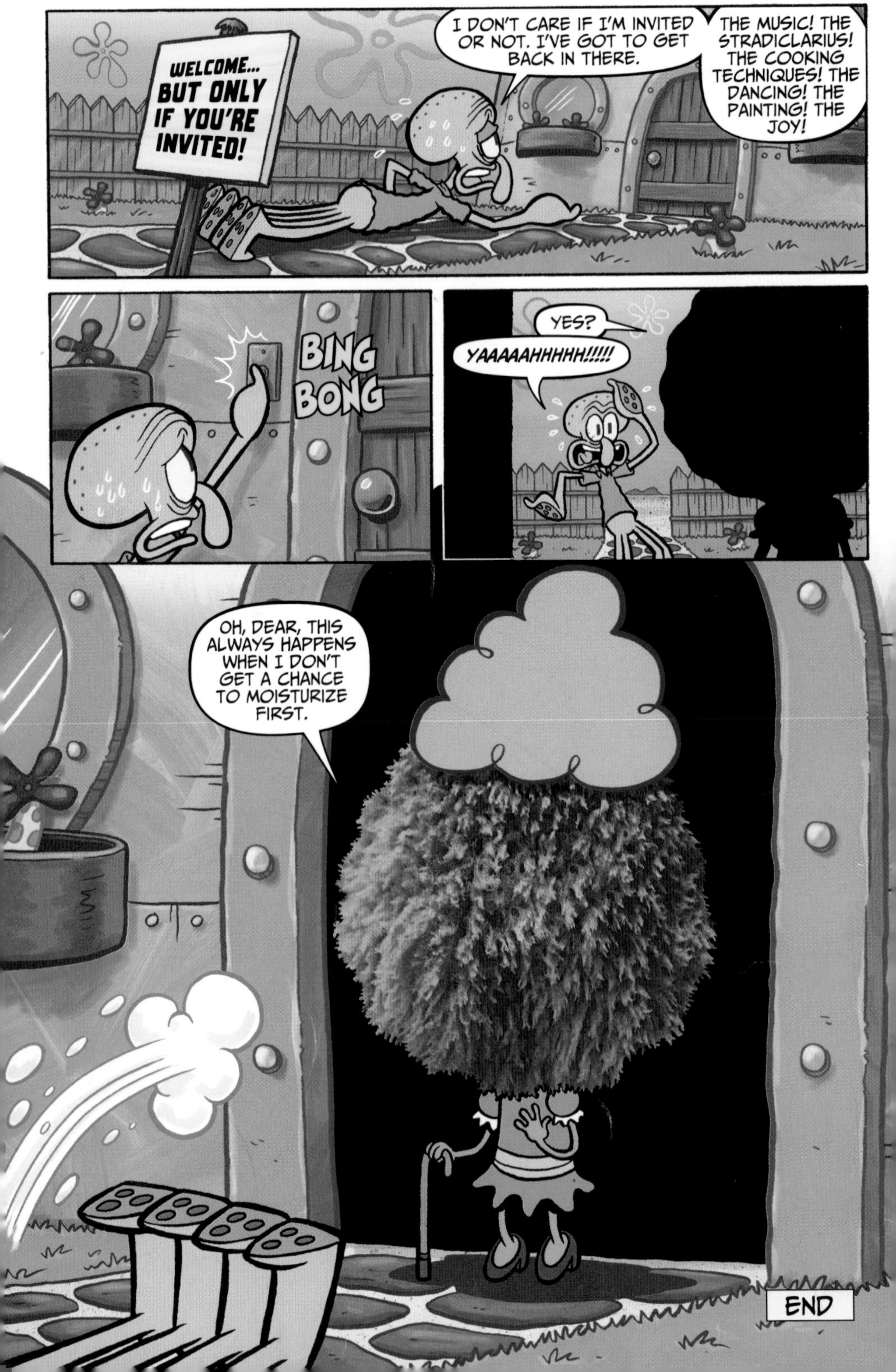
WELCOME... BUT ONLY IF YOU'RE INVITED!
I DON'T CARE IF I'M INVITED OR NOT. I'VE GOT TO GET BACK IN THERE.
THE MUSIC! THE STRADICLARIUS! THE COOKING TECHNIQUES! THE DANCING! THE PAINTING! THE JOY!
BING BONG
YES?
YAAAAAHHHHH!!!!!
OH, DEAR, THIS ALWAYS HAPPENS WHEN I DON'T GET A CHANCE TO MOISTURIZE FIRST.
END

PatStar*NoPants

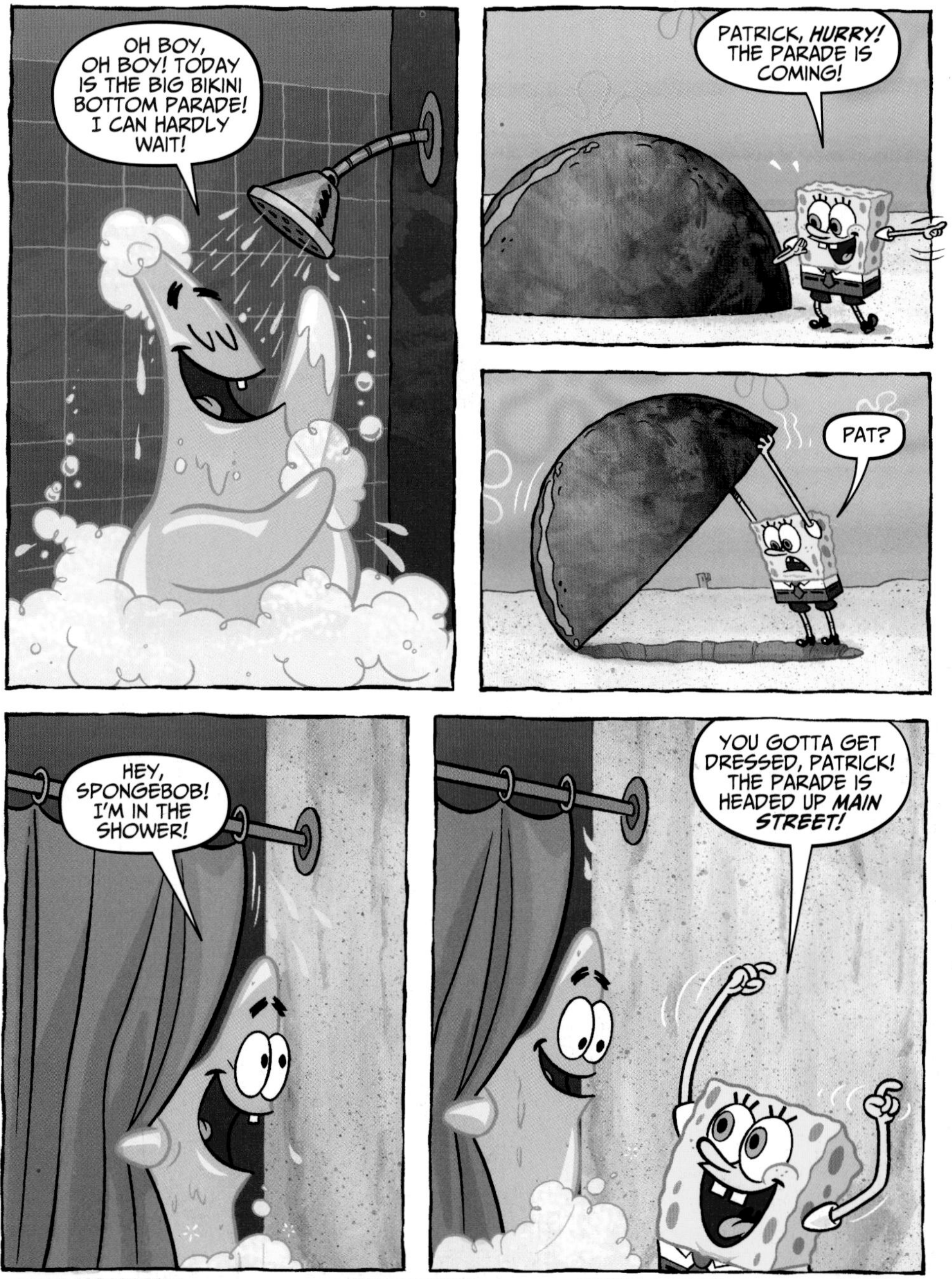

OH BOY, OH BOY! TODAY IS THE BIG BIKINI BOTTOM PARADE! I CAN HARDLY WAIT!
PATRICK, HURRY! THE PARADE IS COMING!
PAT?
HEY, SPONGEBOB! I'M IN THE SHOWER!
YOU GOTTA GET DRESSED, PATRICK! THE PARADE IS HEADED UP MAIN STREET!

STORY: COREY BARBA **PENCILS AND INKS:** VINCE DEPORTER **COLORING:** MICHAEL LAPINSKI **LETTERING:** COMICRAFT

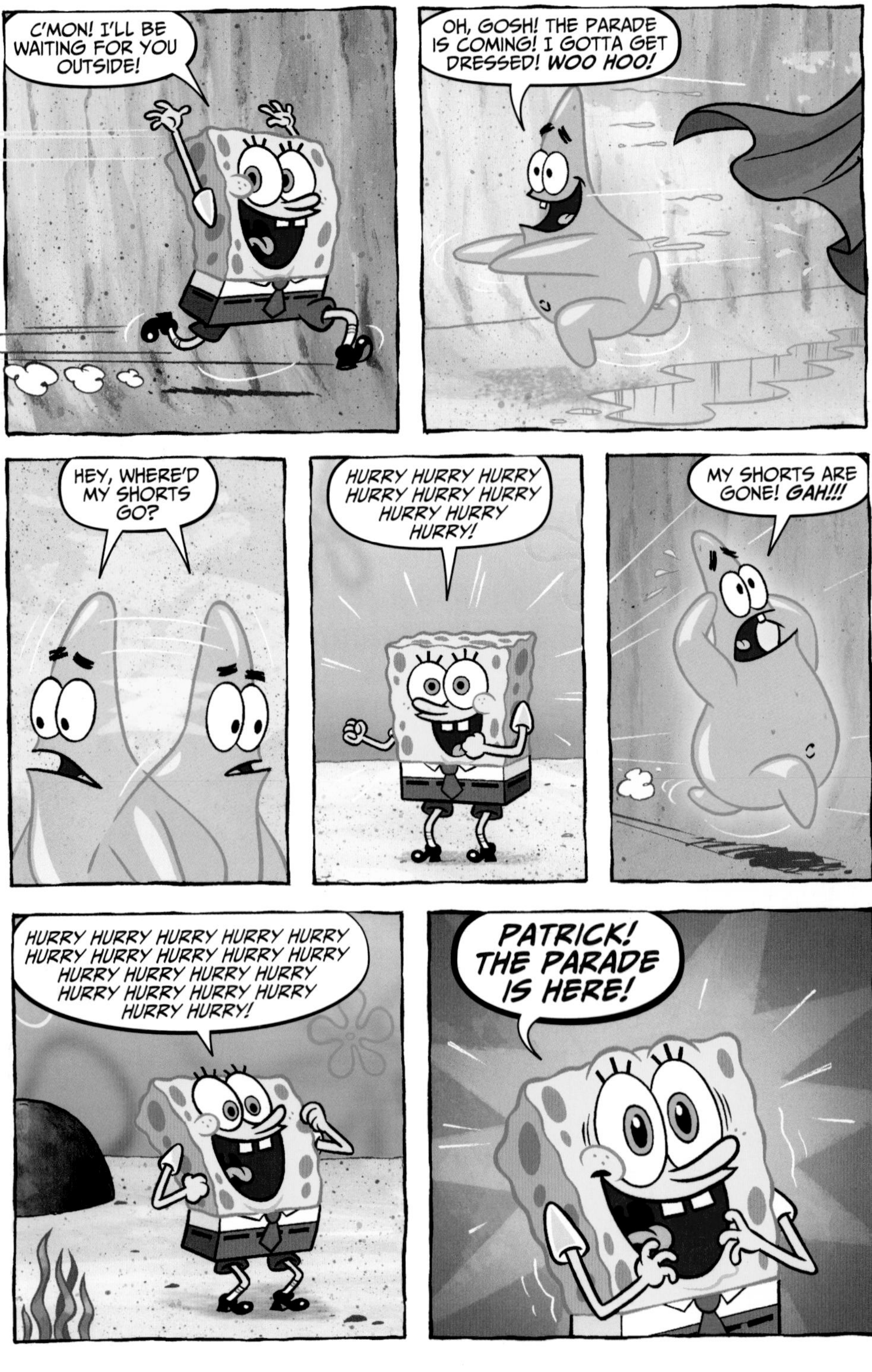
C'MON! I'LL BE WAITING FOR YOU OUTSIDE!
OH, GOSH! THE PARADE IS COMING! I GOTTA GET DRESSED! WOO HOO!
HEY, WHERE'D MY SHORTS GO?
HURRY HURRY HURRY HURRY HURRY HURRY HURRY HURRY HURRY!
MY SHORTS ARE GONE! GAH!!!
HURRY HURRY HURRY HURRY HURRY HURRY HURRY HURRY HURRY HURRY HURRY HURRY HURRY HURRY HURRY HURRY HURRY HURRY HURRY HURRY!
PATRICK! THE PARADE IS HERE!

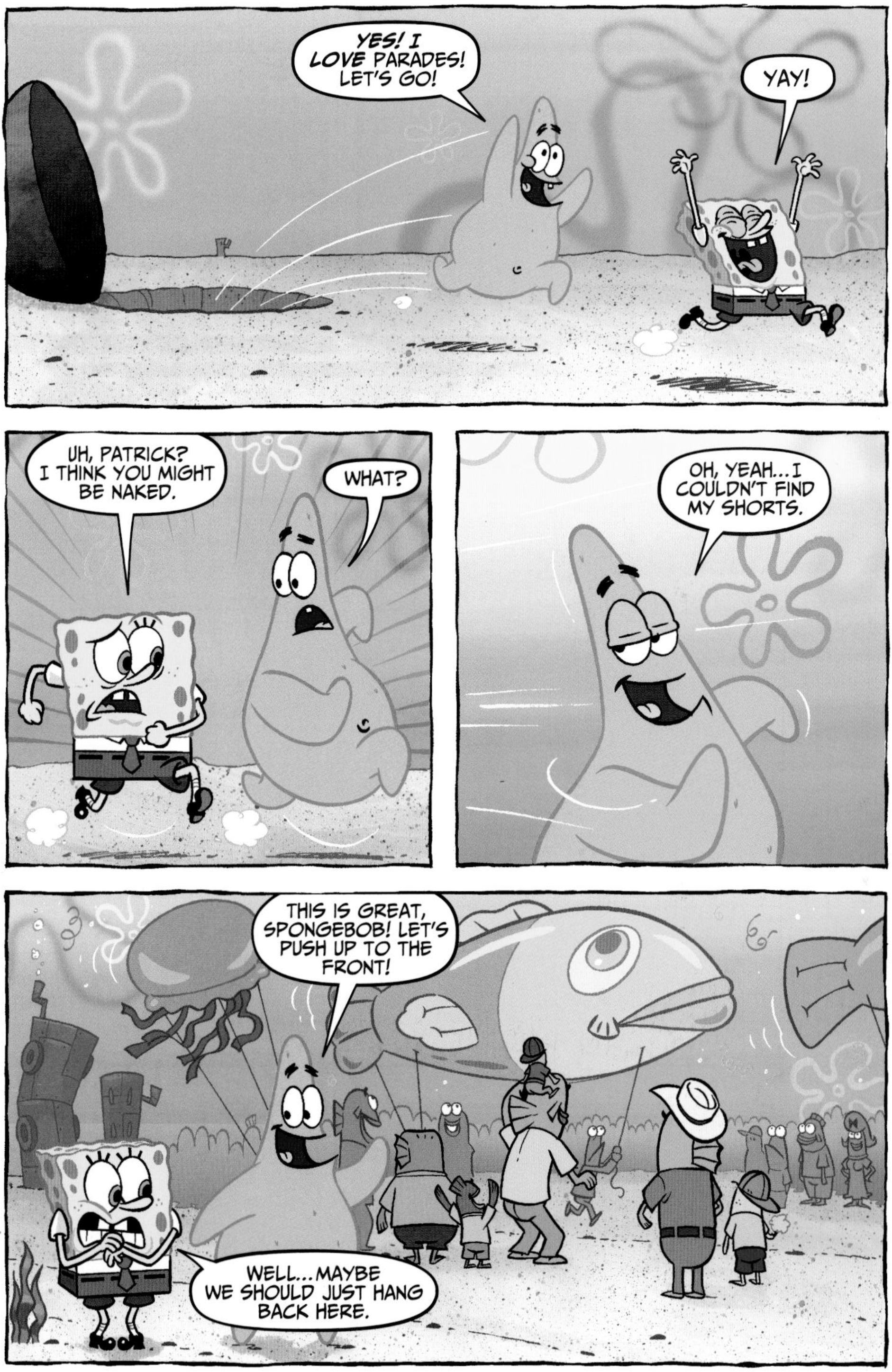
YES! I LOVE PARADES! LET'S GO!
YAY!
UH, PATRICK? I THINK YOU MIGHT BE NAKED.
WHAT?
OH, YEAH... I COULDN'T FIND MY SHORTS.
THIS IS GREAT, SPONGEBOB! LET'S PUSH UP TO THE FRONT!
WELL... MAYBE WE SHOULD JUST HANG BACK HERE.

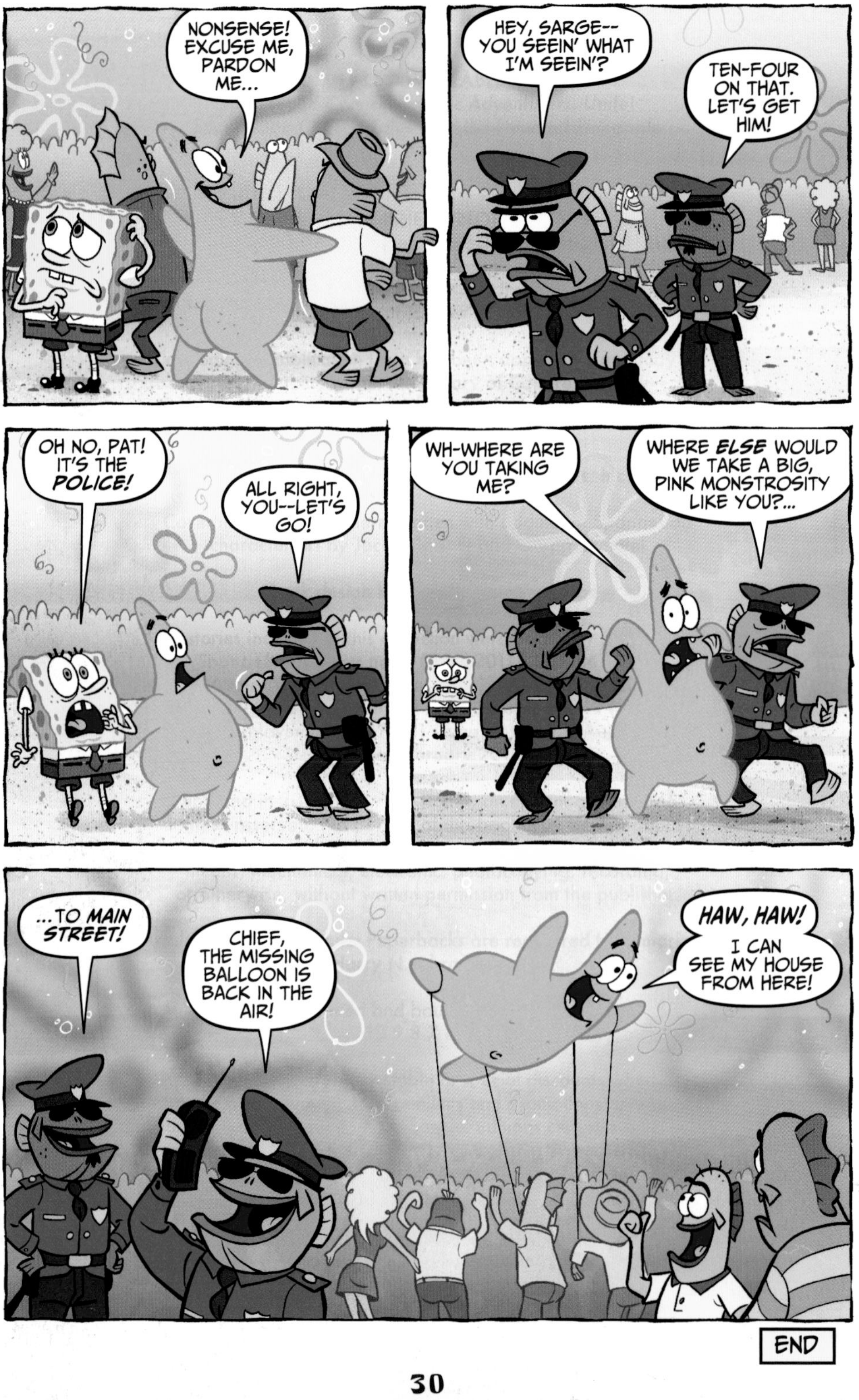
NONSENSE! EXCUSE ME, PARDON ME...
HEY, SARGE-- YOU SEEIN' WHAT I'M SEEIN'?
TEN-FOUR ON THAT. LET'S GET HIM!
OH NO, PAT! IT'S THE POLICE!
ALL RIGHT, YOU--LET'S GO!
WH-WHERE ARE YOU TAKING ME?
WHERE ELSE WOULD WE TAKE A BIG, PINK MONSTROSITY LIKE YOU?...
...TO MAIN STREET!
CHIEF, THE MISSING BALLOON IS BACK IN THE AIR!
HAW, HAW! I CAN SEE MY HOUSE FROM HERE!
END

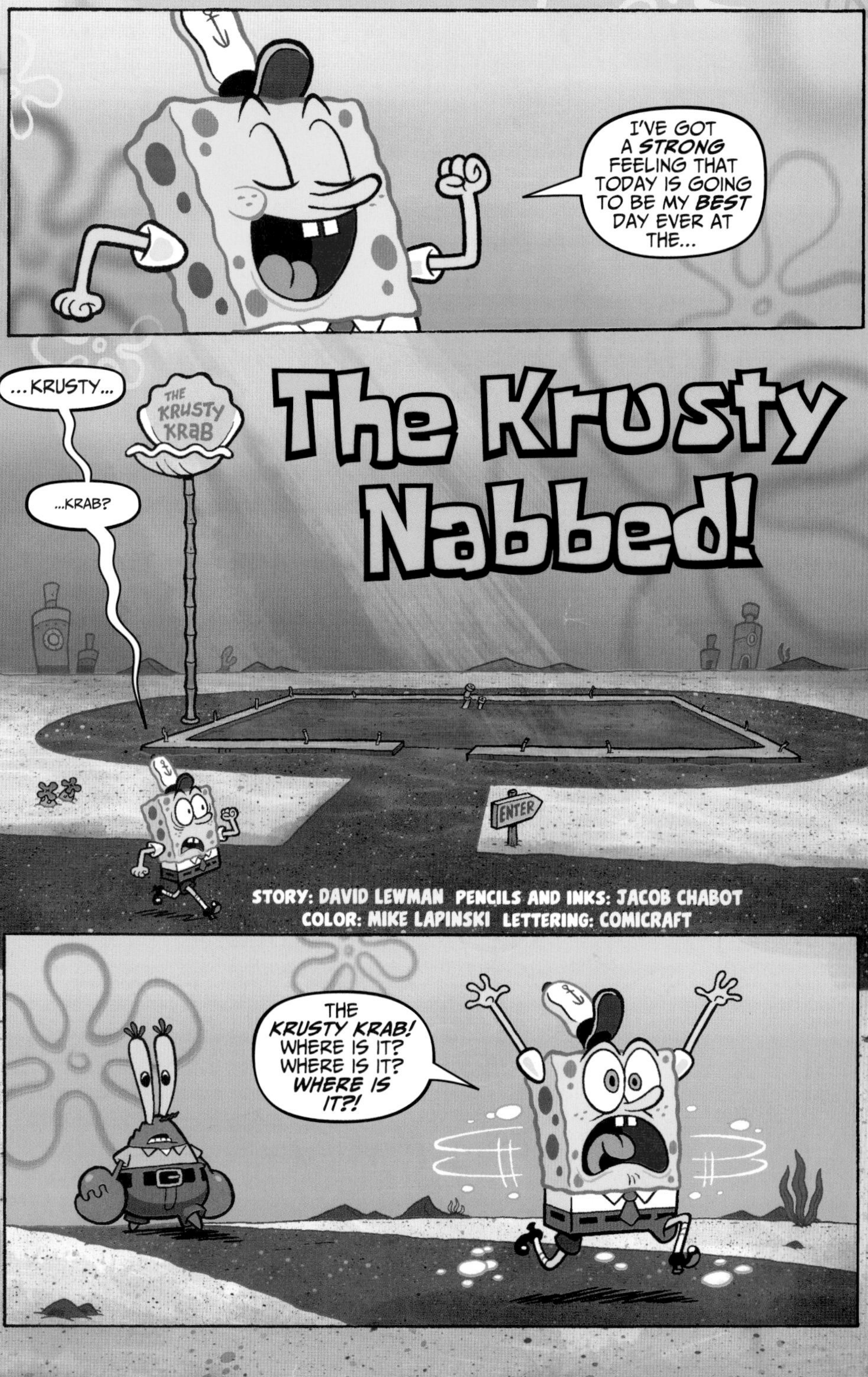
I'VE GOT A STRONG FEELING THAT TODAY IS GOING TO BE MY BEST DAY EVER AT THE...
...KRUSTY...
THE KRUSTY KRAB
...KRAB?
The Krusty Nabbed!
ENTER
STORY: DAVID LEWMAN PENCILS AND INKS: JACOB CHABOT
COLOR: MIKE LAPINSKI LETTERING: COMICRAFT
THE KRUSTY KRAB! WHERE IS IT? WHERE IS IT? WHERE IS IT?!

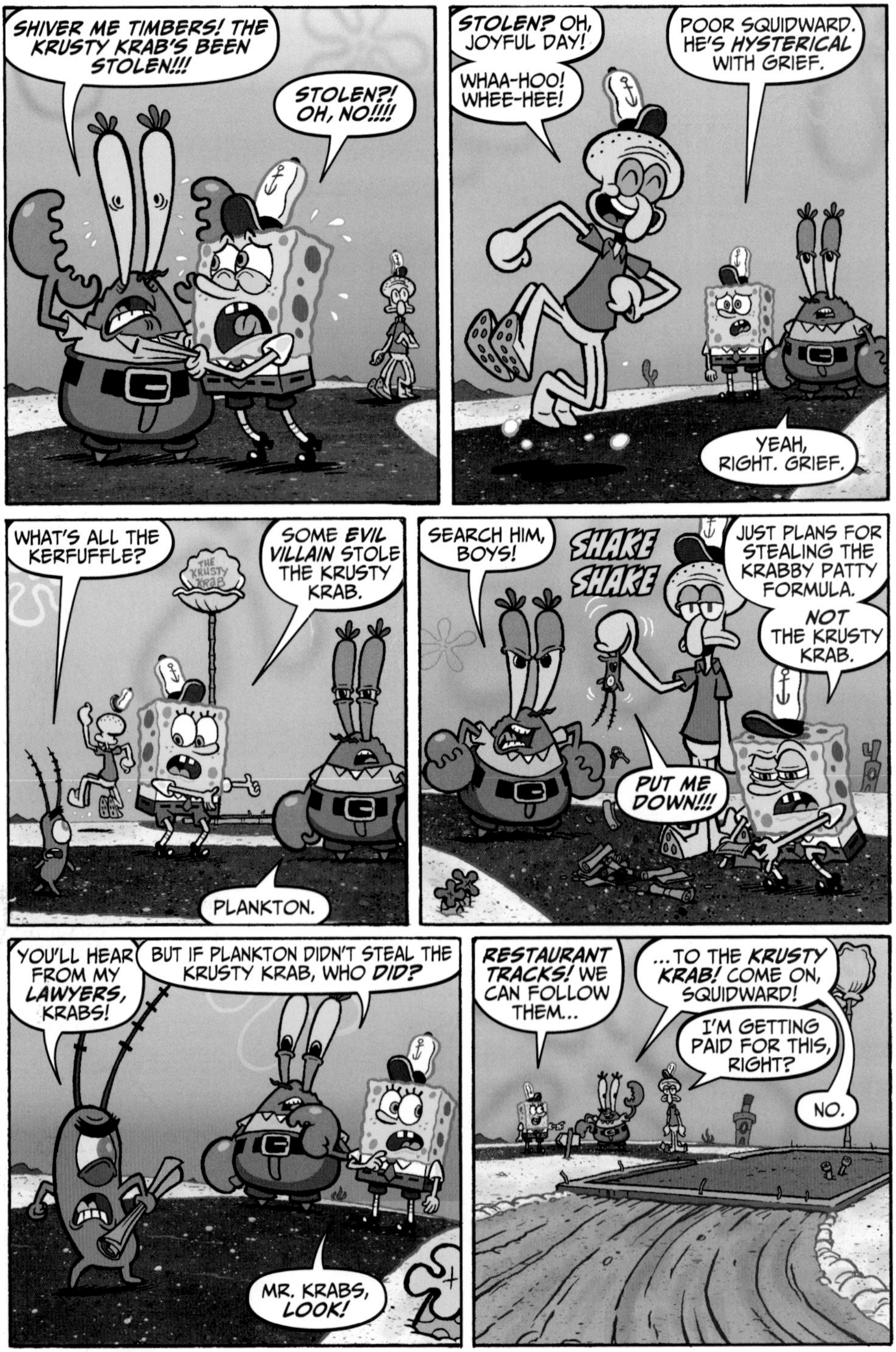
SHIVER ME TIMBERS! THE KRUSTY KRAB'S BEEN STOLEN!!!
STOLEN?! OH, NO!!!!
STOLEN? OH, JOYFUL DAY!
WHAA-HOO! WHEE-HEE!
POOR SQUIDWARD. HE'S HYSTERICAL WITH GRIEF.
YEAH, RIGHT. GRIEF.
WHAT'S ALL THE KERFUFFLE?
SOME EVIL VILLAIN STOLE THE KRUSTY KRAB.
THE KRUSTY KRAB
PLANKTON.
SEARCH HIM, BOYS!
SHAKE SHAKE
JUST PLANS FOR STEALING THE KRABBY PATTY FORMULA.
NOT THE KRUSTY KRAB.
PUT ME DOWN!!!
YOU'LL HEAR FROM MY LAWYERS, KRABS!
BUT IF PLANKTON DIDN'T STEAL THE KRUSTY KRAB, WHO DID?
MR. KRABS, LOOK!
RESTAURANT TRACKS! WE CAN FOLLOW THEM...
...TO THE KRUSTY KRAB! COME ON, SQUIDWARD!
I'M GETTING PAID FOR THIS, RIGHT?
NO.

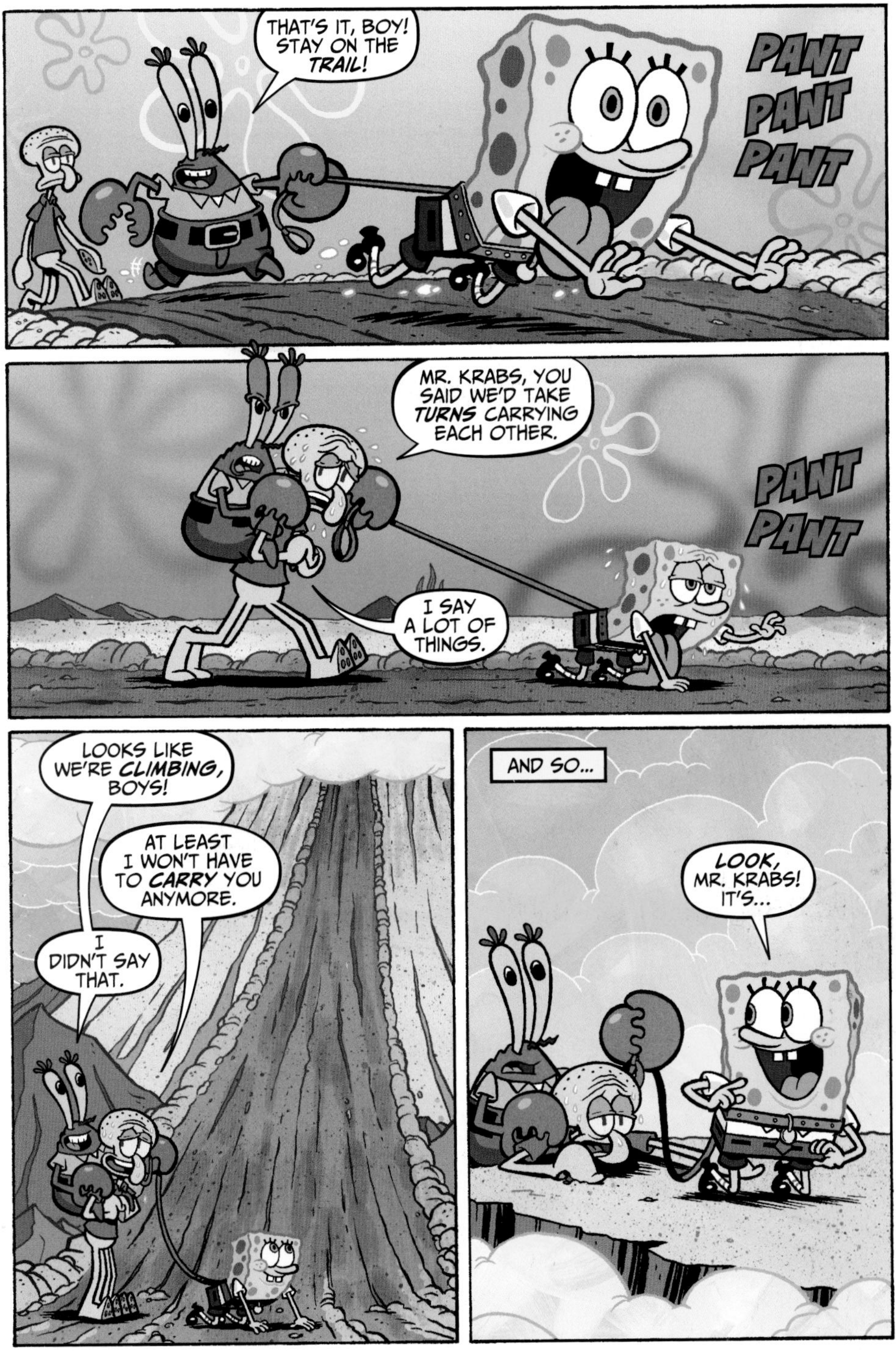
THAT'S IT, BOY! STAY ON THE TRAIL!
PANT PANT PANT
MR. KRABS, YOU SAID WE'D TAKE TURNS CARRYING EACH OTHER.
PANT PANT
I SAY A LOT OF THINGS.
LOOKS LIKE WE'RE CLIMBING, BOYS!
AT LEAST I WON'T HAVE TO CARRY YOU ANYMORE.
I DIDN'T SAY THAT.
AND SO...
LOOK, MR. KRABS! IT'S...

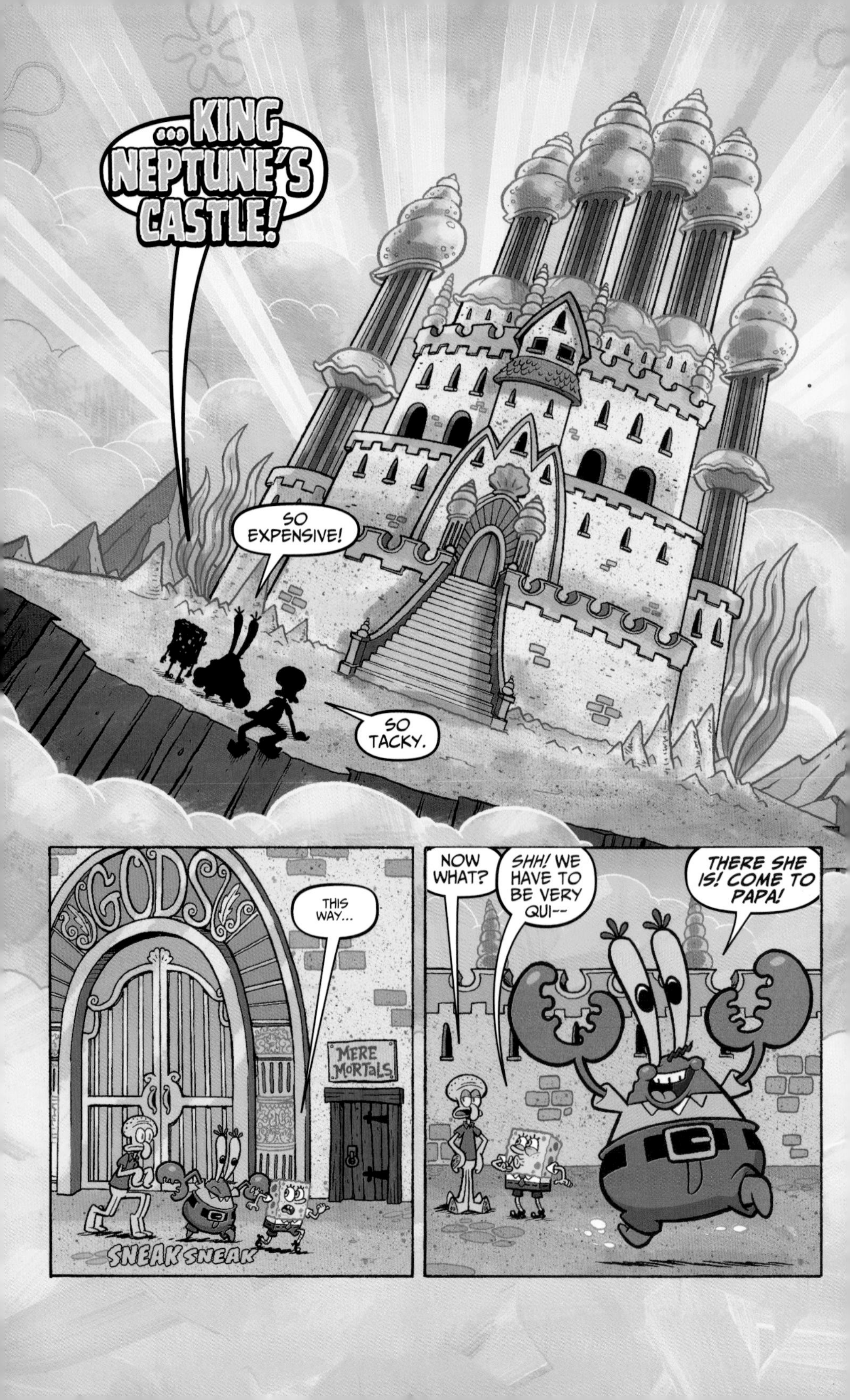
...KING NEPTUNE'S CASTLE!
SO EXPENSIVE!
SO TACKY.
GODS
THIS WAY...
MERE MORTALS
SNEAK SNEAK
NOW WHAT?
SHH! WE HAVE TO BE VERY QUI--
THERE SHE IS! COME TO PAPA!

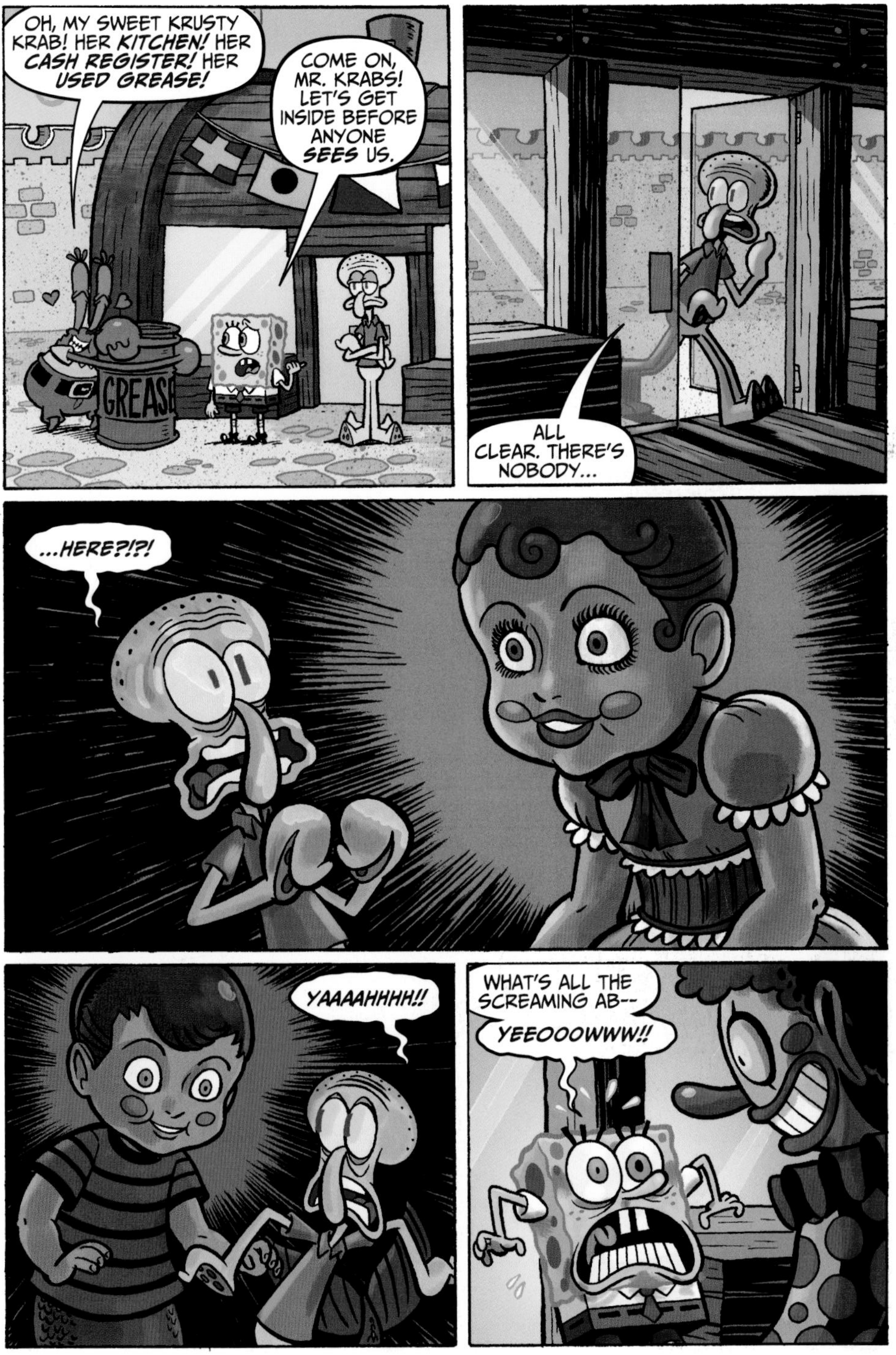
OH, MY SWEET KRUSTY KRAB! HER KITCHEN! HER CASH REGISTER! HER USED GREASE!
COME ON, MR. KRABS! LET'S GET INSIDE BEFORE ANYONE SEES US.
GREASE
ALL CLEAR. THERE'S NOBODY...
...HERE?!?!
YAAAAHHHH!!
WHAT'S ALL THE SCREAMING AB--
YEEOOOWWW!!

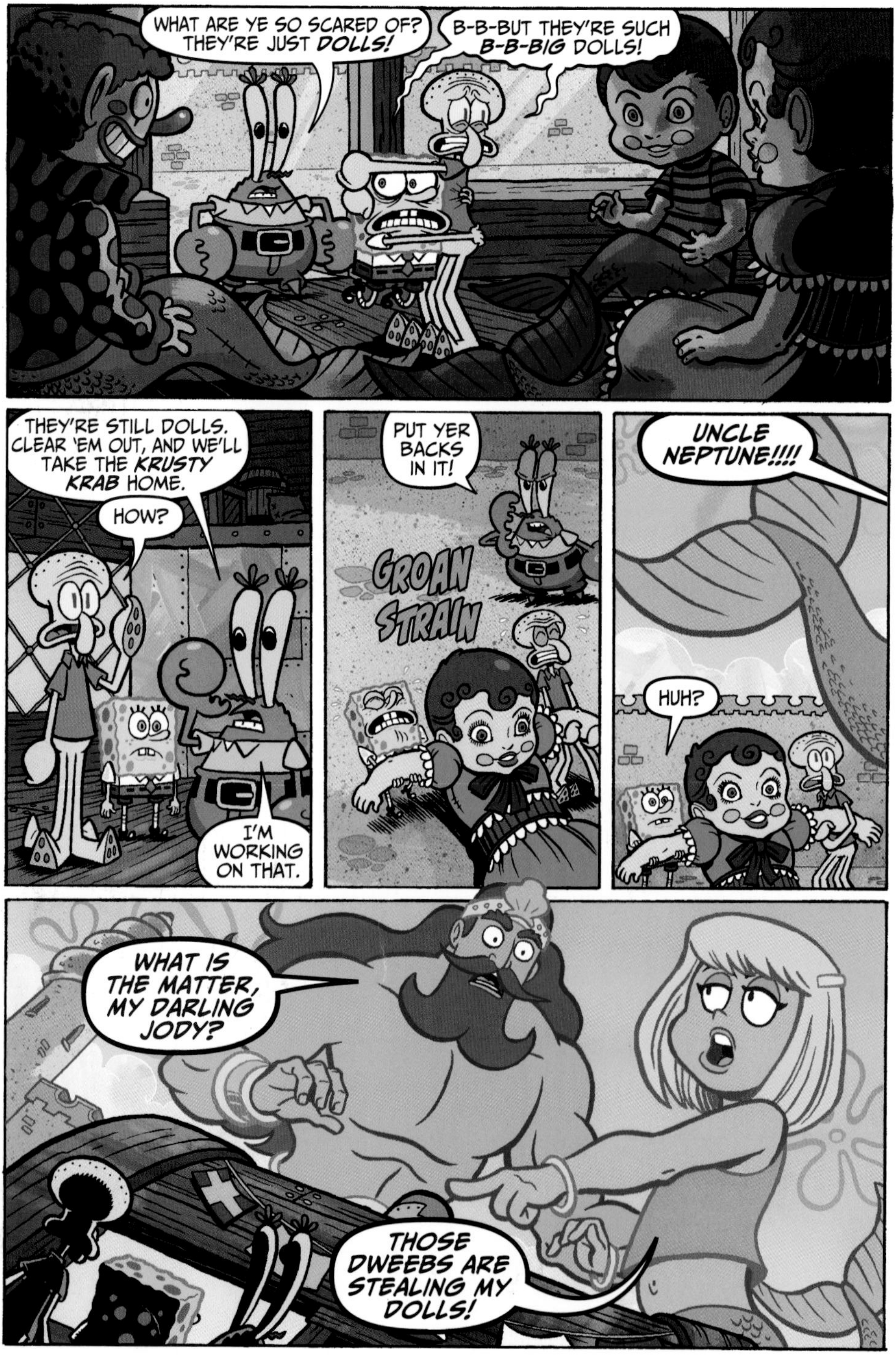
WHAT ARE YE SO SCARED OF? THEY'RE JUST DOLLS!
B-B-BUT THEY'RE SUCH B-B-BIG DOLLS!
THEY'RE STILL DOLLS. CLEAR 'EM OUT, AND WE'LL TAKE THE KRUSTY KRAB HOME.
HOW?
I'M WORKING ON THAT.
PUT YER BACKS IN IT!
GROAN
STRAIN
UNCLE NEPTUNE!!!!
HUH?
WHAT IS THE MATTER, MY DARLING JODY?
THOSE DWEEBS ARE STEALING MY DOLLS!

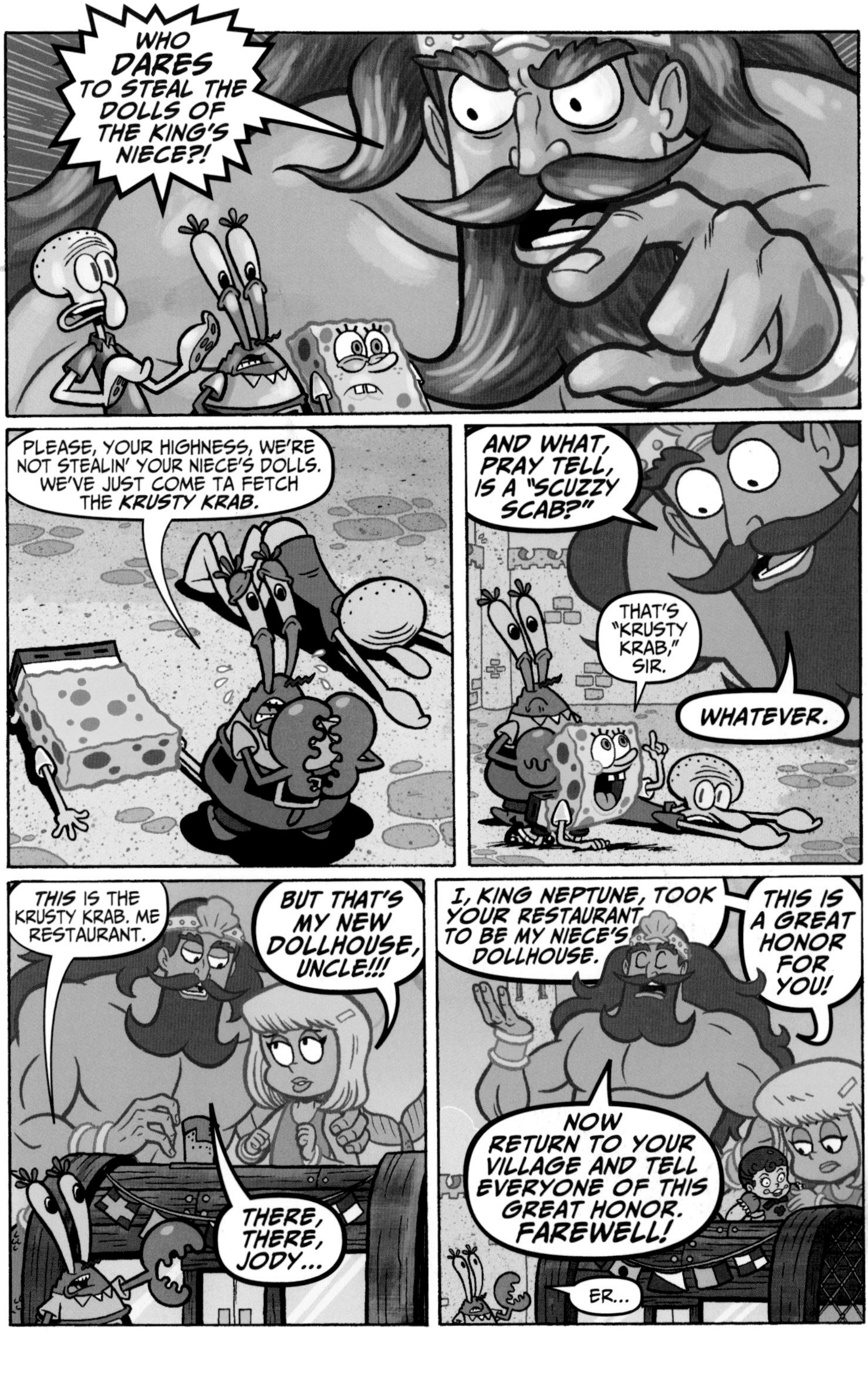
WHO DARES TO STEAL THE DOLLS OF THE KING'S NIECE?!
PLEASE, YOUR HIGHNESS, WE'RE NOT STEALIN' YOUR NIECE'S DOLLS. WE'VE JUST COME TA FETCH THE KRUSTY KRAB.
AND WHAT, PRAY TELL, IS A "SCUZZY SCAB?"
THAT'S "KRUSTY KRAB," SIR.
WHATEVER.
THIS IS THE KRUSTY KRAB. ME RESTAURANT.
BUT THAT'S MY NEW DOLLHOUSE, UNCLE!!!
THERE, THERE, JODY...
I, KING NEPTUNE, TOOK YOUR RESTAURANT TO BE MY NIECE'S DOLLHOUSE.
THIS IS A GREAT HONOR FOR YOU!
NOW RETURN TO YOUR VILLAGE AND TELL EVERYONE OF THIS GREAT HONOR. FAREWELL!
ER...

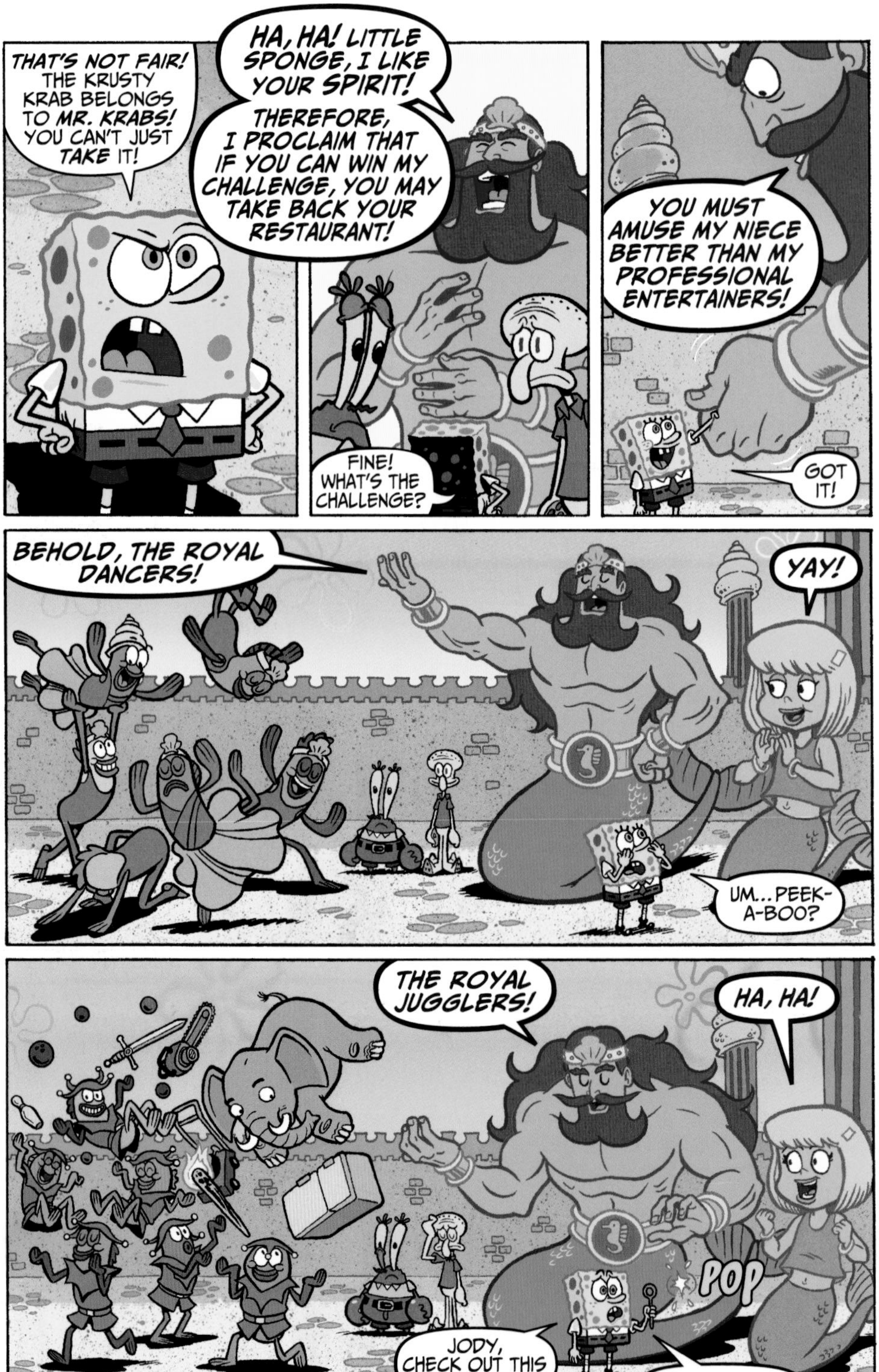
THAT'S NOT FAIR! THE KRUSTY KRAB BELONGS TO MR. KRABS! YOU CAN'T JUST TAKE IT!
HA, HA! LITTLE SPONGE, I LIKE YOUR SPIRIT!
THEREFORE, I PROCLAIM THAT IF YOU CAN WIN MY CHALLENGE, YOU MAY TAKE BACK YOUR RESTAURANT!
FINE! WHAT'S THE CHALLENGE?
YOU MUST AMUSE MY NIECE BETTER THAN MY PROFESSIONAL ENTERTAINERS!
GOT IT!
BEHOLD, THE ROYAL DANCERS!
YAY!
UM... PEEK-A-BOO?
THE ROYAL JUGGLERS!
HA, HA!
POP
JODY, CHECK OUT THIS BUBBLE!
BARNACLES...

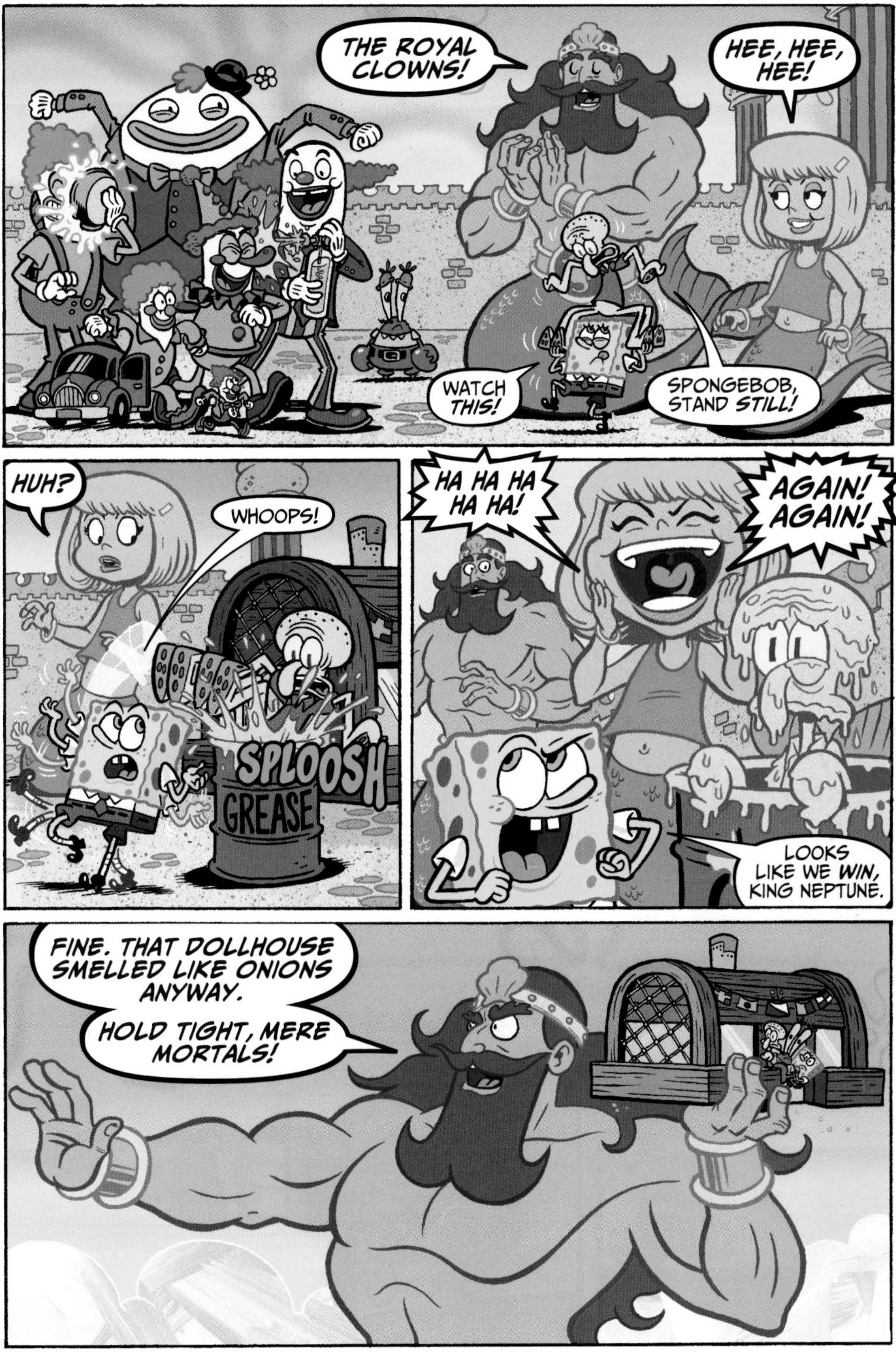
THE ROYAL CLOWNS!
HEE, HEE, HEE!
WATCH THIS!
SPONGEBOB, STAND STILL!
HUH?
WHOOPS!
SPLOOSH
GREASE
HA HA HA HA HA!
AGAIN! AGAIN!
LOOKS LIKE WE WIN, KING NEPTUNE.
FINE. THAT DOLLHOUSE SMELLED LIKE ONIONS ANYWAY.
HOLD TIGHT, MERE MORTALS!

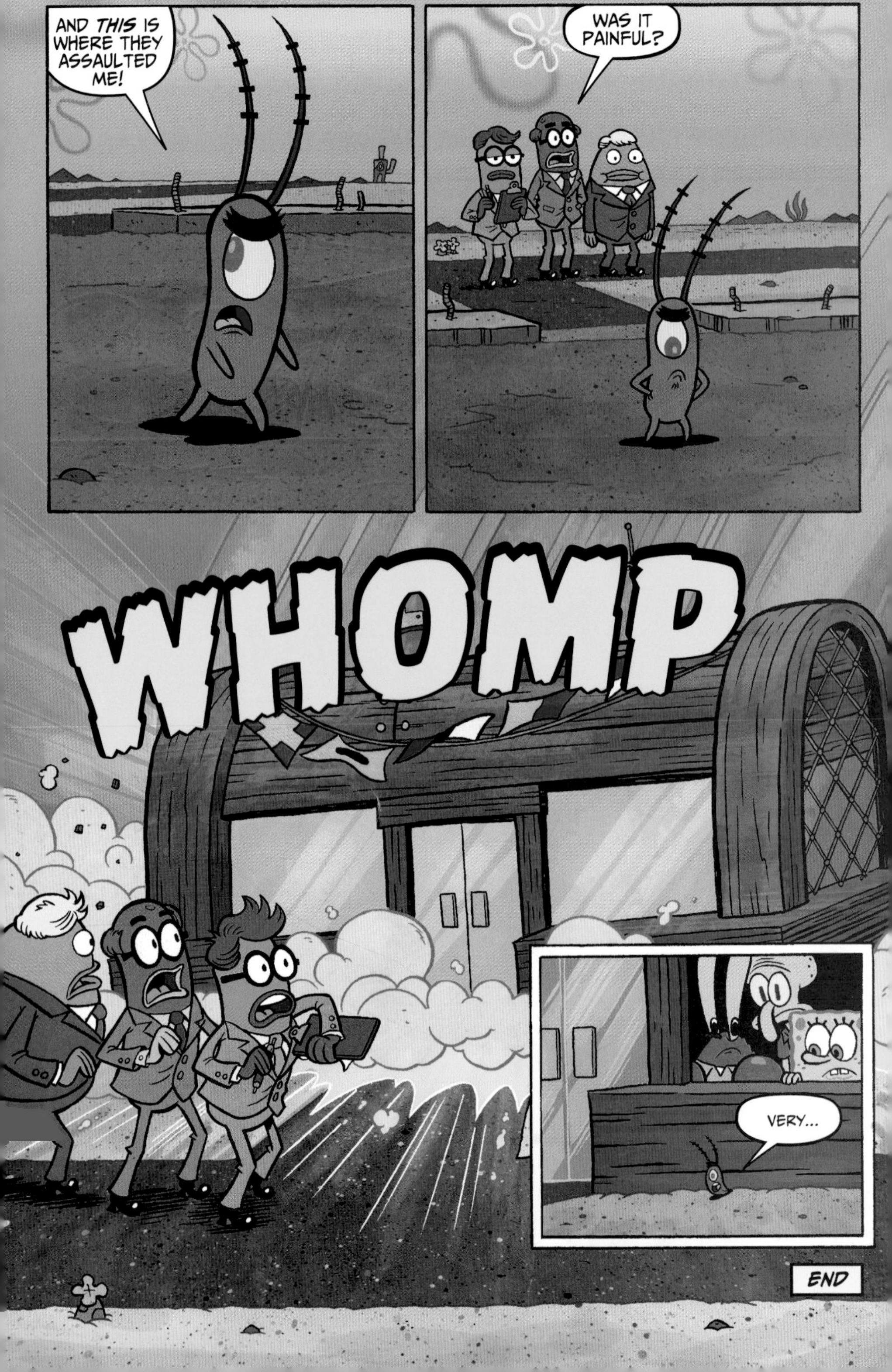
AND THIS IS WHERE THEY ASSAULTED ME!
WAS IT PAINFUL?
WHOMP
VERY...
END

Split Decision

STORY: **ROBERT LEIGHTON** PENCILS AND INKS: **JACOB CHABOT**
LETTERING: **COMICRAFT** COLORING: **MARK MARTIN**

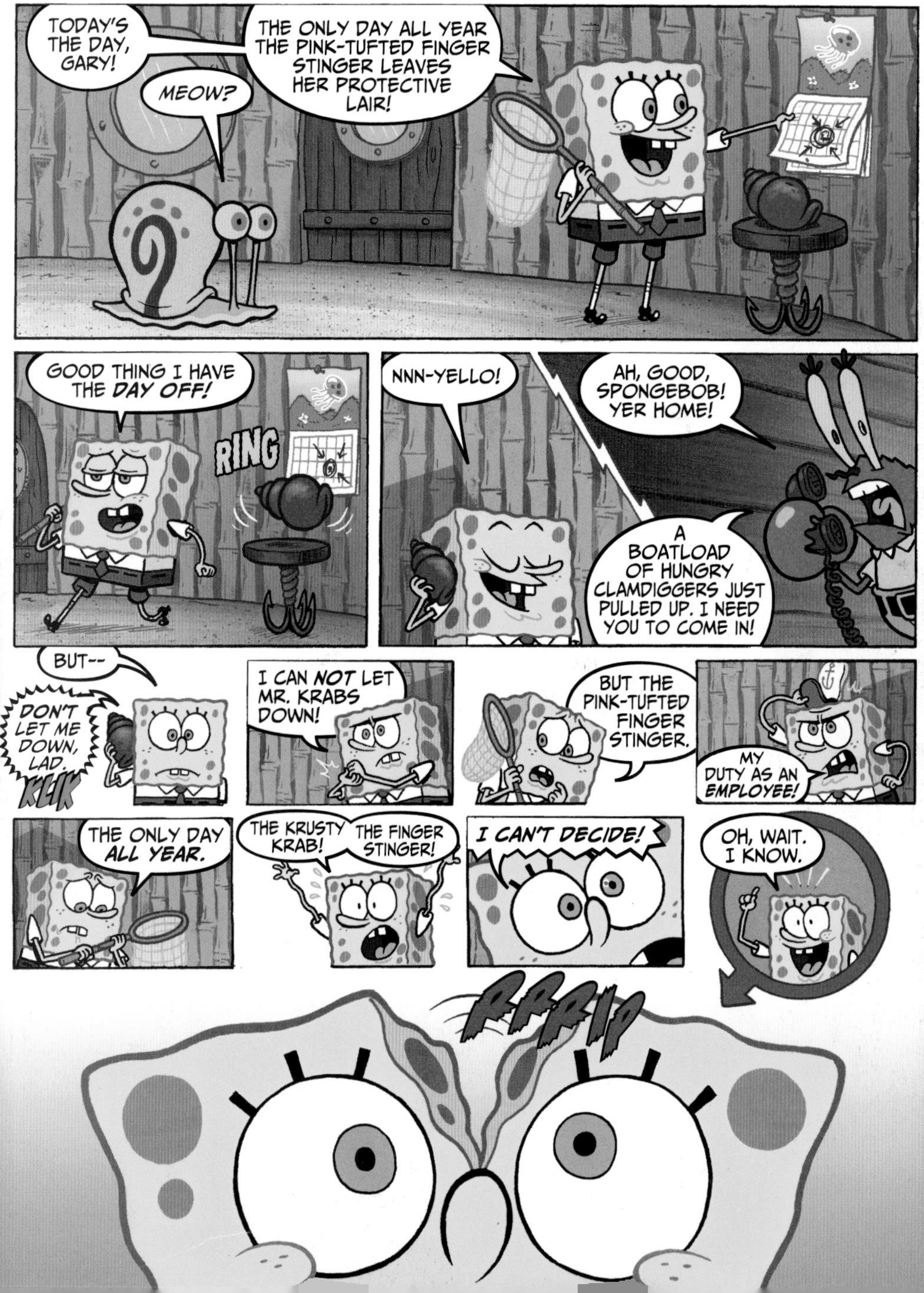
TODAY'S THE DAY, GARY!
MEOW?
THE ONLY DAY ALL YEAR THE PINK-TUFTED FINGER STINGER LEAVES HER PROTECTIVE LAIR!
GOOD THING I HAVE THE DAY OFF!
RING
NNN-YELLO!
AH, GOOD, SPONGEBOB! YER HOME!
A BOATLOAD OF HUNGRY CLAMDIGGERS JUST PULLED UP. I NEED YOU TO COME IN!
BUT--
DON'T LET ME DOWN, LAD.
KLIK
I CAN NOT LET MR. KRABS DOWN!
BUT THE PINK-TUFTED FINGER STINGER.
MY DUTY AS AN EMPLOYEE!
THE ONLY DAY ALL YEAR.
THE KRUSTY KRAB!
THE FINGER STINGER!
I CAN'T DECIDE!
OH, WAIT. I KNOW.
RRRIP

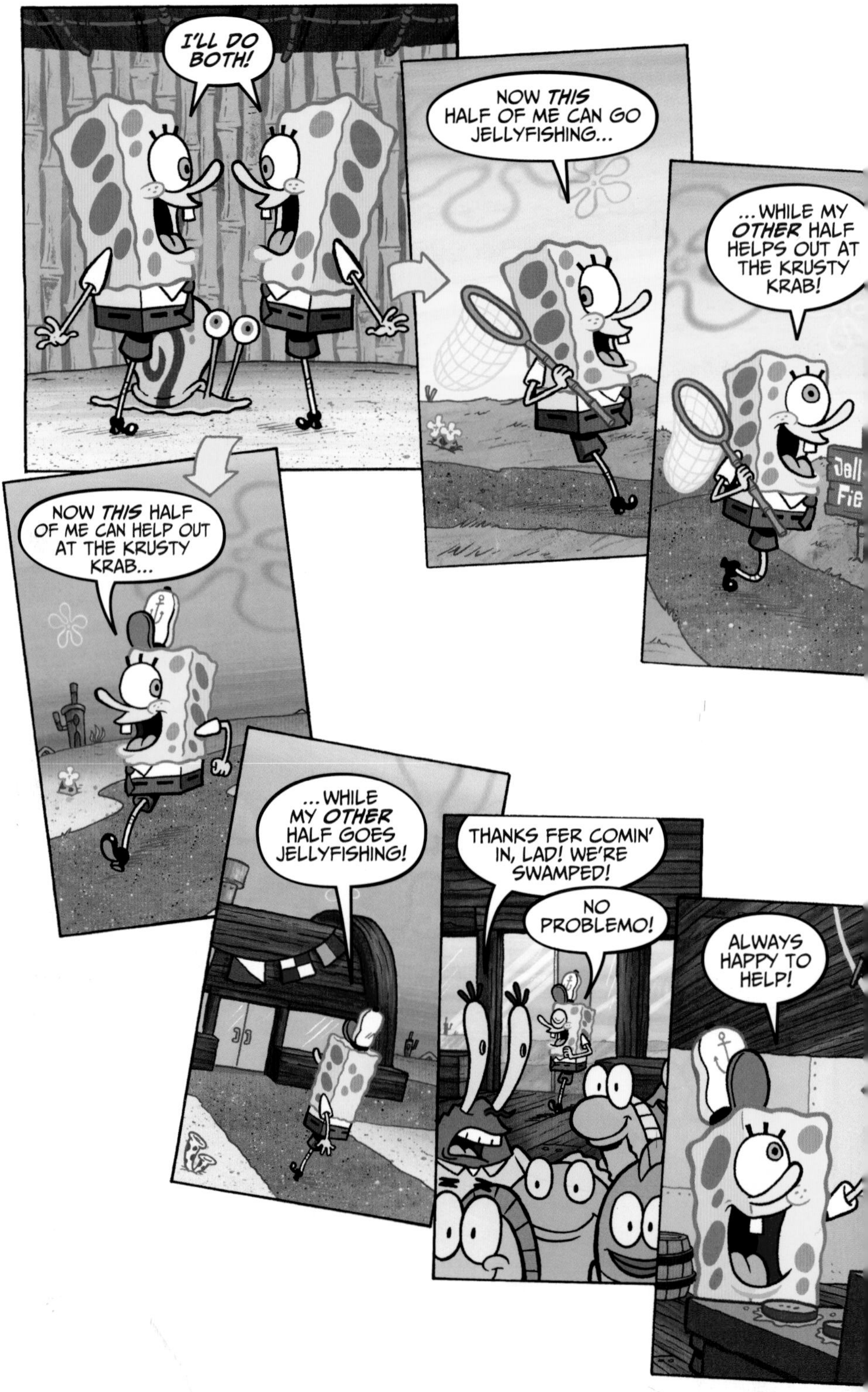
I'LL DO BOTH!
NOW THIS HALF OF ME CAN GO JELLYFISHING...
...WHILE MY OTHER HALF HELPS OUT AT THE KRUSTY KRAB!
NOW THIS HALF OF ME CAN HELP OUT AT THE KRUSTY KRAB...
...WHILE MY OTHER HALF GOES JELLYFISHING!
THANKS FER COMIN' IN, LAD! WE'RE SWAMPED!
NO PROBLEMO!
ALWAYS HAPPY TO HELP!

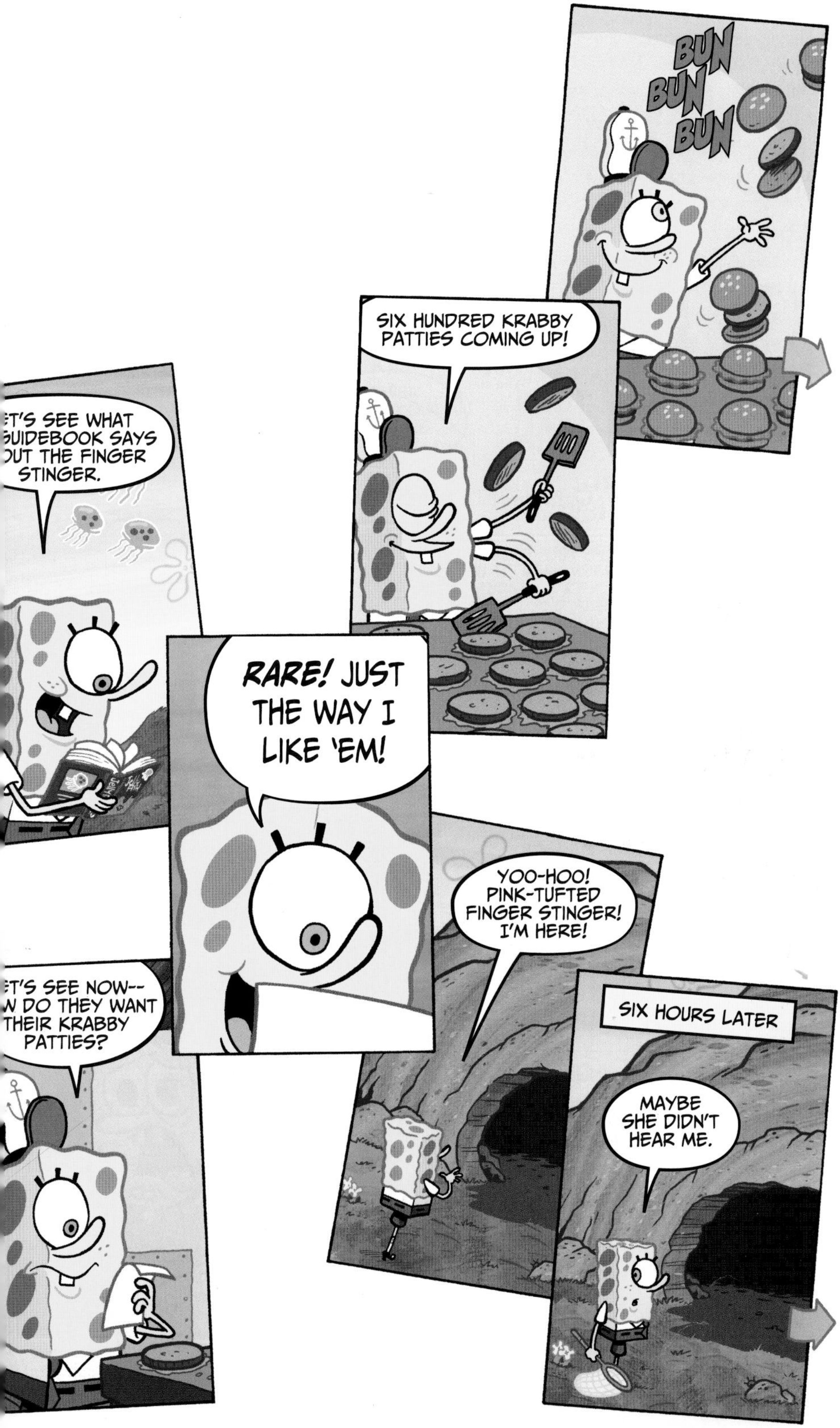
ET'S SEE WHAT
GUIDEBOOK SAYS
OUT THE FINGER
STINGER.
ET'S SEE NOW--
W DO THEY WANT
THEIR KRABBY
PATTIES?
RARE! JUST THE WAY I LIKE 'EM!
SIX HUNDRED KRABBY PATTIES COMING UP!
BUN BUN BUN
YOO-HOO! PINK-TUFTED FINGER STINGER! I'M HERE!
SIX HOURS LATER
MAYBE SHE DIDN'T HEAR ME.

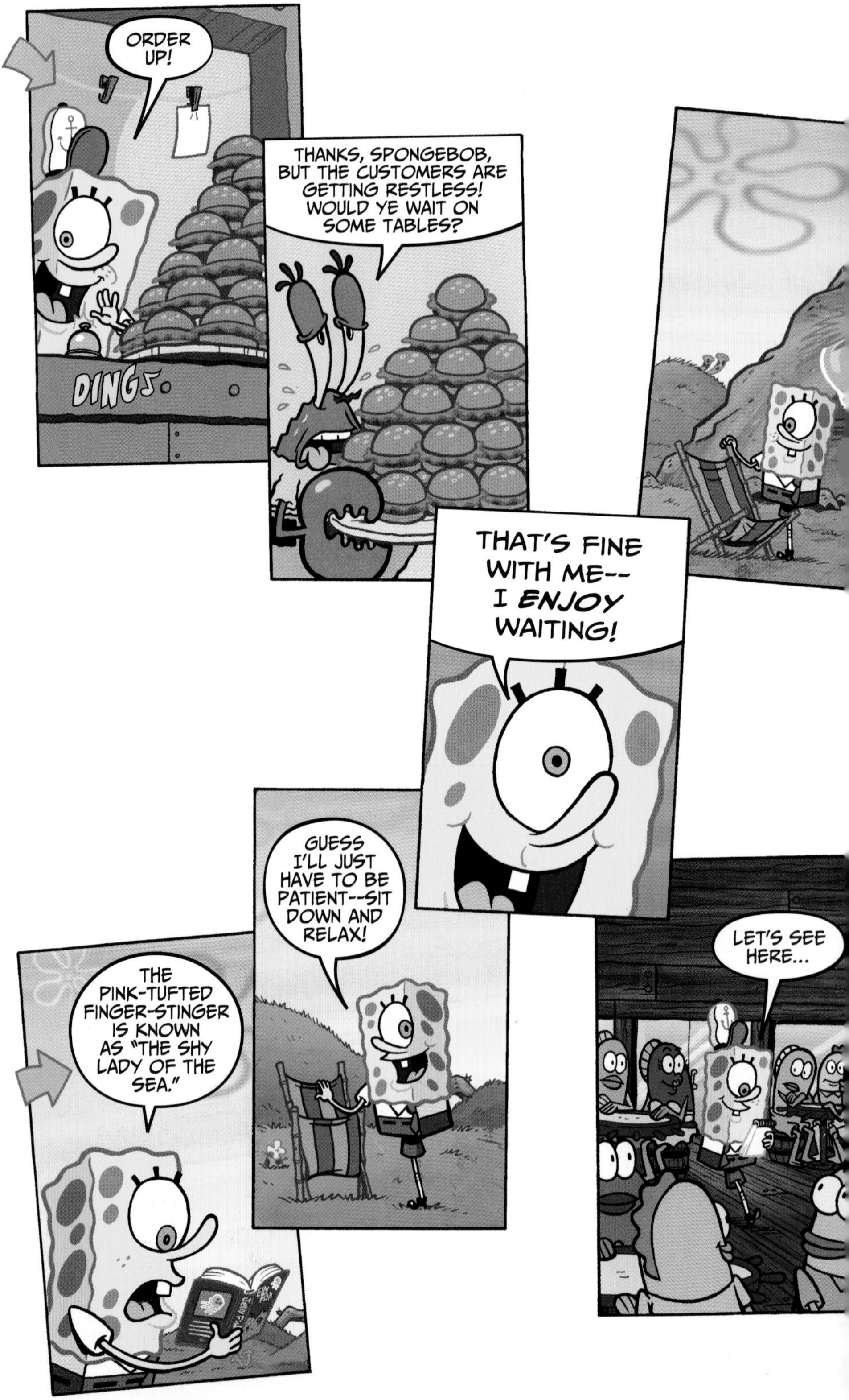
ORDER UP!
DINGS
THANKS, SPONGEBOB, BUT THE CUSTOMERS ARE GETTING RESTLESS! WOULD YE WAIT ON SOME TABLES?
THAT'S FINE WITH ME-- I *ENJOY* WAITING!
LET'S SEE HERE...
THE PINK-TUFTED FINGER-STINGER IS KNOWN AS "THE SHY LADY OF THE SEA."
GUESS I'LL JUST HAVE TO BE PATIENT--SIT DOWN AND RELAX!

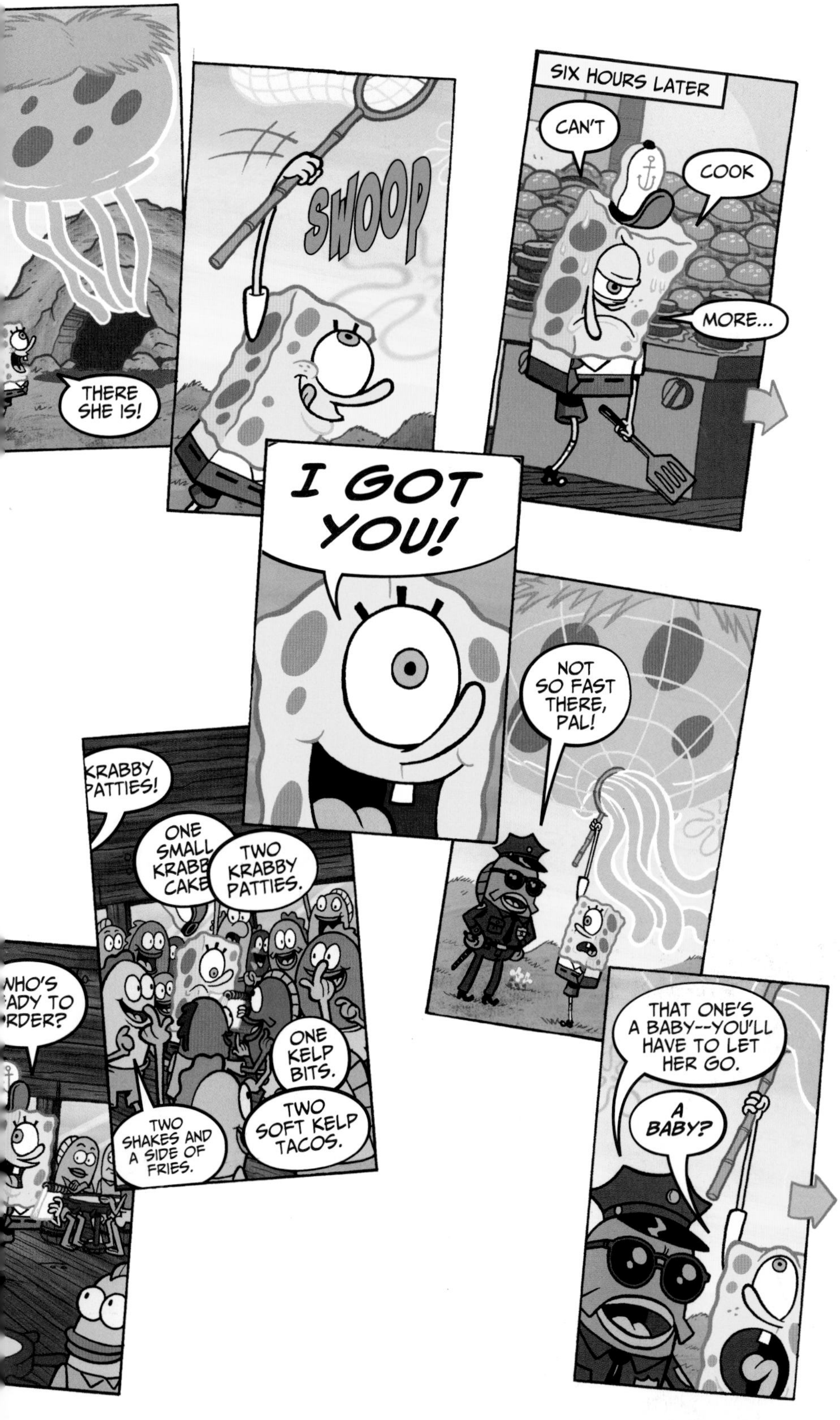
THERE SHE IS!
SWOOP
I GOT YOU!
SIX HOURS LATER
CAN'T
COOK
MORE...
NOT SO FAST THERE, PAL!
THAT ONE'S A BABY--YOU'LL HAVE TO LET HER GO.
A BABY?
KRABBY PATTIES!
ONE SMALL KRABB CAKE
TWO KRABBY PATTIES.
ONE KELP BITS.
TWO SHAKES AND A SIDE OF FRIES.
TWO SOFT KELP TACOS.

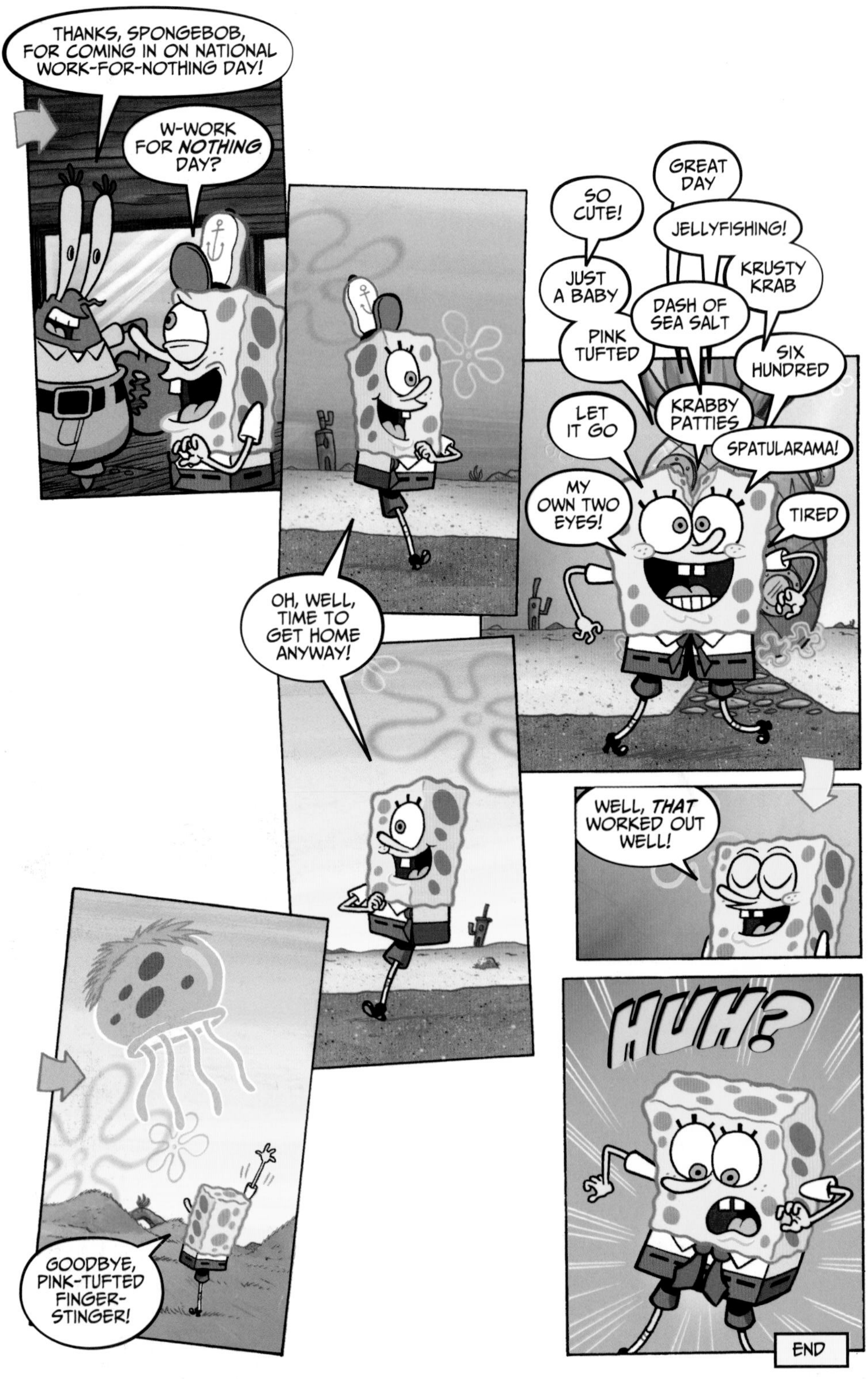
THANKS, SPONGEBOB, FOR COMING IN ON NATIONAL WORK-FOR-NOTHING DAY!
W-WORK FOR *NOTHING* DAY?
OH, WELL, TIME TO GET HOME ANYWAY!
GOODBYE, PINK-TUFTED FINGER-STINGER!
SO CUTE!
GREAT DAY
JELLYFISHING!
JUST A BABY
KRUSTY KRAB
DASH OF SEA SALT
PINK TUFTED
SIX HUNDRED
LET IT GO
KRABBY PATTIES
SPATULARAMA!
MY OWN TWO EYES!
TIRED
WELL, *THAT* WORKED OUT WELL!
HUH?
END

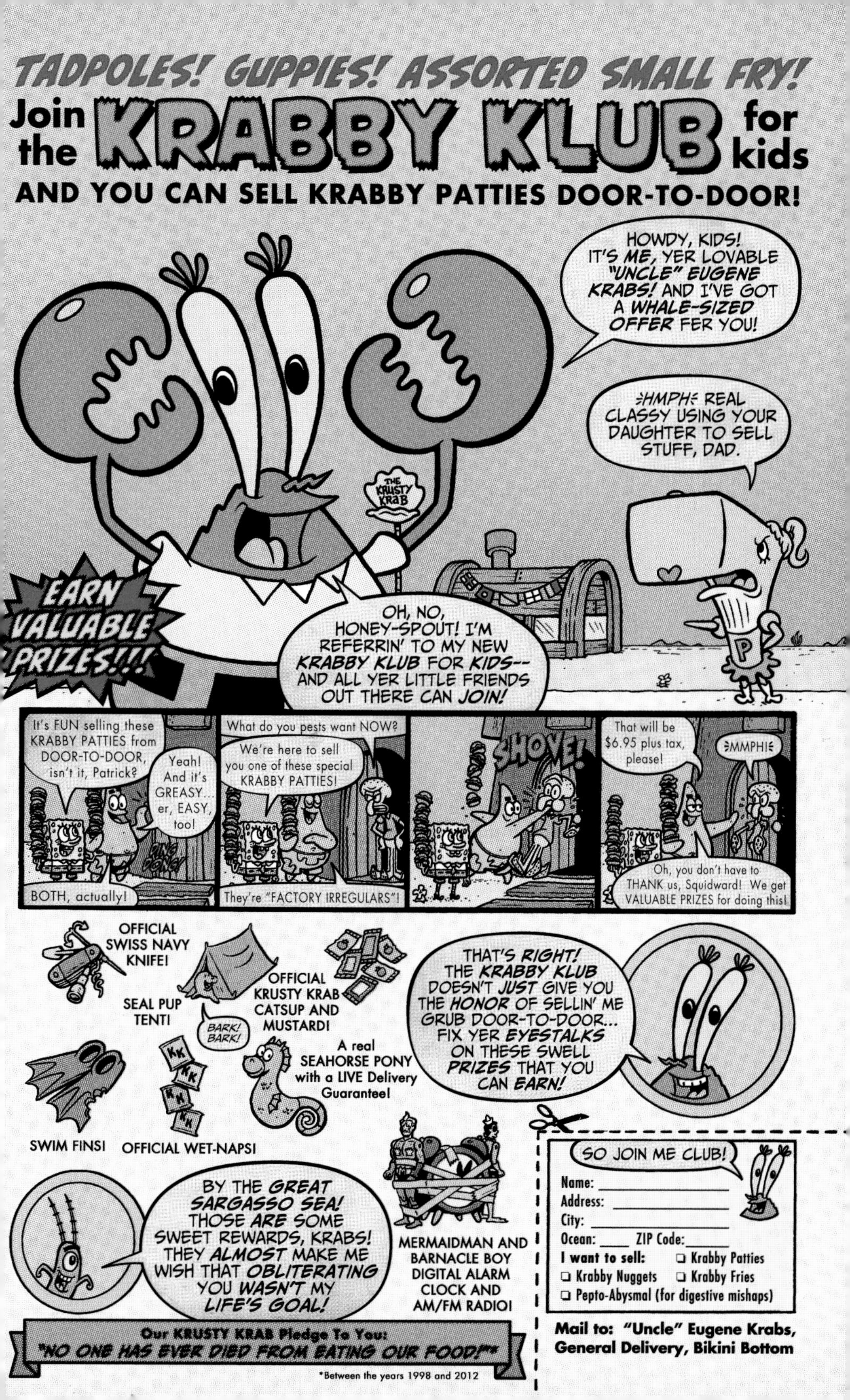

TADPOLES! GUPPIES! ASSORTED SMALL FRY!
Join the KRABBY KLUB for kids
AND YOU CAN SELL KRABBY PATTIES DOOR-TO-DOOR!
HOWDY, KIDS! IT'S ME, YER LOVABLE "UNCLE" EUGENE KRABS! AND I'VE GOT A WHALE-SIZED OFFER FER YOU!
HMPH REAL CLASSY USING YOUR DAUGHTER TO SELL STUFF, DAD.
THE KRUSTY KRAB
EARN VALUABLE PRIZES!!!
OH, NO, HONEY-SPOUT! I'M REFERRIN' TO MY NEW KRABBY KLUB FOR KIDS-- AND ALL YER LITTLE FRIENDS OUT THERE CAN JOIN!
It's FUN selling these KRABBY PATTIES from DOOR-TO-DOOR, isn't it, Patrick?
Yeah! And it's GREASY... er, EASY, too!
DING DONG!
BOTH, actually!
What do you pests want NOW?
We're here to sell you one of these special KRABBY PATTIES!
They're "FACTORY IRREGULARS"!
SHOVE!
That will be $6.95 plus tax, please!
MMPH!
Oh, you don't have to THANK us, Squidward! We get VALUABLE PRIZES for doing this!
OFFICIAL SWISS NAVY KNIFE!
SEAL PUP TENT!
BARK! BARK!
OFFICIAL KRUSTY KRAB CATSUP AND MUSTARD!
A real SEAHORSE PONY with a LIVE Delivery Guarantee!
SWIM FINS!
OFFICIAL WET-NAPS!
THAT'S RIGHT! THE KRABBY KLUB DOESN'T JUST GIVE YOU THE HONOR OF SELLIN' ME GRUB DOOR-TO-DOOR... FIX YER EYESTALKS ON THESE SWELL PRIZES THAT YOU CAN EARN!
BY THE GREAT SARGASSO SEA! THOSE ARE SOME SWEET REWARDS, KRABS! THEY ALMOST MAKE ME WISH THAT OBLITERATING YOU WASN'T MY LIFE'S GOAL!
MERMAIDMAN AND BARNACLE BOY DIGITAL ALARM CLOCK AND AM/FM RADIO!
SO JOIN ME CLUB!
Name:
Address:
City:
Ocean: ZIP Code:
I want to sell: ❑ Krabby Patties
❑ Krabby Nuggets ❑ Krabby Fries
❑ Pepto-Abysmal (for digestive mishaps)
Mail to: "Uncle" Eugene Krabs, General Delivery, Bikini Bottom
Our KRUSTY KRAB Pledge To You:
"NO ONE HAS EVER DIED FROM EATING OUR FOOD!"*
*Between the years 1998 and 2012

MONKEY SEA, MONKEY DO!

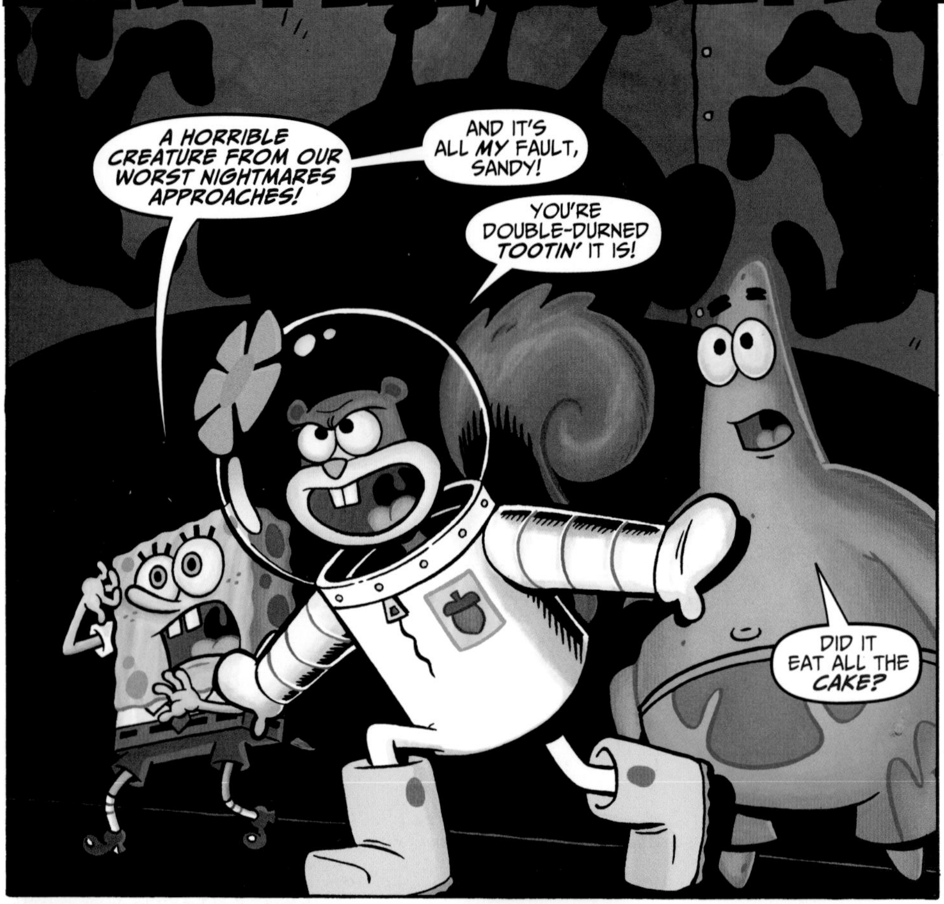
A HORRIBLE CREATURE FROM OUR WORST NIGHTMARES APPROACHES!
AND IT'S ALL MY FAULT, SANDY!
YOU'RE DOUBLE-DURNED TOOTIN' IT IS!
DID IT EAT ALL THE CAKE?

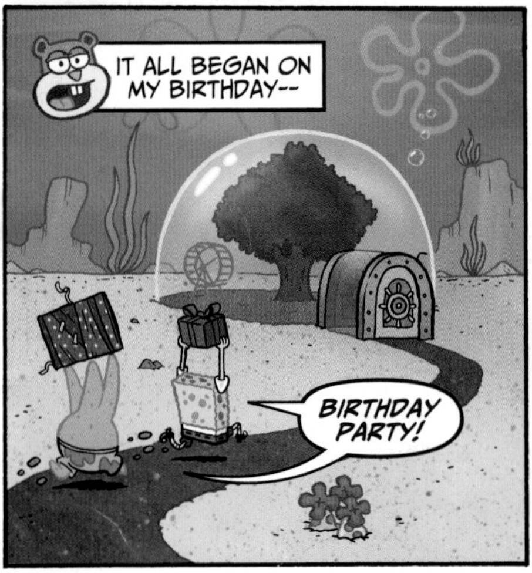
IT ALL BEGAN ON MY BIRTHDAY--
BIRTHDAY PARTY!

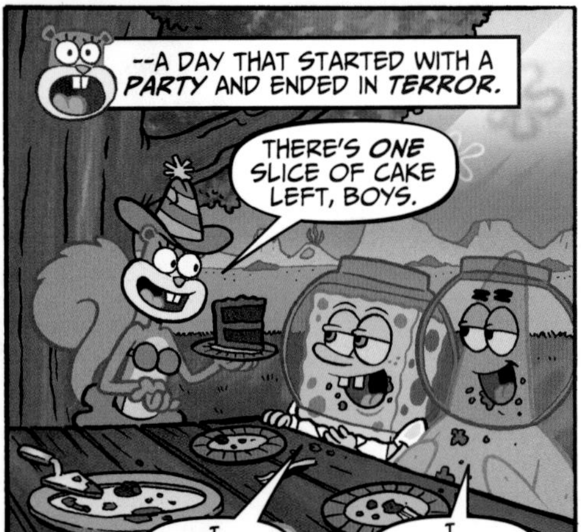
--A DAY THAT STARTED WITH A PARTY AND ENDED IN TERROR.
THERE'S ONE SLICE OF CAKE LEFT, BOYS.
I COULDN'T!
I SHOULDN'T!

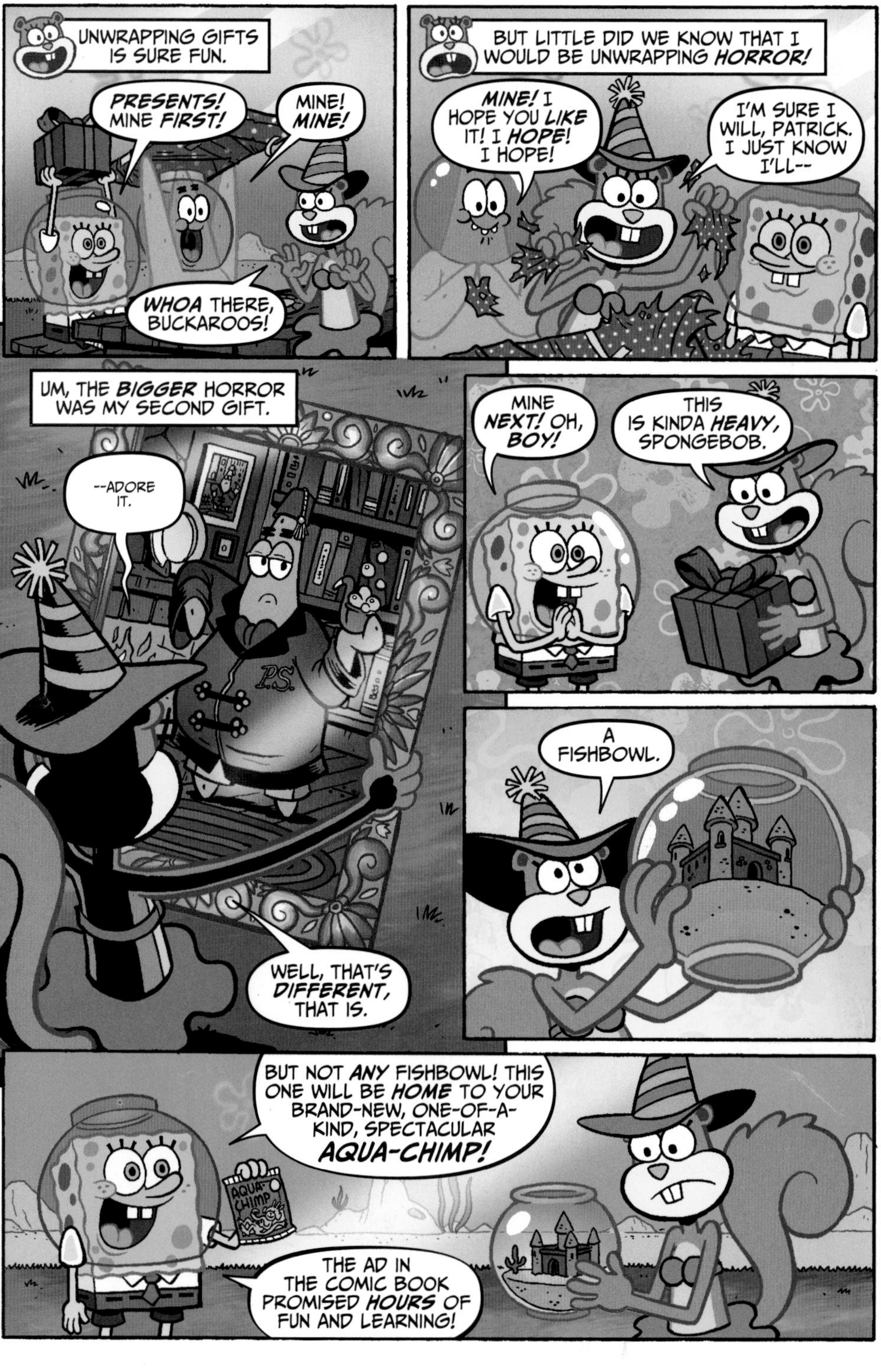

UNWRAPPING GIFTS IS SURE FUN.
PRESENTS! MINE FIRST!
MINE! MINE!
WHOA THERE, BUCKAROOS!
BUT LITTLE DID WE KNOW THAT I WOULD BE UNWRAPPING HORROR!
MINE! I HOPE YOU LIKE IT! I HOPE! I HOPE!
I'M SURE I WILL, PATRICK. I JUST KNOW I'LL--
UM, THE BIGGER HORROR WAS MY SECOND GIFT.
--ADORE IT.
P.S.
WELL, THAT'S DIFFERENT, THAT IS.
MINE NEXT! OH, BOY!
THIS IS KINDA HEAVY, SPONGEBOB.
A FISHBOWL.
BUT NOT ANY FISHBOWL! THIS ONE WILL BE HOME TO YOUR BRAND-NEW, ONE-OF-A-KIND, SPECTACULAR AQUA-CHIMP!
AQUA-CHIMP
THE AD IN THE COMIC BOOK PROMISED HOURS OF FUN AND LEARNING!

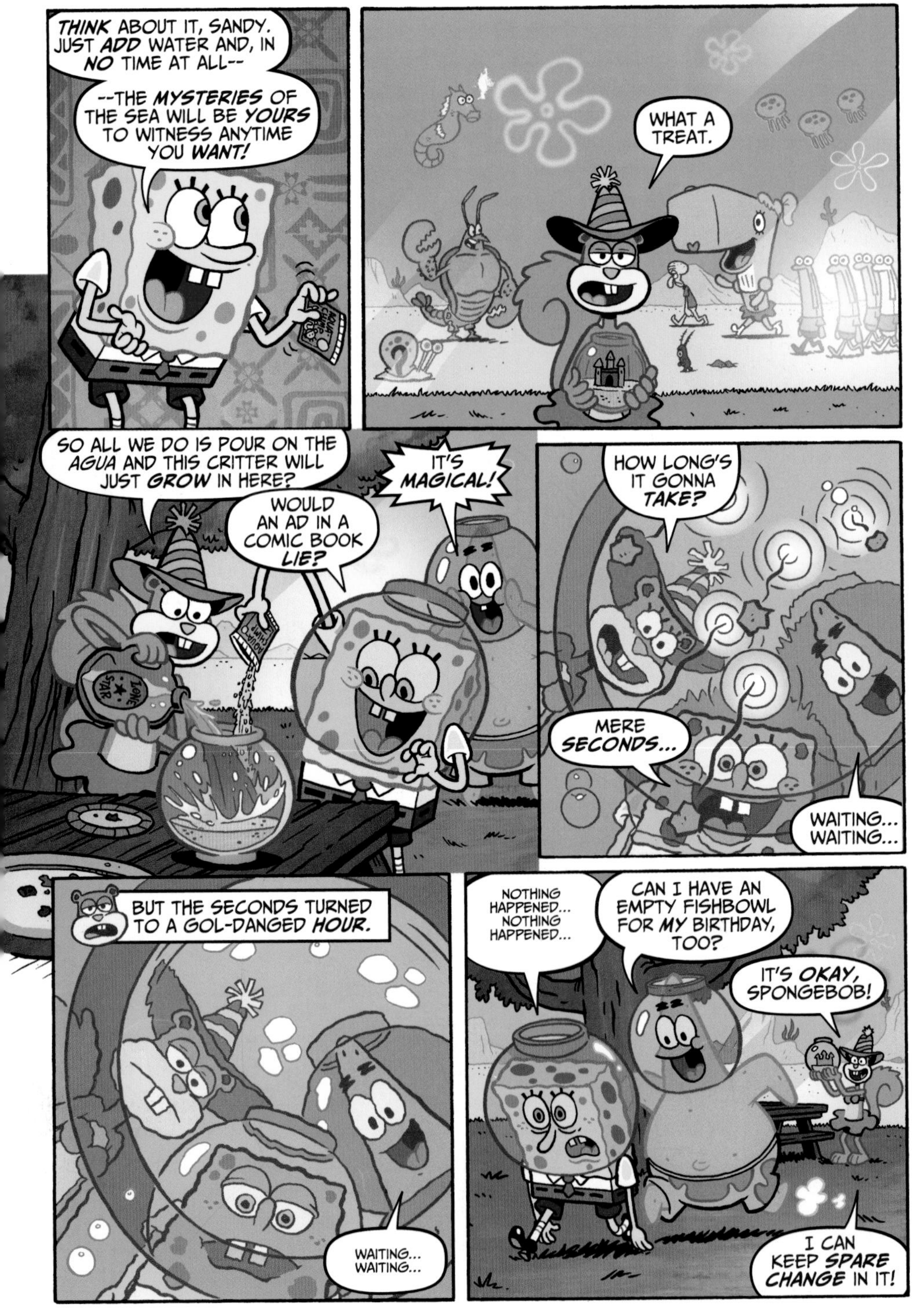
THINK ABOUT IT, SANDY. JUST ADD WATER AND, IN NO TIME AT ALL--
--THE MYSTERIES OF THE SEA WILL BE YOURS TO WITNESS ANYTIME YOU WANT!
WHAT A TREAT.
SO ALL WE DO IS POUR ON THE AGUA AND THIS CRITTER WILL JUST GROW IN HERE?
IT'S MAGICAL!
WOULD AN AD IN A COMIC BOOK LIE?
HOW LONG'S IT GONNA TAKE?
MERE SECONDS...
WAITING... WAITING...
BUT THE SECONDS TURNED TO A GOL-DANGED HOUR.
WAITING... WAITING...
NOTHING HAPPENED... NOTHING HAPPENED...
CAN I HAVE AN EMPTY FISHBOWL FOR MY BIRTHDAY, TOO?
IT'S OKAY, SPONGEBOB!
I CAN KEEP SPARE CHANGE IN IT!

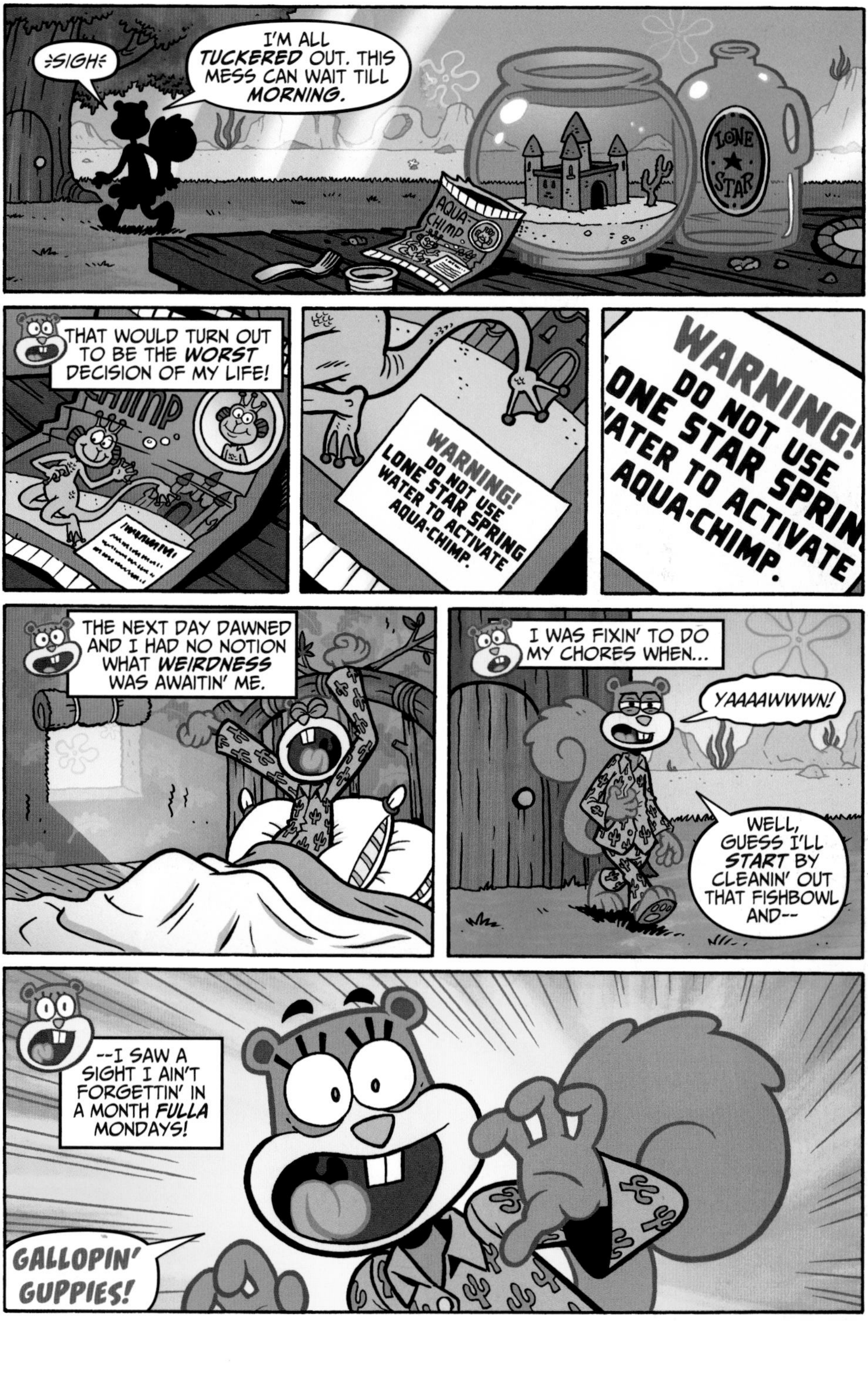

SIGH
I'M ALL TUCKERED OUT. THIS MESS CAN WAIT TILL MORNING.
LONE STAR
AQUA-CHIMP
THAT WOULD TURN OUT TO BE THE WORST DECISION OF MY LIFE!
WARNING! DO NOT USE LONE STAR SPRING WATER TO ACTIVATE AQUA-CHIMP.
WARNING! DO NOT USE LONE STAR SPRING WATER TO ACTIVATE AQUA-CHIMP.
THE NEXT DAY DAWNED AND I HAD NO NOTION WHAT WEIRDNESS WAS AWAITIN' ME.
I WAS FIXIN' TO DO MY CHORES WHEN...
YAAAAWWWN!
WELL, GUESS I'LL START BY CLEANIN' OUT THAT FISHBOWL AND--
--I SAW A SIGHT I AIN'T FORGETTIN' IN A MONTH FULLA MONDAYS!
GALLOPIN' GUPPIES!

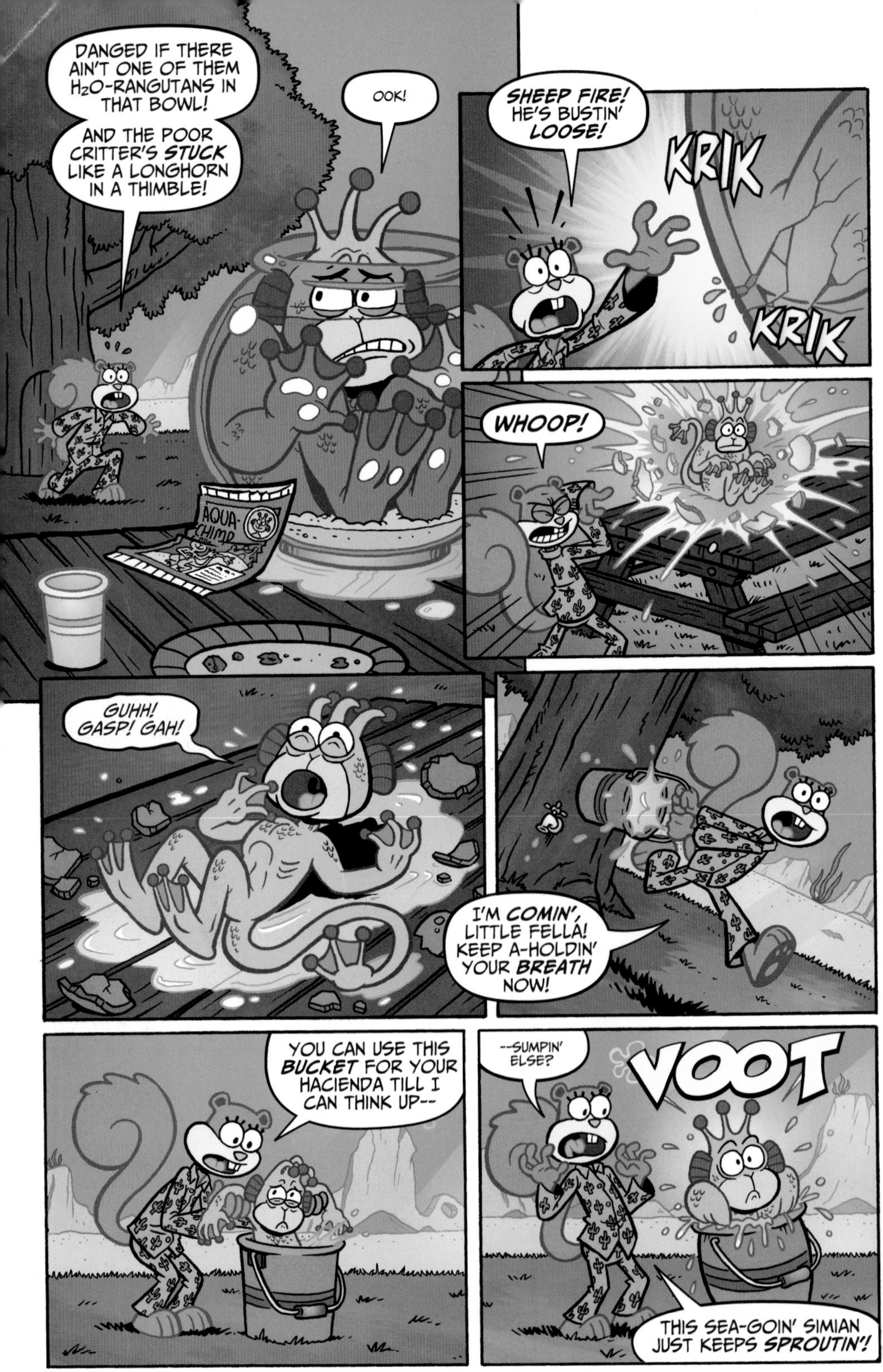
DANGED IF THERE AIN'T ONE OF THEM H_2O-RANGUTANS IN THAT BOWL!
AND THE POOR CRITTER'S **STUCK** LIKE A LONGHORN IN A THIMBLE!
OOK!
AQUA-CHIMP
SHEEP FIRE! HE'S BUSTIN' ***LOOSE!***
KRIK
KRIK
WHOOP!
GUHH! GASP! GAH!
I'M ***COMIN'***, LITTLE FELLA! KEEP A-HOLDIN' YOUR ***BREATH*** NOW!
YOU CAN USE THIS ***BUCKET*** FOR YOUR HACIENDA TILL I CAN THINK UP--
--SUMPIN' ELSE?
VOOT
THIS SEA-GOIN' SIMIAN JUST KEEPS ***SPROUTIN'***!

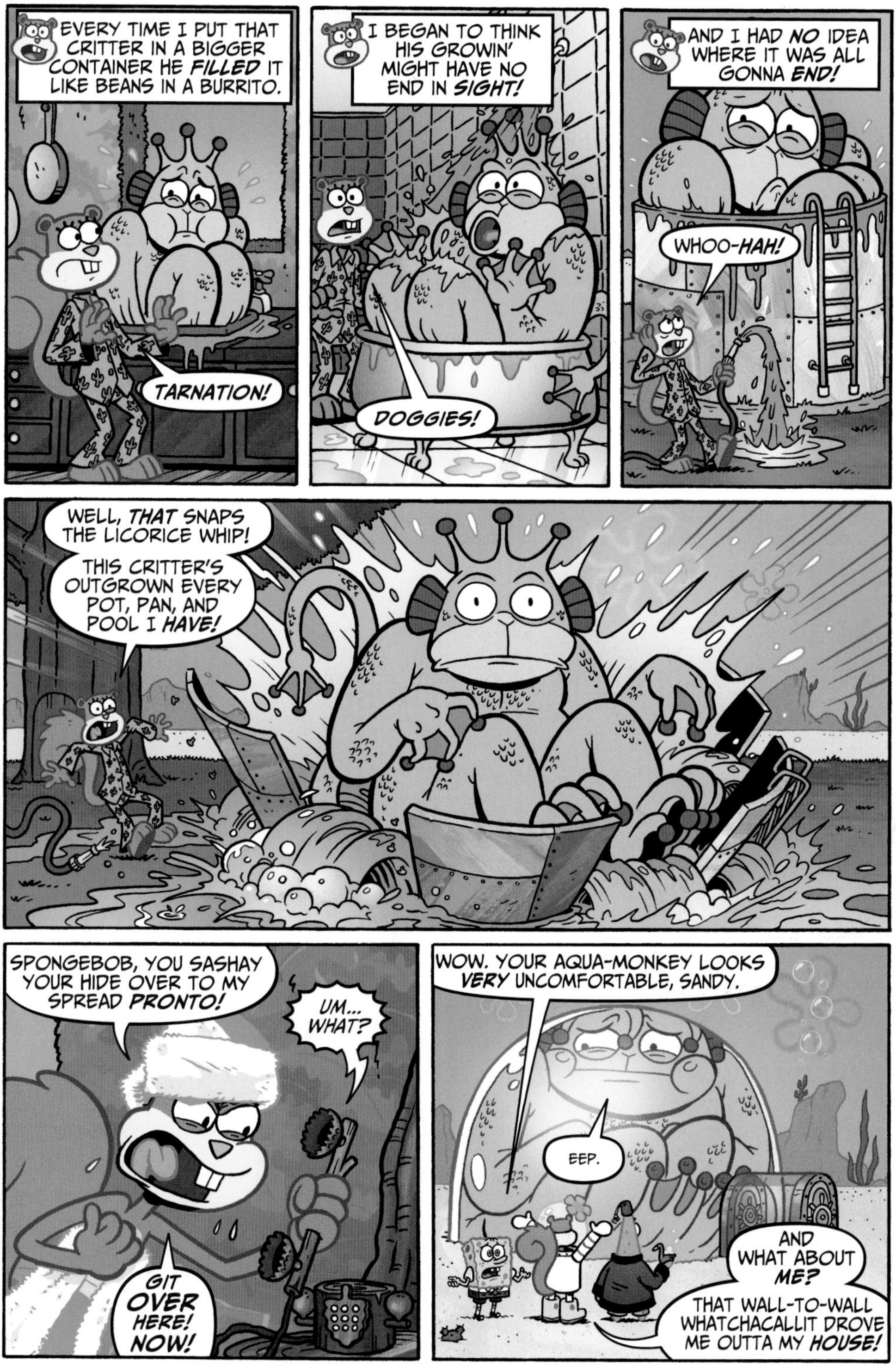
EVERY TIME I PUT THAT CRITTER IN A BIGGER CONTAINER HE FILLED IT LIKE BEANS IN A BURRITO.
TARNATION!
I BEGAN TO THINK HIS GROWIN' MIGHT HAVE NO END IN SIGHT!
DOGGIES!
AND I HAD NO IDEA WHERE IT WAS ALL GONNA END!
WHOO-HAH!
WELL, THAT SNAPS THE LICORICE WHIP!
THIS CRITTER'S OUTGROWN EVERY POT, PAN, AND POOL I HAVE!
SPONGEBOB, YOU SASHAY YOUR HIDE OVER TO MY SPREAD PRONTO!
UM... WHAT?
GIT OVER HERE! NOW!
WOW. YOUR AQUA-MONKEY LOOKS VERY UNCOMFORTABLE, SANDY.
EEP.
AND WHAT ABOUT ME?
THAT WALL-TO-WALL WHATCHACALLIT DROVE ME OUTTA MY HOUSE!

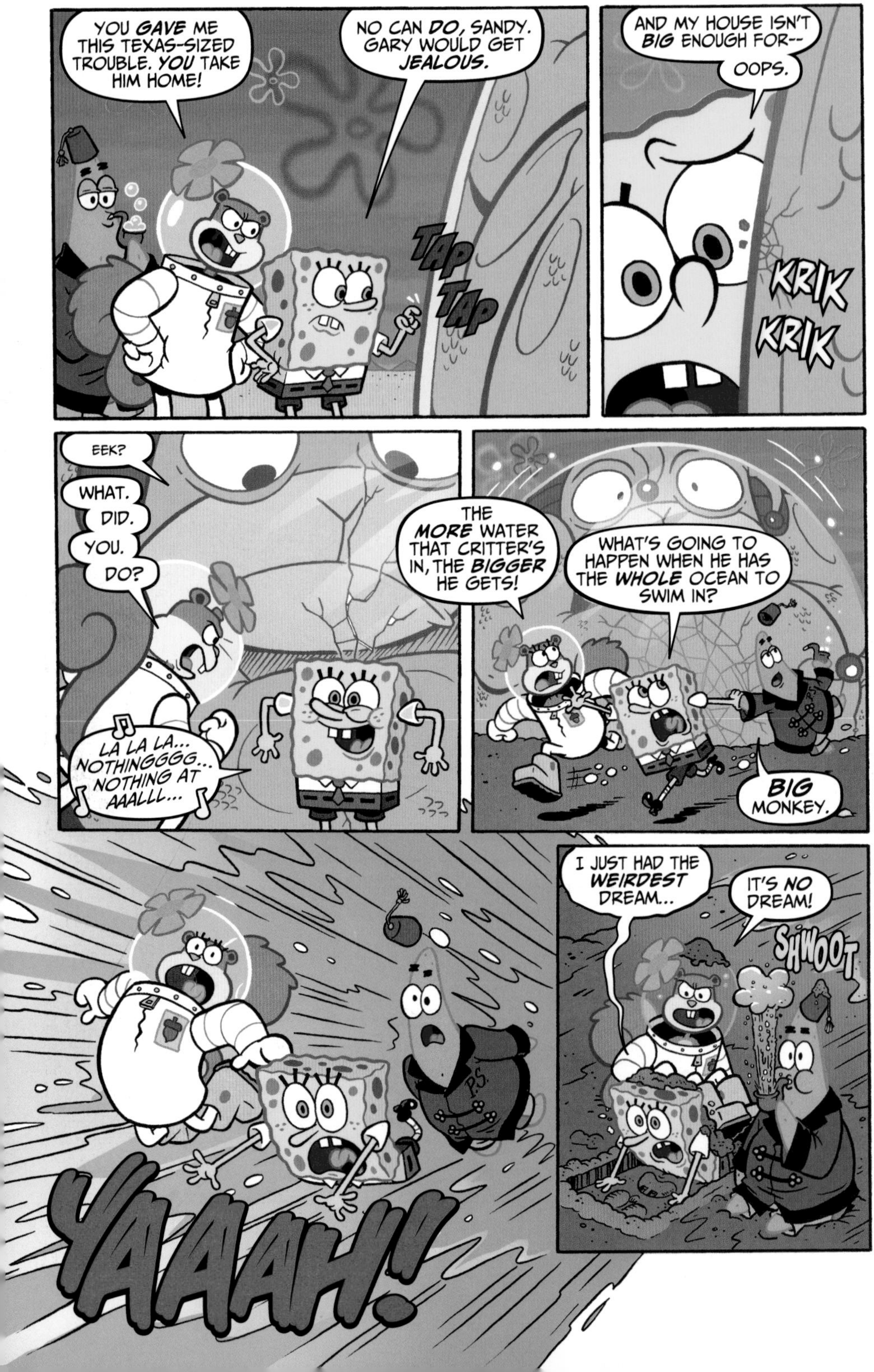
YOU GAVE ME THIS TEXAS-SIZED TROUBLE. YOU TAKE HIM HOME!
NO CAN DO, SANDY. GARY WOULD GET JEALOUS.
TAP TAP
AND MY HOUSE ISN'T BIG ENOUGH FOR--
OOPS.
KRIK KRIK
EEK?
WHAT.
DID.
YOU.
DO?
LA LA LA... NOTHINGGGG... NOTHING AT AAALLL...
THE MORE WATER THAT CRITTER'S IN, THE BIGGER HE GETS!
WHAT'S GOING TO HAPPEN WHEN HE HAS THE WHOLE OCEAN TO SWIM IN?
BIG MONKEY.
YAAAH!
I JUST HAD THE WEIRDEST DREAM...
IT'S NO DREAM!
SHWOOT

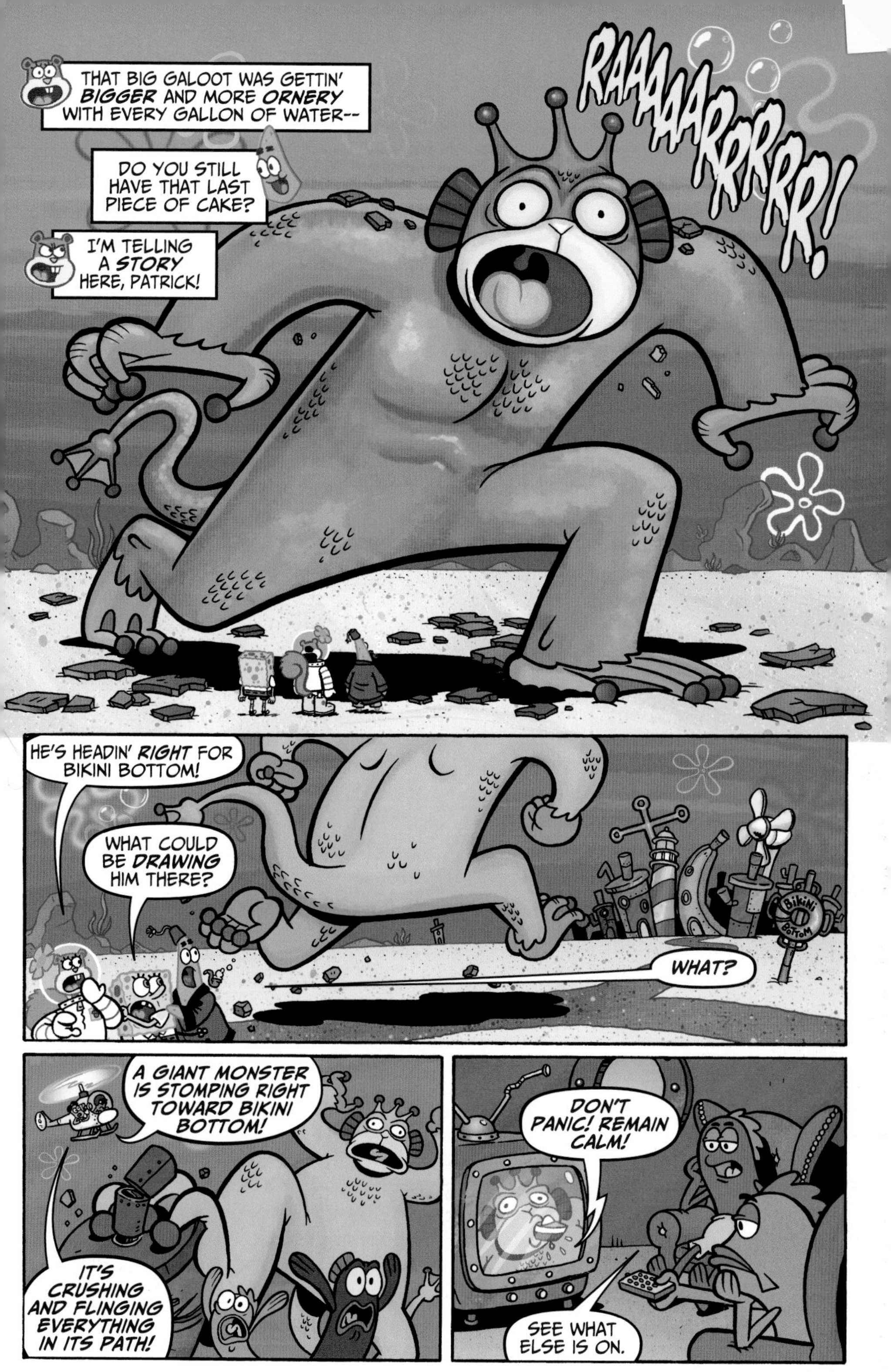
THAT BIG GALOOT WAS GETTIN' BIGGER AND MORE ORNERY WITH EVERY GALLON OF WATER--
RAAAAARRRRR!
DO YOU STILL HAVE THAT LAST PIECE OF CAKE?
I'M TELLING A STORY HERE, PATRICK!
HE'S HEADIN' RIGHT FOR BIKINI BOTTOM!
WHAT COULD BE DRAWING HIM THERE?
WHAT?
BIKINI BOTTOM
A GIANT MONSTER IS STOMPING RIGHT TOWARD BIKINI BOTTOM!
IT'S CRUSHING AND FLINGING EVERYTHING IN ITS PATH!
DON'T PANIC! REMAIN CALM!
SEE WHAT ELSE IS ON.

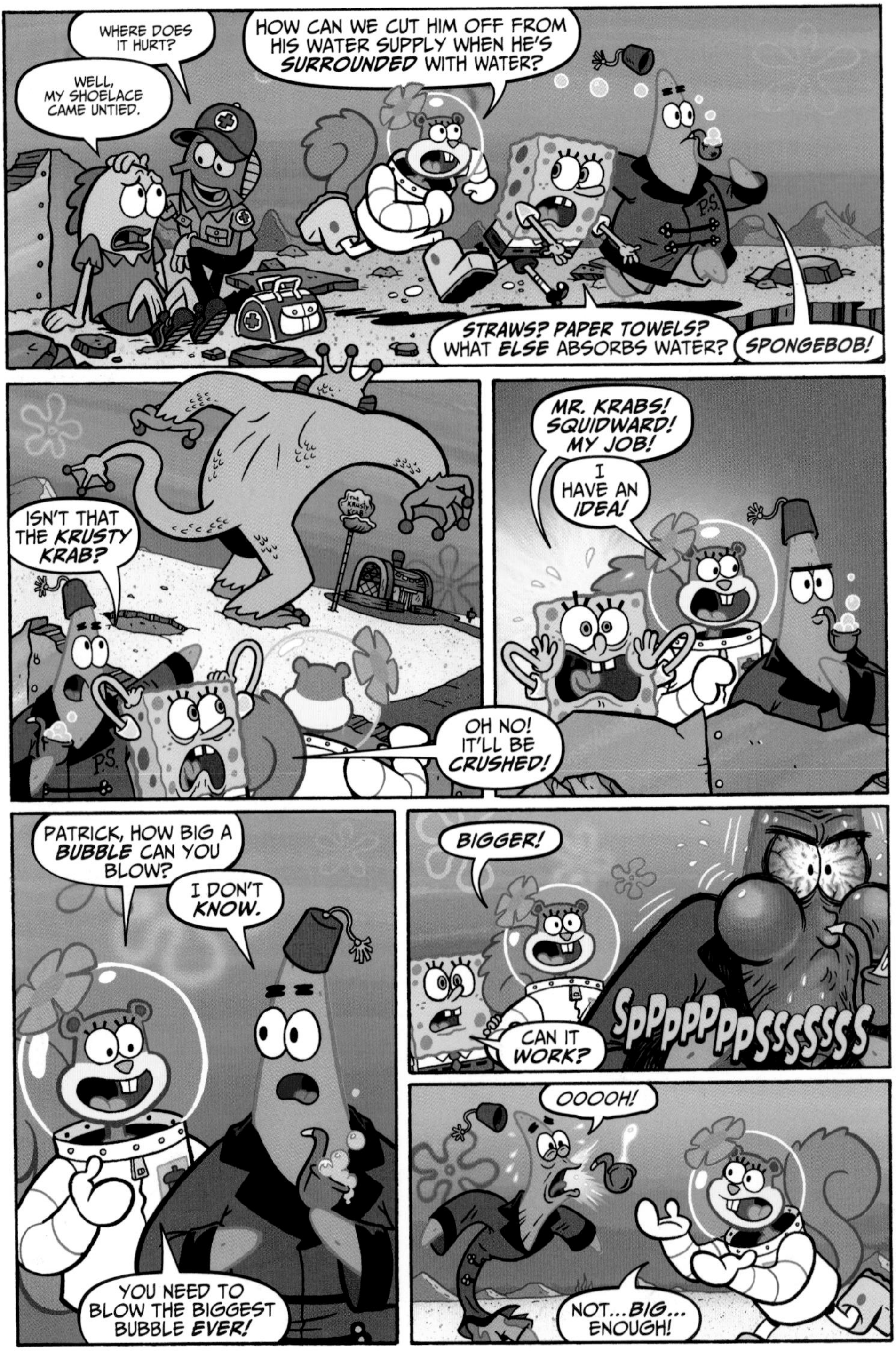
WHERE DOES IT HURT?
WELL, MY SHOELACE CAME UNTIED.
HOW CAN WE CUT HIM OFF FROM HIS WATER SUPPLY WHEN HE'S SURROUNDED WITH WATER?
STRAWS? PAPER TOWELS? WHAT ELSE ABSORBS WATER?
SPONGEBOB!
ISN'T THAT THE KRUSTY KRAB?
OH NO! IT'LL BE CRUSHED!
MR. KRABS! SQUIDWARD! MY JOB!
I HAVE AN IDEA!
PATRICK, HOW BIG A BUBBLE CAN YOU BLOW?
I DON'T KNOW.
YOU NEED TO BLOW THE BIGGEST BUBBLE EVER!
BIGGER!
CAN IT WORK?
SPPPPPPPSSSSSSS
OOOOH!
NOT...BIG... ENOUGH!

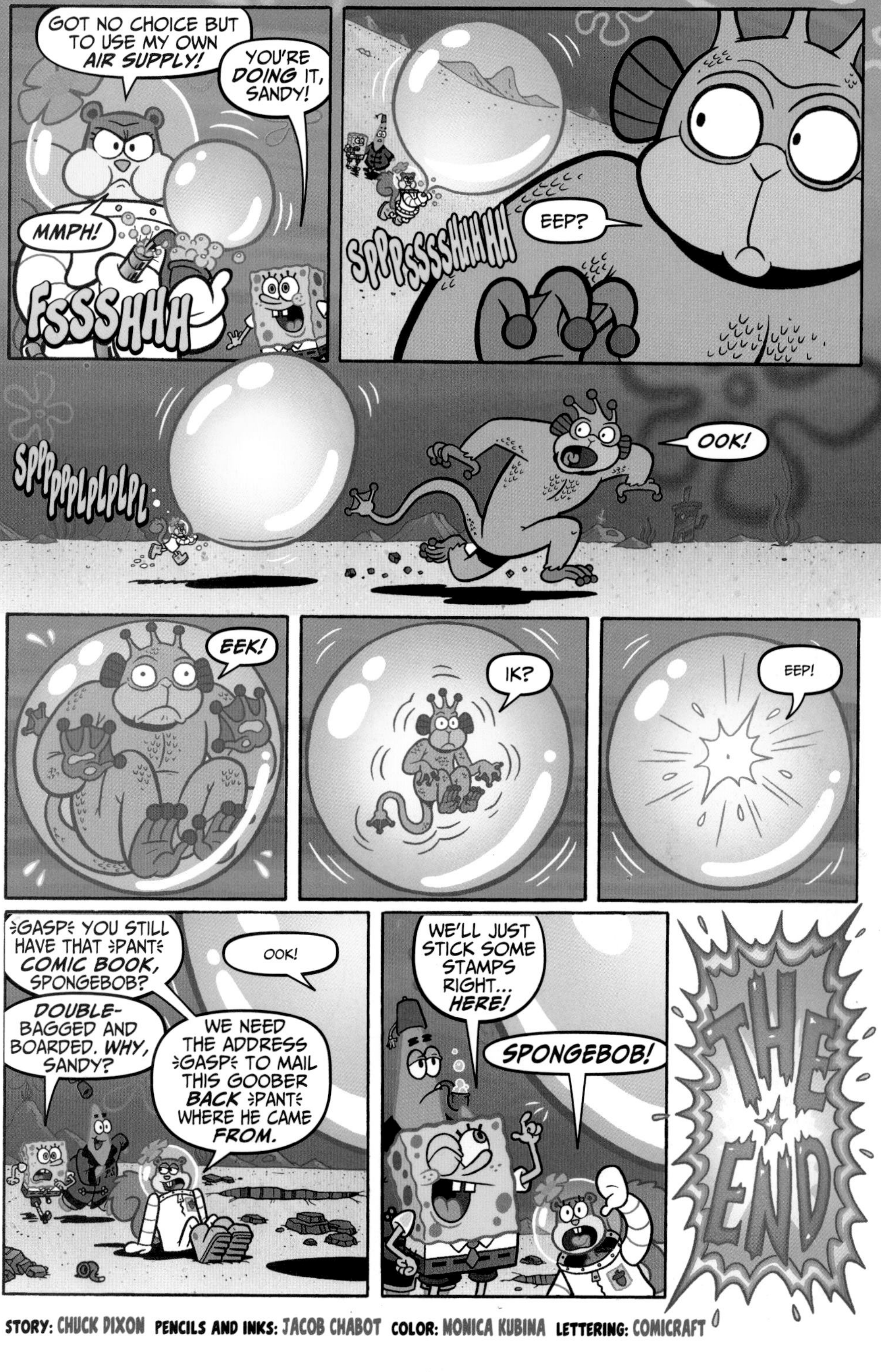
GOT NO CHOICE BUT TO USE MY OWN AIR SUPPLY!
YOU'RE DOING IT, SANDY!
MMPH!
FSSSHHH
SPPPSSSSHHHHH
EEP?
SPPPPPLPLPLPL
OOK!
EEK!
IK?
EEP!
ﾐGASPﾐ YOU STILL HAVE THAT ﾐPANTﾐ COMIC BOOK, SPONGEBOB?
OOK!
DOUBLE-BAGGED AND BOARDED. WHY, SANDY?
WE NEED THE ADDRESS ﾐGASPﾐ TO MAIL THIS GOOBER BACK ﾐPANTﾐ WHERE HE CAME FROM.
WE'LL JUST STICK SOME STAMPS RIGHT... HERE!
SPONGEBOB!
THE END

STORY: CHUCK DIXON **PENCILS AND INKS:** JACOB CHABOT **COLOR:** MONICA KUBINA **LETTERING:** COMICRAFT

Where's Penny?

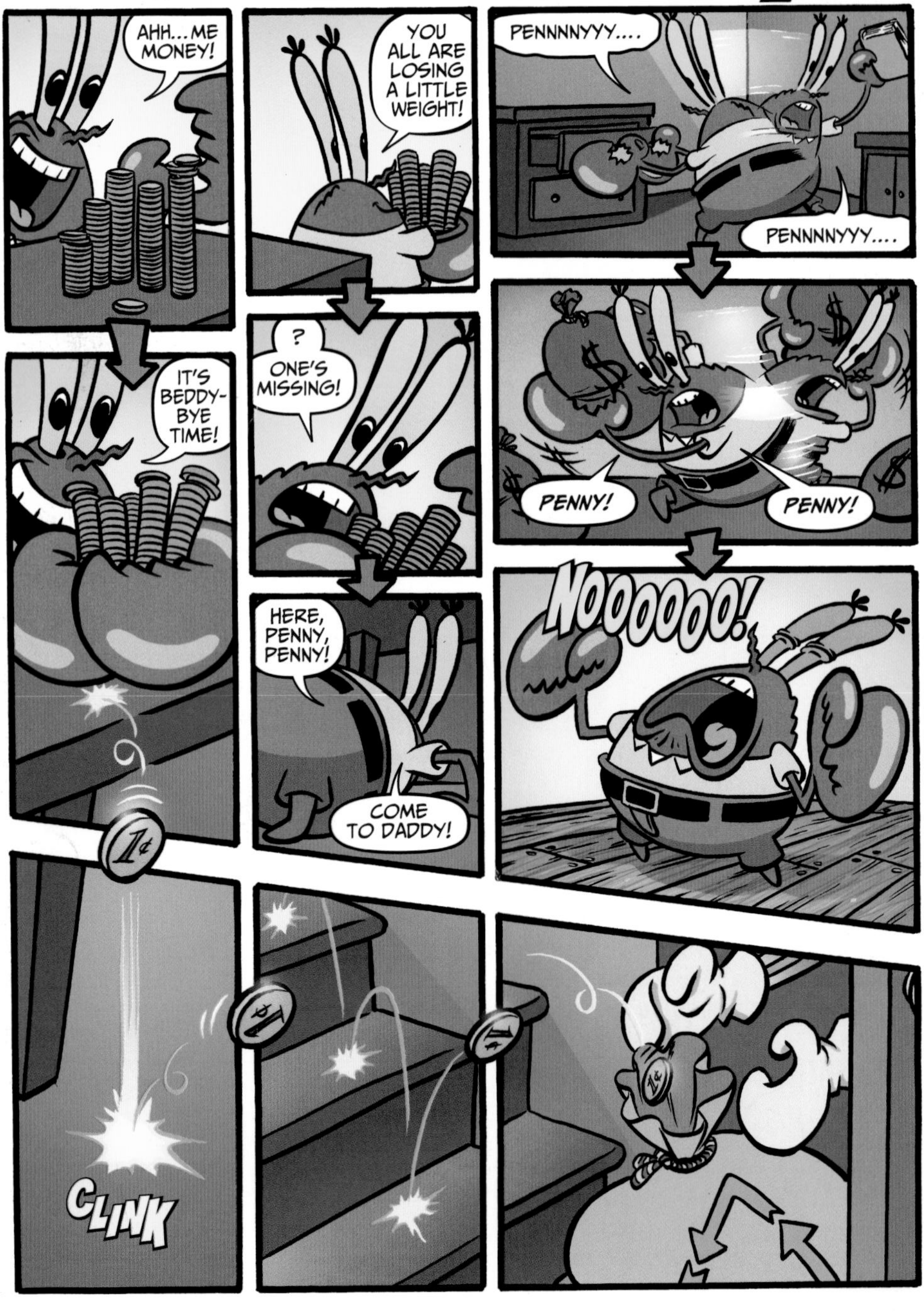
AHH...ME MONEY!
YOU ALL ARE LOSING A LITTLE WEIGHT!
PENNNNYYY....
PENNNNYYY....
IT'S BEDDY-BYE TIME!
?
ONE'S MISSING!
PENNY!
PENNY!
HERE, PENNY, PENNY!
COME TO DADDY!
NOOOOOO!
CLINK

STORY: ROBERT LEIGHTON **PENCILS AND INKS:** GREGG SCHIGIEL
COLOR: MONICA KUBINA **LETTERING:** COMICRAFT

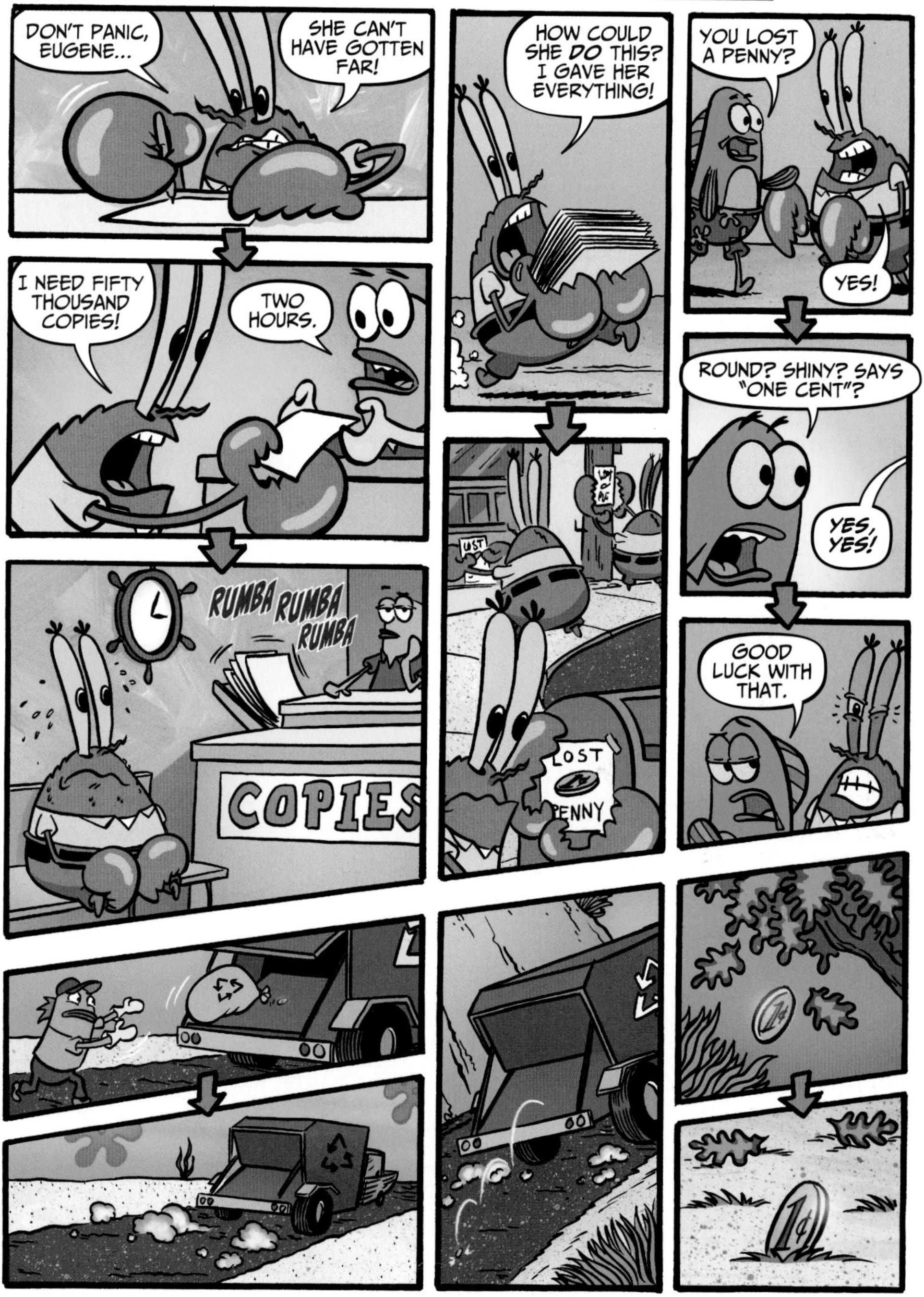

DON'T PANIC, EUGENE...
SHE CAN'T HAVE GOTTEN FAR!
I NEED FIFTY THOUSAND COPIES!
TWO HOURS.
RUMBA RUMBA RUMBA
COPIES
HOW COULD SHE *DO* THIS? I GAVE HER EVERYTHING!
LOST PENNY
YOU LOST A PENNY?
YES!
ROUND? SHINY? SAYS "ONE CENT"?
YES, YES!
GOOD LUCK WITH THAT.

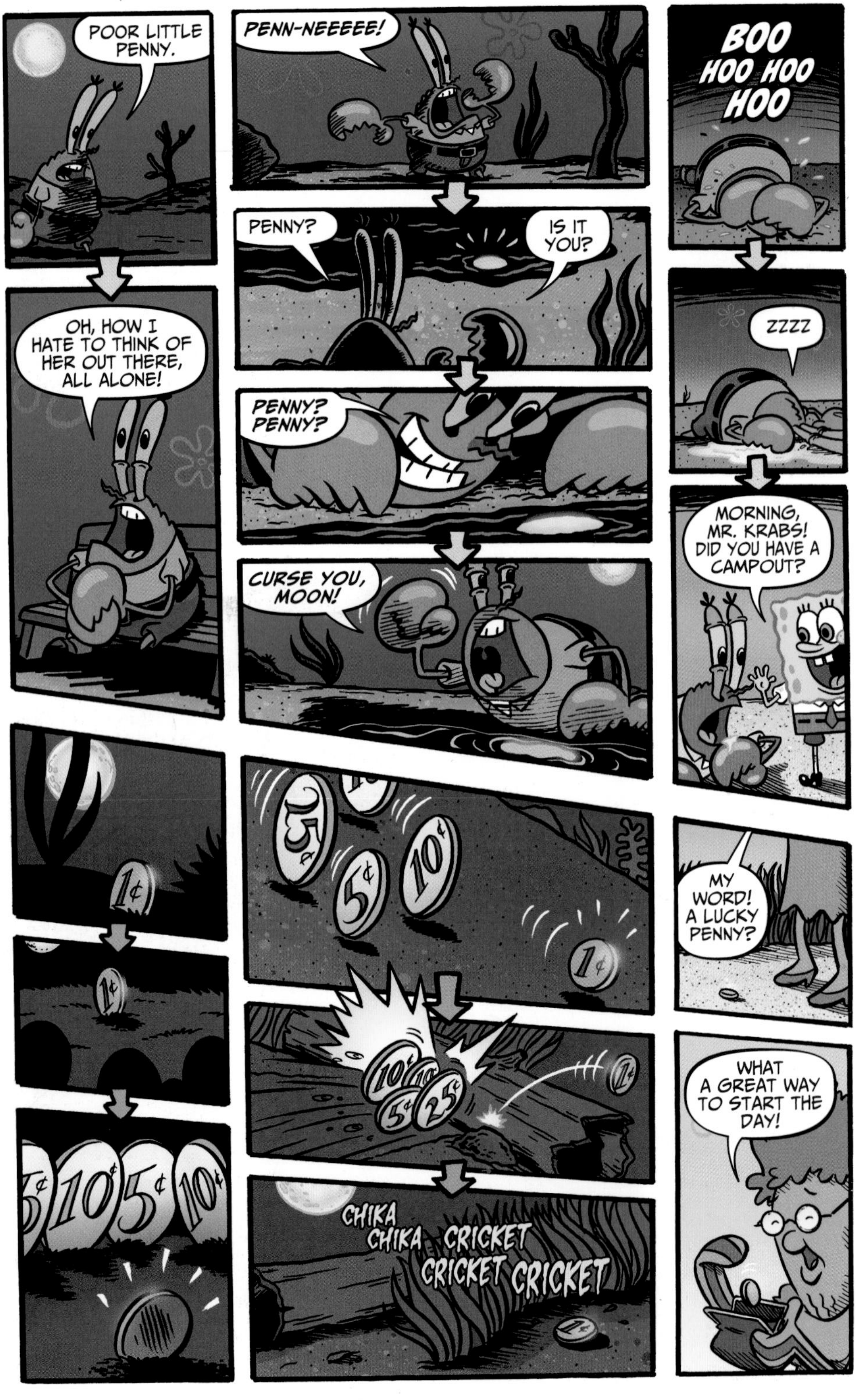
POOR LITTLE PENNY.
OH, HOW I HATE TO THINK OF HER OUT THERE, ALL ALONE!
PENN-NEEEEE!
PENNY?
IS IT YOU?
PENNY? PENNY?
CURSE YOU, MOON!
BOO HOO HOO HOO
ZZZZ
MORNING, MR. KRABS! DID YOU HAVE A CAMPOUT?
1¢
1¢
5¢ 10¢ 5¢ 10¢
5¢ 5¢ 10¢ 10¢
1¢
10¢ 10¢ 5¢ 25¢
1¢
CHIKA CHIKA CRICKET CRICKET CRICKET
MY WORD! A LUCKY PENNY?
WHAT A GREAT WAY TO START THE DAY!

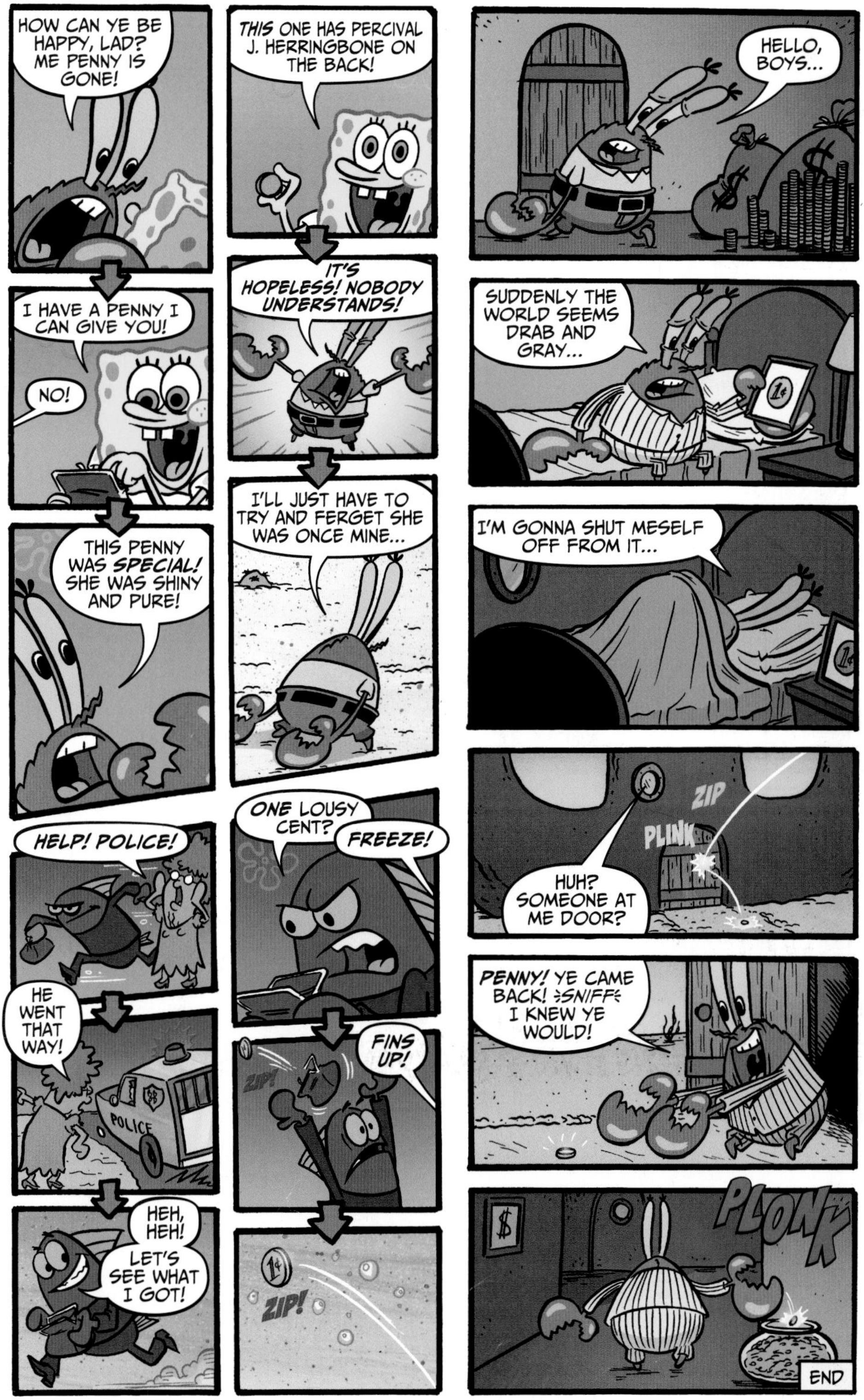
HOW CAN YE BE HAPPY, LAD? ME PENNY IS GONE!
I HAVE A PENNY I CAN GIVE YOU!
NO!
THIS PENNY WAS SPECIAL! SHE WAS SHINY AND PURE!
HELP! POLICE!
HE WENT THAT WAY!
POLICE
HEH, HEH!
LET'S SEE WHAT I GOT!
THIS ONE HAS PERCIVAL J. HERRINGBONE ON THE BACK!
IT'S HOPELESS! NOBODY UNDERSTANDS!
I'LL JUST HAVE TO TRY AND FERGET SHE WAS ONCE MINE...
ONE LOUSY CENT?
FREEZE!
ZIP!
FINS UP!
1¢
ZIP!
HELLO, BOYS...
SUDDENLY THE WORLD SEEMS DRAB AND GRAY...
I'M GONNA SHUT MESELF OFF FROM IT...
ZIP
PLINK
HUH? SOMEONE AT ME DOOR?
PENNY! YE CAME BACK! *SNIFF* I KNEW YE WOULD!
PLONK
END

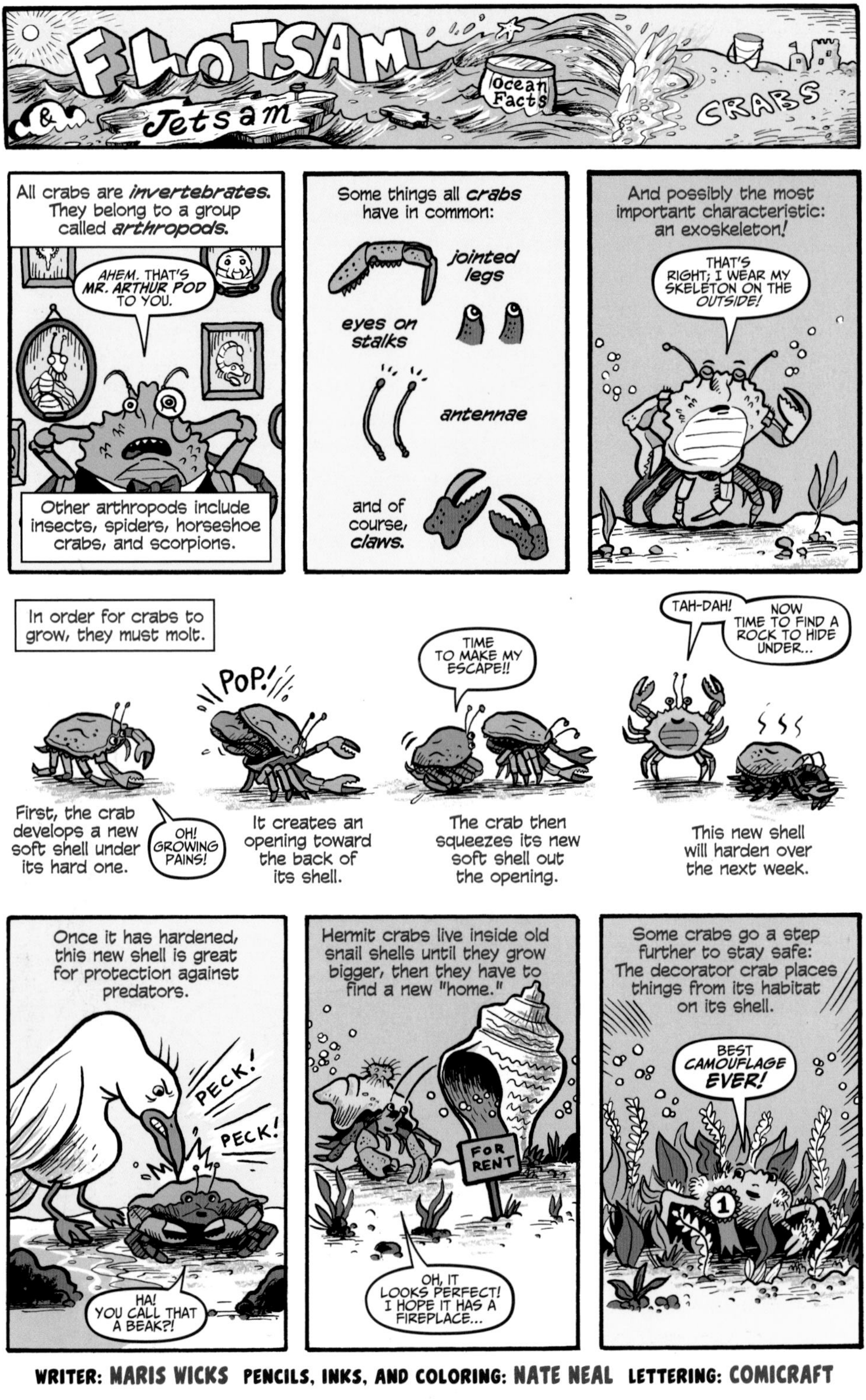
FLOTSAM
& Jetsam
Ocean Facts
CRABS
All crabs are *invertebrates.* They belong to a group called *arthropods.*
AHEM. THAT'S MR. ARTHUR POD TO YOU.
Other arthropods include insects, spiders, horseshoe crabs, and scorpions.
Some things all *crabs* have in common:
jointed legs
eyes on stalks
antennae
and of course, claws.
And possibly the most important characteristic: an exoskeleton!
THAT'S RIGHT; I WEAR MY SKELETON ON THE *OUTSIDE!*
In order for crabs to grow, they must molt.
First, the crab develops a new soft shell under its hard one.
OH! GROWING PAINS!
POP!
It creates an opening toward the back of its shell.
TIME TO MAKE MY ESCAPE!!
The crab then squeezes its new soft shell out the opening.
TAH-DAH!
NOW TIME TO FIND A ROCK TO HIDE UNDER...
This new shell will harden over the next week.
Once it has hardened, this new shell is great for protection against predators.
PECK!
PECK!
HA! YOU CALL THAT A BEAK?!
Hermit crabs live inside old snail shells until they grow bigger, then they have to find a new "home."
FOR RENT
OH, IT LOOKS PERFECT! I HOPE IT HAS A FIREPLACE...
Some crabs go a step further to stay safe: The decorator crab places things from its habitat on its shell.
BEST CAMOUFLAGE EVER!
1

WRITER: MARIS WICKS PENCILS, INKS, AND COLORING: NATE NEAL LETTERING: COMICRAFT

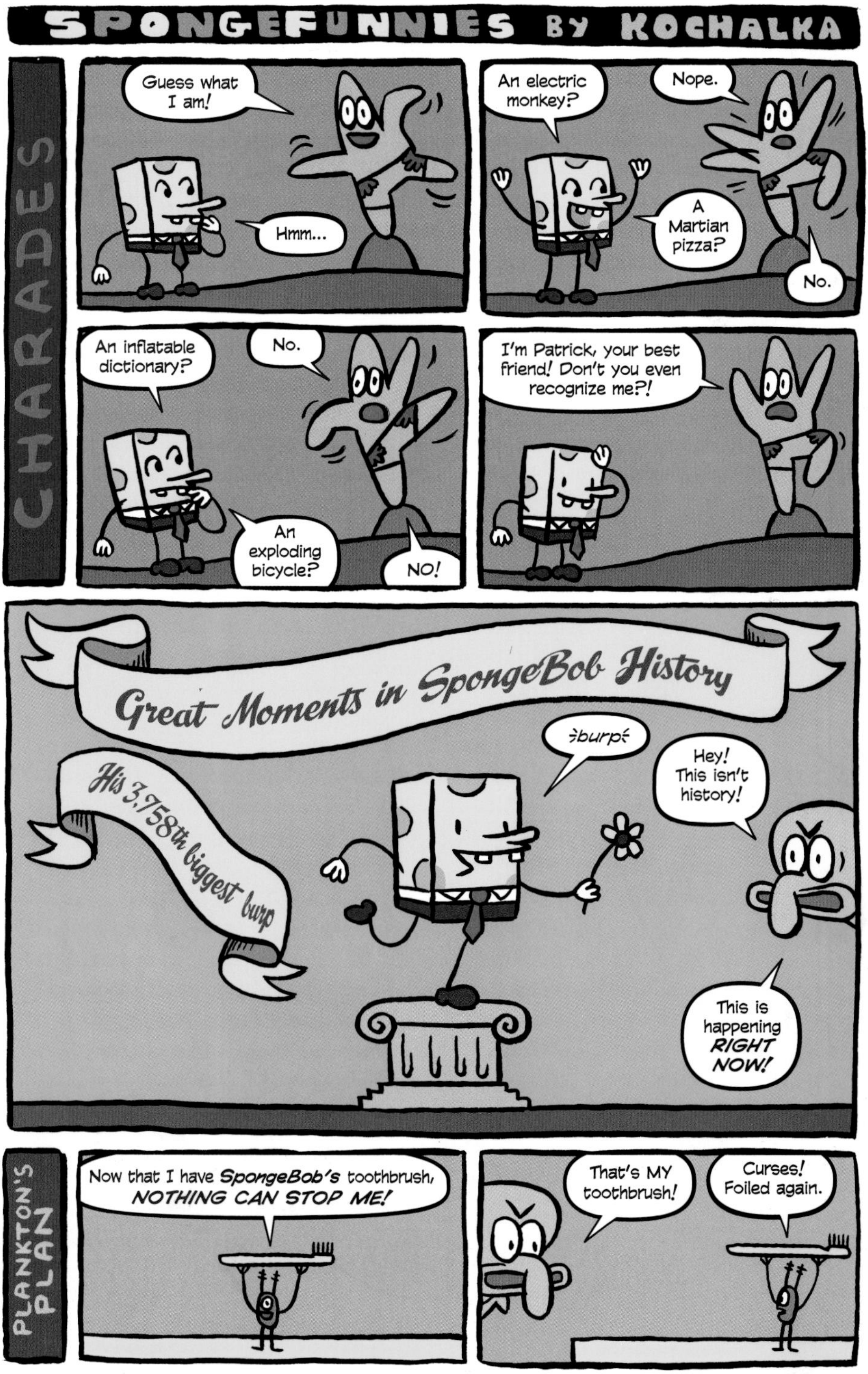
SPONGEFUNNIES BY KOCHALKA
CHARADES
Guess what I am!
Hmm...
An electric monkey?
Nope.
A Martian pizza?
No.
An inflatable dictionary?
No.
An exploding bicycle?
NO!
I'm Patrick, your best friend! Don't you even recognize me?!
Great Moments in SpongeBob History
His 3,758th biggest burp
≥burp≤
Hey! This isn't history!
This is happening RIGHT NOW!
PLANKTON'S PLAN
Now that I have SpongeBob's toothbrush, NOTHING CAN STOP ME!
That's MY toothbrush!
Curses! Foiled again.

Story and art: James Kochalka Lettering: Comicraft

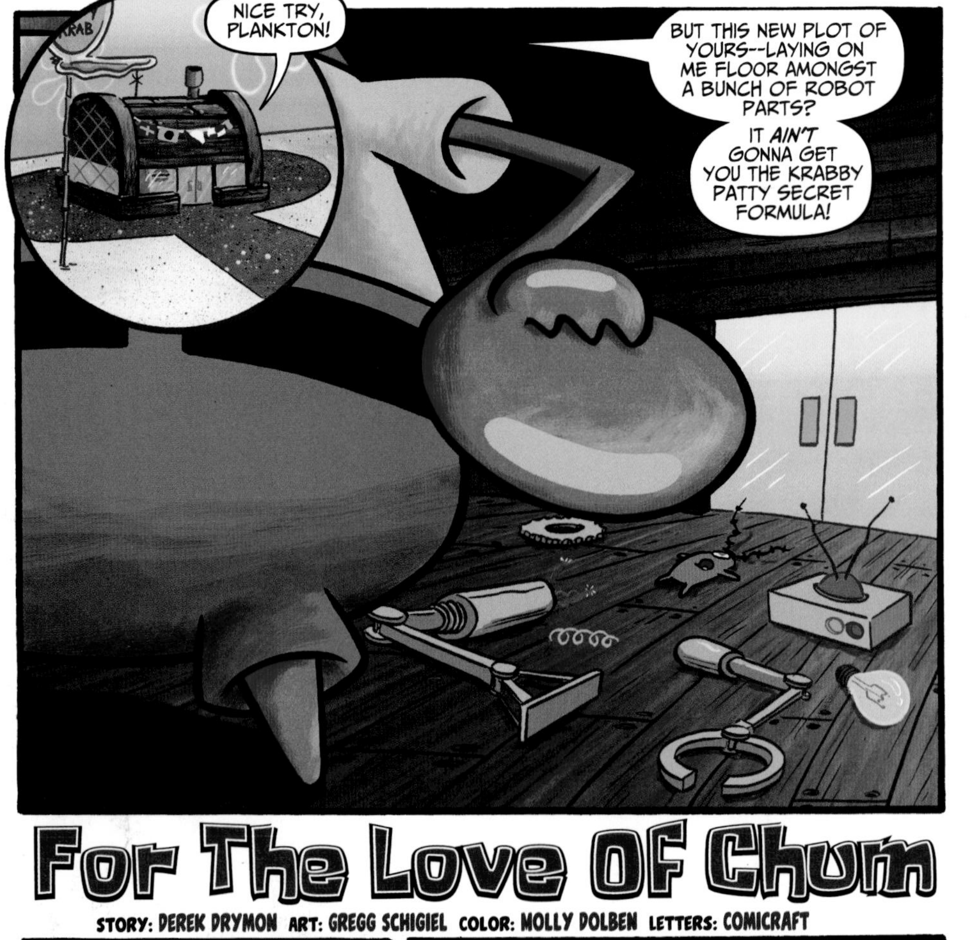
NICE TRY, PLANKTON!
BUT THIS NEW PLOT OF YOURS--LAYING ON ME FLOOR AMONGST A BUNCH OF ROBOT PARTS?
IT *AIN'T* GONNA GET YOU THE KRABBY PATTY SECRET FORMULA!

For The Love Of Chum

STORY: DEREK DRYMON **ART:** GREGG SCHIGIEL **COLOR:** MOLLY DOLBEN **LETTERS:** COMICRAFT

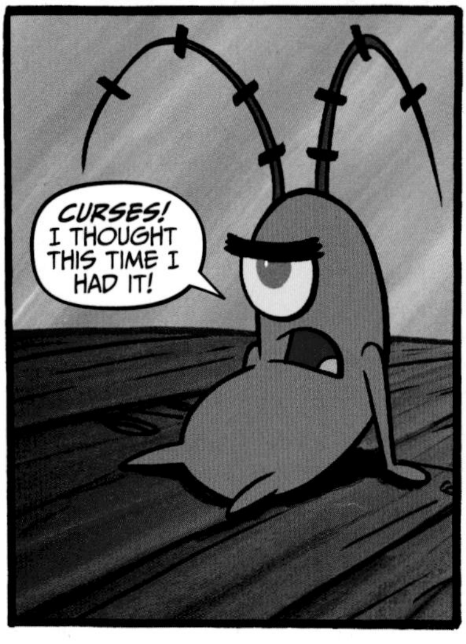
CURSES! I THOUGHT THIS TIME I HAD IT!

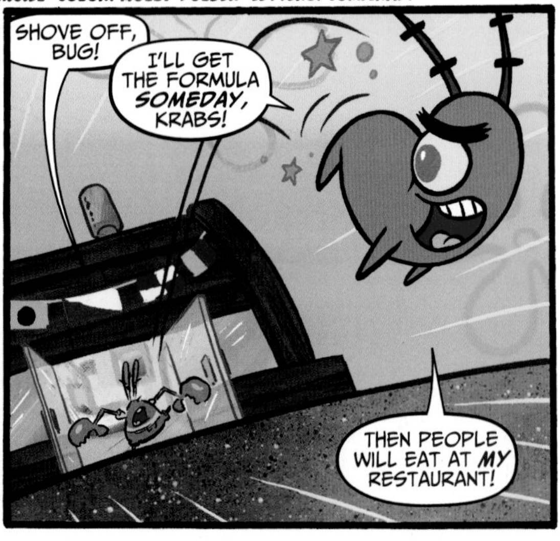
SHOVE OFF, BUG!
I'LL GET THE FORMULA *SOMEDAY,* KRABS!
THEN PEOPLE WILL EAT AT *MY* RESTAURANT!

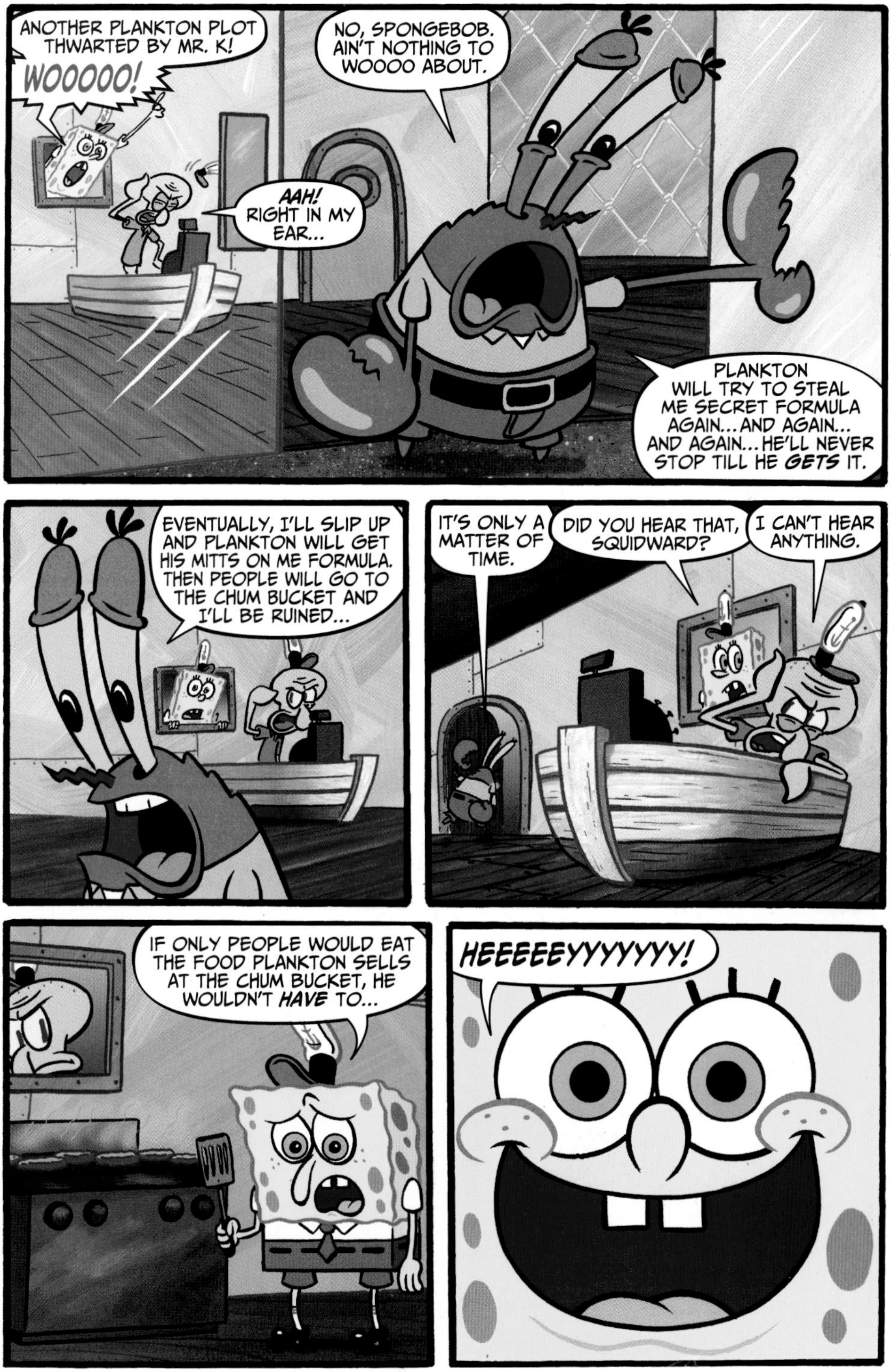
ANOTHER PLANKTON PLOT THWARTED BY MR. K!
WOOOOO!
NO, SPONGEBOB. AIN'T NOTHING TO WOOOO ABOUT.
AAH! RIGHT IN MY EAR...
PLANKTON WILL TRY TO STEAL ME SECRET FORMULA AGAIN... AND AGAIN... AND AGAIN... HE'LL NEVER STOP TILL HE GETS IT.
EVENTUALLY, I'LL SLIP UP AND PLANKTON WILL GET HIS MITTS ON ME FORMULA. THEN PEOPLE WILL GO TO THE CHUM BUCKET AND I'LL BE RUINED...
IT'S ONLY A MATTER OF TIME.
DID YOU HEAR THAT, SQUIDWARD?
I CAN'T HEAR ANYTHING.
IF ONLY PEOPLE WOULD EAT THE FOOD PLANKTON SELLS AT THE CHUM BUCKET, HE WOULDN'T HAVE TO...
HEEEEEYYYYYYY!

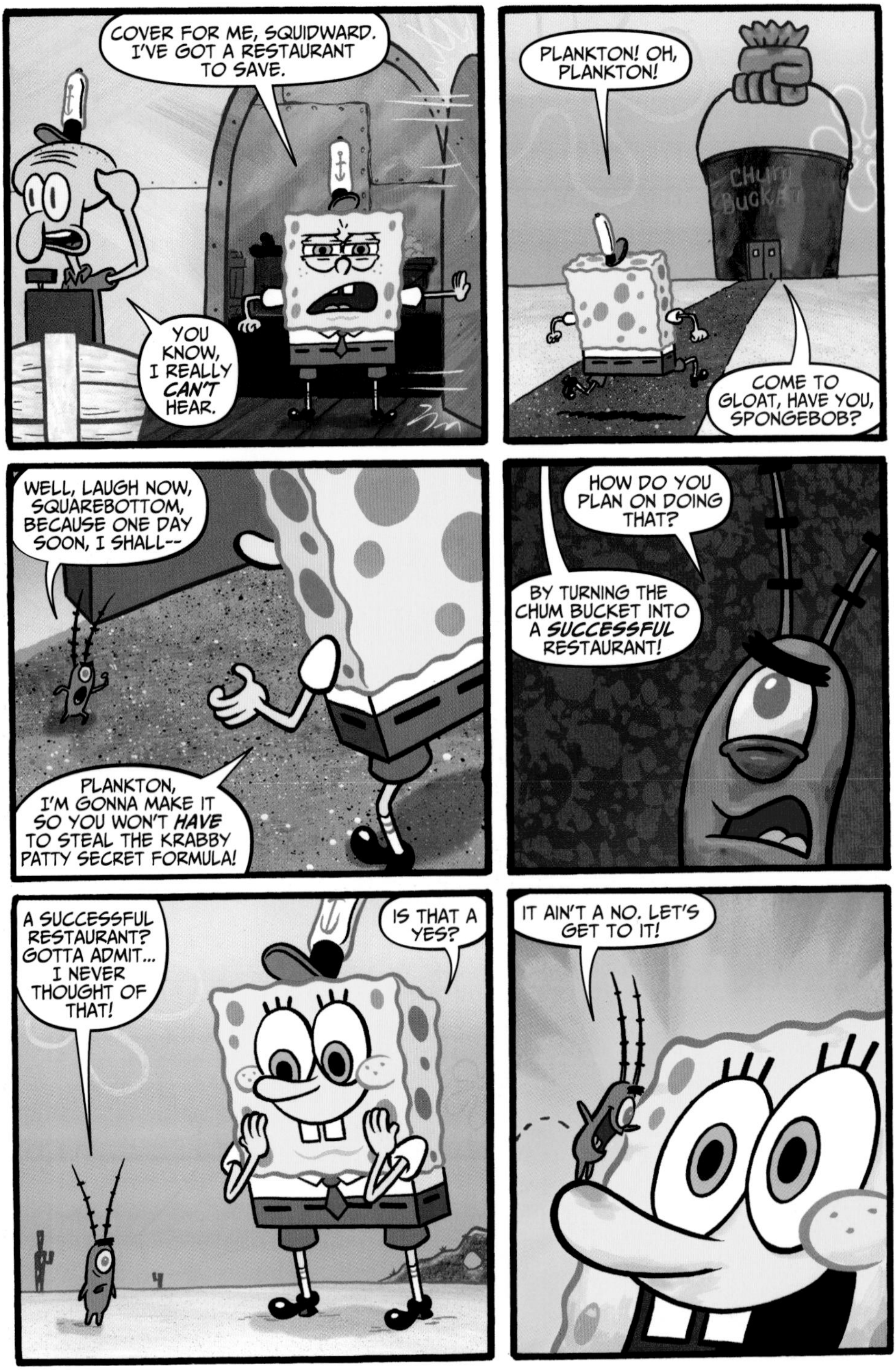
COVER FOR ME, SQUIDWARD. I'VE GOT A RESTAURANT TO SAVE.
YOU KNOW, I REALLY *CAN'T* HEAR.
PLANKTON! OH, PLANKTON!
CHUM BUCKET
COME TO GLOAT, HAVE YOU, SPONGEBOB?
WELL, LAUGH NOW, SQUAREBOTTOM, BECAUSE ONE DAY SOON, I SHALL--
PLANKTON, I'M GONNA MAKE IT SO YOU WON'T *HAVE* TO STEAL THE KRABBY PATTY SECRET FORMULA!
HOW DO YOU PLAN ON DOING THAT?
BY TURNING THE CHUM BUCKET INTO A *SUCCESSFUL* RESTAURANT!
A SUCCESSFUL RESTAURANT? GOTTA ADMIT... I NEVER THOUGHT OF THAT!
IS THAT A YES?
IT AIN'T A NO. LET'S GET TO IT!

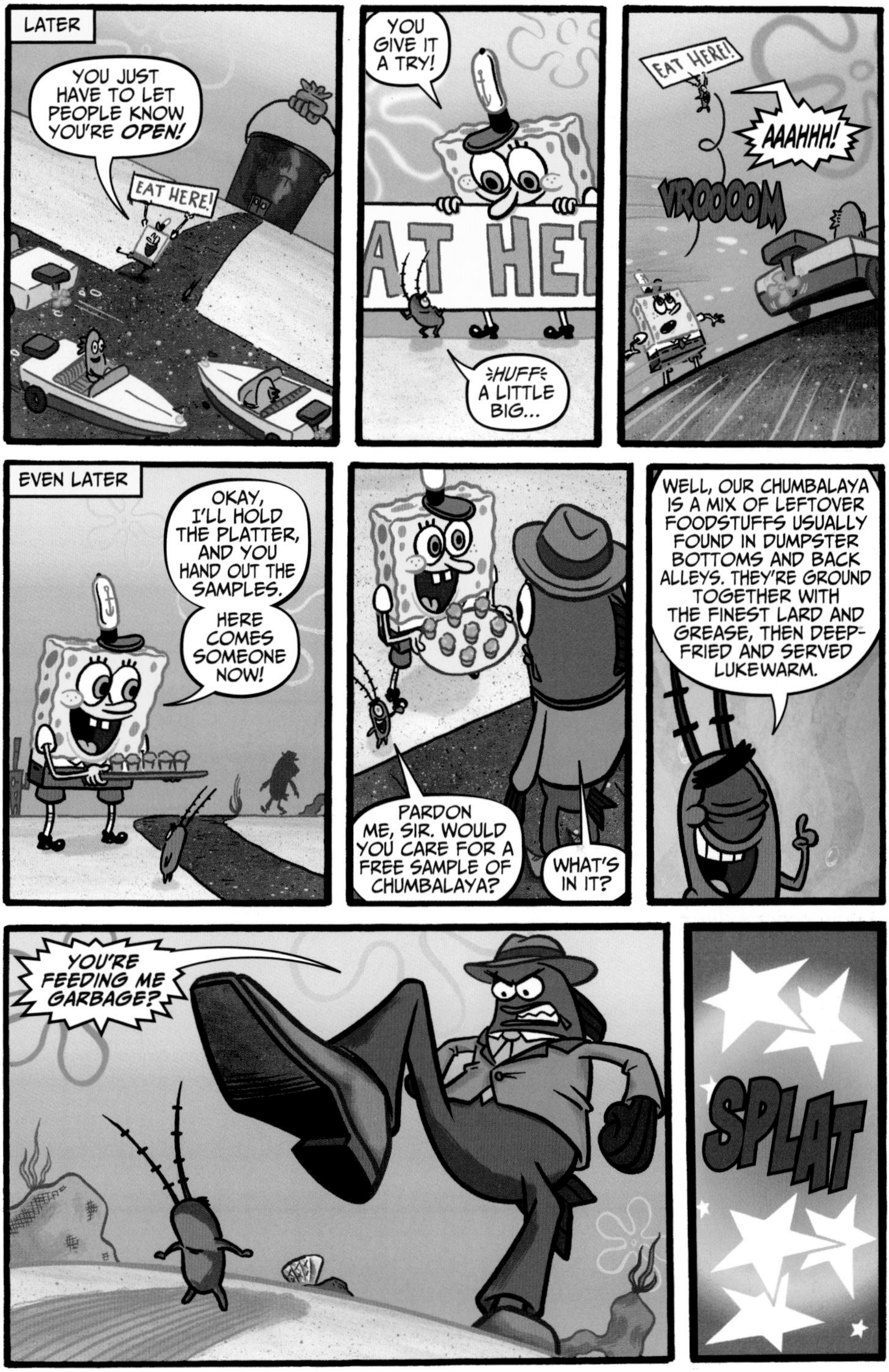
LATER
YOU JUST HAVE TO LET PEOPLE KNOW YOU'RE *OPEN!*
EAT HERE!
YOU GIVE IT A TRY!
HUFF A LITTLE BIG...
EAT HERE!
AAAHHH!
VROOOOM
EVEN LATER
OKAY, I'LL HOLD THE PLATTER, AND YOU HAND OUT THE SAMPLES.
HERE COMES SOMEONE NOW!
PARDON ME, SIR. WOULD YOU CARE FOR A FREE SAMPLE OF CHUMBALAYA?
WHAT'S IN IT?
WELL, OUR CHUMBALAYA IS A MIX OF LEFTOVER FOODSTUFFS USUALLY FOUND IN DUMPSTER BOTTOMS AND BACK ALLEYS. THEY'RE GROUND TOGETHER WITH THE FINEST LARD AND GREASE, THEN DEEP-FRIED AND SERVED LUKEWARM.
YOU'RE FEEDING ME GARBAGE?
SPLAT

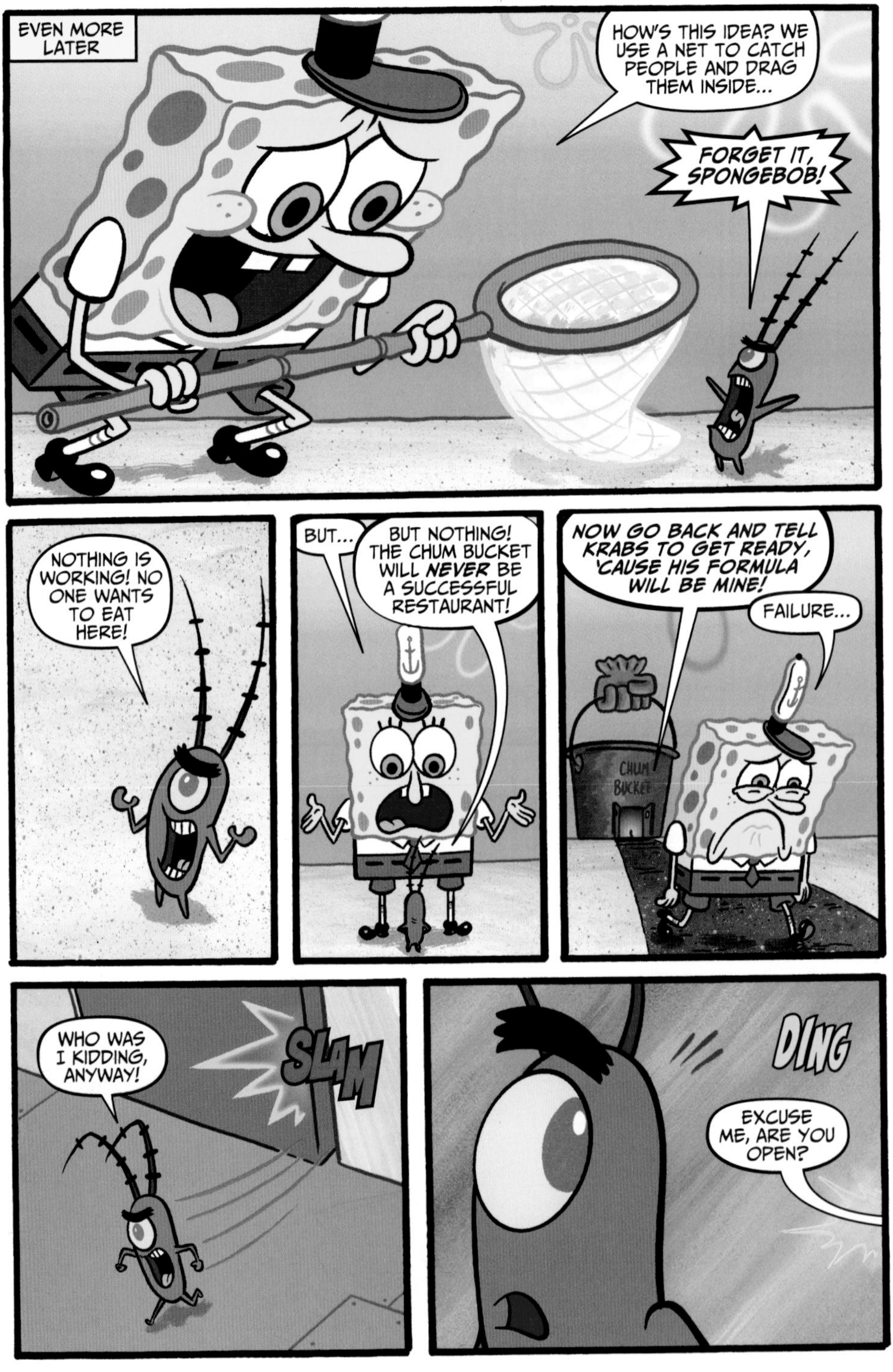
EVEN MORE LATER
HOW'S THIS IDEA? WE USE A NET TO CATCH PEOPLE AND DRAG THEM INSIDE...
FORGET IT, SPONGEBOB!
NOTHING IS WORKING! NO ONE WANTS TO EAT HERE!
BUT...
BUT NOTHING! THE CHUM BUCKET WILL NEVER BE A SUCCESSFUL RESTAURANT!
NOW GO BACK AND TELL KRABS TO GET READY, 'CAUSE HIS FORMULA WILL BE MINE!
FAILURE...
CHUM BUCKET
WHO WAS I KIDDING, ANYWAY!
SLAM
DING
EXCUSE ME, ARE YOU OPEN?

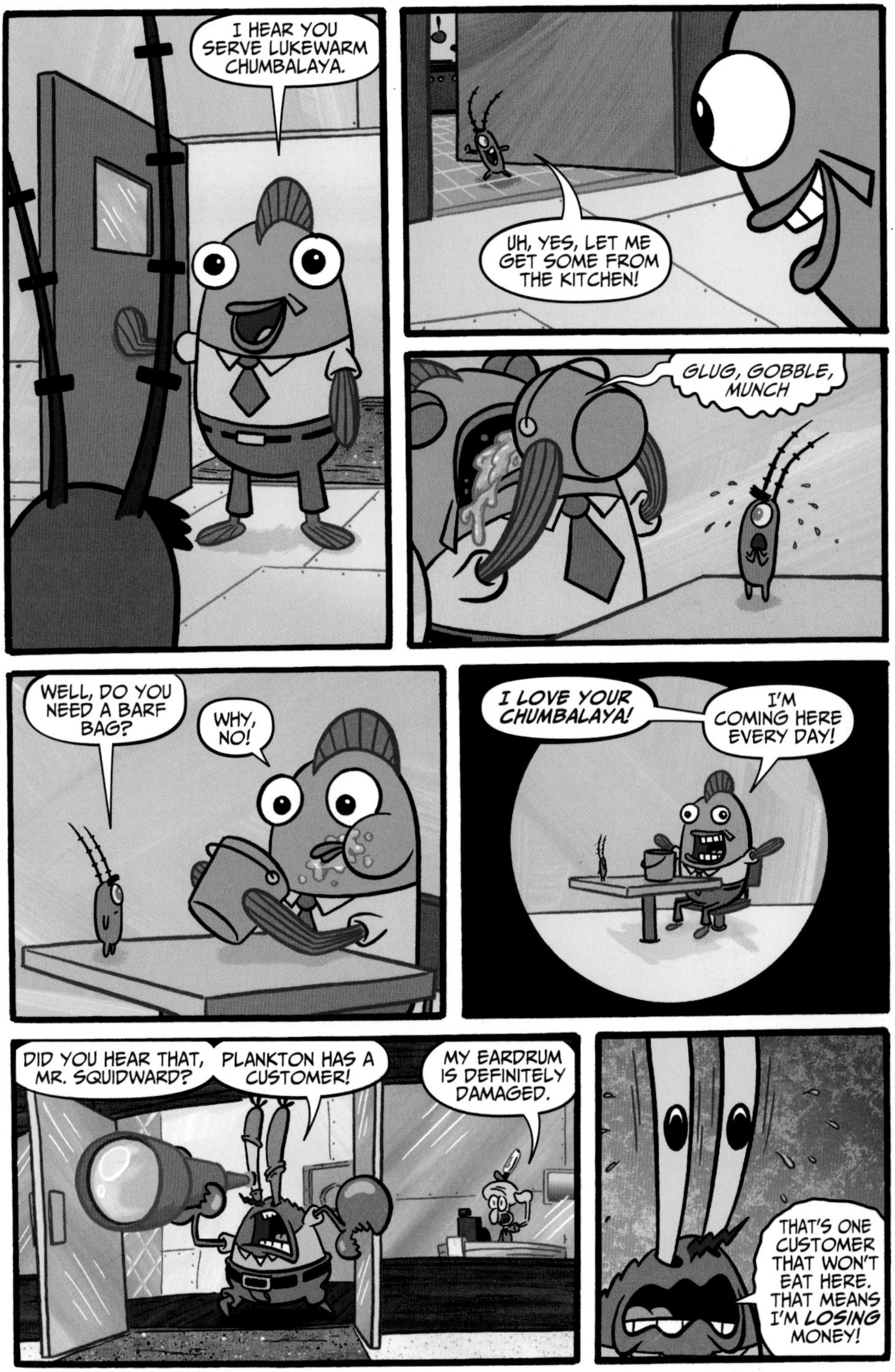
I HEAR YOU SERVE LUKEWARM CHUMBALAYA.
UH, YES, LET ME GET SOME FROM THE KITCHEN!
GLUG, GOBBLE, MUNCH
WELL, DO YOU NEED A BARF BAG?
WHY, NO!
I LOVE YOUR CHUMBALAYA!
I'M COMING HERE EVERY DAY!
DID YOU HEAR THAT, MR. SQUIDWARD?
PLANKTON HAS A CUSTOMER!
MY EARDRUM IS DEFINITELY DAMAGED.
THAT'S ONE CUSTOMER THAT WON'T EAT HERE. THAT MEANS I'M LOSING MONEY!

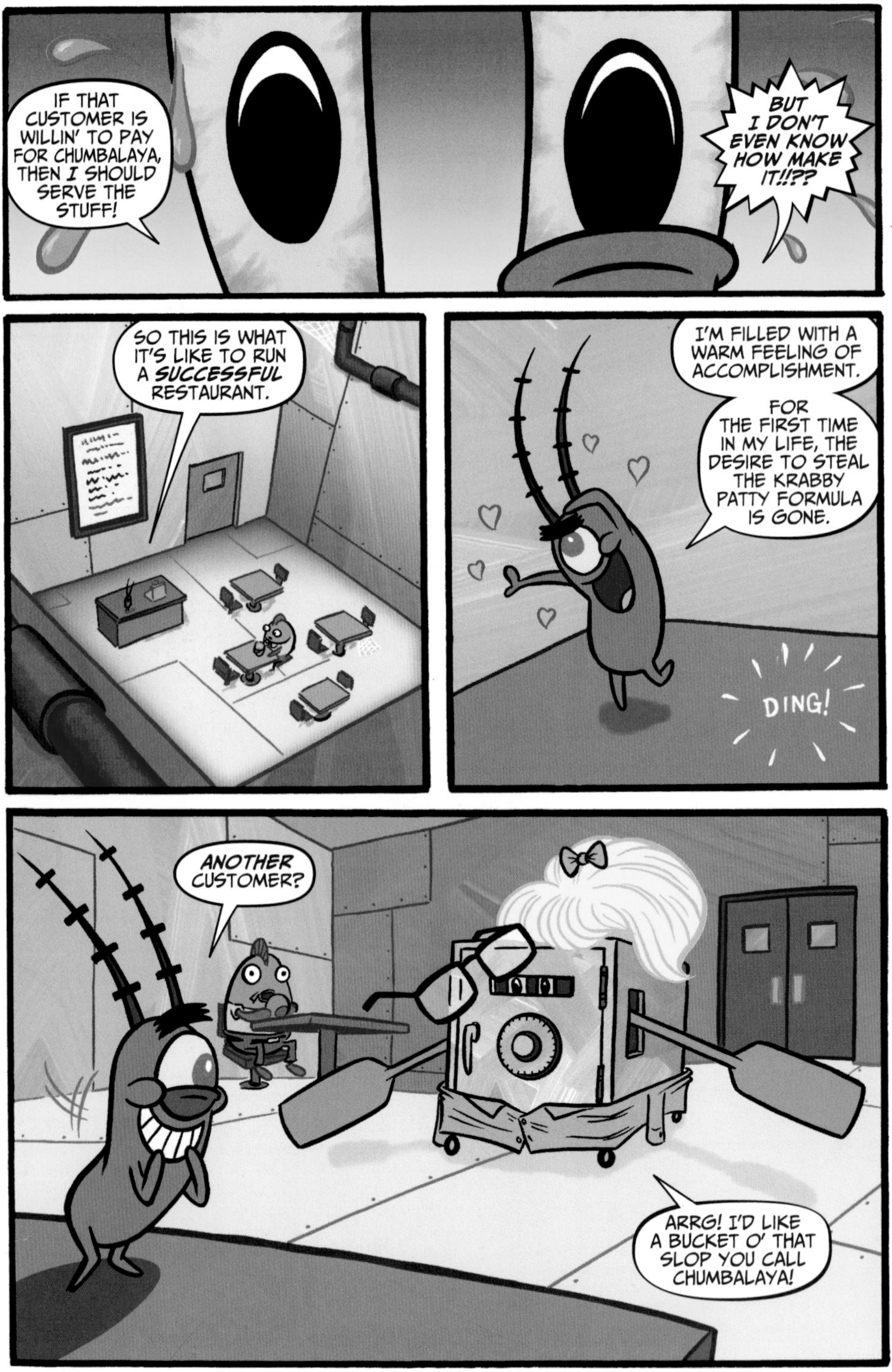

IF THAT CUSTOMER IS WILLIN' TO PAY FOR CHUMBALAYA, THEN *I* SHOULD SERVE THE STUFF!
BUT I DON'T EVEN KNOW HOW MAKE IT!!??
SO THIS IS WHAT IT'S LIKE TO RUN A *SUCCESSFUL* RESTAURANT.
I'M FILLED WITH A WARM FEELING OF ACCOMPLISHMENT.
FOR THE FIRST TIME IN MY LIFE, THE DESIRE TO STEAL THE KRABBY PATTY FORMULA IS GONE.
DING!
ANOTHER CUSTOMER?
ARRG! I'D LIKE A BUCKET O' THAT SLOP YOU CALL CHUMBALAYA!

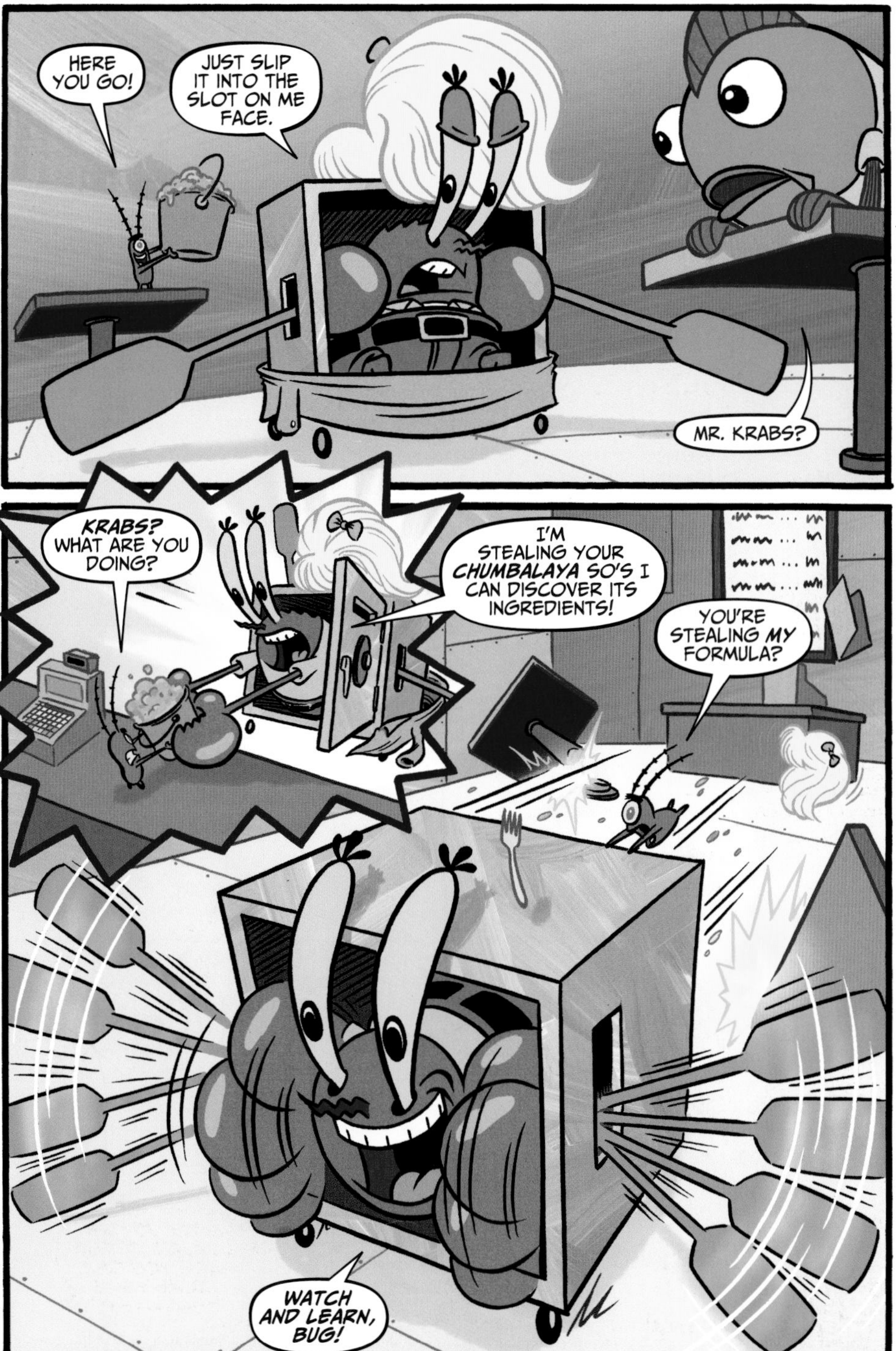
HERE YOU GO!
JUST SLIP IT INTO THE SLOT ON ME FACE.
MR. KRABS?
KRABS? WHAT ARE YOU DOING?
I'M STEALING YOUR CHUMBALAYA SO'S I CAN DISCOVER ITS INGREDIENTS!
YOU'RE STEALING MY FORMULA?
WATCH AND LEARN, BUG!

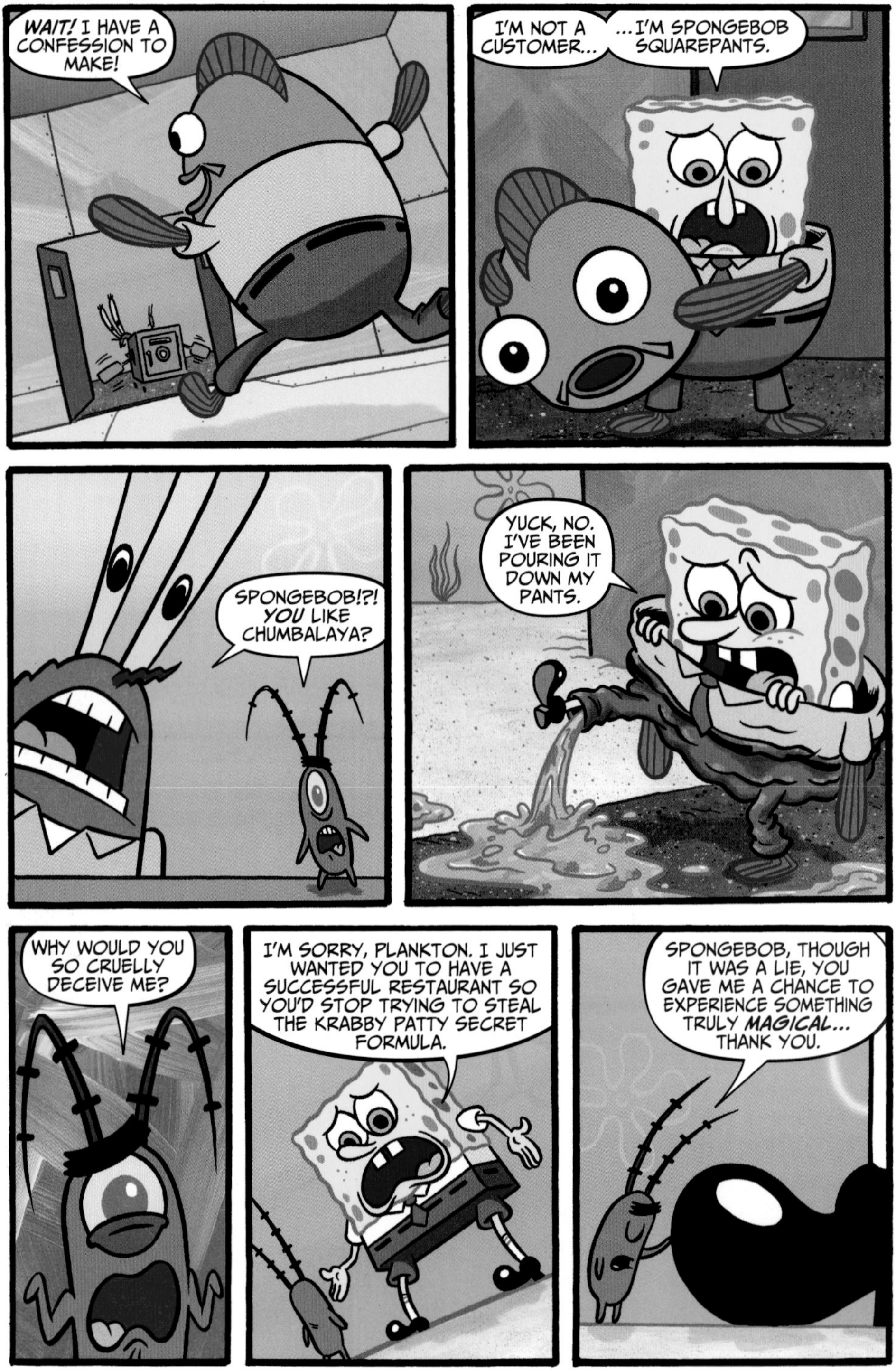
WAIT! I HAVE A CONFESSION TO MAKE!
I'M NOT A CUSTOMER...
...I'M SPONGEBOB SQUAREPANTS.
SPONGEBOB!?! YOU LIKE CHUMBALAYA?
YUCK, NO. I'VE BEEN POURING IT DOWN MY PANTS.
WHY WOULD YOU SO CRUELLY DECEIVE ME?
I'M SORRY, PLANKTON. I JUST WANTED YOU TO HAVE A SUCCESSFUL RESTAURANT SO YOU'D STOP TRYING TO STEAL THE KRABBY PATTY SECRET FORMULA.
SPONGEBOB, THOUGH IT WAS A LIE, YOU GAVE ME A CHANCE TO EXPERIENCE SOMETHING TRULY MAGICAL... THANK YOU.

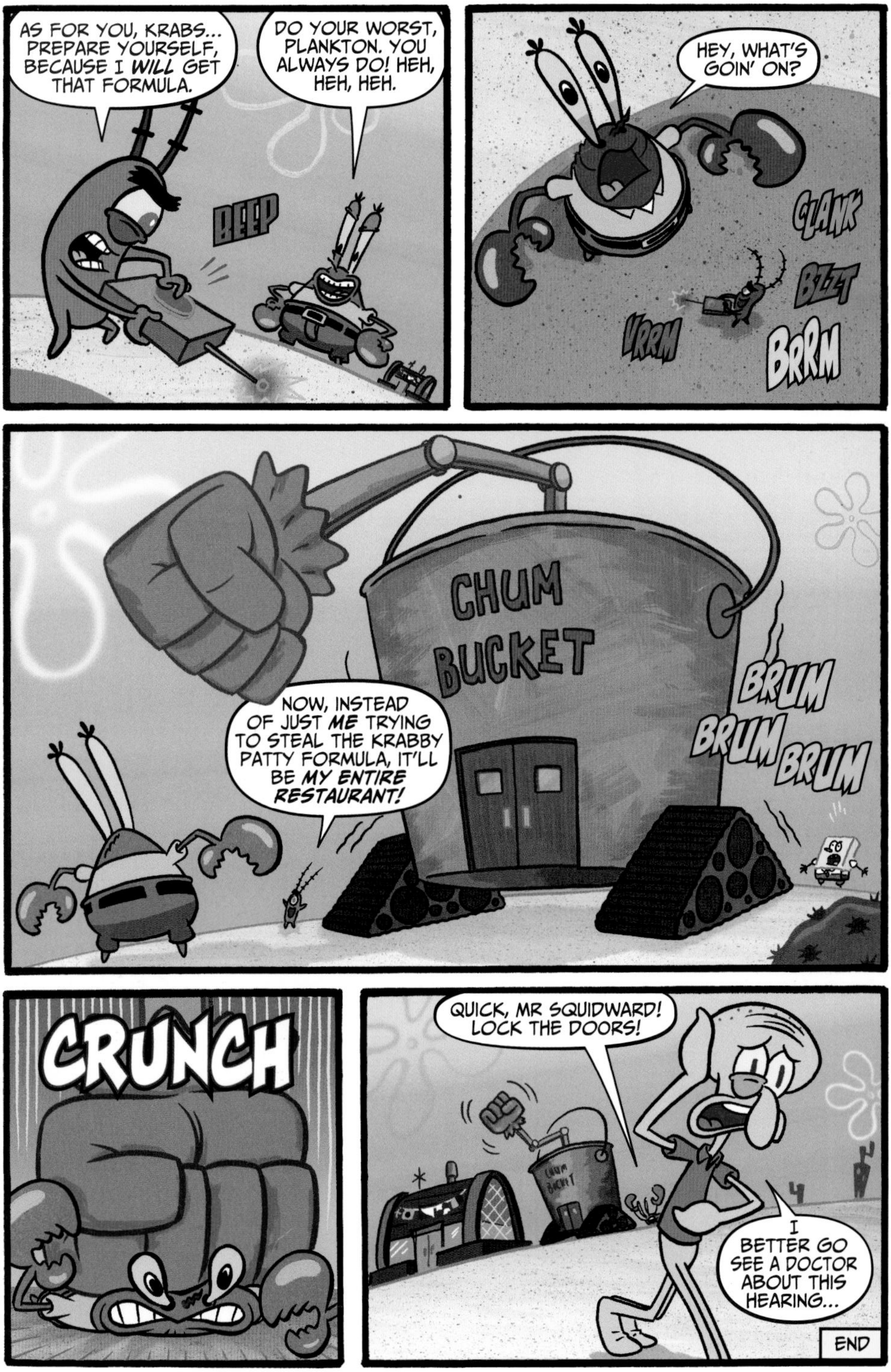
AS FOR YOU, KRABS... PREPARE YOURSELF, BECAUSE I *WILL* GET THAT FORMULA.
DO YOUR WORST, PLANKTON. YOU ALWAYS DO! HEH, HEH, HEH.
BEEP
HEY, WHAT'S GOIN' ON?
CLANK
BZZT
VRRM
BRRM
CHUM BUCKET
BRUM
BRUM BRUM
NOW, INSTEAD OF JUST *ME* TRYING TO STEAL THE KRABBY PATTY FORMULA, IT'LL BE *MY ENTIRE RESTAURANT!*
CRUNCH
QUICK, MR SQUIDWARD! LOCK THE DOORS!
I BETTER GO SEE A DOCTOR ABOUT THIS HEARING...
END

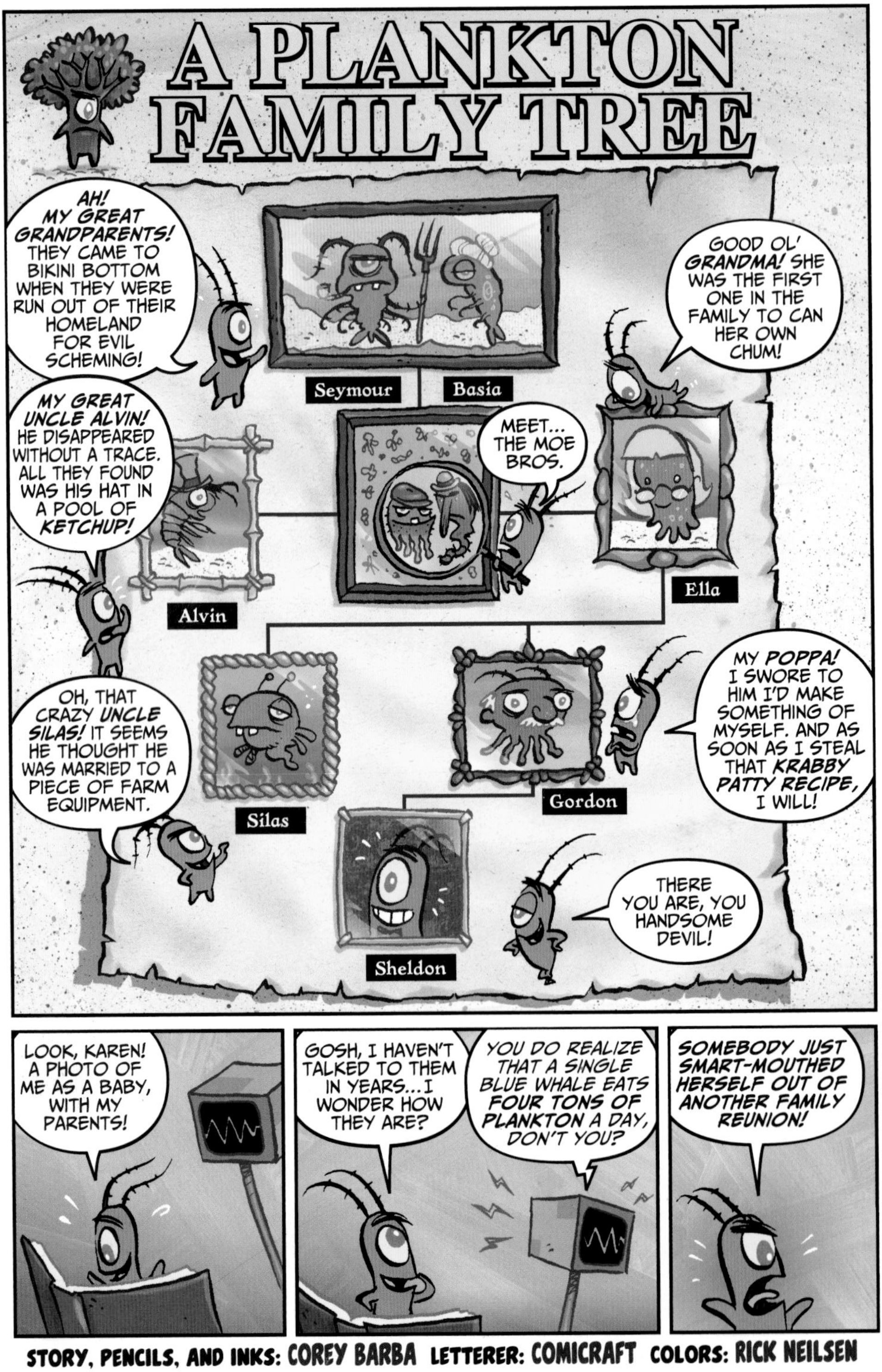
A PLANKTON FAMILY TREE
AH! MY GREAT GRANDPARENTS! THEY CAME TO BIKINI BOTTOM WHEN THEY WERE RUN OUT OF THEIR HOMELAND FOR EVIL SCHEMING!
Seymour
Basia
GOOD OL' GRANDMA! SHE WAS THE FIRST ONE IN THE FAMILY TO CAN HER OWN CHUM!
MY GREAT UNCLE ALVIN! HE DISAPPEARED WITHOUT A TRACE. ALL THEY FOUND WAS HIS HAT IN A POOL OF KETCHUP!
MEET... THE MOE BROS.
Alvin
Ella
OH, THAT CRAZY UNCLE SILAS! IT SEEMS HE THOUGHT HE WAS MARRIED TO A PIECE OF FARM EQUIPMENT.
MY POPPA! I SWORE TO HIM I'D MAKE SOMETHING OF MYSELF. AND AS SOON AS I STEAL THAT KRABBY PATTY RECIPE, I WILL!
Silas
Gordon
Sheldon
THERE YOU ARE, YOU HANDSOME DEVIL!
LOOK, KAREN! A PHOTO OF ME AS A BABY, WITH MY PARENTS!
GOSH, I HAVEN'T TALKED TO THEM IN YEARS... I WONDER HOW THEY ARE?
YOU DO REALIZE THAT A SINGLE BLUE WHALE EATS FOUR TONS OF PLANKTON A DAY, DON'T YOU?
SOMEBODY JUST SMART-MOUTHED HERSELF OUT OF ANOTHER FAMILY REUNION!

STORY, PENCILS, AND INKS: COREY BARBA LETTERER: COMICRAFT COLORS: RICK NEILSEN

A PEEK INSIDE THE MIND OF PATRICK

A TYPICAL MOMENT IN PATRICK'S DAY...

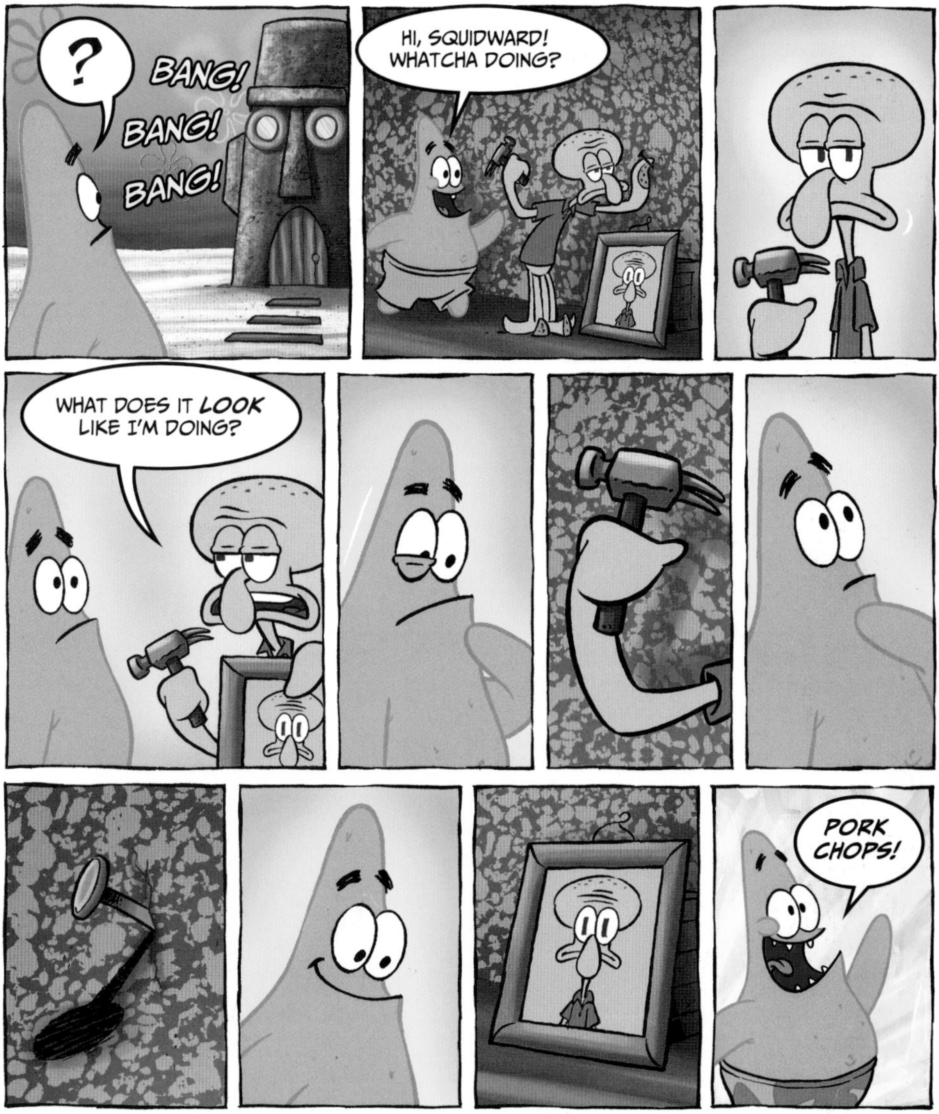
?
BANG!
BANG!
BANG!
HI, SQUIDWARD! WHATCHA DOING?
WHAT DOES IT *LOOK* LIKE I'M DOING?
PORK CHOPS!

LET'S TAKE A LOOK INSIDE, SHALL WE?

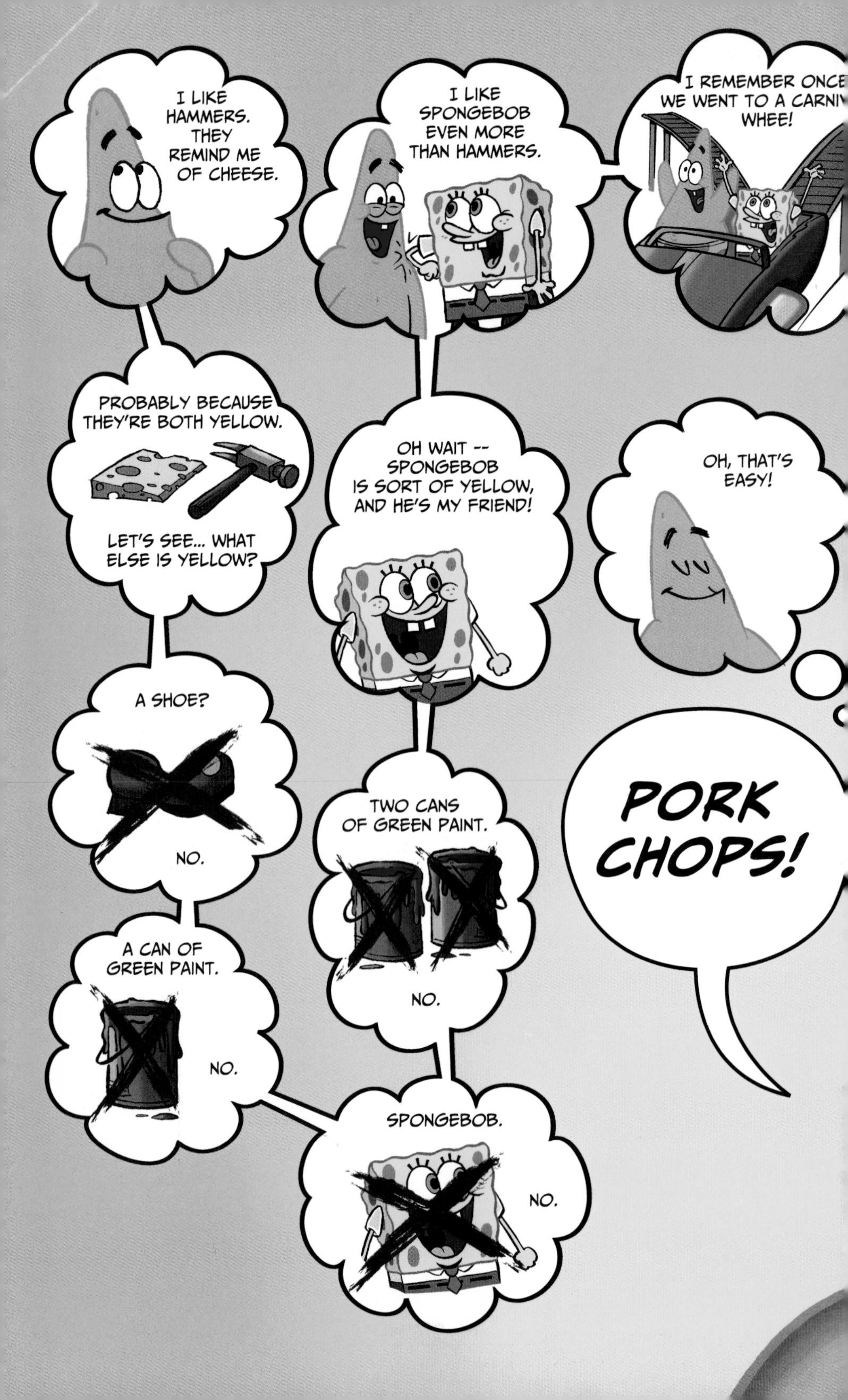
I LIKE HAMMERS. THEY REMIND ME OF CHEESE.
PROBABLY BECAUSE THEY'RE BOTH YELLOW.
LET'S SEE... WHAT ELSE IS YELLOW?
A SHOE?
NO.
A CAN OF GREEN PAINT.
NO.
SPONGEBOB.
NO.
TWO CANS OF GREEN PAINT.
NO.
OH WAIT -- SPONGEBOB IS SORT OF YELLOW, AND HE'S MY FRIEND!
I LIKE SPONGEBOB EVEN MORE THAN HAMMERS.
WHEE!
OH, THAT'S EASY!
PORK CHOPS!

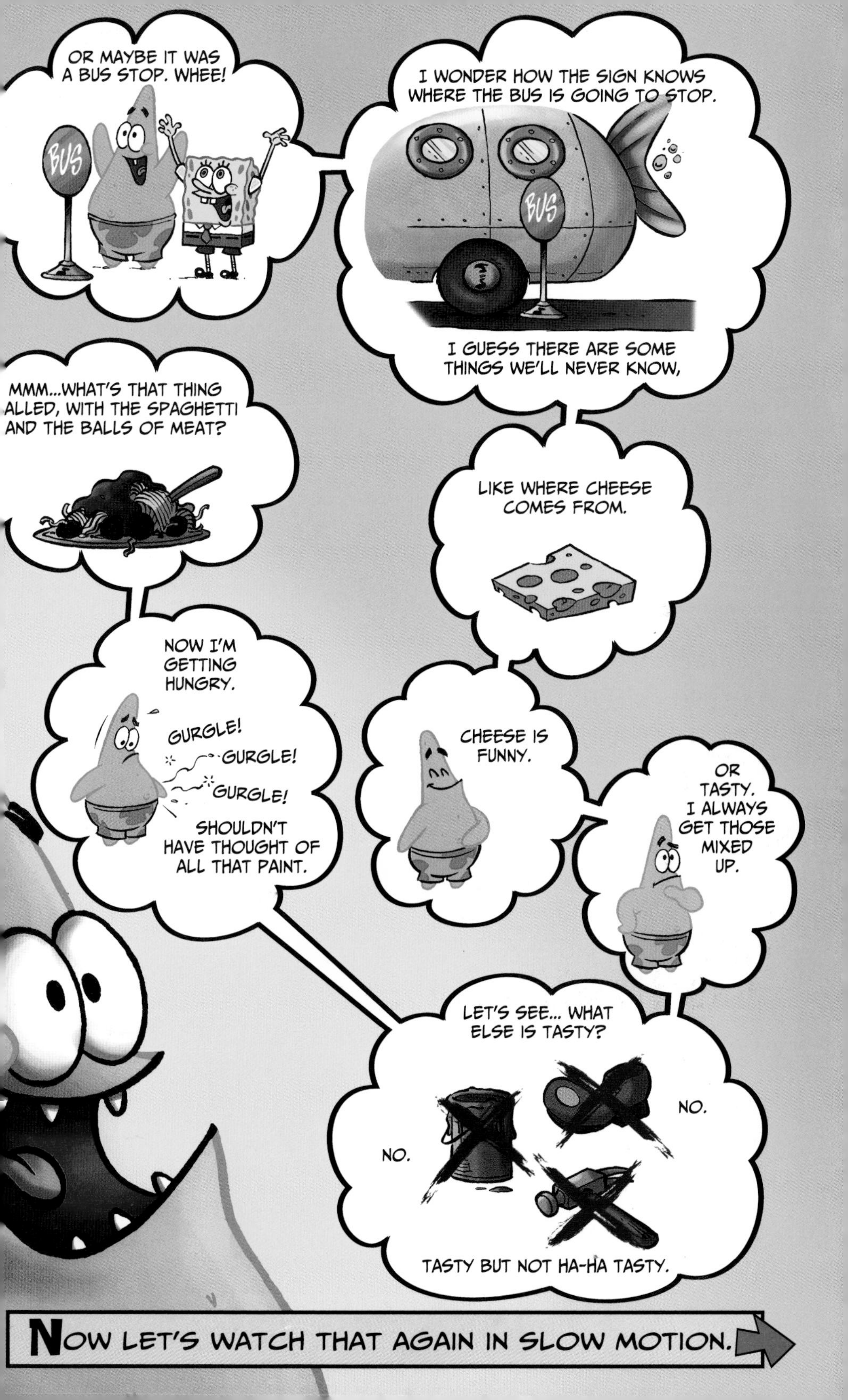
OR MAYBE IT WAS A BUS STOP. WHEE!
BUS
I WONDER HOW THE SIGN KNOWS WHERE THE BUS IS GOING TO STOP.
BUS
I GUESS THERE ARE SOME THINGS WE'LL NEVER KNOW,
LIKE WHERE CHEESE COMES FROM.
CHEESE IS FUNNY.
OR TASTY. I ALWAYS GET THOSE MIXED UP.
LET'S SEE... WHAT ELSE IS TASTY?
NO.
NO.
TASTY BUT NOT HA-HA TASTY.
MMM...WHAT'S THAT THING ALLED, WITH THE SPAGHETTI AND THE BALLS OF MEAT?
NOW I'M GETTING HUNGRY.
GURGLE!
GURGLE!
GURGLE!
SHOULDN'T HAVE THOUGHT OF ALL THAT PAINT.
NOW LET'S WATCH THAT AGAIN IN SLOW MOTION.

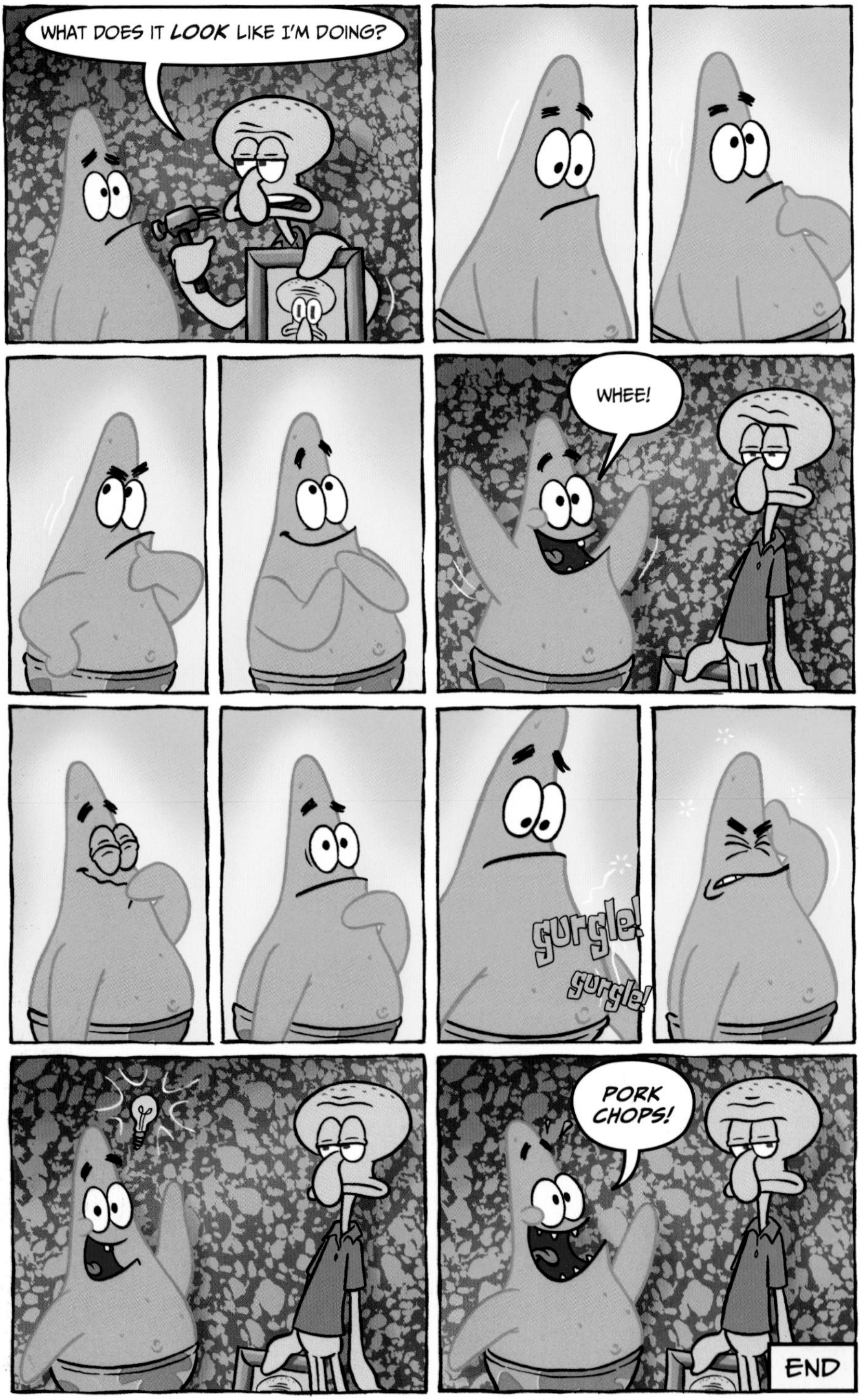
WHAT DOES IT LOOK LIKE I'M DOING?
WHEE!
gurgle!
gurgle!
PORK CHOPS!
END

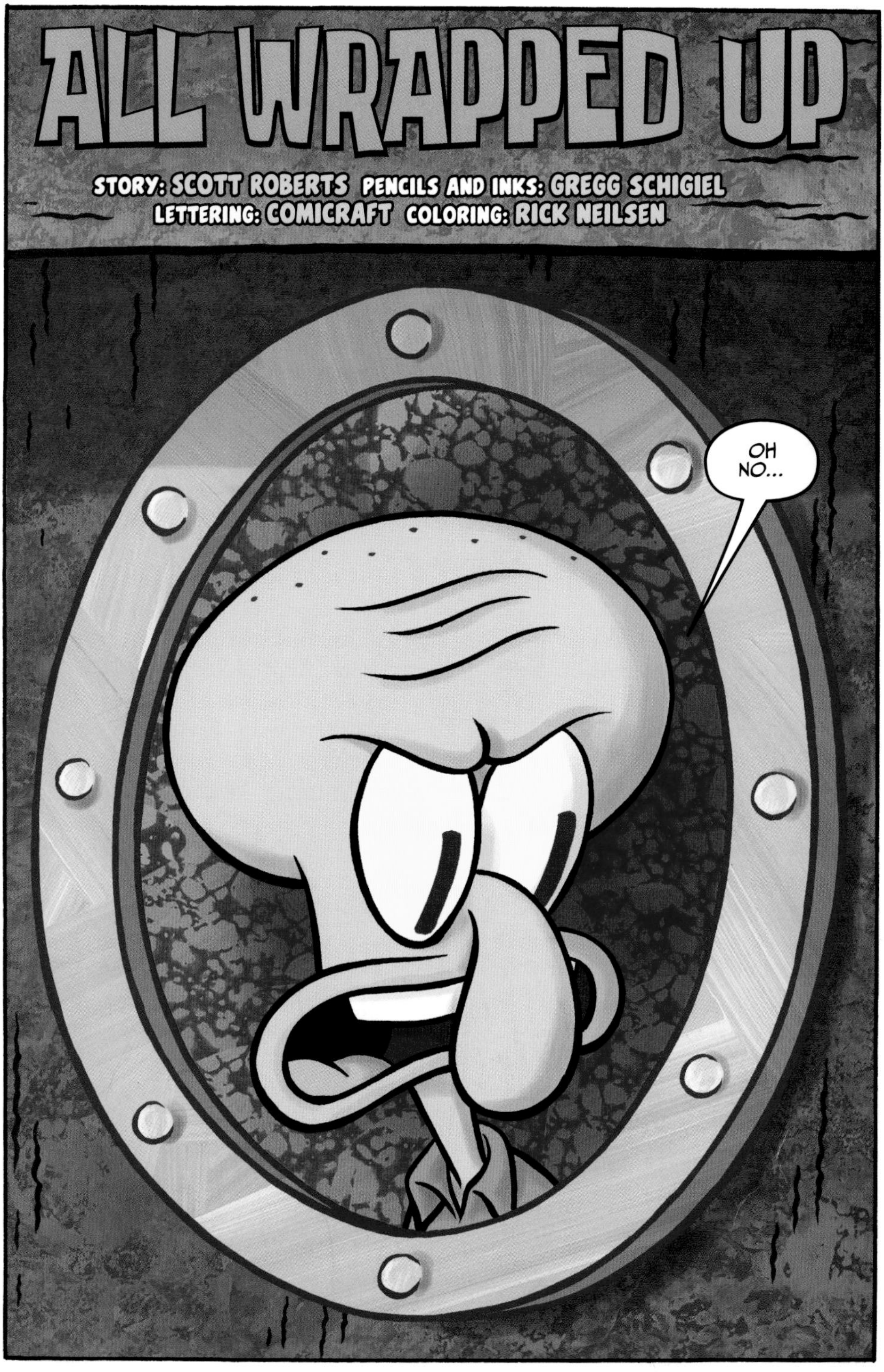
ALL WRAPPED UP
STORY: SCOTT ROBERTS PENCILS AND INKS: GREGG SCHIGIEL
LETTERING: COMICRAFT COLORING: RICK NEILSEN
OH NO...

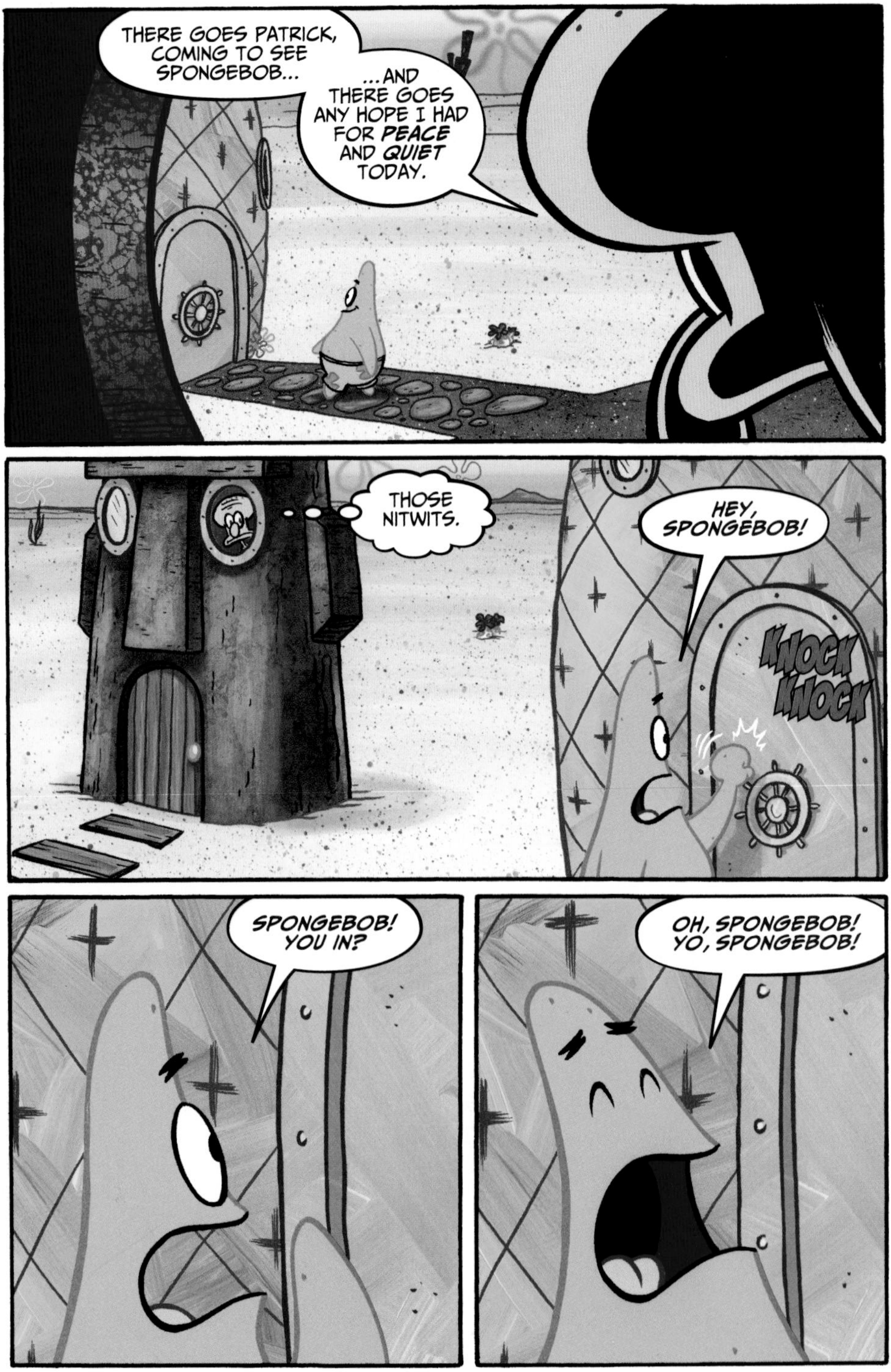
THERE GOES PATRICK, COMING TO SEE SPONGEBOB...
...AND THERE GOES ANY HOPE I HAD FOR PEACE AND QUIET TODAY.
THOSE NITWITS.
HEY, SPONGEBOB!
KNOCK KNOCK
SPONGEBOB! YOU IN?
OH, SPONGEBOB! YO, SPONGEBOB!

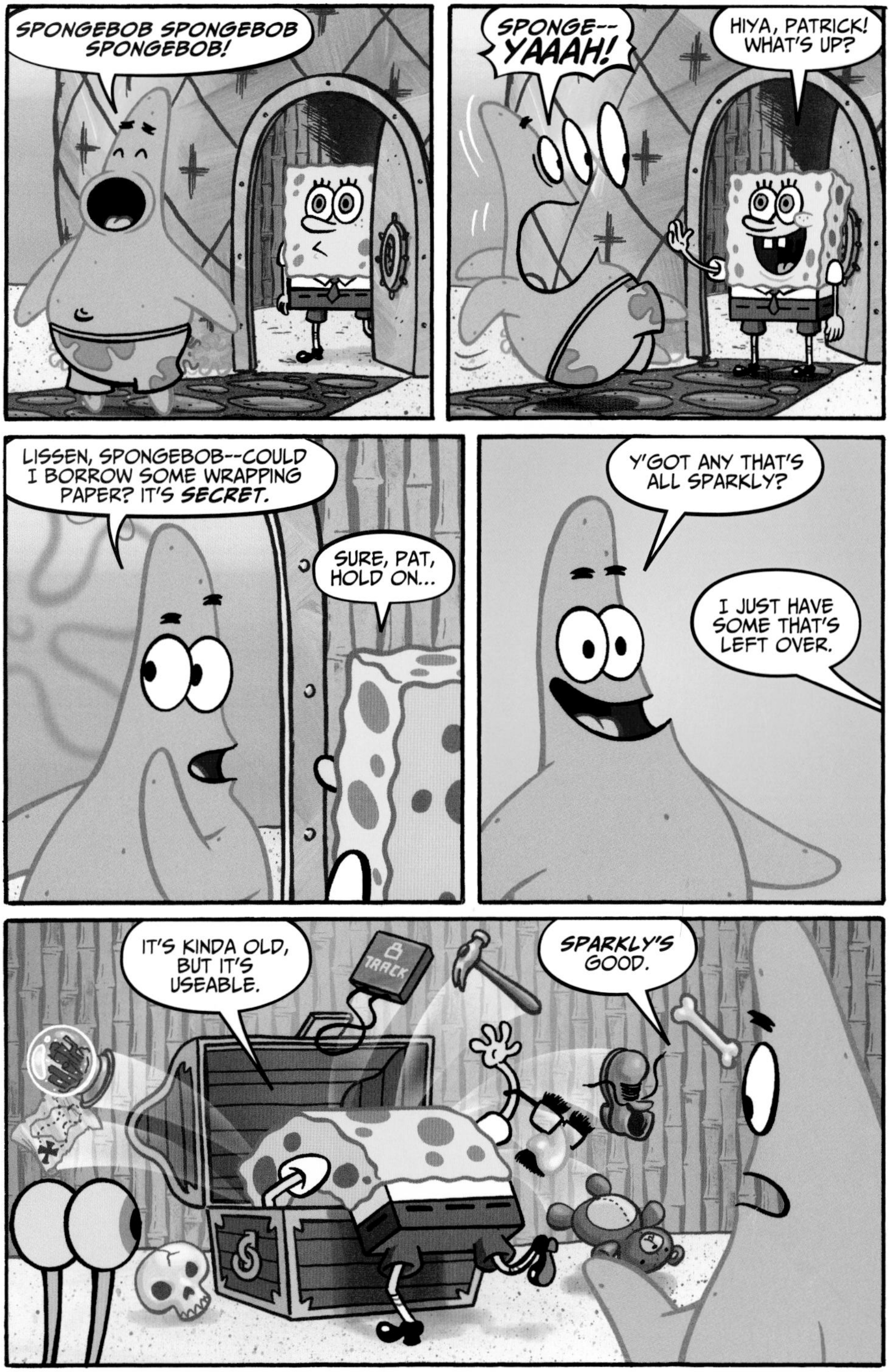
SPONGEBOB SPONGEBOB SPONGEBOB!
SPONGE-- YAAAH!
HIYA, PATRICK! WHAT'S UP?
LISSEN, SPONGEBOB--COULD I BORROW SOME WRAPPING PAPER? IT'S SECRET.
SURE, PAT, HOLD ON...
Y'GOT ANY THAT'S ALL SPARKLY?
I JUST HAVE SOME THAT'S LEFT OVER.
IT'S KINDA OLD, BUT IT'S USEABLE.
TRACK
SPARKLY'S GOOD.

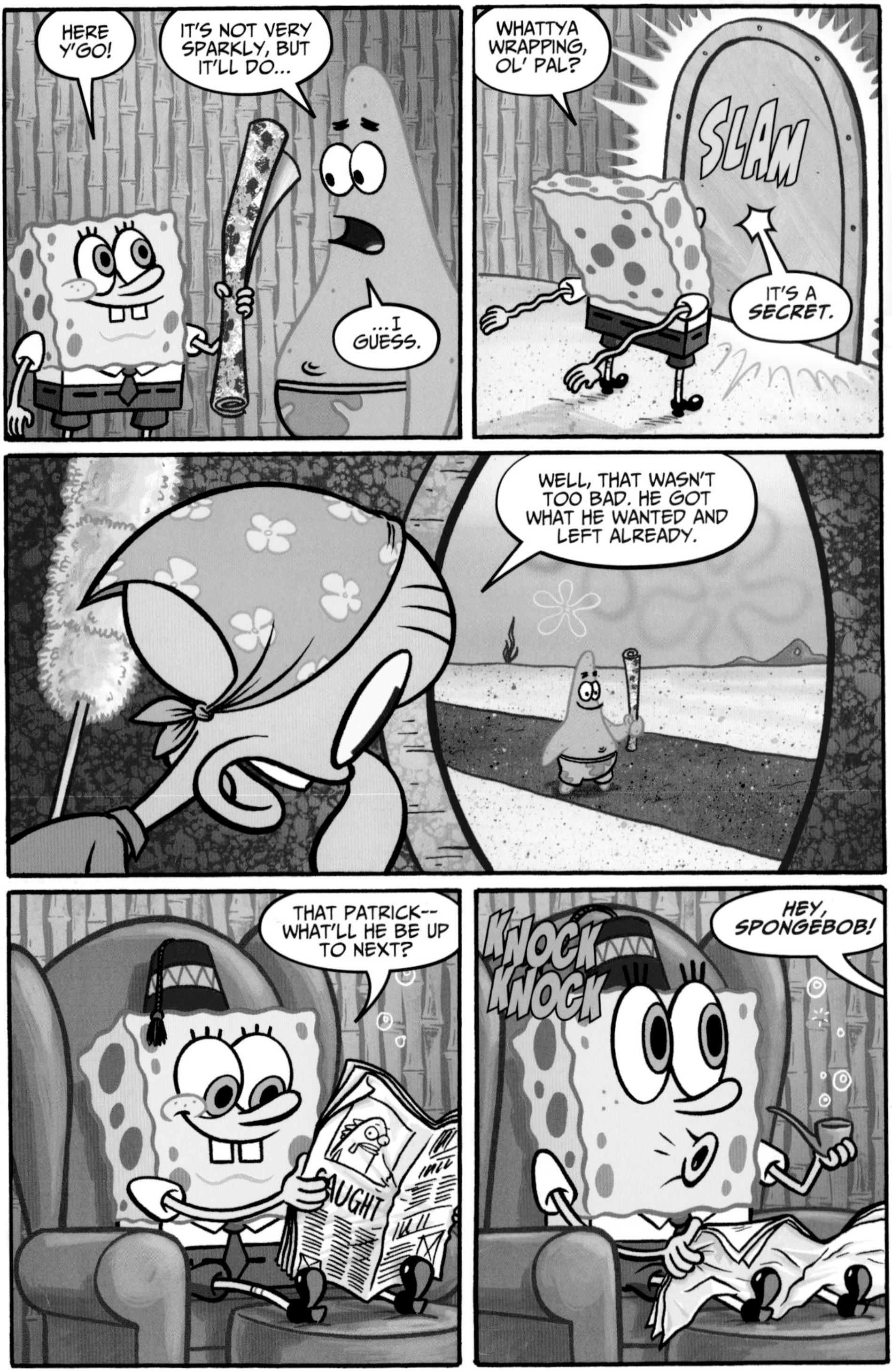
HERE Y'GO!
IT'S NOT VERY SPARKLY, BUT IT'LL DO...
...I GUESS.
WHATTYA WRAPPING, OL' PAL?
SLAM
IT'S A SECRET.
WELL, THAT WASN'T TOO BAD. HE GOT WHAT HE WANTED AND LEFT ALREADY.
THAT PATRICK-- WHAT'LL HE BE UP TO NEXT?
CAUGHT
KNOCK KNOCK
HEY, SPONGEBOB!

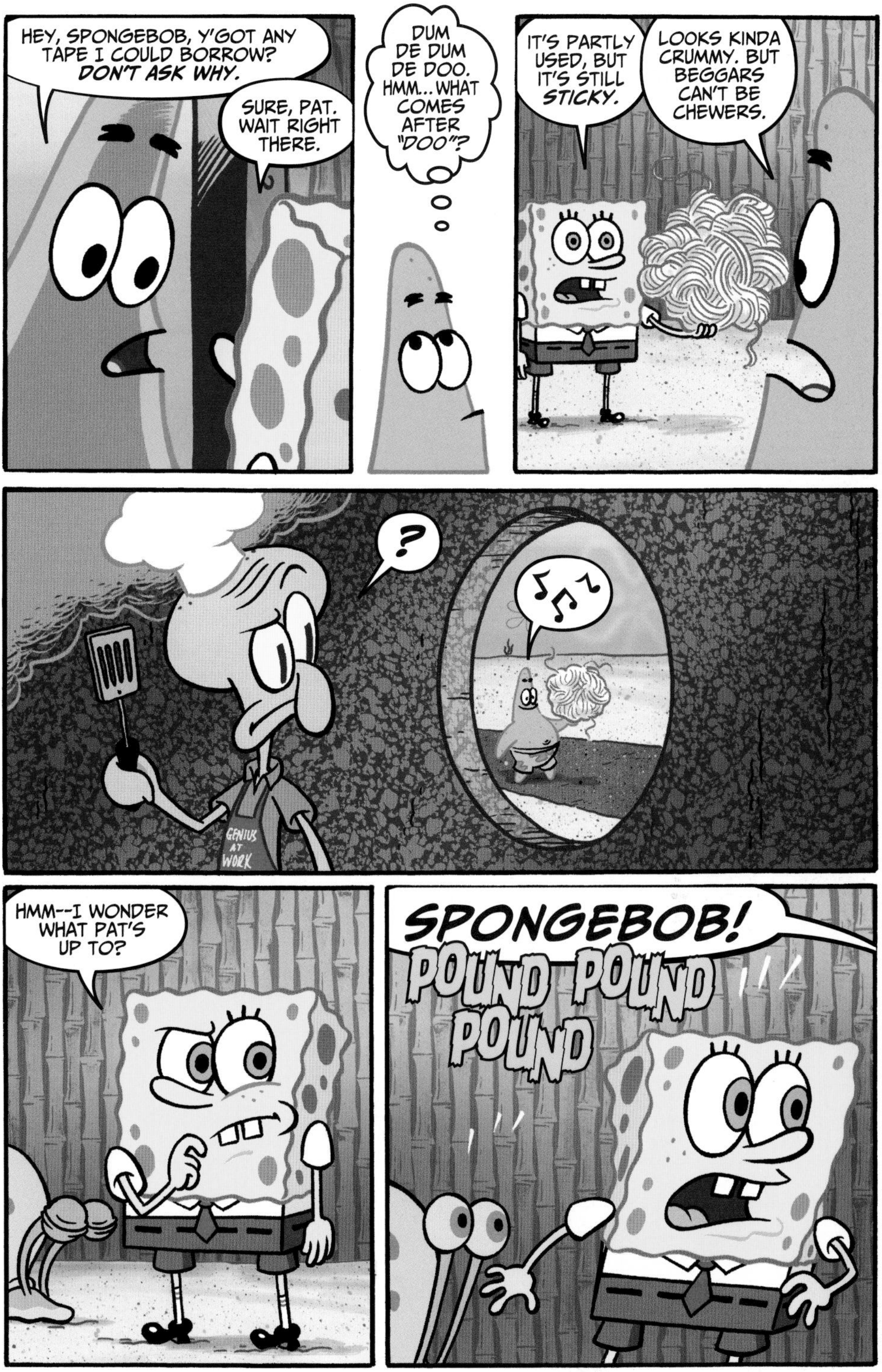
HEY, SPONGEBOB, Y'GOT ANY TAPE I COULD BORROW? DON'T ASK WHY.
SURE, PAT. WAIT RIGHT THERE.
DUM DE DUM DE DOO. HMM...WHAT COMES AFTER "DOO"?
IT'S PARTLY USED, BUT IT'S STILL STICKY.
LOOKS KINDA CRUMMY. BUT BEGGARS CAN'T BE CHEWERS.
?
GENIUS AT WORK
HMM--I WONDER WHAT PAT'S UP TO?
SPONGEBOB!
POUND POUND POUND

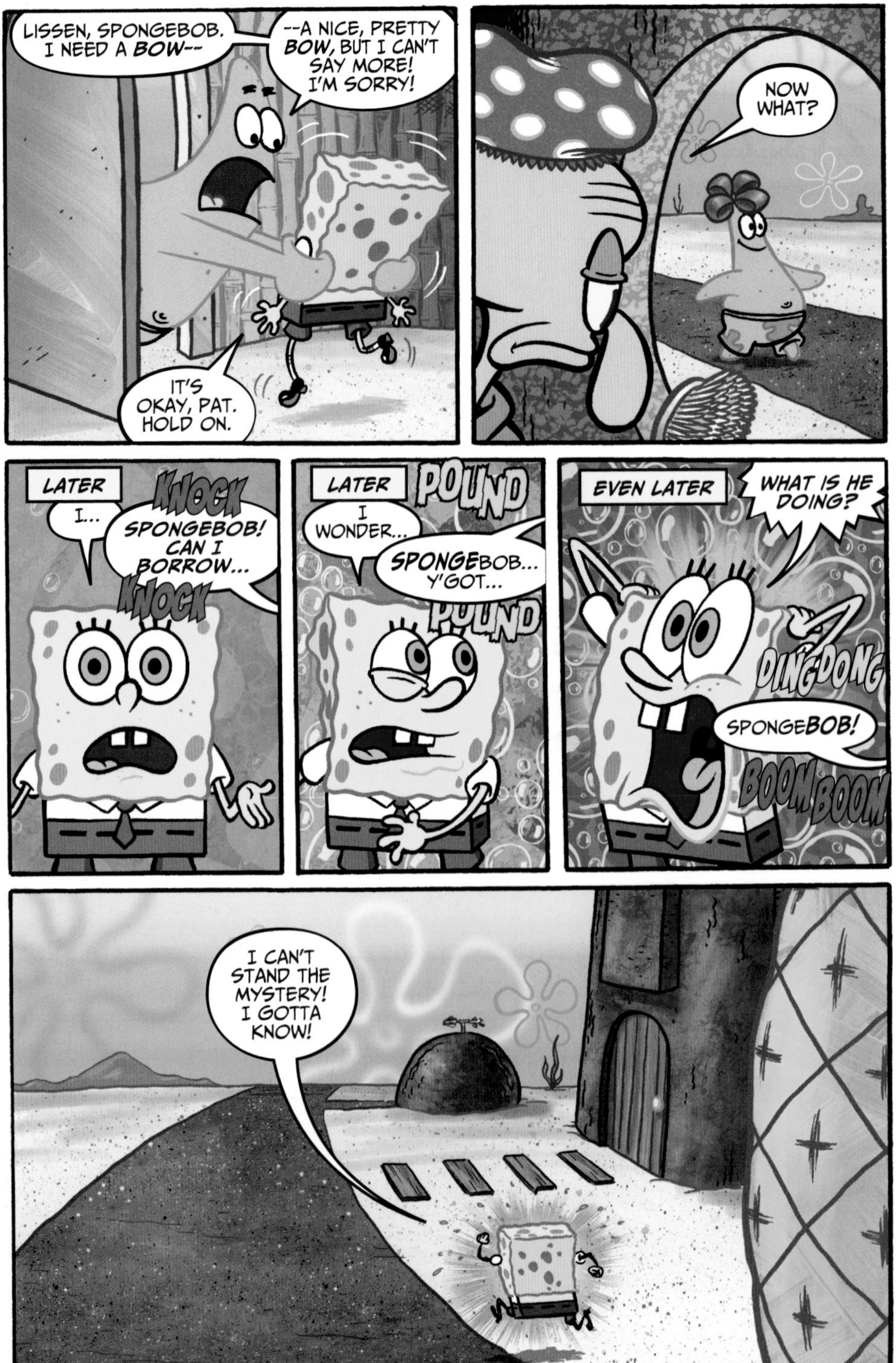
LISSEN, SPONGEBOB. I NEED A *BOW*--
--A NICE, PRETTY *BOW*, BUT I CAN'T SAY MORE! I'M SORRY!
IT'S OKAY, PAT. HOLD ON.
NOW WHAT?
LATER
KNOCK
I...
SPONGEBOB! CAN I BORROW...
KNOCK
LATER
POUND
I WONDER...
SPONGEBOB... Y'GOT...
POUND
EVEN LATER
WHAT IS HE DOING?
DING DONG
SPONGEBOB!
BOOM BOOM
I CAN'T STAND THE MYSTERY! I GOTTA KNOW!

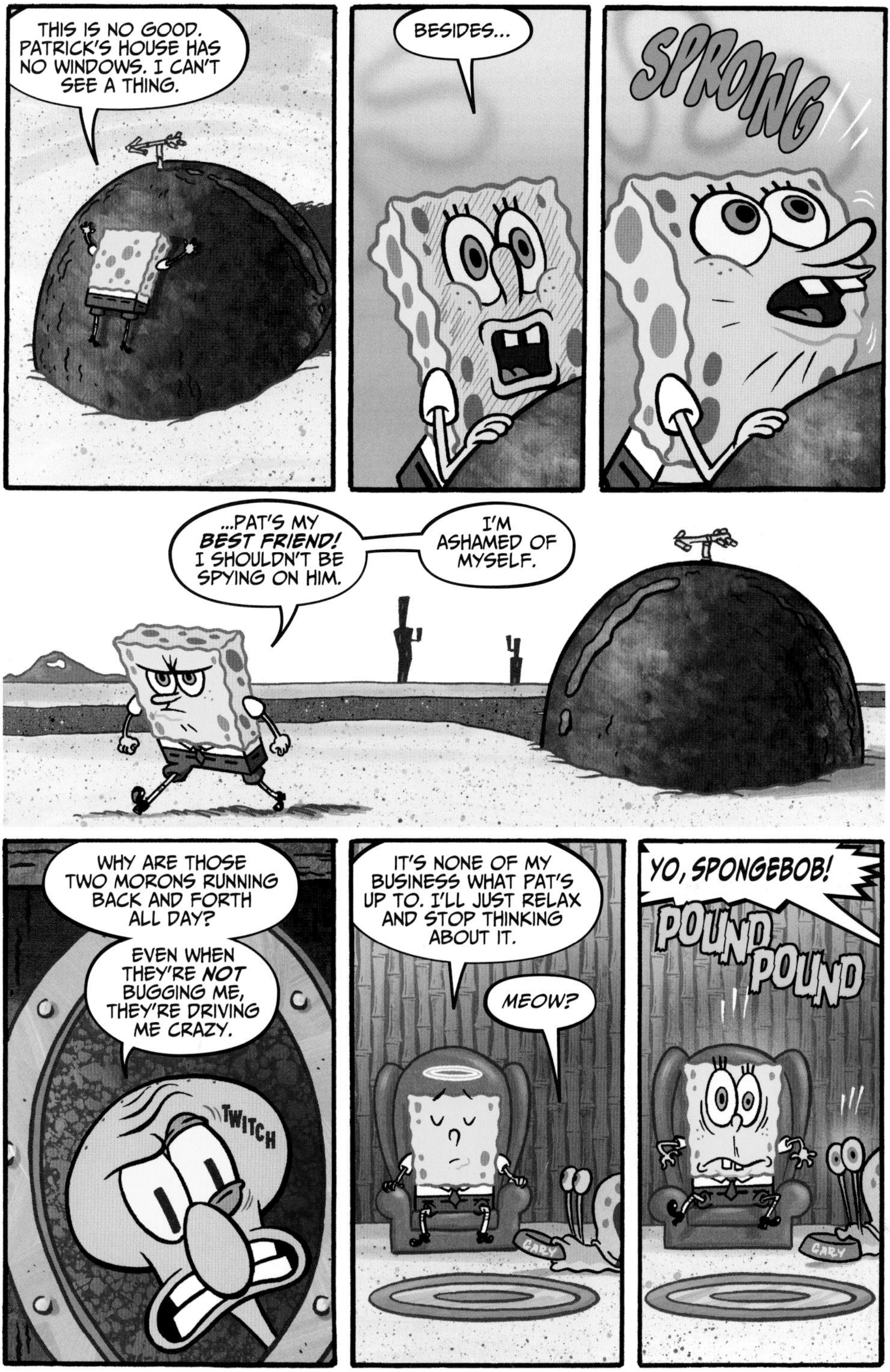
THIS IS NO GOOD. PATRICK'S HOUSE HAS NO WINDOWS. I CAN'T SEE A THING.
BESIDES...
SPROING
...PAT'S MY BEST FRIEND! I SHOULDN'T BE SPYING ON HIM.
I'M ASHAMED OF MYSELF.
WHY ARE THOSE TWO MORONS RUNNING BACK AND FORTH ALL DAY?
EVEN WHEN THEY'RE NOT BUGGING ME, THEY'RE DRIVING ME CRAZY.
TWITCH
IT'S NONE OF MY BUSINESS WHAT PAT'S UP TO. I'LL JUST RELAX AND STOP THINKING ABOUT IT.
MEOW?
GARY
YO, SPONGEBOB!
POUND POUND
GARY

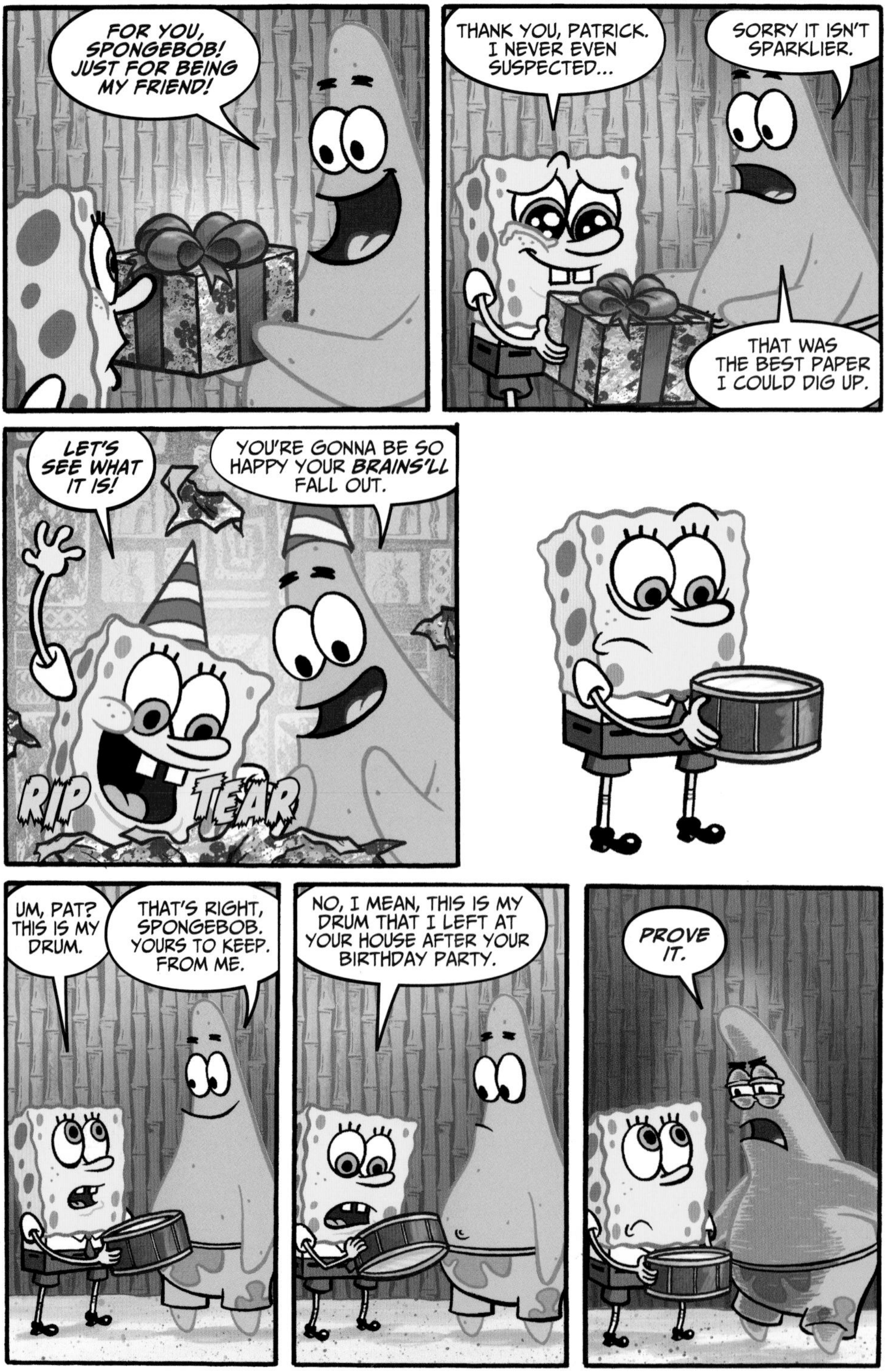
FOR YOU, SPONGEBOB! JUST FOR BEING MY FRIEND!
THANK YOU, PATRICK. I NEVER EVEN SUSPECTED...
SORRY IT ISN'T SPARKLIER.
THAT WAS THE BEST PAPER I COULD DIG UP.
LET'S SEE WHAT IT IS!
YOU'RE GONNA BE SO HAPPY YOUR BRAINS'LL FALL OUT.
RIP
TEAR
UM, PAT? THIS IS MY DRUM.
THAT'S RIGHT, SPONGEBOB. YOURS TO KEEP. FROM ME.
NO, I MEAN, THIS IS MY DRUM THAT I LEFT AT YOUR HOUSE AFTER YOUR BIRTHDAY PARTY.
PROVE IT.

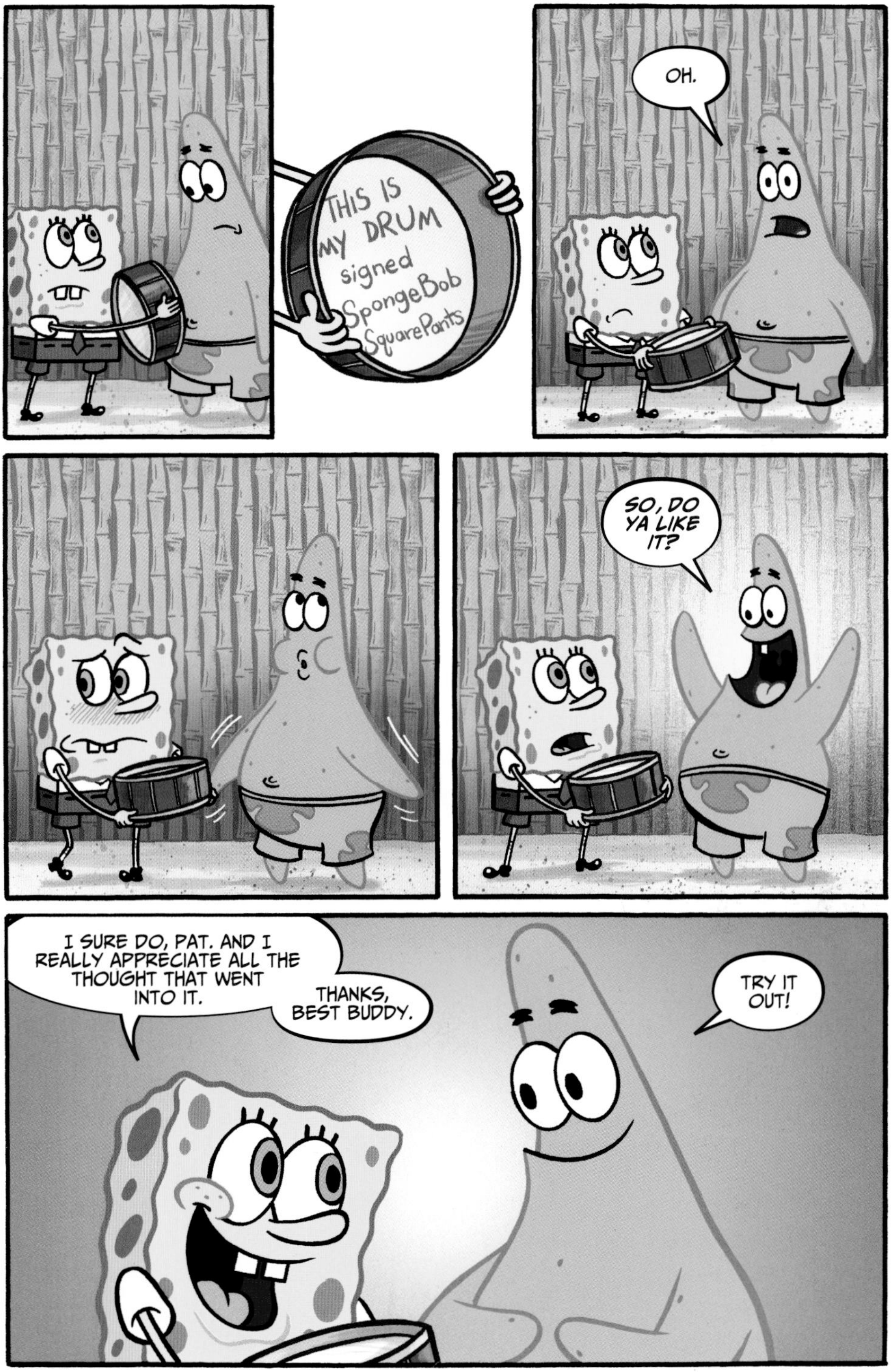
THIS IS MY DRUM signed SpongeBob SquarePants
OH.
SO, DO YA LIKE IT?
I SURE DO, PAT. AND I REALLY APPRECIATE ALL THE THOUGHT THAT WENT INTO IT.
THANKS, BEST BUDDY.
TRY IT OUT!

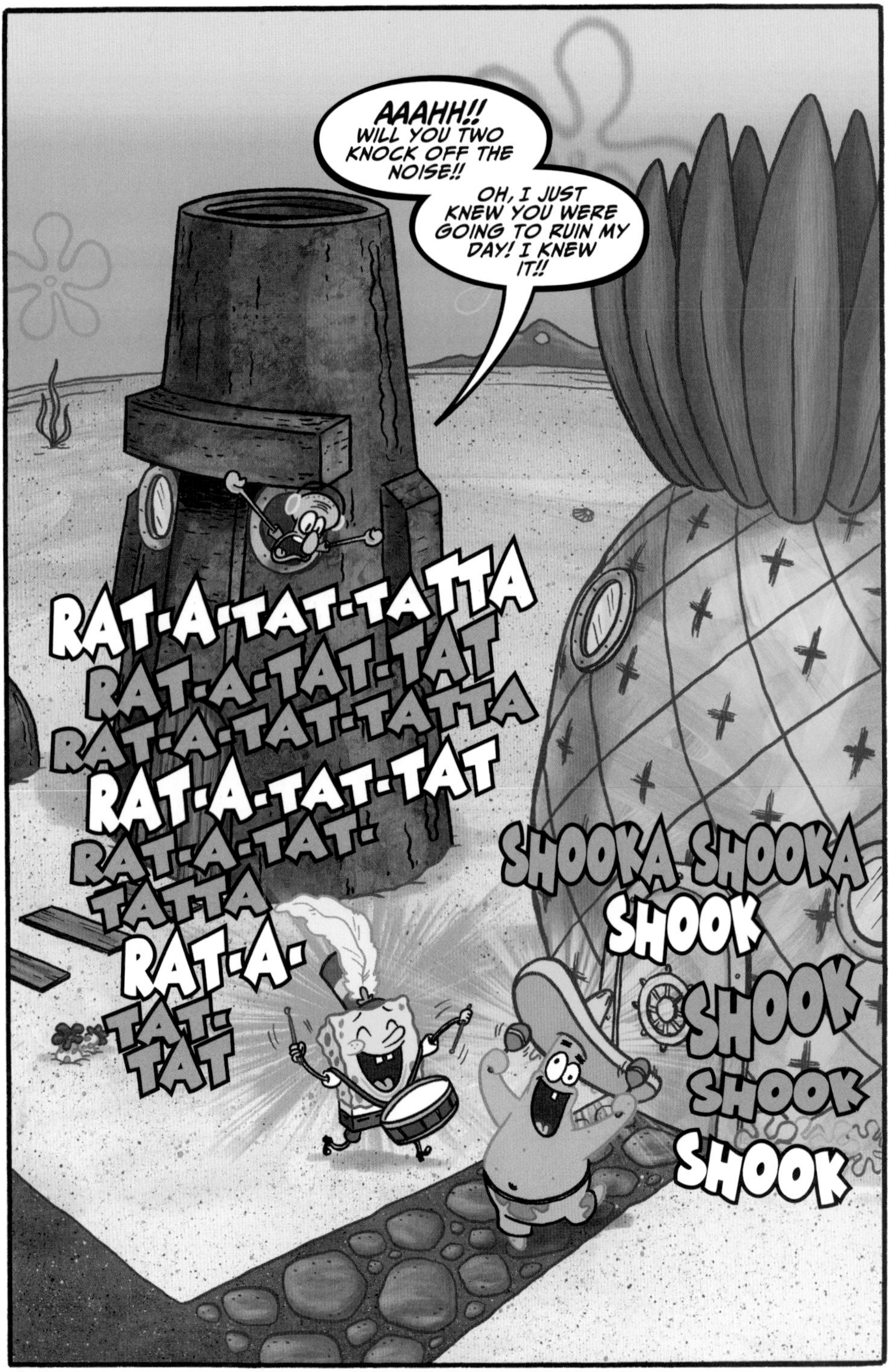
AAAHH!! WILL YOU TWO KNOCK OFF THE NOISE!!
OH, I JUST KNEW YOU WERE GOING TO RUIN MY DAY! I KNEW IT!!
RAT-A-TAT-TATTA
RAT-A-TAT-TAT
RAT-A-TAT-TATTA
RAT-A-TAT-TAT
RAT-A-TAT-TATTA
RAT-A-TAT-TAT
SHOOKA SHOOKA
SHOOK
SHOOK
SHOOK
SHOOK

END

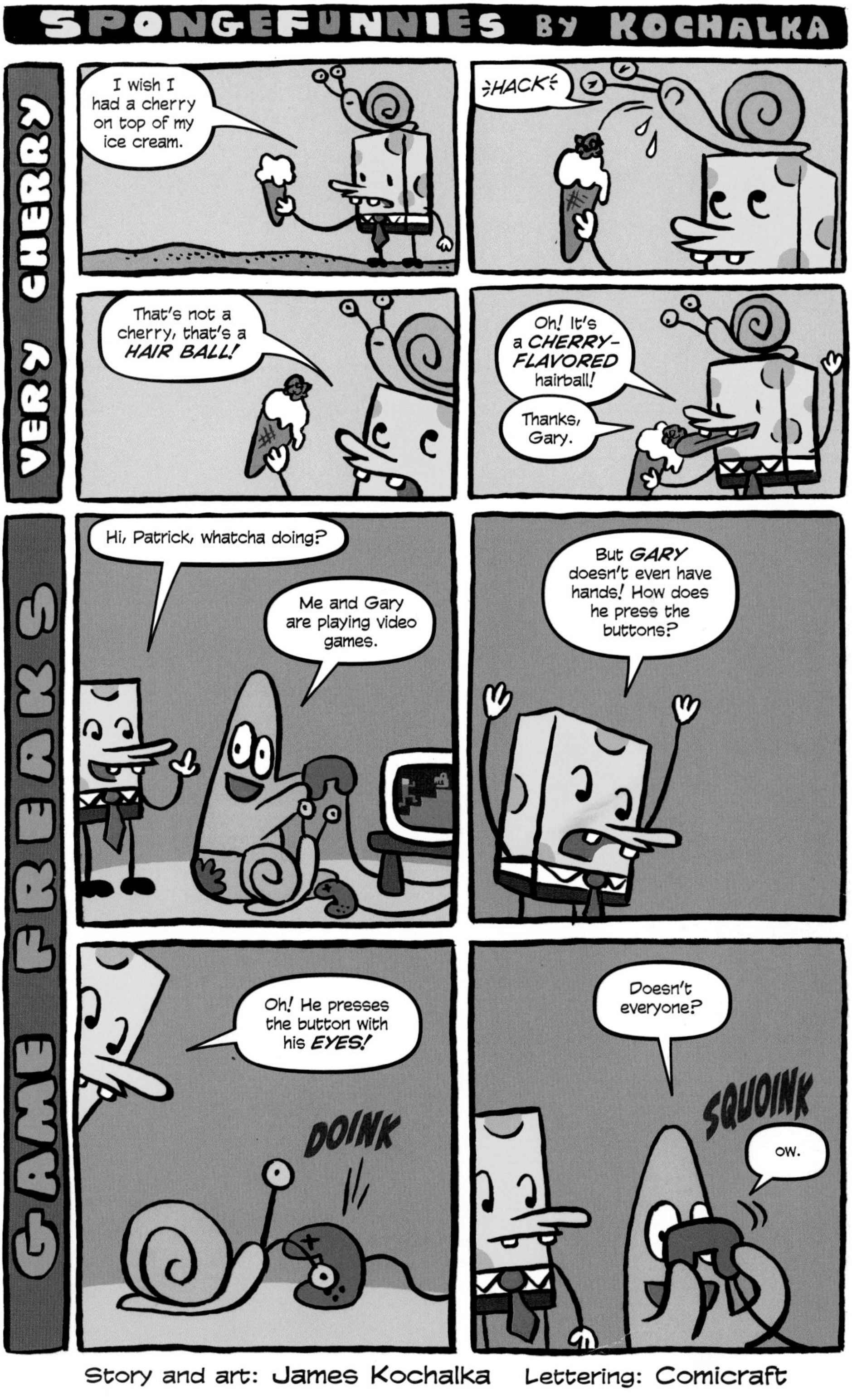
SPONGEFUNNIES BY KOCHALKA
VERY CHERRY
I wish I had a cherry on top of my ice cream.
HACK
That's not a cherry, that's a HAIR BALL!
Oh! It's a CHERRY-FLAVORED hairball!
Thanks, Gary.
GAME FREAKS
Hi, Patrick, whatcha doing?
Me and Gary are playing video games.
But GARY doesn't even have hands! How does he press the buttons?
Oh! He presses the button with his EYES!
DOINK
Doesn't everyone?
SQUOINK
ow.

Story and art: James Kochalka Lettering: Comicraft

The Tooth Shall Set You Free

STORY: COREY BARBA PENCILS AND INKS: JACOB CHABOT COLOR: MICHAEL DEVITO LETTERING: COMICRAFT

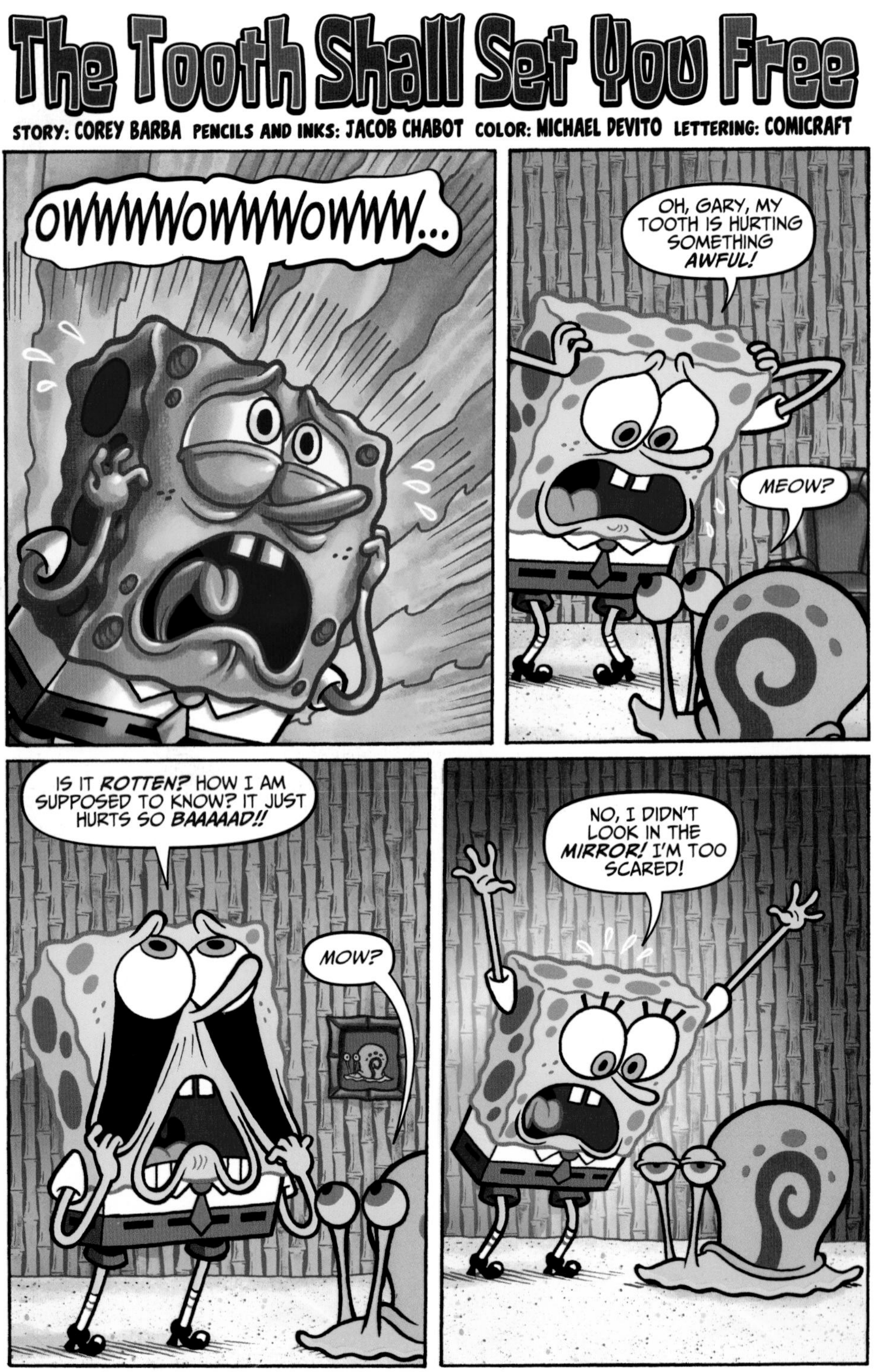
OWWWWOWWWOWWW...
OH, GARY, MY TOOTH IS HURTING SOMETHING AWFUL!
MEOW?
IS IT ROTTEN? HOW I AM SUPPOSED TO KNOW? IT JUST HURTS SO BAAAAAD!!
MOW?
NO, I DIDN'T LOOK IN THE MIRROR! I'M TOO SCARED!

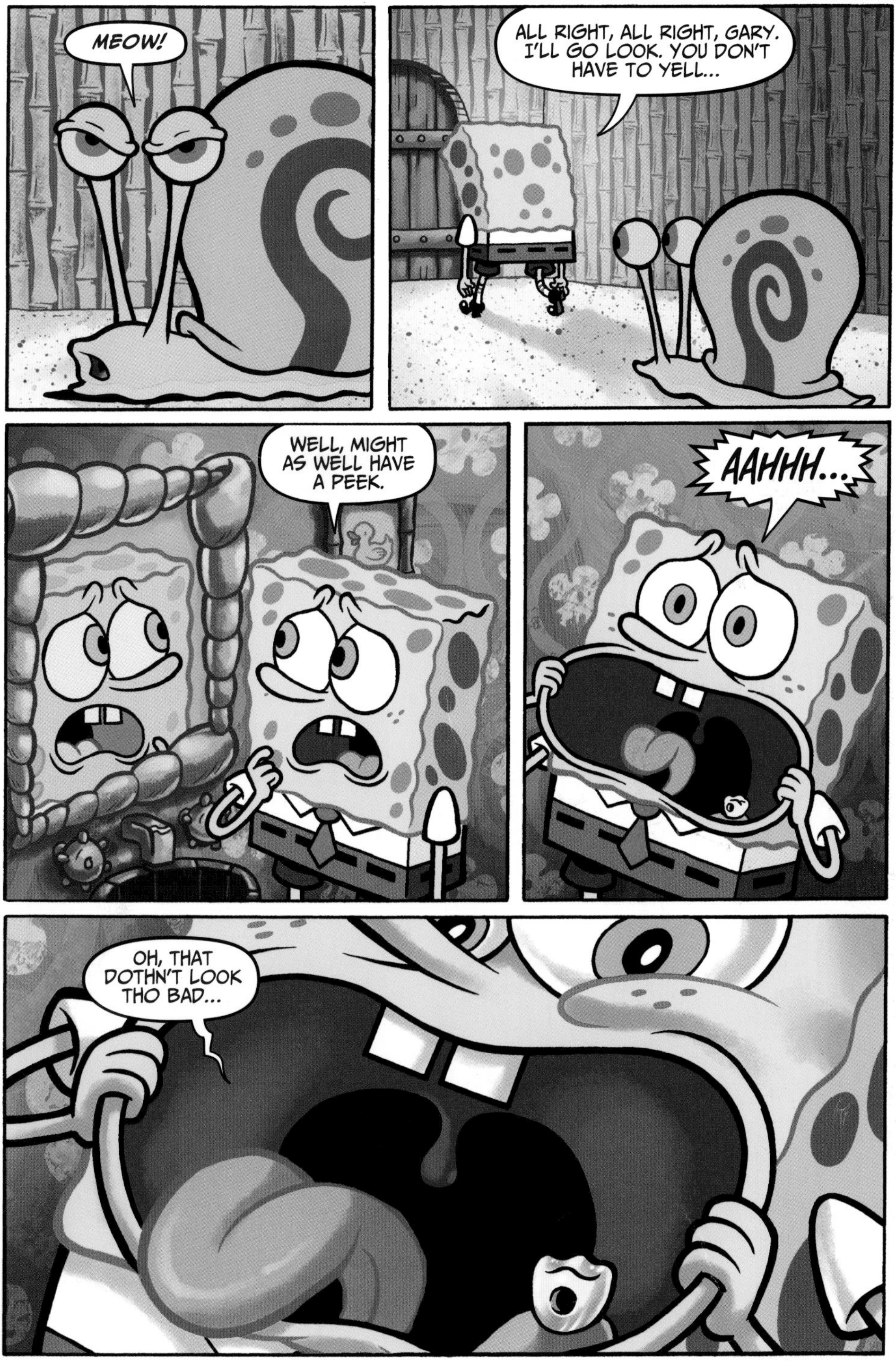
MEOW!
ALL RIGHT, ALL RIGHT, GARY. I'LL GO LOOK. YOU DON'T HAVE TO YELL...
WELL, MIGHT AS WELL HAVE A PEEK.
AAHHH...
OH, THAT DOTHN'T LOOK THO BAD...

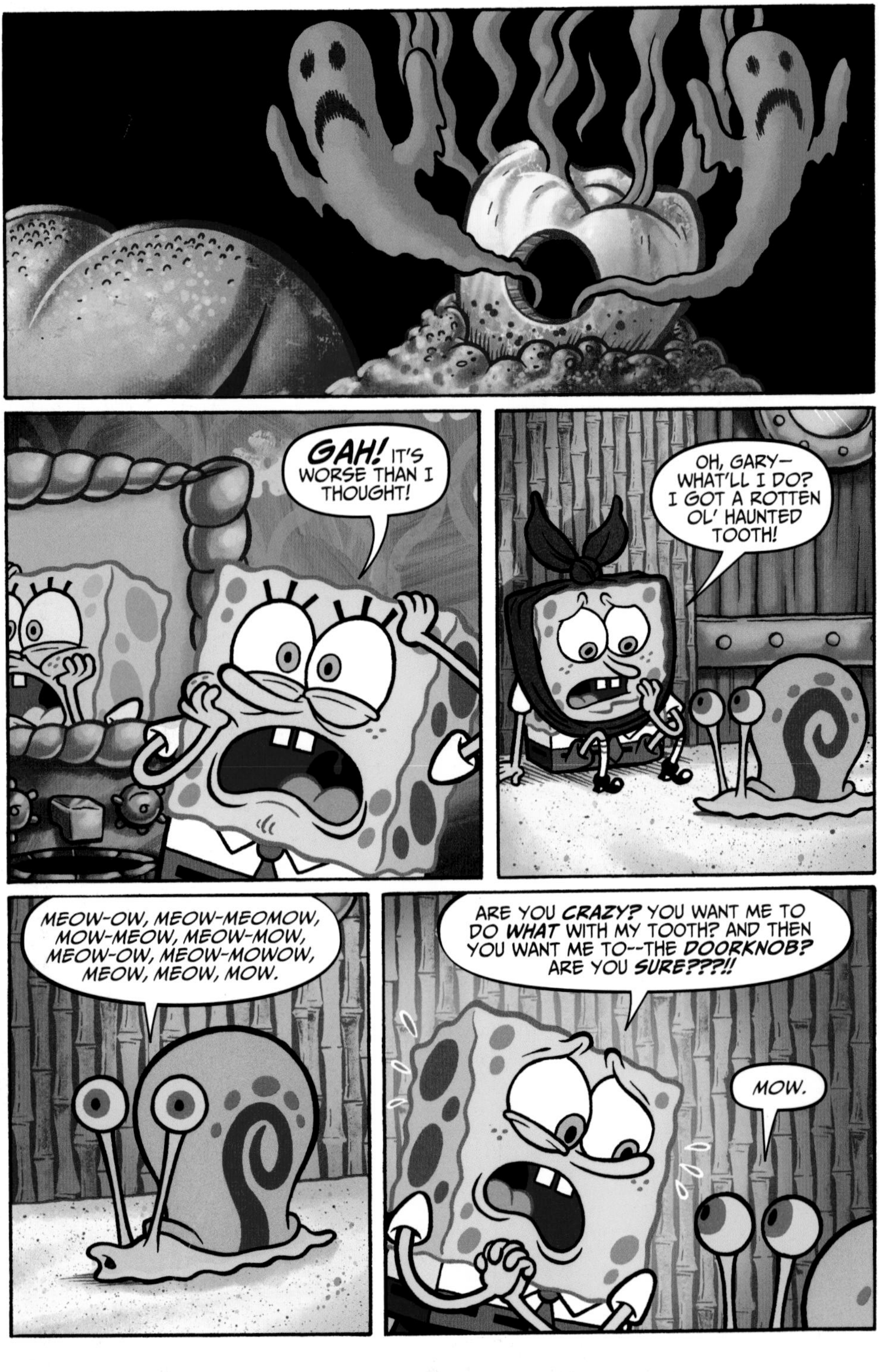
GAH! IT'S WORSE THAN I THOUGHT!
OH, GARY— WHAT'LL I DO? I GOT A ROTTEN OL' HAUNTED TOOTH!
MEOW-OW, MEOW-MEOMOW, MOW-MEOW, MEOW-MOW, MEOW-OW, MEOW-MOWOW, MEOW, MEOW, MOW.
ARE YOU CRAZY? YOU WANT ME TO DO WHAT WITH MY TOOTH? AND THEN YOU WANT ME TO--THE DOORKNOB? ARE YOU SURE???!!
MOW.

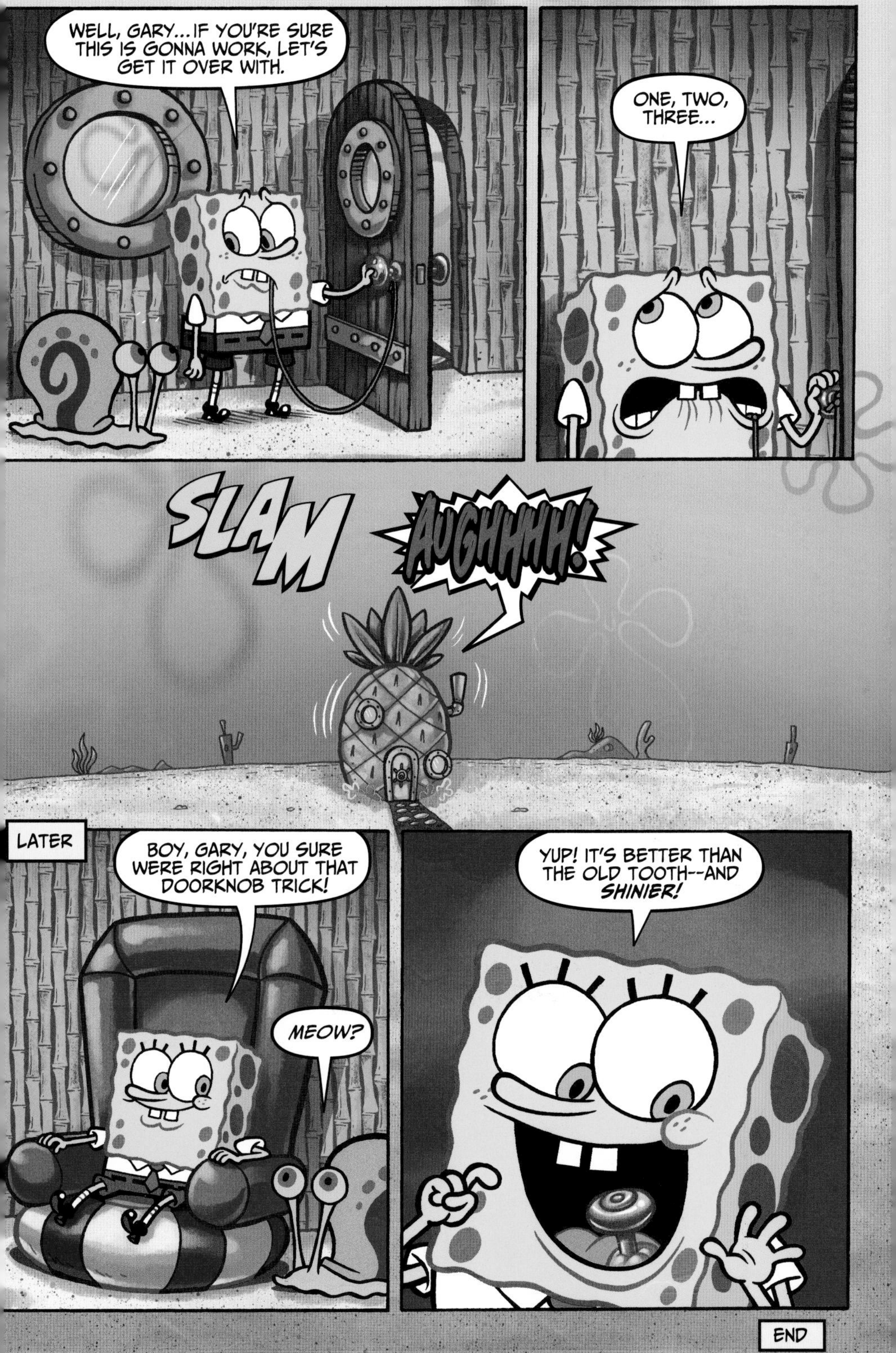
WELL, GARY... IF YOU'RE SURE THIS IS GONNA WORK, LET'S GET IT OVER WITH.
ONE, TWO, THREE...
SLAM
AUGHHHH!
LATER
BOY, GARY, YOU SURE WERE RIGHT ABOUT THAT DOORKNOB TRICK!
MEOW?
YUP! IT'S BETTER THAN THE OLD TOOTH--AND SHINIER!
END

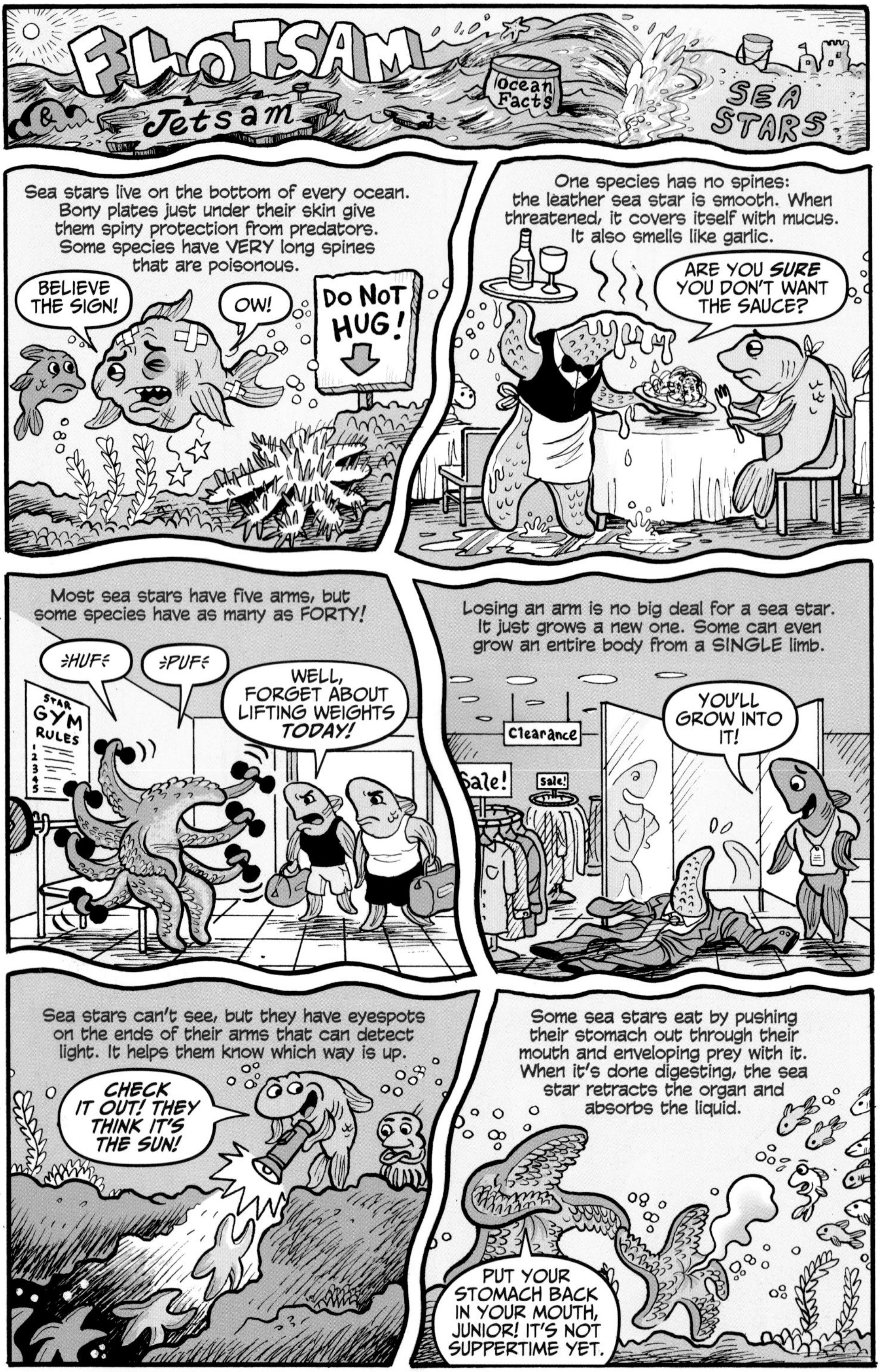
FLOTSAM & Jetsam
Ocean Facts
SEA STARS
Sea stars live on the bottom of every ocean. Bony plates just under their skin give them spiny protection from predators. Some species have VERY long spines that are poisonous.
BELIEVE THE SIGN!
OW!
Do Not HUG!
One species has no spines: the leather sea star is smooth. When threatened, it covers itself with mucus. It also smells like garlic.
ARE YOU SURE YOU DON'T WANT THE SAUCE?
Most sea stars have five arms, but some species have as many as FORTY!
STAR GYM RULES
HUF
PUF
WELL, FORGET ABOUT LIFTING WEIGHTS TODAY!
Losing an arm is no big deal for a sea star. It just grows a new one. Some can even grow an entire body from a SINGLE limb.
Clearance
Sale!
Sale!
YOU'LL GROW INTO IT!
Sea stars can't see, but they have eyespots on the ends of their arms that can detect light. It helps them know which way is up.
CHECK IT OUT! THEY THINK IT'S THE SUN!
Some sea stars eat by pushing their stomach out through their mouth and enveloping prey with it. When it's done digesting, the sea star retracts the organ and absorbs the liquid.
PUT YOUR STOMACH BACK IN YOUR MOUTH, JUNIOR! IT'S NOT SUPPERTIME YET.

WRITER: JULIE WINTERBOTTOM PENCILS, INKS, AND COLOR: NATE NEAL LETTERING: COMICRAFT

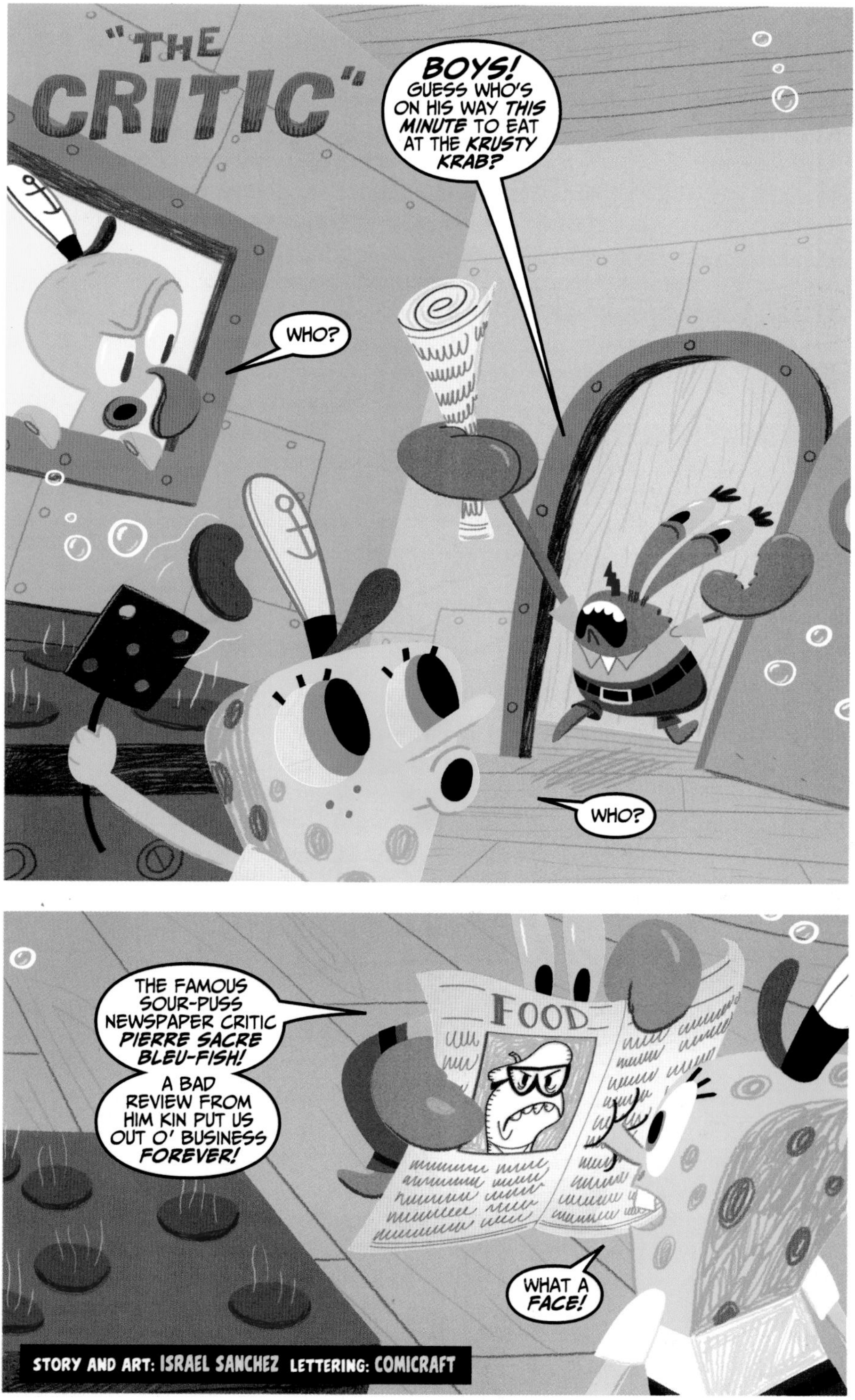
"THE CRITIC"
BOYS! GUESS WHO'S ON HIS WAY THIS MINUTE TO EAT AT THE KRUSTY KRAB?
WHO?
WHO?
THE FAMOUS SOUR-PUSS NEWSPAPER CRITIC PIERRE SACRE BLEU-FISH!
A BAD REVIEW FROM HIM KIN PUT US OUT O' BUSINESS FOREVER!
FOOD
WHAT A FACE!
STORY AND ART: ISRAEL SANCHEZ LETTERING: COMICRAFT

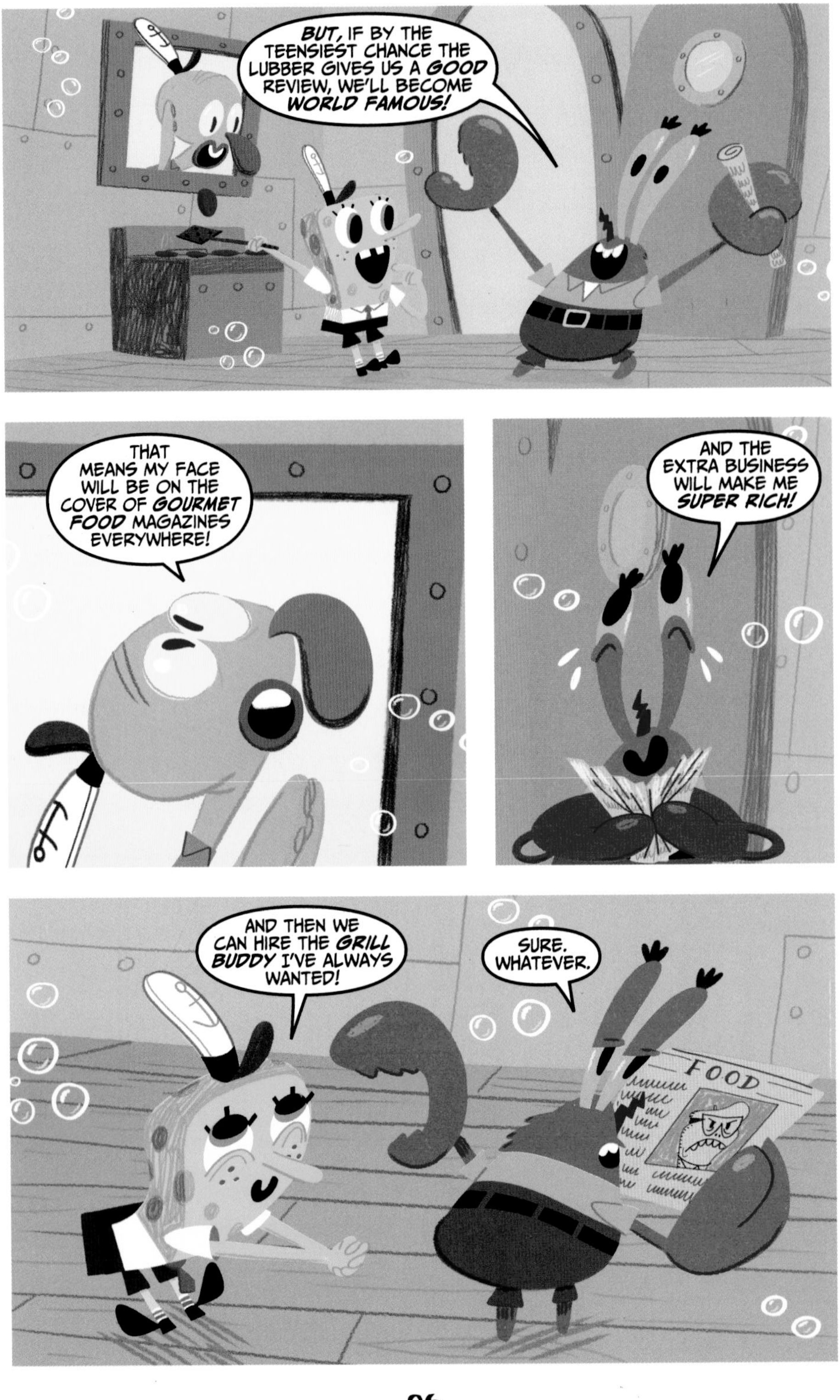
BUT, IF BY THE TEENSIEST CHANCE THE LUBBER GIVES US A GOOD REVIEW, WE'LL BECOME WORLD FAMOUS!
THAT MEANS MY FACE WILL BE ON THE COVER OF GOURMET FOOD MAGAZINES EVERYWHERE!
AND THE EXTRA BUSINESS WILL MAKE ME SUPER RICH!
AND THEN WE CAN HIRE THE GRILL BUDDY I'VE ALWAYS WANTED!
SURE. WHATEVER.
FOOD

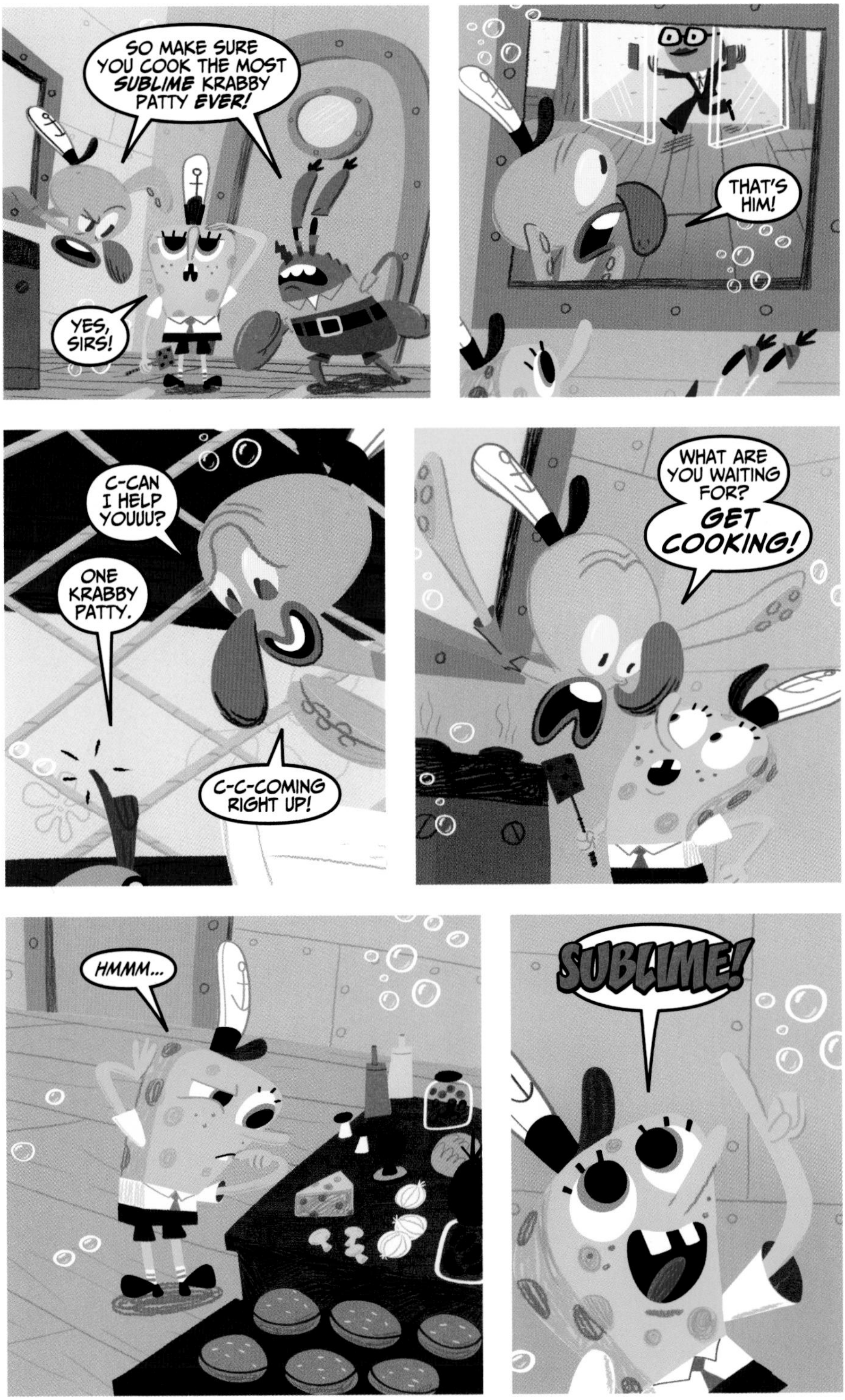
SO MAKE SURE YOU COOK THE MOST SUBLIME KRABBY PATTY EVER!
YES, SIRS!
THAT'S HIM!
C-CAN I HELP YOUUU?
ONE KRABBY PATTY.
C-C-COMING RIGHT UP!
WHAT ARE YOU WAITING FOR? GET COOKING!
HMMM...
SUBLIME!

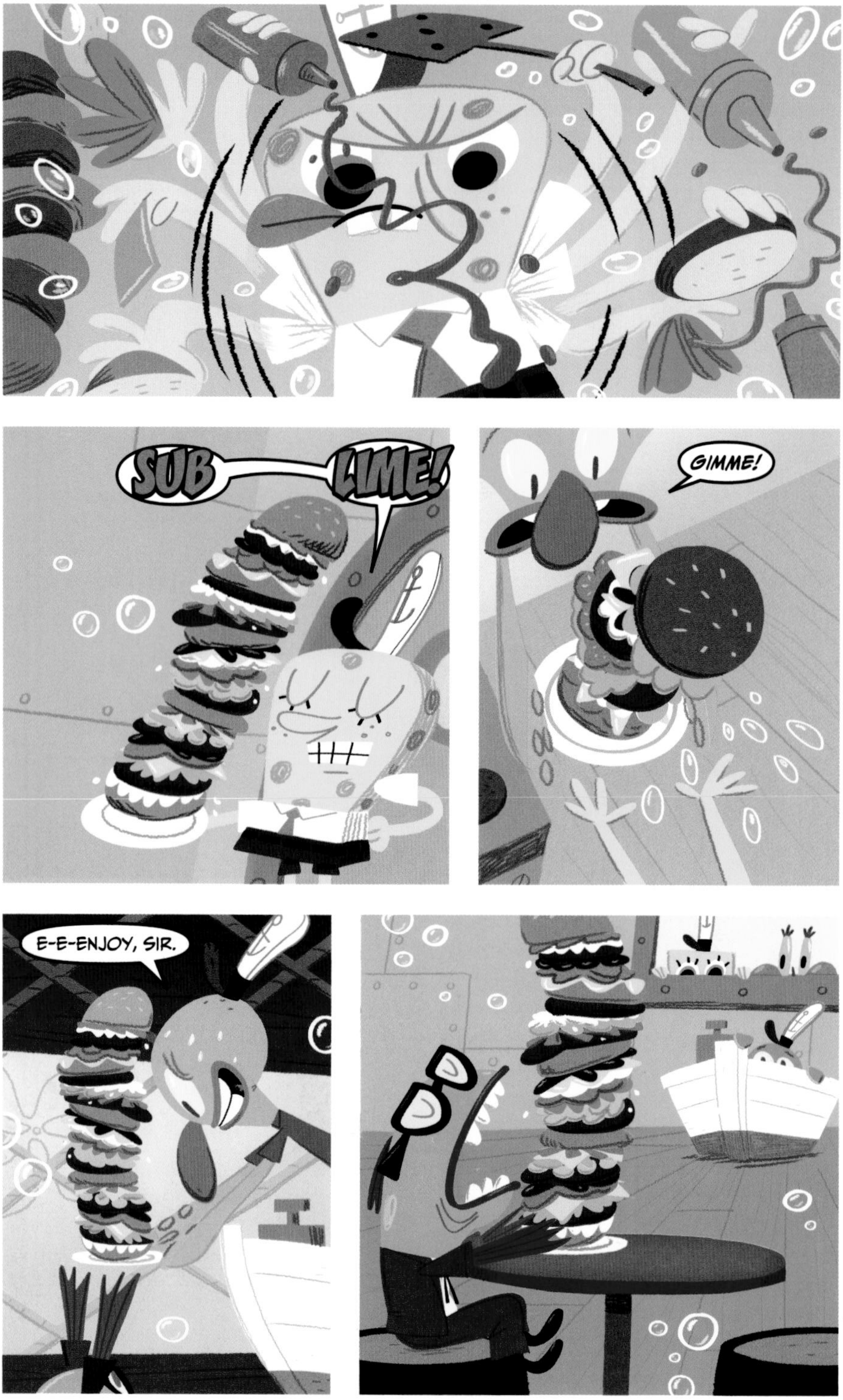
SUB LIME!
GIMME!
E-E-ENJOY, SIR.

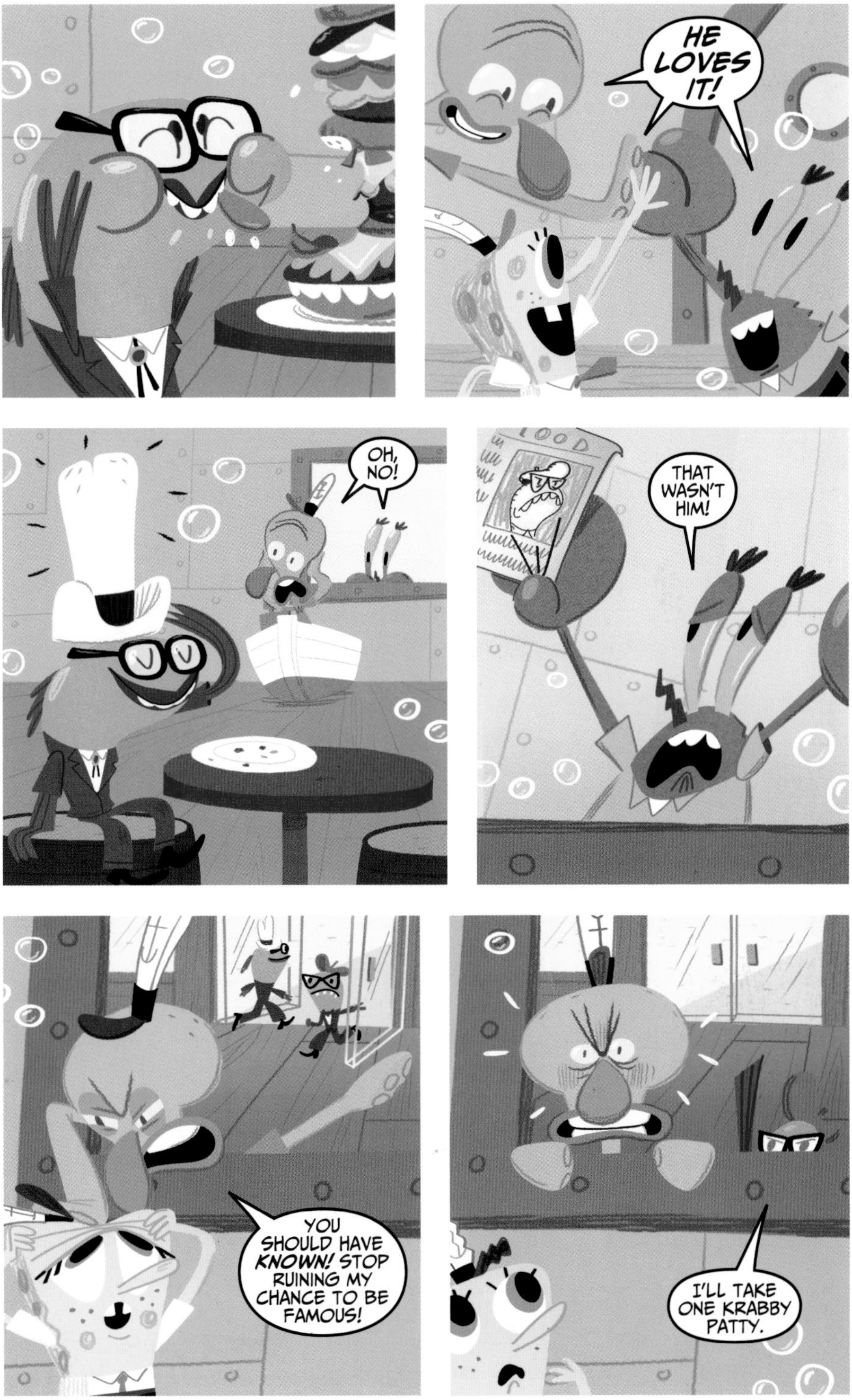
HE LOVES IT!
OH, NO!
THAT WASN'T HIM!
YOU SHOULD HAVE KNOWN! STOP RUINING MY CHANCE TO BE FAMOUS!
I'LL TAKE ONE KRABBY PATTY.

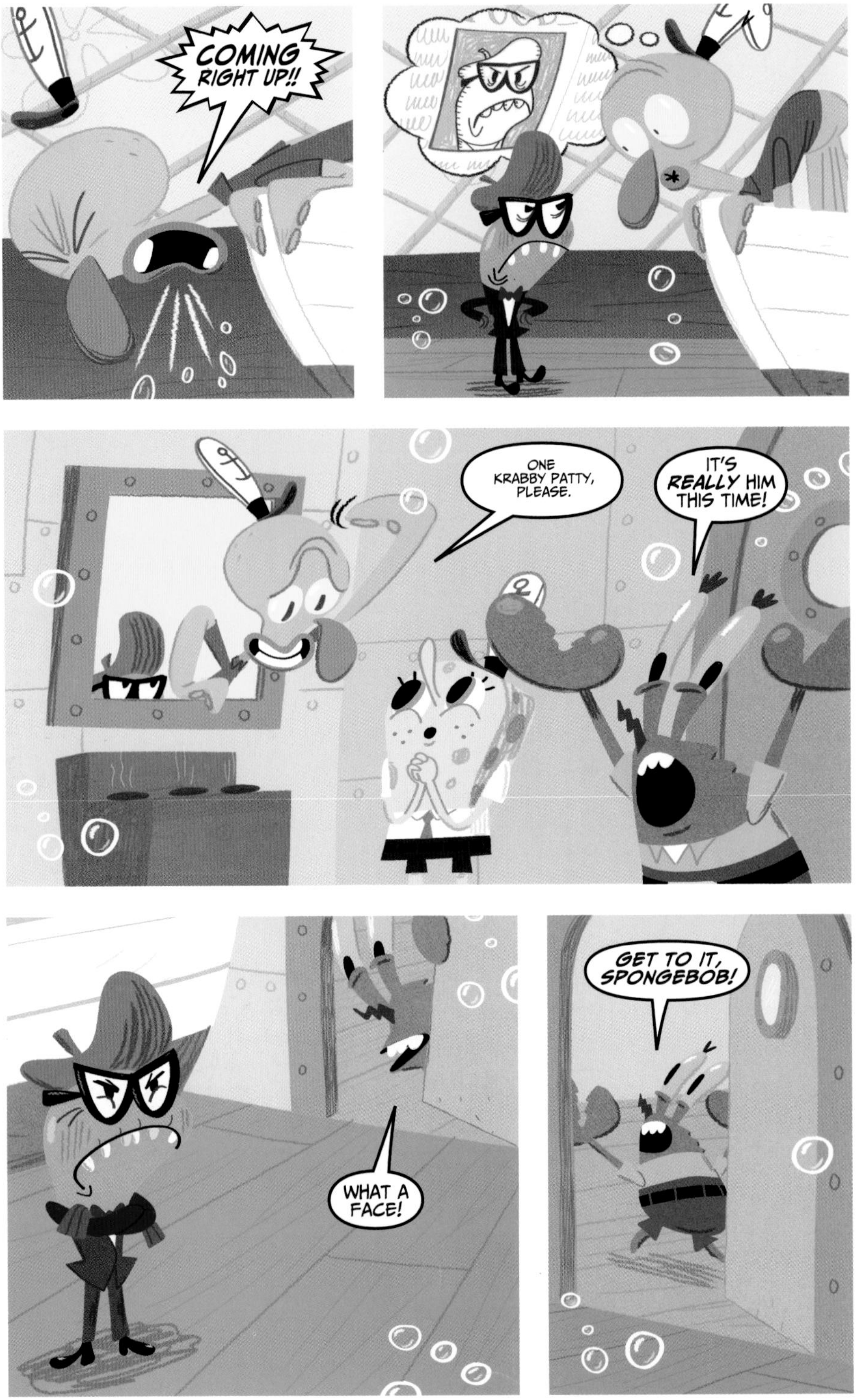
COMING RIGHT UP!!
ONE KRABBY PATTY, PLEASE.
IT'S REALLY HIM THIS TIME!
WHAT A FACE!
GET TO IT, SPONGEBOB!

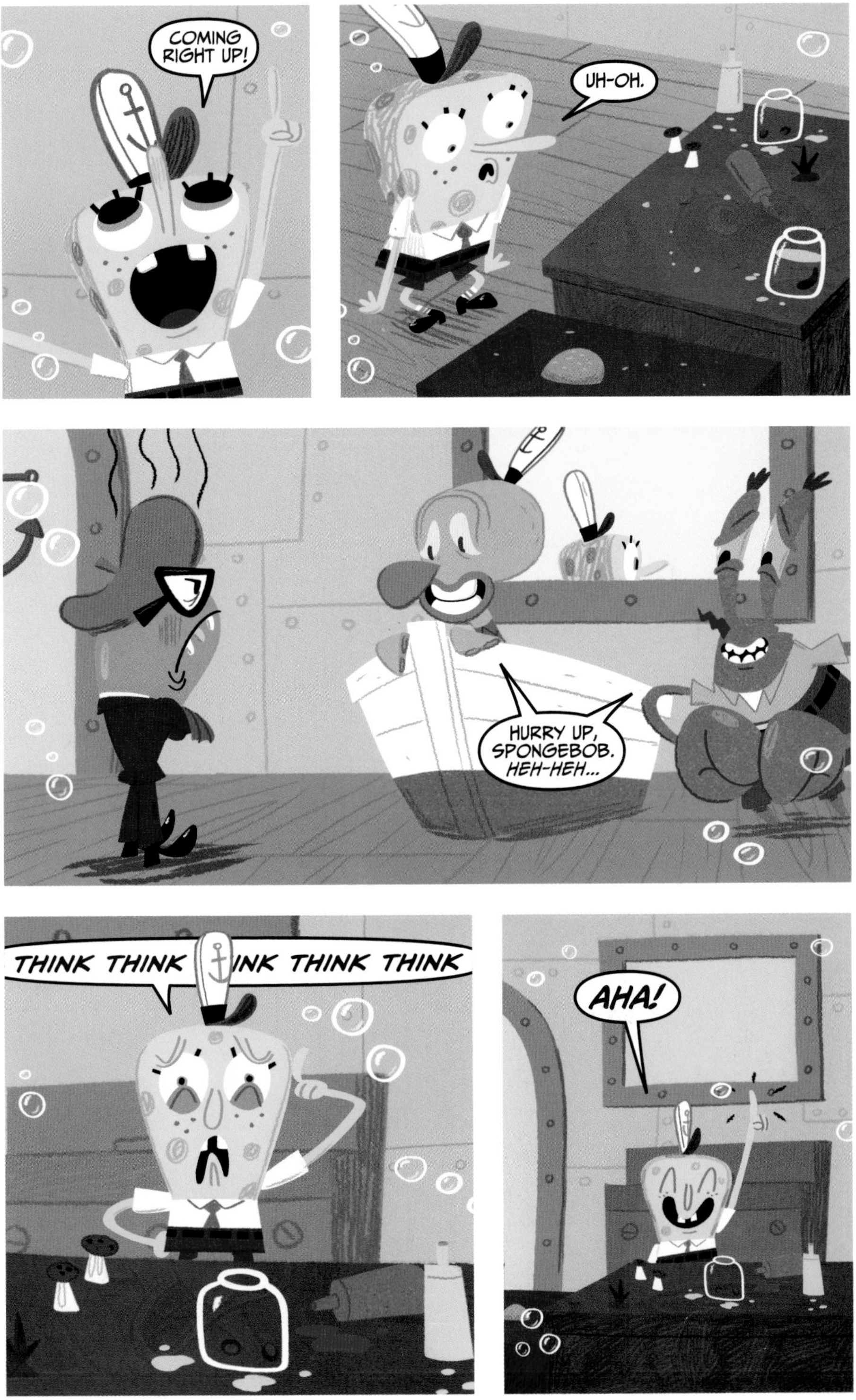
COMING RIGHT UP!
UH-OH.
HURRY UP, SPONGEBOB. HEH-HEH...
THINK THINK THINK THINK THINK
AHA!

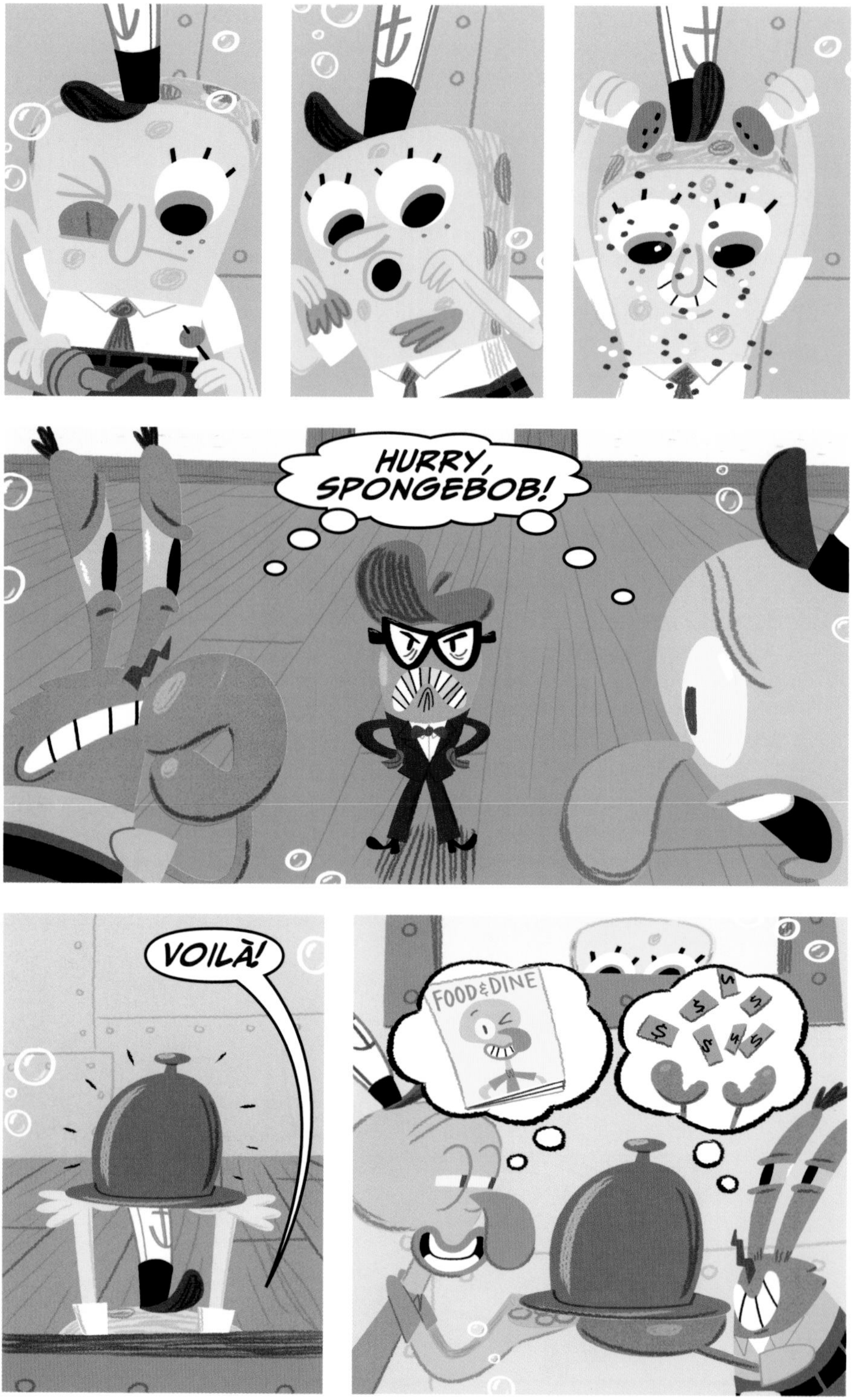
HURRY, SPONGEBOB!
VOILÀ!
FOOD & DINE

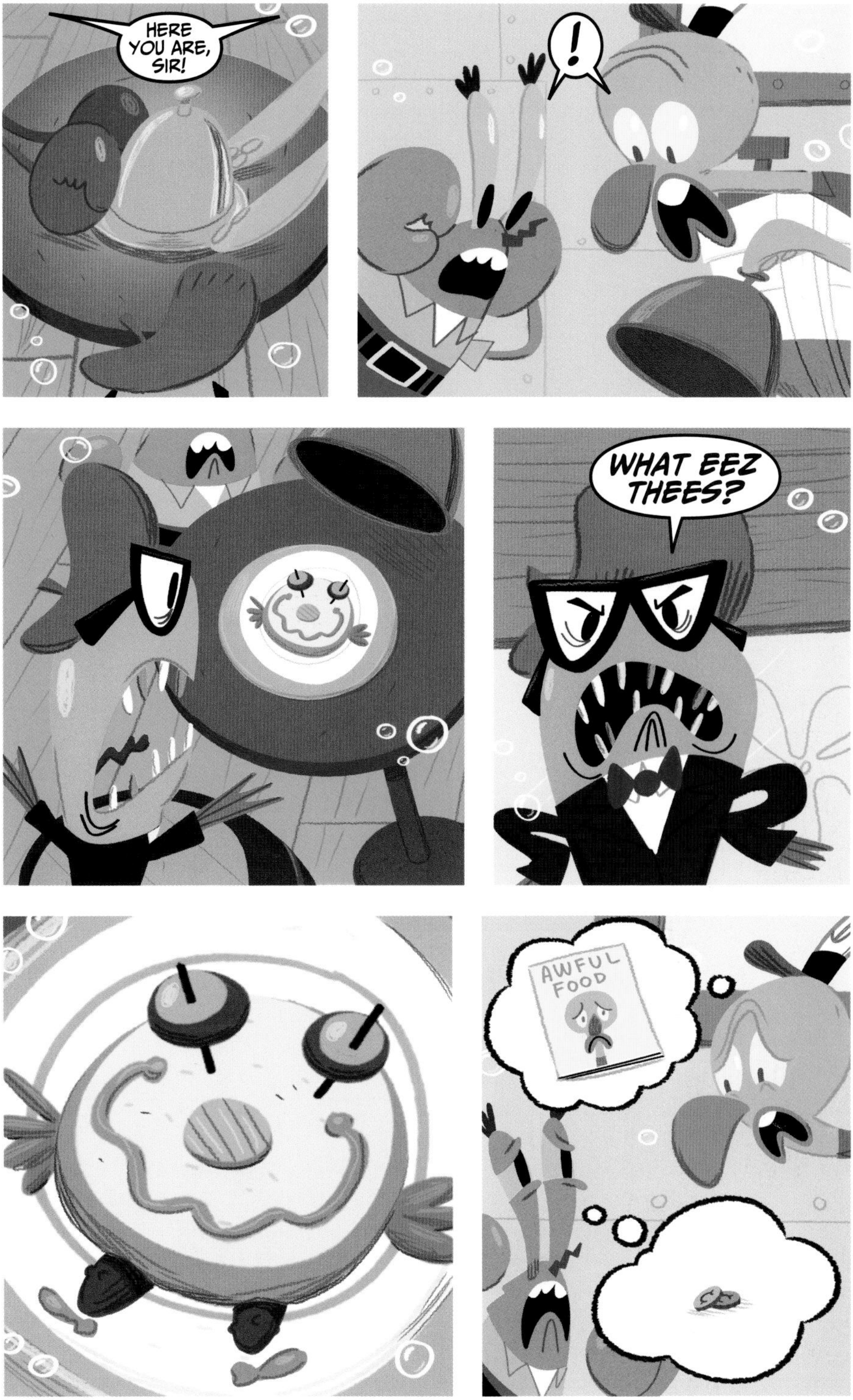
HERE YOU ARE, SIR!
!
WHAT EEZ THEES?
AWFUL FOOD

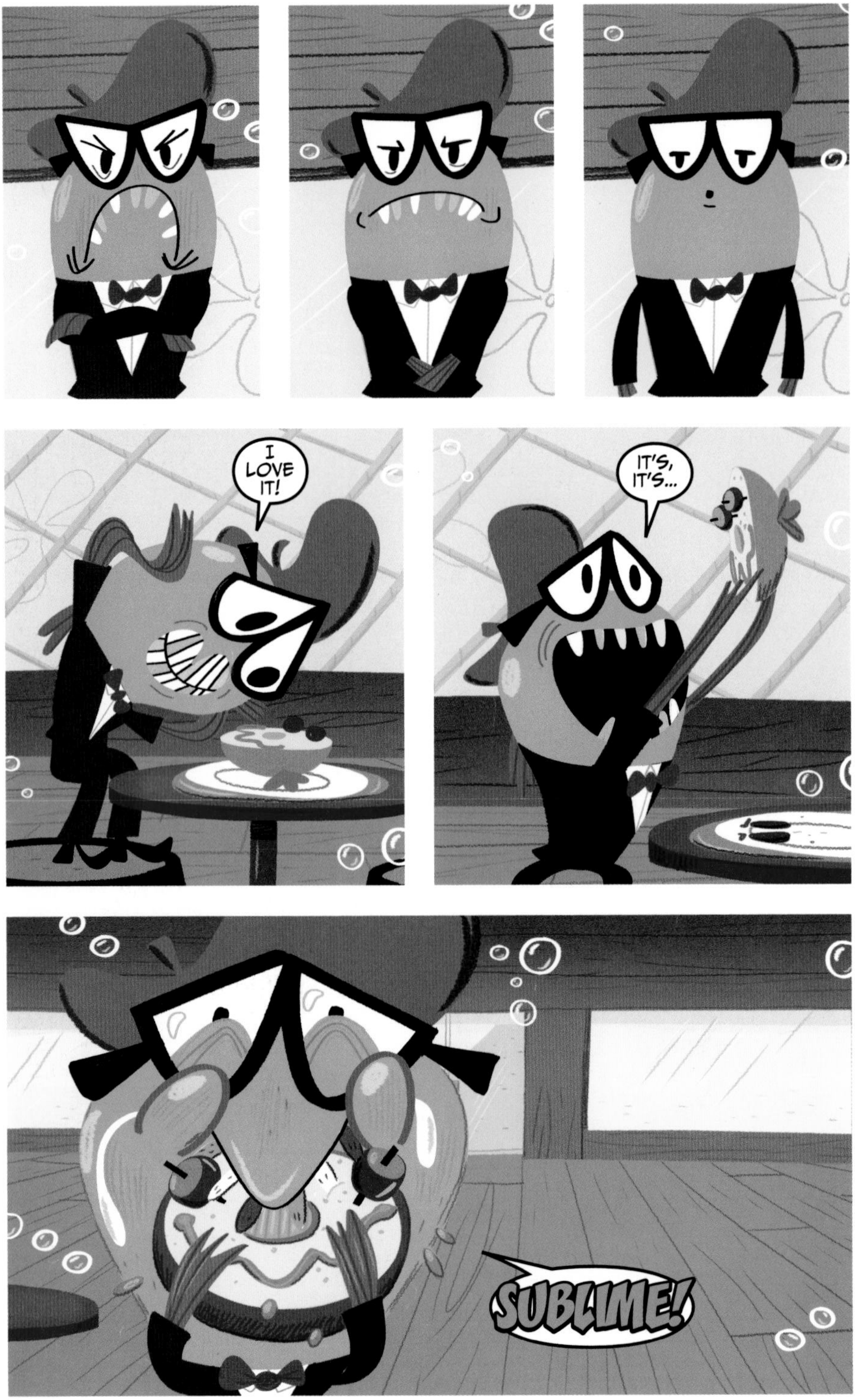
I LOVE IT!
IT'S, IT'S...
SUBLIME!

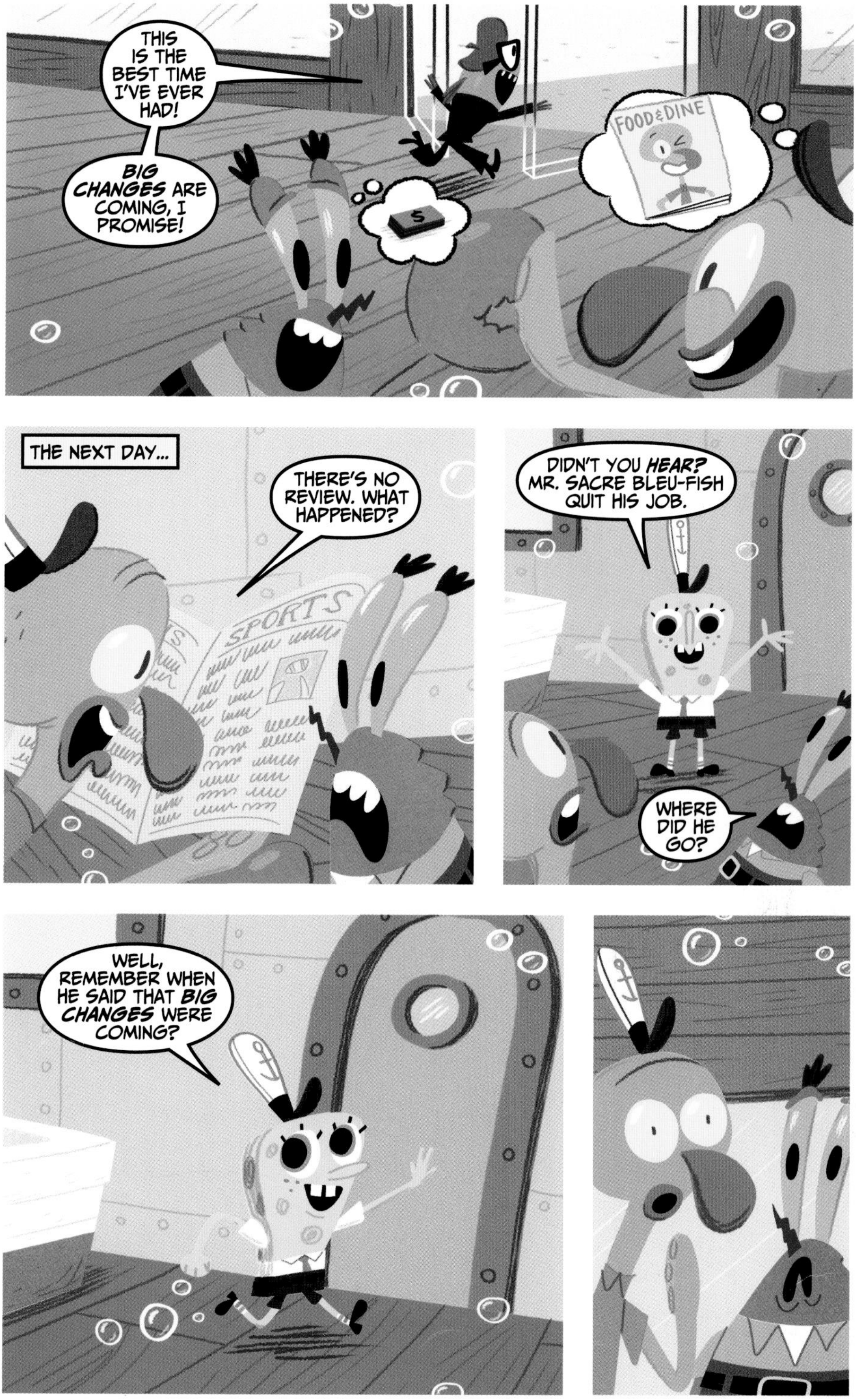
THIS IS THE BEST TIME I'VE EVER HAD!
BIG CHANGES ARE COMING, I PROMISE!
FOOD&DINE
THE NEXT DAY...
THERE'S NO REVIEW. WHAT HAPPENED?
SPORTS
DIDN'T YOU HEAR? MR. SACRE BLEU-FISH QUIT HIS JOB.
WHERE DID HE GO?
WELL, REMEMBER WHEN HE SAID THAT BIG CHANGES WERE COMING?

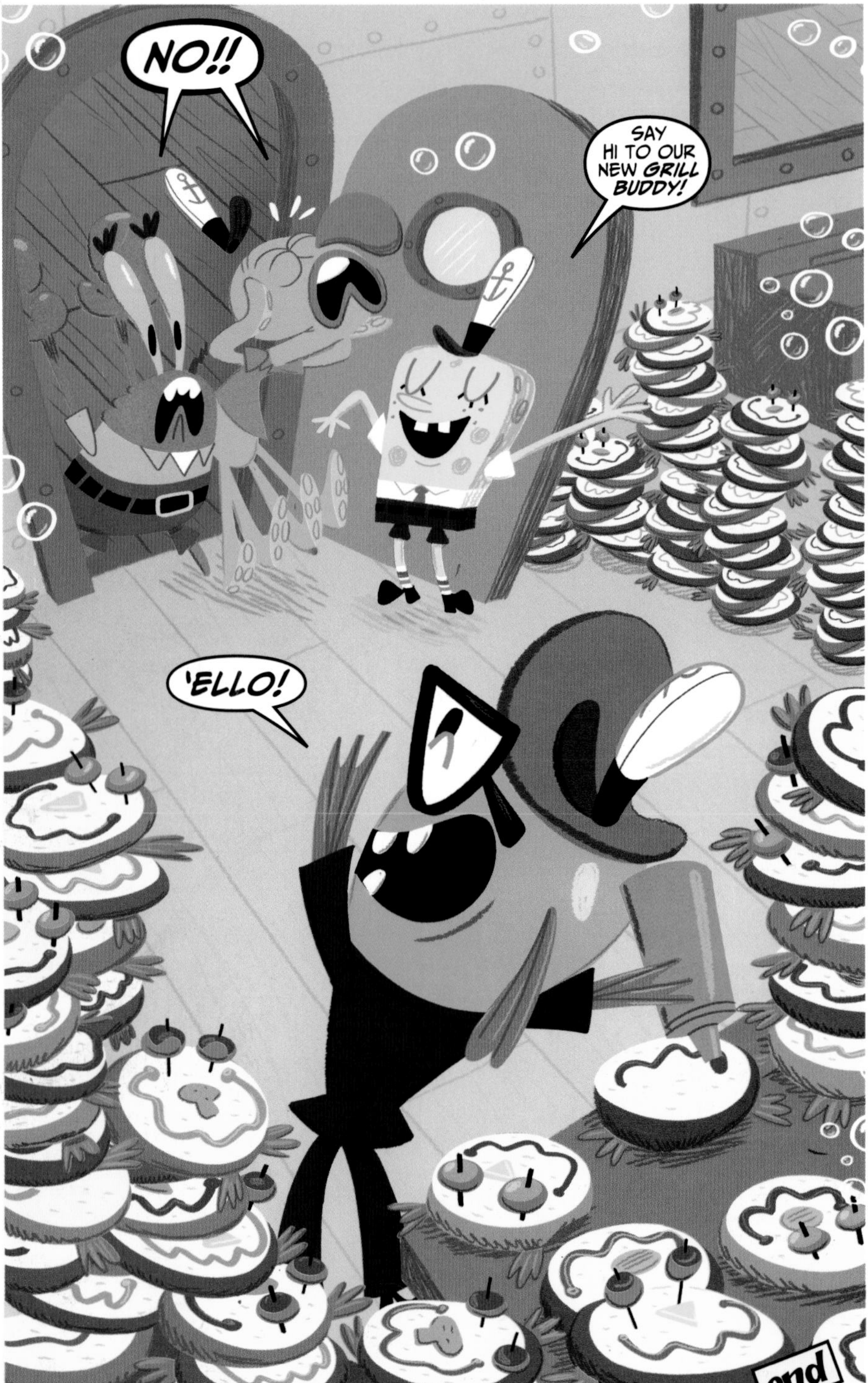
NO!!
SAY HI TO OUR NEW GRILL BUDDY!
'ELLO!
end

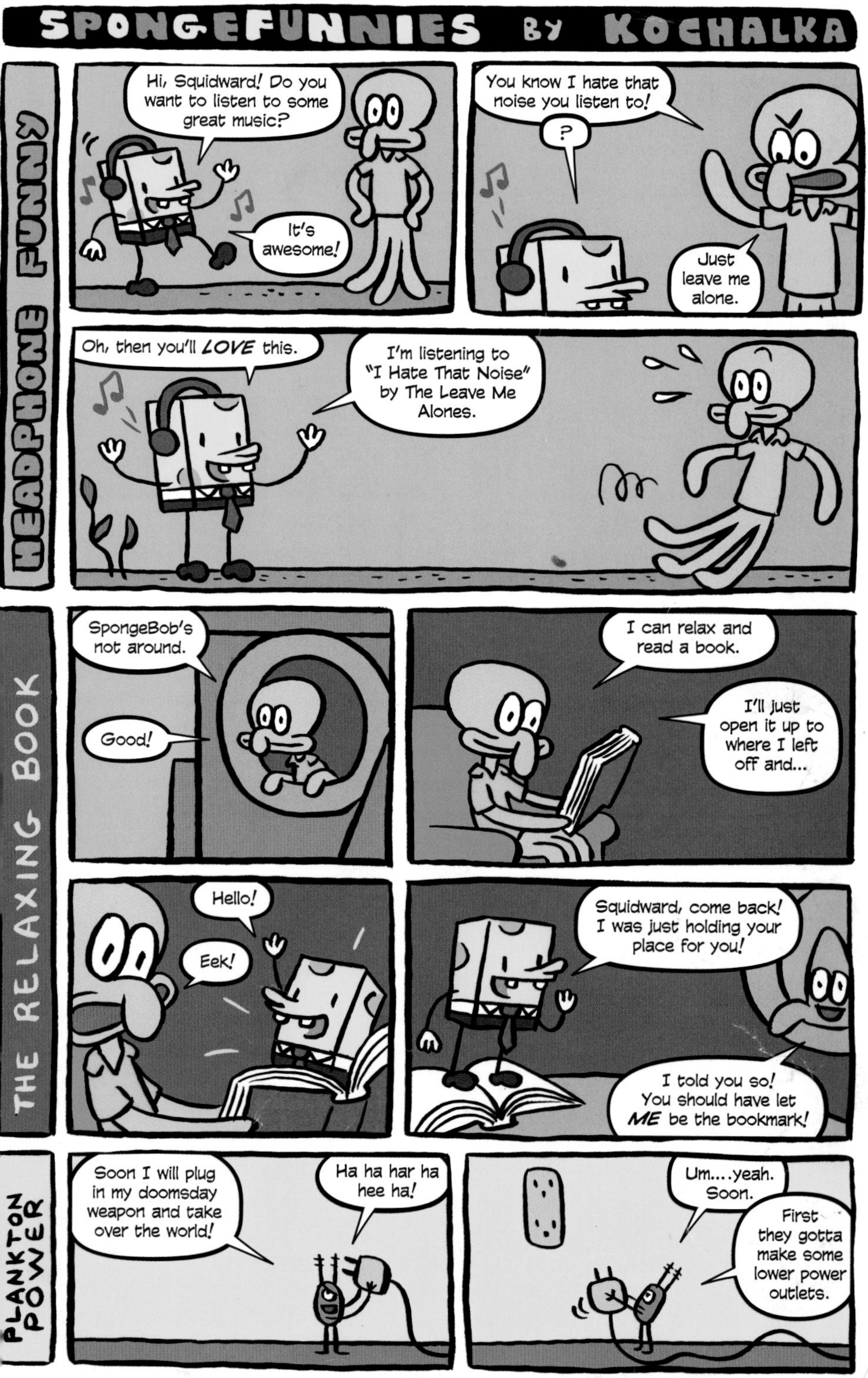
SPONGEFUNNIES BY KOCHALKA
HEADPHONE FUNNY
Hi, Squidward! Do you want to listen to some great music?
It's awesome!
You know I hate that noise you listen to!
?
Just leave me alone.
Oh, then you'll LOVE this.
I'm listening to "I Hate That Noise" by The Leave Me Alones.
THE RELAXING BOOK
SpongeBob's not around.
Good!
I can relax and read a book.
I'll just open it up to where I left off and...
Hello!
Eek!
Squidward, come back! I was just holding your place for you!
I told you so! You should have let ME be the bookmark!
PLANKTON POWER
Soon I will plug in my doomsday weapon and take over the world!
Ha ha har ha hee ha!
Um....yeah. Soon.
First they gotta make some lower power outlets.

Story and art: James Kochalka Lettering: Comicraft

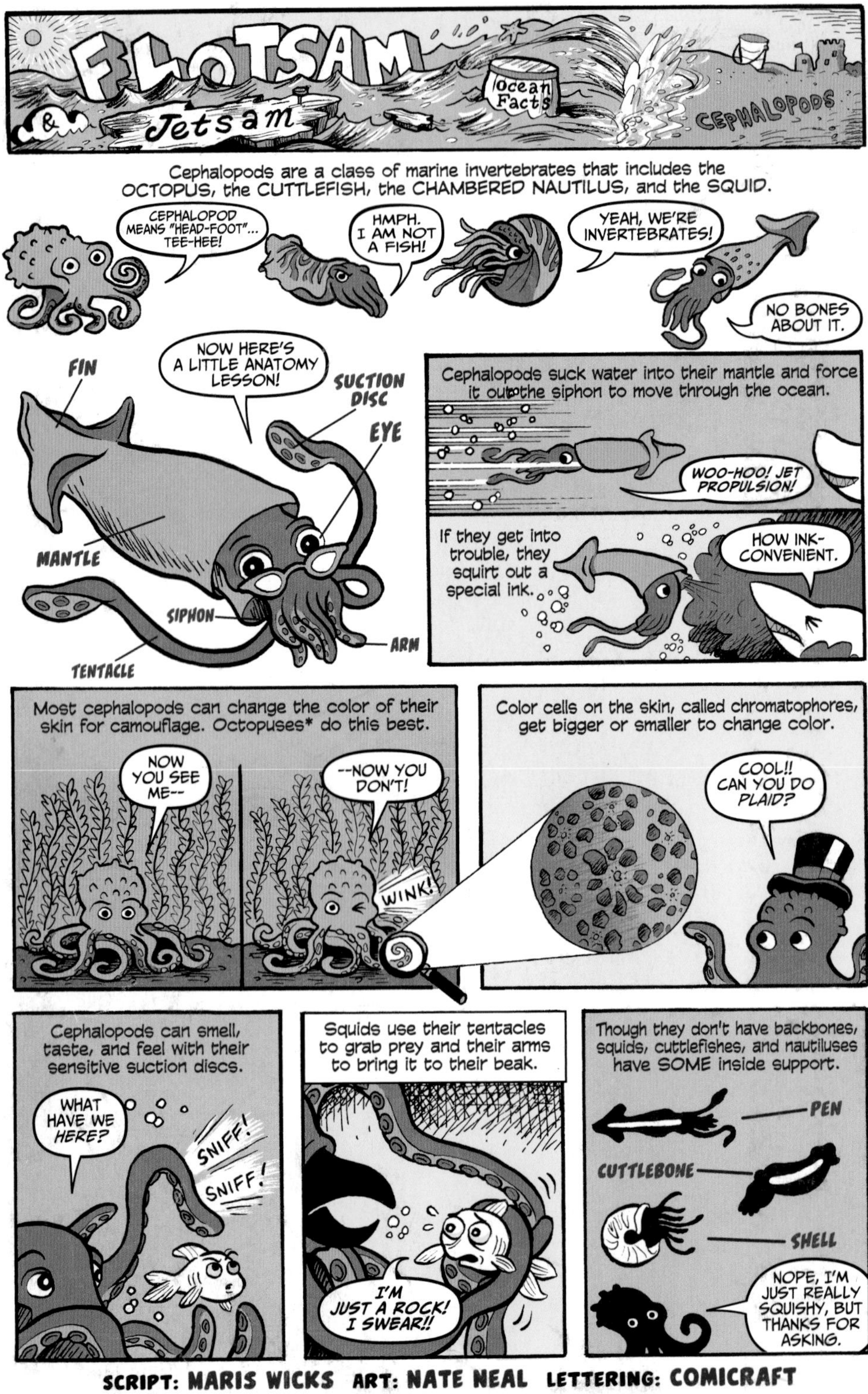
FLOTSAM
&
Jetsam
Ocean Facts
CEPHALOPODS
Cephalopods are a class of marine invertebrates that includes the OCTOPUS, the CUTTLEFISH, the CHAMBERED NAUTILUS, and the SQUID.
CEPHALOPOD MEANS "HEAD-FOOT"... TEE-HEE!
HMPH. I AM NOT A FISH!
YEAH, WE'RE INVERTEBRATES!
NO BONES ABOUT IT.
NOW HERE'S A LITTLE ANATOMY LESSON!
FIN
SUCTION DISC
EYE
MANTLE
SIPHON
ARM
TENTACLE
Cephalopods suck water into their mantle and force it out the siphon to move through the ocean.
WOO-HOO! JET PROPULSION!
If they get into trouble, they squirt out a special ink.
HOW INK-CONVENIENT.
Most cephalopods can change the color of their skin for camouflage. Octopuses* do this best.
NOW YOU SEE ME--
--NOW YOU DON'T!
WINK!
Color cells on the skin, called chromatophores, get bigger or smaller to change color.
COOL!! CAN YOU DO PLAID?
Cephalopods can smell, taste, and feel with their sensitive suction discs.
WHAT HAVE WE HERE?
SNIFF!
SNIFF!
Squids use their tentacles to grab prey and their arms to bring it to their beak.
I'M JUST A ROCK! I SWEAR!!
Though they don't have backbones, squids, cuttlefishes, and nautiluses have SOME inside support.
PEN
CUTTLEBONE
SHELL
NOPE, I'M JUST REALLY SQUISHY, BUT THANKS FOR ASKING.

*Attention grammar nerds: *Octopuses*, *octopi*, and *octopodes* are all correct plural forms of *octopus*.

SCRIPT: MARIS WICKS ART: NATE NEAL LETTERING: COMICRAFT